THREE EXTRAORDINARY LIVES,
THREE EXTRAORDINARY STORIES . . .

Adam Coopersmith. He is that rare combination of brilliant researcher and caring physician. His floundering marriage explodes when he falls in love with another woman, jeopardizing a lifetime's career. And then his *own* life is threatened. . . .

Sandy Raven. A researcher on the cutting edge, Sandy's devotion is matched only by his genius. Yet at the moment of his greatest discovery, he will experience his most profound betrayal—and the disaster that every scientist fears. Will he now abandon his dreams to pursue more worldly prizes?

Isabel da Costa. A child prodigy, she is constantly pushed by her domineering father. Though she becomes a world-renowned physicist, all the adulation in the world cannot compensate for her lost childhood. In the end, she is torn between loyalty to her father and the young man who holds the key to her happiness . . . until a shocking revelation changes her life forever.

Their stories make PRIZES a gripping, emotionally charged experience, a novel that proves once again that Erich Segal is the unsurpassed master of laughter and tears, tragedy and triumph.

By Erich Segal:

Novels:
LOVE STORY
OLIVER'S STORY
MAN, WOMAN AND CHILD
THE CLASS
DOCTORS
ACTS OF FAITH
PRIZES*

For Children:
FAIRY TALE

Academic Books:
ROMAN LAUGHTER: The Comedy of Plautus
EURIPIDES: A Collection of Critical Essays (Ed.)
PLAUTUS: Three Comedies (Ed. and Trans.)
THE OXFORD READINGS IN GREEK TRAGEDY
(Ed.)
CAESAR AUGUSTUS: Seven Aspects (Co ed.)
PLATO'S DIALOGUES (Ed.)
THE OXFORD READINGS IN ARISTOPHANES (Ed.)
PLAUTUS: Four Comedies (Ed. and Trans.)
[THE OXFORD WORLD'S CLASSICS SERIES]

*Published by Ivy Books

PRIZES

Erich Segal

IVY BOOKS • NEW YORK

Ivy Books
Published by Ballantine Books
Copyright © 1995 by Ploys, Inc.

All rights reserved under International and Pan-American Copyright Conventions. Published in the United States by Ballantine Books, a division of Random House, Inc., New York, and simultaneously in Canada by Random House of Canada Limited, Toronto.

Grateful acknowledgment is made to Random House, Inc. for permission to reprint an excerpt from *Babar and His Children* by Jean de Brunhoff. Copyright © 1938 and renewed 1966 by Random House, Inc. Reprinted by permission of Random House, Inc.

http://www.randomhouse.com

Library of Congress Catalog Card Number: 95-95305

ISBN 0-8041-1427-7

Manufactured in the United States of America

First Hardcover Edition: May 1995
First Mass Market Edition: June 1996

10 9 8 7 6 5 4 3 2 1

To Karen,
Francesca, and Miranda—
my Prizes

What's the rush?

Ask the cancer patient who has only a few months to live. Ask the AIDS patient whose body is shriveling . . . the "rush" arises from our human compassion for our fellow man who needs help now.

PROFESSOR W. FRENCH ANDERSON
GENETICS PIONEER

PROLOGUE

> Diseases desperate grown
> By desperate appliances are relieved,
> Or not at all.
>
> Hamlet, ACT IV SCENE 3

THE BOSS was dying.

He was losing weight, growing paler and thinner. And feeling an exhaustion no amount of sleep could relieve.

"Skipper," he confided to his closest friend, "Boyd Penrose is a lousy liar."

"Come on. He's not the White House physician for nothing."

"Listen, I'm dying and I know it."

"No—"

"Yes, dammit. There's a cold black wind tearing down the corridor of my chest. I can even hear the wings of the Angel of Death flapping in my bedroom when I'm left alone."

"I'll call Penrose."

"No. If I can't wring it out of him, nobody can."

"We'll double-team him. He can't outface both of us."

Forty-five minutes later a bedraggled Penrose, looking not at all like the admiral of the Navy that he was, stood straight-backed and tight-lipped in the regal bedroom.

"You rang, sir?" The physician injected his tone with as much sarcasm as he dared display to his powerful patient.

"Sit down, you lousy quack," the sick man snapped. The admiral obeyed.

"Come clean, Boyd," Skipper demanded. "You're hiding something. Has he got some fatal condition you're too chickenshit to divulge?"

Penrose was cowed. He lowered his head and sighed. "Skip, I wish to God you didn't have to hear this." The doctor had to summon the courage to continue. "He's got lymphosarcoma—it's a cancer of the blood and tissues."

There was a shocked silence.

"All right, hold the sackcloth and ashes a minute," said the patient at last, trying to camouflage his fear with bravado. "Let me hear the wretched details." Turning to the physician, he asked, "What are my chances of recovery?"

"That's just it, Boss," Penrose answered. "This isn't one of those numbers you get out of alive."

Another silence.

"How long have I got?"

"About five, maybe six months at the outside."

"Great. If I'm lucky, at least I'll get my Christmas presents. Skip, be a pal and give me a shot of Jack Daniel's. Pour one for yourself and Penrose too."

"No, I can't," the doctor protested.

"Drink it, Boyd, goddammit. Show me I still have some authority around here."

The Navy man acquiesced.

Skipper's face was gray. "I don't get it. Why are you guys taking this lying down? There must be some way of fighting this monster."

They looked toward the doctor again. "As a matter of fact," he confessed, "there are three different labs—Harvard, Stanford, and Rockefeller—that are all developing experimental drugs to combat this mother. But they're still a long way from getting FDA approval."

"Screw the formalities, Boyd," the Boss growled. "The White House can get me anything we ask for."

"No, no, it isn't a question of just having the influence to get it, which I know you could swing. But once we do, there's simply no way of knowing which of these techniques—if any—will do the job. And even if we could choose the best, we still wouldn't know how much to administer. We might kill you then and there."

"Okay. Strike the carpet-bombing approach. How do you decide which is the best gamble?"

Some color returned to Penrose's face, perhaps because he finally felt there was something he could *do*.

"Well, I can call up a couple of heavyweights and, keeping total anonymity, find out what they think of the relative merits of the three medications."

"Good idea. Why don't you start right away," Skipper suggested. "Use the Boss's office. The phone's secure. Only get us some answers."

The moment the admiral departed, the patient turned to his companion and demanded, "Be a pal, Skipper, let me have a refill of that hooch and turn on my TV."

Penrose was back in less than an hour. "I don't believe it," he mumbled, shaking his head.

"What exactly do you find so amazing?" Skipper demanded.

"The first choice of all the guys I called was the same character—Max Rudolph. He's the immunologist at Harvard who's developed those special mice."

"Mice?" the sick man asked with exasperation. "What in hell's name do mice have to do with my goddamn life?"

Penrose looked his patient straight in the eye and said softly, "They could save it."

1
ADAM

MAX RUDOLPH sat alone in his darkened penthouse lab at Harvard Medical School, staring into the velvet sky, waiting for signs of daybreak over the Charles River.

Having been informed that the blood and other tissue samples would be delivered at precisely six A.M., he had arrived early to be sure that none of the conscientious night owls on his staff would be working at their benches when the courier arrived.

There was a single exception: he had summoned his protégé, Adam Coopersmith, to meet him at five A.M.

Physically they made an odd couple: Max, mid-sixties, short, bespectacled, and almost bald. Adam, tall, wiry, with a shock of dark brown hair, younger-looking than his twenty-eight years, eyes still disconcertingly innocent.

"Max, you pulled me out of the operating room—this better be important."

"It is," his mentor announced.

"You sounded so mysterious on the phone. What the hell is going on?" Adam demanded.

"My boy," Max answered gravely. "For the first time in our professional lives we're going to do something unethical."

Adam was startled. "Did I hear you right—you, who sprints after the mailman when he forgets to collect postage due on a letter?"

4

"A life is at stake," the older man answered somberly. "Certain corners will have to be cut."

"You've never done that."

"Yes, but I've never had the President of the United States as a patient before."

"What do you mean?"

"Admiral Penrose called me from the White House about a patient he described only as 'a senior Washington personage.' He insisted that I not ask any more."

Max conveyed to Adam verbatim the medical information given on the phone by the Washington physician. And their awesome assignment.

"God, that's an enormous responsibility."

"I know, that's why I had to share it with somebody."

"Am I supposed to thank you for that?" Adam smiled.

They were interrupted by a loud grating sound at the end of the hall. They watched mutely as the elevator doors opened and a black-leather-jacketed creature of the night appeared. In one hand he carried a helmet and in the other a carton about the size of a cigar box.

"Dr. Rudolph?" he asked in a subdued monotone.

"Yes."

"Do you have some sort of ID?"

Max pulled out his wallet and showed the envoy his driver's license.

The courier checked it with a quick intense look, handed over the package, and quickly receded into the shadows. The two scientists exchanged glances.

"And it's not even Halloween," Max whispered. "Let's get to work."

They walked slowly down the corridor, an obstacle course of dry-ice chests, refrigerated centrifuges, and tanks of nitrogen, helium, and oxygen splayed chaotically like large metal tenpins.

Adam snapped on the lights of a room stacked floor to ceiling with cages of mice, all scampering to and fro, blissfully unaware of their unique qualities.

When transfused with human blood and other tissue, their systems became carbon copies of the donors. This meant reactions to whatever they were subsequently given were miniature but precise reflections of their human model.

"All right Adam, we have three possibilities. They could cure, kill, or even do nothing. What do you suggest?"

"Four sets of six mice each. We inject them all with the patient's blood and then treat each group with varying strengths of the medications. The fourth crew obviously gets placebos."

"But they still get their share of good cheese," Max admonished.

Adam grinned. "Always the friend of the downtrodden."

By seven-thirty, when day staff began to straggle in, they had already infected a third of the mice. To avoid arousing suspicion, they merely handed over case AC/1068/24 to the technicians who normally performed this sort of mundane procedure.

Adam called the obstetrics ward. He listened for a moment, and then announced with evident pleasure, "All's well—eight pounds, eight ounces."

"Lucky people," the professor murmured.

As they descended in the elevator, Max permitted himself the luxury of a yawn.

"Shall we visit the House of Pancakes before we turn in?"

"Don't do this to me," Adam protested. "I promised Lisl I'd watch your cholesterol."

"But we're scientific outlaws at the moment." Max laughed. "Can't you let a nervous old man calm himself with some blintzes and sour cream?"

"No, ethics are one thing, but I don't want to lose my best friend to a lipid-soaked pancake."

"Okay." Max sighed histrionically. "To salve your conscience I'll eat them with margarine."

* * *

Two weeks passed slowly and painfully. At precisely eleven-thirty each evening the two men would meet at the lab to endure a telephonic dressing-down from Admiral Penrose, whose increasingly strained voice reflected the growing apprehension in Washington.

At one point Penrose's tirade grew so loud and acrimonious that Adam snatched the receiver and growled, "Dammit, Admiral. You've got to impress on your patient that in a very real sense these mice are acting as his understudies."

"He knows that," the Navy man replied with annoyance.

"Then perhaps he might just appreciate the fact that we've held off treating him." He paused for effect and then continued quietly, "All the Rockefeller mice died last night."

"All?" The physician's voice quavered.

"I'm afraid so. But it's better than a President, don't you agree?"

Penrose hesitated. "Yes ... yes, I suppose so," he conceded after a moment. "But what do you suggest I report back?"

"The truth," Adam answered. "Only remind him he's still got two more bullets. Good night, Admiral."

He hung up and looked at his mentor. "Well, Max?"

"Very impressive, Doctor. Now let's get our lab books up to date."

"That's okay. Why don't you go home to your anxious wife while I transcribe the unhappy necrology into the computer."

The senior man nodded. "I'm not doing my share of the drone work, but I gratefully cede to your excess energy. By the way, what makes you feel that Lisl is concerned about me?"

"It's her job," Adam retorted. "She's told me hundreds of times: 'My husband worries about the world, and I worry about my husband.'"

Max smiled, turned up the collar of his trench coat and began to trudge slowly down the hall.

Adam's eyes followed the receding figure with an unexpected touch of sadness. He looks so small and vulnerable, he thought. Why can't I give him some of my youth?

2

ISABEL

ISABEL'S DIARY

November 16

My name is Isabel da Costa. I am four years old and live with my parents and big brother Peter in Clairemont Mesa, California. About a year ago, Mom and Dad found out that I could read on my own. They got very excited and took me to see a lot of people who gave me all sorts of different things to read.

I really wish this hadn't happened. Because Peter doesn't want to play with me anymore. Maybe if I keep this diary a secret, he might like me again.

As it is, I mostly play by myself, making up stories—and thinking. Like one of the lines in the song "Twinkle, Twinkle" really bothers me. It asks "How I wonder what you are?"—but never gives an answer.

Then my dad, who is very smart, explained that stars are big hot glowing balls of gas. They are so far away that we see them as only tiny bits of light. And even though light travels faster than anything else in the world, it might take years and years for it to reach us.

I wanted to know more. So Dad promised to teach me

about the solar system—if I got out of the sand pit and washed my hands for dinner.

We had chocolate pudding, my favorite.

It is a terrible thing to be born mentally handicapped. Few people realize, however, that it is also an affliction to be born a genius. Isabel da Costa knew.

Nothing in her parents' backgrounds suggested that their child would someday be called a "female Einstein." Indeed, her father Raymond twice failed the qualifying exam for a doctorate in physics at U.C. San Diego.

Yet the department admired his unabated enthusiasm and offered him the nonfaculty position of Junior Development Engineer—which involved the preparation of apparatus for lectures and experiments.

This was not what Ray had dreamed of. But at least he had a legitimate connection with a university lab. He was so dedicated that he soon became indispensable. His reward was Muriel Haverstock.

One day this plump, vivacious brunette music major, suffering from the common female phobia for science, pleaded for Raymond's assistance.

"Oh please, Mr. D.," she begged the stocky, red-haired supervisor. "I need this course to graduate, and if you don't help me I'll never get this oscilloscope to work."

By the time Ray had shown her how to measure the resonance of RLC circuits, he was smitten.

As the bell rang he gathered his courage, then invited her for a cup of coffee.

"Sure," she answered. "If you don't mind waiting till after my orchestra rehearsal."

His heart leapt. "That'd be great."

"Okay, why not drop by the auditorium around seven-thirty," she continued. "You might even be able to catch some of our scratchings and wheezings."

Raymond arrived early and sat in the back row,

watching Edmundo Zimmer conduct Bach's D Minor Double Concerto. To his surprise, Muriel had been chosen to join the Concert Mistress in playing the exquisite duet in the largo movement.

"Actually, I came here to study English," she explained over dinner. "But when I got into the orchestra, Edmundo completely converted me to music. He's so charismatic—and not even bitter about his accident."

"What happened?" Raymond inquired. "All I could see was that his arms were kind of stiff."

"He was a rising young cellist in Argentina when he was in a car crash. He fell against the dashboard and paralyzed both his forearms. So now the closest he can come to being a musician is conducting our bunch of amateurs. I really admire his courage."

As they got to know one another, Raymond confessed that he was already mired in scientific failure; that he would never rise above his current station.

Paradoxically, this made Muriel admire him more. For Raymond seemed to accept professional disappointment with a strength of character similar to Edmundo's.

They married.

And lived unhappily ever after.

After graduation, Muriel found a job teaching music at the Hanover Day School and continued playing with the orchestra until late in her first pregnancy.

On July 10, 1967, Raymond da Costa became the proud father of a son, already sprouting wisps of red hair like his own. He vowed that Peter would have the advantages he himself had been denied when growing up. And pillaged the library for books on enhancing a child's brainpower.

Muriel was pleased that he was taking such an interest in Peter's development—until she noticed the darker side.

"Raymond, in heaven's name, what is this sinister document?" she exclaimed after accidentally coming across a lab notebook containing the detailed day-by-day account of their son's intellectual progress.

Or, as the father saw it, the deficiencies.

He was in no mood for explanations. "Muriel, I'm going to have the kid evaluated. I don't think he's living up to his potential."

"But he's barely two years old," she reprimanded him. "What on earth do you expect him to be doing—nuclear physics?"

The severity of his reply disconcerted her. "No—but it wouldn't be unprecedented if he could do simple arithmetic with these colored blocks. Frankly, Muriel, I'm afraid Peter's no genius."

"So what? He's still a sweet, adorable child. Do you think I would love you more if you were professor of Physics at Princeton?"

He looked her straight in the eye and answered, "Yes."

Muriel felt Raymond would be less preoccupied with little Peter's mind if they had another child.

When she mentioned it, Ray was so enthusiastic that the next day he came home from the lab with a gift-wrapped present—an ovulation thermometer. And his lovemaking seemed to have regained its initial ardor as his enthusiasm grew for their new experiment.

She announced her pregnancy almost immediately.

During the months that followed, Ray was warm and caring. No effort was too great. He scoured the health food shops for vitamins, went with her to every doctor's appointment, helped her practice her Lamaze exercises, and soothed her when she was anxious.

On the·Ides of March, 1972, she went into labor and shortly afterward brought forth a bouncing baby girl.

A *girl*.

Raymond had been unprepared for this possibility. His own idiosyncratic, unscientific expectation was that he would have only sons.

Muriel, on the other hand, was overjoyed. She was sure that Ray would quickly be captivated by their new baby's charm, as well as her long dark curls, and not cherish any absurd fantasies of sending her to Yale while she was still in Pampers.

At first her instinct seemed correct. Raymond was attentive and affectionate to his bright-eyed little girl, whom they named Isabel after his mother. Muriel spent many happy hours reading to her lovely, lively daughter, who seemed fascinated by words and rather adept with them.

At first Raymond did not seem aware that, even as she played in the garden with other toddlers whose vocabulary was limited to monosyllables, Isabel was speaking complete sentences.

But the most astounding discovery was yet to come.

As Muriel was cleaning up the multicolored remnants after Isabel's third birthday, scraping ice cream off the rug and scrubbing jellied fingerprints from the wall, she overheard a tiny bell-like voice.

" 'Babar is trying to read, but finds it difficult to concentrate; his thoughts are elsewhere. He tries to write, but again his thoughts wander. He is thinking of his wife and the little baby soon to be born. Will it be handsome and strong? Oh, how hard it is to wait for one's heart's desire!' "

She had never read this story to Isabel. Clearly her daughter had simply unwrapped a gift and decided to peruse it herself.

At first she was stunned, unsure of what to do. And though reluctant to call this amazing event to her husband's attention, she wanted corroboration that it was not her imagination.

She quietly slipped from the room and summoned Raymond from his study. Now both parents stood in the doorway dumbstruck, watching their pretty little girl— whose previous exposure to the alphabet had been merely watching "Sesame Street"—recite flawlessly from a book intended for adults to entertain their children.

"How could she learn all this without us noticing?" Muriel asked, this time sharing her husband's elation.

Raymond did not answer. He did not know how bright his daughter was.

But he was resolved to spare no effort to find out.

3
SANDY

TIME
SCIENCE

COVER STORY
The Man Who Discovered Immortality
"The most important breakthrough of the decade in the battle against cancer"   -

"When I was a kid in the Bronx, I was a classic example of the guy who got sand kicked in his face."

Nobody kicks sand in this man's face anymore.

The acknowledged leader in the brave new science of genetic engineering, Professor Sandy Raven has already made history by receiving the first federal approval for clinical trials on reversing the aging process.

Still in his early forties, with many more productive years in front of him, Raven has paved the way not only for increased human life span, but for the potential arrest of fatal illnesses and the regeneration of tissue in wasting diseases like muscular dystrophy and, ultimately, Alzheimer's.

Raven has received numerous awards and is widely regarded as a likely Nobel winner—if the selectors in Stockholm don't see his near-billionaire status as compensation enough.

In many ways, his personality is reminiscent of Bill Gates's, another unconventional genius-magnate (*Time* April 16, 1984) who, as a college dropout, founded Microsoft Corporation, the computing software giant, and is now one of the wealthiest men in the world.

Raven's lifestyle is fairly eccentric. Though Cal Tech, where he is a professor of Microbiology and Director of the Institute of Gerontology, provides him with sixteen thousand square feet of laboratory space on two floors of the tallest structure on campus, he prefers to work in the special building he constructed for himself on his seventeen-acre walled estate near Santa Barbara.

Raven is fanatical about privacy. The grounds of his palatial estate are patrolled around the clock by an undisclosed number of security guards. The security measures can, in part, be attributed to the enormous commercial potential of his research, but sources close to him—who emphasize

that "nobody but his father is *really* close to him"—suggest that Raven has personal motives for his obsession.

Yet, on the rare occasions he appears in public, he is affable and good-natured. With engaging self-deprecation, he describes his own somewhat inauspicious beginnings: "Like one scientific view of the creation of the world, my career began with a Big Bang." At the age of eleven, he tried to make hydrogen and oxygen by the electrolysis of water. "Unfortunately," he recalls with a sheepish smile, "I sort of just missed by a molecule and nearly blew up my parents' kitchen."

Raven brackets this with a more traumatic explosion. Psychologists have noted that many of the most creative minds have come from affection-starved childhoods—Sir Isaac Newton, abandoned at birth, is the classic example. Raven seems to fit this paradigm. He recalls his single respite from scientific studies was "daydreaming."

The only child of Pauline and Sidney Raven, he had just entered Bronx High School of Science when his parents divorced. Shortly thereafter, his mother married a wealthy jeweler and relinquished custody of her young son.

Sandy could have gone to

live with his father, who had moved to Los Angeles, but he was determined to finish at Bronx Science, and he spent the rest of his childhood shuttling from one grudging relative to another.

The elder Raven—whose name may be familiar to film buffs as the producer of the cult movie *Godzilla Meets Hercules*—began as manager of Loew's Grand theater.

Indeed, Sandy's fondest early memories are of the Saturday afternoons father and son spent together, "munching endless boxes of popcorn" and watching Burt Lancaster dueling with brigands and Gene Kelly leaping over fire hydrants as he sang in the rain.

In his senior year, young Sandy's project on the transmission of genes in fruit flies won him a Westinghouse Scholarship to MIT. By the time he was studying for his doctorate, the scientific world was about to experiment on *humans*.

The field of genetic engineering seemed not to have existed as a discipline when Sandy was growing up, although some of its techniques, used to breed corn and cattle, had been practiced for millennia. Now, the "new farmers" wore white coats and worked indoors.

Spending a dozen years on the MIT faculty, Raven was able to observe pioneering research firsthand when working under Professor Gregory Morgenstern, who eventually won the Nobel Prize in 1983 for his findings on liver cancer.

During this period Raven married Morgenstern's daughter Judy. The union produced a girl—and a divorce. Dr. Raven is adamantly silent about both.

At the age of thirty-two, he was offered a full professorship at Cal Tech in Pasadena, where he began to assemble a team for his new area of research— the fight against aging.

Raven was not the first gladiator in this arena. In recent years, geneticists the world over have been making hitherto undreamed-of strides in what is arguably the greatest—and most difficult—challenge ever to face mankind.

Unlike certain diseases that can be pinpointed to specific places on a particular chromosome, the aging process is controlled from at least a hundred different sites on the human genome—the sum total of genes in a person's body.

Several important discoveries served as point of departure for Raven's own work. At the National Institute of Environmental Health Sciences, Dr. Carl Barrett located an area that determines longevity on

Chromosome One. Doctors James Smith and Olivia Pereira-Smith of Baylor have traced another to Chromosome Four.

Raven's first major breakthrough came when he identified a group of genes that caused degeneration in skin cells. In various trials he succeeded in reversing it, at least temporarily. But he entered a domain entirely his own when he succeeded in "immortalizing" some of the genetic components of skin rejuvenation.

This "Ponce de Leon" discovery—a media coinage that makes the scientist cringe—has turned Sandy Raven into a kind of folk hero. The press has touted him as the creator of the ultimate Hollywood dream: a chemical that holds out the promise of eternal youth.

Though he announced his discovery in a highly technical article in the academic journal *Experimental Gerontology*, his biochemical magic was quickly translated into headlines for laymen and disseminated by the wire services of the world.

The reaction was electrifying. Calls flooded the university switchboard. Mail came to his lab literally by the sackful. Curiously, this proved a disheartening experience for Raven.

"Instead of feeling proud, I felt guilty that I had not done enough. I mean these were not just women wanting to lose their wrinkles. Most of the messages were desperate cries from people who wrongly presumed that I was already capable of reversing *any* soft tissue damage. They pleaded with me to save their loved ones' lives, and I was left with a feeling of terrible frustration and—yes—failure."

Both the sensitivity and humility characterize the man.

And yet, despite Raven's disconsolate air, he has in fact prepared the way for the development of genetic procedures to conquer many killer pathologies.

Raven remains a reluctant hero, still quixotically determined to avoid the limelight. He wryly dismisses his new celebrity status with typical self-effacing good humor:

"Let's face it, I have the charisma of a soggy bagel. If I can make the cover of *Time*, the nerds are conquering the world."

Other major figures in the field have a more respectful attitude.

"Sandy's achievement was probably the most important breakthrough of the decade in the battle against cancer," says his admirer and former father-in-law, Gregory Morgenstern of MIT. "It dwarfs anything I've ever done. He deserves all the honor and glory—and money—that I'm sure he's going to get."

"Jesus, Dad. Did you see how they ended the article?" Sandy fumed.

"Yes, sonny boy," the older man muttered uncomfortably. "But it's only natural for a cover story that they would trace your career and go back and speak to the people who knew you along the way. After all, Morgenstern did win the Big One. How the hell are they supposed to know the skeletons in his closet? Actually, this would have been the chance for you to tell them."

"What good would that have been? Besides, I somehow thought they would dig it up on their own. But I guess there are limits to what even the press can find out."

"Listen, it could have been worse."

"How?"

"Look at it this way, kiddo. They could have mentioned Rochelle."

"Yeah," Sandy acknowledged. "Thank God for that."

4

ADAM

SUDDENLY, AT the beginning of the third week, the blood count in category two of the Stanford mice began to improve dramatically.

At first Max and Adam kept this information from the others in case it turned out to be a false dawn. But forty-eight hours later it was certain: the animals' systems were clear.

The human cancer had been cured in its mouse surrogate.

They were now as confident as any laboratory could make them that their drug would work on the patient himself. Of course, there was an element of uncertainty since they had not completed the normal cycle of FDA trials.

But then, they had a White House concession.

With the generosity that characterized his relationship with Adam, Max Rudolph deputized him to deliver the serum personally to Washington. For though he deferred to no man in matters of scientific knowledge and technique, he knew that sending his assistant might also be a kind of therapeutic measure.

What had distinguished Adam from all Rudolph's other pupils was the young man's extraordinary sensitivity and almost-religious desire to heal. Just meeting him and looking into his compassionate gray-green eyes would immediately reassure a patient.

"But Max," Adam had protested, "couldn't we send it by the same courier who brought the blood?"

"Yes," the older man granted. "But even the best messenger services are unable to detect an incipient toxic reaction in an untried drug."

"Then why don't *you* go?"

"I'm old and tired and I don't want to leave Lisl," he replied. "Tell me the truth, are you nervous about meeting such wielders of power?"

"Frankly, yes."

"Well, that's another reason to make the journey. You'll quickly learn that they're just like ordinary human beings." To which he added with a mischievous smile, "Some even less so."

The admiral was puzzled when he stepped forward to meet Adam as he deplaned at National Airport.

In addition to his overnight case, the lanky Harvard doctor was carrying what looked like a square lamp shade with a handle.

"What's that?"

"It's a surprise for the patient," Adam answered with a tiny smile. "I think you'll like it too."

"Do you have any more luggage?"

"No, I travel light."

Penrose nodded, and led his Boston colleague to a limousine waiting on the tarmac.

The two men rode in silence for several minutes before Adam glanced out the window and suddenly realized that the lights of Washington had receded and they were now in the countryside.

"Hey," he said, confused, "what's going on? Are we going to Camp David or something?"

"No," the admiral answered, "the patient's in Virginia." He paused and then confided, "And it's not the President."

"What? Who else has got the clout to get hold of three unapproved drugs?"

"When I tell you, Dr. Coopersmith, you'll realize that in this country the king-makers are more powerful than the kings. Our patient is Thomas Deely Hartnell."

Adam's jaw dropped. "Otherwise known as 'the Boss'? Former Ambassador to the Court of Saint James? Adviser to every President, right and left?"

Penrose nodded. "And a man to whom you say no at your peril. I hope you'll forgive the subterfuge, but I somehow sensed that Dr. Rudolph would not have extended his patriotism beyond the Oval Office."

Neither would I, Adam thought to himself with annoyance. This revelation disquieted him, and as the limousine navigated still narrower and darker roads, he grew more apprehensive. What if the Navy physician was still lying? What if this was some mafioso don?

But then he realized that in a way it *was*. After all, Hartnell was an old-style power broker. This was far from the first time he would have twisted rules to get his own way.

Perhaps the admiral read his thoughts, because a few minutes later he said earnestly, "Let me assure you, Dr. Coopersmith, Thomas Hartnell is a very worthy human being—and a valuable asset to this country. You should have no qualms about what you're doing."

In moments they reached the imposing gates of Clifton House, which instantly opened to admit the men who had come to heal the lord of the manor.

"Ow!"

Adam stood silently in the elegant bedroom as Penrose injected the serum into Hartnell's buttock. Then the two men turned the dignitary onto his back, and when Hartnell was comfortable, Adam, with the panache of a magician, whisked away the cloth from the object he had carried into the room and announced:

"Voilà, Mr. Hartnell, a gift from Immunology Lab 808, and specifically its director, Max Rudolph."

"A mouse . . . ?"

"Well yes, zoologically speaking, I suppose so. But this little fella's rather unusual—he has the same blood chemistry as you do, and we thought if you saw him frisking around, it might give you an idea of what you'll be like in a couple of weeks."

"Now tell me," the Boss questioned imperiously, "how soon do I get better?"

"I can't answer that, sir," Adam replied. "Unfortunately, you're not a mouse."

After waiting for the sedative to take effect, Penrose led the visiting scientist to a majestic drawing room where members of the patient's inner circle were tensely waiting by the fireplace. They were all anxious to hear what had transpired. The admiral quickly made the introductions.

"All we can say at this point is that he's resting comfortably," he declared by way of overture. "And now, I'll leave it to my learned colleague to spell out the procedure we've put into effect."

He gracefully yielded to Adam, who looked around, trying to gauge his audience, then began.

"I don't have to tell you that we're skating on thin ice in total darkness. But I'll be glad to share with you what little we do know."

Despite the lateness of the hour, Adam felt an unexpected surge of energy. Until now, he had been operating under enormous pressure. Not merely the tension of running so great a medical risk, but the unfamiliarity of his surroundings. These people were from another world. Their status intimidated him.

But now they had entered a domain in which he was the master and they the wide-eyed tourists, looking at him with awe and hanging on his every word. When it came to discussing genetic engineering, his enthusiasm always went into overdrive.

Moreover, he was a born teacher, and his manner charmed the audience.

He discoursed on the development of a retrovirus that

could be transported directly to the cancer cells that had gone amok. Its "disguise" would allow it to penetrate the nucleus of the malignant cell where the alchemy of DNA transformed foe back into friend. Pausing, he smiled.

"In other words, it makes a bunch of Hell's Angels suddenly turn into the Vienna Boys Choir."

Surveying his high-powered audience, Adam was puzzled by the presence of a tall, striking blonde. Her horn-rimmed glasses and conservative suit seemed to him deliberate attempts to camouflage her beauty.

Yet Antonia Nielson was far too young—a fairly recent graduate of Georgetown Law School, it later emerged—to hold important government office. And she was even too youthful to be a politically acceptable wife for a sixty-year-old man.

But she was the ideal vintage for a cabinet-level mistress.

The only question was: Whose?

In any case, she seemed to fill an important role, even meriting a private whispered chat with Boyd Penrose, who gave her a mock salute before they returned to the others.

As Adam spoke, she smiled several times at his witticisms, and he began to think that he had seen her somewhere before.

And then it struck him. To set the mouse cage down on the patient's night table, he'd had to displace a leather-framed photograph of Hartnell and a ravishing young woman. He now realized it was Antonia, without spectacles. His question was answered.

Under any other circumstances, Adam would have been tempted to claim her as his reward. But somehow in this grandiose—and somewhat menacing—atmosphere, he found himself intimidated. After all, he reminded himself, you also trifle with the Boss's girl at your even greater peril.

As the various guests departed, none of them neglected to kiss Antonia. It all appeared perfectly friendly, except the way the Attorney General held her. Indeed, if she had not been so clearly involved with the Boss, Adam would have suspected a liaison with the country's chief legal officer.

Unexpectedly, she took the initiative as they emerged from the mansion to a blue sky marbled with the first pink streaks of morning.

Adam's driver was waiting patiently. As if he'd been watching all evening, he sprang from the car and opened the back door for his passenger. Before Adam could climb inside, Antonia materialized next to him and asked in soft, confident tones, "Doctor, I know you're staying at the Watergate. May I offer you a ride?"

Adam smiled. This was an unexpected gift. "Only if you'll agree to have a very early breakfast with me."

"Fine," she answered. "I'll even make it for you myself. But in return, you'll have to let me cross-examine you like hell while we drive."

"With pleasure," Adam responded. "Just let me retrieve my impedimenta and liberate the driver."

As they sped toward the capital, Adam quickly realized that her gesture was not romantically inspired. To be sure, she was desperately anxious to talk to him, but as a *doctor*.

"Nobody tells me anything," she complained. "I mean, even Boyd still treats me like a child. Would you mind terribly explaining the exact nature of what you're doing?"

Though she had listened raptly to the earlier account, she now made him review it point by point in even greater detail. When he'd finished, she said, as a kind of feverish command, "He's *got* to live, Adam. You mustn't let him die. Now honestly, what do you think his chances really are?"

It was as if she was trying to persuade him to use other magic he might have been holding back. Still, though they had covered this ground before, he answered her question again, attempting to sympathize with her distracted concern.

"Miss Nielson—"

"Please call me Toni."

"Well, Toni, I can only say that what Max has done gives Mr. Hartnell a better shot of licking this killer than any other man on the planet."

"Oh Christ, that's wonderful," she exclaimed. As they stopped for a traffic light, she squeezed his hand. Yet even this wordless act was not an invitation, merely an impassioned thank-you. "I mean he's such a good person. No one knows him better than I. Beneath that gruff exterior, he's loving and sensitive."

Forty minutes later they were in her small, expensively decorated flat. Books formed much of the decor and reflected the wide variety of Toni's interests.

Her eclectic library included not only history and biography, but fiction of both Americas. She also offered some engaging literary interpretations. (On García Marquez's *One Hundred Years of Solitude*: "The diary of my social life." On *Moby Dick*: "An allegory of Richard Nixon's political career.")

While she stirred the batter for oatmeal pancakes, Adam excused himself to wash up. When he returned, she was placing the first flapjacks on his plate.

"Butter? Syrup?" she inquired.

"Thanks. I'll help myself. This looks terrific. Hey, I wish Max were here—this is his favorite food, and he deserves his share of the spoils."

"Have you spoken to him?"

"I checked in before we left Virginia, but I think I ought to get over to my hotel pretty soon. There's always a chance that one of my patients has had a crisis."

"That's unusual. I thought all doctors were incommunicado if they went out of town."

"No," he replied. "Not real doctors."

"Why don't you just call over to see if you have any

messages?" she suggested, revealing her anxiety at the thought of letting go of the Boss's medical consultant.

"Thanks, Toni, but I'm kind of bushed and think I ought to get some sleep. Besides, Mr. Hartnell's watchful gaze is beginning to give me the willies." He pointed to a copy of the same photograph he'd seen in the sick man's bedroom. This time it was placed center stage near the sofa.

"Well," she joked, "it's one way of keeping an eye on your patient. But may I delay your departure with another cup of coffee?"

"Sure, fine."

Moments later, as she was in the kitchen area, the phone rang.

"My God," Adam remarked, "your day starts early."

She smiled. "No, it's my evenings that are long. Take it, Adam. My hands are full."

"Are you sure?"

"Go on, answer or they'll hang up."

He picked up the receiver, listened for an instant and said, "Are you sure you have the right number?"

"Who is it?" she asked in a stage whisper.

Adam covered the phone. "Sounds like a mistake. Some secretary's asking for 'Skipper.' "

"Oh," she said casually, taking the phone from him. "That's me. It's my old tomboy nickname."

Then, speaking to the caller, "Morning, Cecily, put him right on, please." She paused for a moment and then exclaimed warmly, "Hi sweetheart, feeling better yet? Yes, I'm here with Dr. Coopersmith. We have to be sure he doesn't walk under a bus or something. He's a very precious commodity."

She listened for a minute and then asserted, "Yes, yes I *did* notice he's attractive. What should matter to you is that he really knows his stuff and I honestly think this drug is going to work."

Then, abruptly, her voice became severe. "No—you listen to me. You will *not* have guests to dinner, especially not in your bedroom. Furthermore, when I get there I'm going to confiscate your booze. Now that you're going to live, I don't want you to die from cirrhosis."

In another minute they were exchanging kisses down the line. Toni hung up in a buoyant mood.

"I guess you know who that was?" She smiled.

"Yeah," Adam responded, trying to mask his disappointment. "Everybody's Boss."

"Except mine." Toni grinned.

"What makes you so special?" Adam asked, with an unmistakable tinge of jealousy.

"I'm his daughter," she replied.

Well, well—Hartnell was her father. That changed things somewhat. No. That changed things completely.

Except where did "Nielson" come from? That, at least, was a mystery easily dispelled nine hours later when they were returning to the Virginia estate.

"Mr. Jack Nielson was a childhood folly," she explained. "We were at law school together, and quite frankly, I think he was more in love with my father's influence than he was with me. It was the only time the Boss and I disagreed."

"You mean he disapproved?"

"No, as a matter of fact he thought Jack was terrific and practically pushed me into his arms. Anyway, my husband turned out to be such a louse that he was into philandering before we even got back from the honeymoon."

"I'm sorry," Adam commiserated. "I mean, he was pretty stupid."

"Well," she said breezily, "it was what they call a learning experience. And now I'm immunized."

"Against what?"

She looked at the road ahead and then said quietly, "Against emotional involvements."

There was a dinner party at the mansion, after all. The only concession the Boss had made to doctor's orders was that he did not attend in person.

It was a high-level evening by any standard, a kind of elite circle of courtiers, befitting the nature of the house: two senators, a senior columnist from the *New York Times*, the Secretary of State. And the Attorney General. All except the last had brought a companion. Conversation was lively, if provincial—at least in Adam's view. Their stock-in-trade was governmental gossip—small talk about big names.

Before the evening ended, Admiral Penrose turned up in time to join Adam in a thorough examination of the patient, and then immediately departed.

Toni stayed a bit longer, but she beckoned Adam into a corner for a rapid confidential chat. Pressing something metallic into his hand, she murmured, "Take my car and just leave it in the garage. I've got a spare set of keys. Will you be able to find your way back?"

He nodded, understanding all too well what was happening and unable to keep from feeling hurt.

"Yeah," he muttered. "I suppose so. How will you—" He stopped himself. "I guess that's none of my business, huh?"

"I guess," she whispered.

Okay, he consoled himself, it was all a meaningless tease. Or a figment of his imagination. Toni was not available, after all. She had unblushingly gone off hand in hand with the Attorney General.

Yet the next night, she insisted upon taking him to dinner at La Renaissance.

He was puzzled by her unexpected interest, but had already seen enough of her lifestyle to permit himself a few cynical observations at the end of the evening.

"Does your father approve of you going out with a married man?"

"He's no one to talk," she replied casually. "He stopped supervising my social life when I broke up with Jack. Anyway, he and . . . my friend were college classmates. So how can he object?"

She was not the least self-conscious in discussing

these details. On the other hand, she did not seem over-joyed, but rather philosophical about this relationship, which clearly was dependent on her "friend's" domestic obligations. As it would turn out, there were even several nights in a row when Toni was unfettered and could invite Adam to one or another Washington festivity.

His every attempt to elicit personal details of her life—except for what she had told him about her marriage—was met with a perfunctory rendition of her curriculum vitae, until finally he said in frustration, "This is supposed to be a conversation, not a job interview."

One evening, as they were walking home from a performance of *Swan Lake* at the Kennedy Center, he was in a carefree mood and actually danced for a few seconds in imitation of the prince. She surprised him by executing several steps in response.

The whole incident was out of character for them both. Their defenses were suddenly down and they confessed to one another that, as children, they had each studied ballet.

"What made you quit?" he asked. "I mean, you have a perfect dancer's body."

She smiled. "Thanks for the compliment. The stupid truth is that I was always so tall that none of the boys could lift me. What stopped you from becoming the American Baryshnikov?"

"Actually," he answered, trying to sound mysterious, "I had an ulterior motive for taking lessons."

"Which was?"

"I'll tell you another time." He grinned. And then, a few paces later, he scolded her, "Now can you see what a pain in the ass it is when you deliberately classify harmless information?"

That night, Boyd Penrose phoned at three A.M.

Without apology or preface he reported, "Cooper-smith, I've just read the Boss's numbers, and those lymphocytes are definitely making a comeback. I think we've turned the corner, old buddy."

Overflowing with euphoria, Adam called Boston and conveyed the good news to Max. As he hung up, there was another ring.

"Hi, I got Boyd's message too, your line was busy," Toni said ecstatically. "Were you on with Max?"

"Yes, I just reported to him."

"I figured as much. Would you like to report to *me* for an impromptu party?"

"Why not," Adam agreed.

Toni was intoxicated with joy. "Oh, Adam," she wept, hurling her arms around him as he entered her apartment. "You've done it—you've saved my father!"

Suddenly she was kissing him on the lips.

It was unexpected, but far from undesirable. He'd been happy to begin with, but this amorous gesture added a new dimension.

Which he welcomed wholeheartedly.

The next morning, Toni put her arms around him and pleaded, "*Now* will you tell me why you took ballet?"

"Two reasons. To begin with, my mother was the pianist for the class and I joined as an act of loyalty. Also it was a way to hurt my father for the shabby way he treated her. I punished him—imagine an Indiana steelworker having to tell his buddies that his son was a fruitcake who pranced around in tights."

"Well, I can vouch for your masculinity," she said, beaming. "And I'll be happy to sign an affidavit. Anyway, what happened to your mom?"

"She died when I was twelve. He killed her."

"What? You can't be serious."

"She was trying to bear him another kid, and she got toxemia in the late stages of pregnancy." His anger was emerging now. "I mean, it was a heartless thing from start to finish—when she got into trouble, he bullied the doctor to hold off delivery to make sure the baby she was carrying would live. In the end they lost both of them."

"Who took care of you?"

"I took care of myself."

"That's impossible."

"Yes. I found that out. So, unlikely as it sounds, I took up a sport—platform diving."

"Ah-ha," she replied with admiration. "I guess you wanted to flirt with danger, huh?"

"Sort of. But it meant that for at least a couple of seconds—in my head—I could be completely alone, thirty-three feet above the rest of the world."

"I knew you were a kindred spirit," she murmured. "We're both closet loners."

She continued her interrogation at breakfast.

"Did your dad ever find out you were really a daring young diver?"

"Yes," Adam said, his face revealing some of his deeply repressed sadness. "He was studying the only section of the paper he ever read, and discovered I was competing in the state championships. He showed up with two of his drinking buddies. But they had never been to a meet, and cheered in all the wrong places. It made me so nervous, I dove like a whale and really screwed up my point total."

She could tell from his eyes that the memory of his failure still plagued him.

"After that, all I wanted to do was get the hell away from home. And at that point my only chance was getting an academic scholarship. My grades were better than my diving. Ever hear of Shimer College?"

"Frankly, no."

"Nobody has. But it's a small, progressive offshoot of the University of Chicago. They believed if you could pass their test, you were ready for college. It was a kind of incubator for premeds anxious to save a few years. I was so keen to be a doctor that I worked as an orderly in Michael Reese Hospital in the summers—

which gave me a respectable excuse for not going home. I channeled my anger into studying, and by some miracle I got into Harvard Med."

"No doubt with the goal of keeping women from dying of toxemia," Toni suggested gently.

"And saving babies," Adam added. "I was a grand old man of nineteen. I may have been academically prepared, but I was a social misfit. Especially among all those smooth Ivy League graduates who'd never even heard of Shimer. I suppose that's why I only felt at home with the other lab rats."

"Is that how you met Max?"

Adam nodded. "I finally found a father I respected. While I was finishing my residency in OB/GYN, Max wangled me a research fellowship. He didn't just teach me immunology, he taught me life. I mean, the first time I was invited to his house for dinner, I knew that Max and Lisl had the kind of relationship that gave marriage a good name.

"She's a Kleinian analyst—does wonders with children. They took me under their wing. She introduced me to the late quartets of Beethoven."

"They're really difficult," Toni remarked.

"Yeah," Adam agreed, again impressed by the breadth of her knowledge. "And most especially since I didn't even know the *early* quartets."

"Do they have any kids?" Toni asked.

"Me, I guess."

"Then you gave them something very special too."

"I hope so, and if I ever qualify for the title of human being, it's because of their generosity."

"And?" Toni queried.

"And now it's your turn to be up close and personal," he responded, hoping his candor had eased her own inhibitions.

But she suddenly pleaded lateness for work, she had to be at the Department of Justice in fifteen minutes. They would talk again that evening. Adam let go reluc-

tantly, half suspecting that she would use the day to rebuild her psychic barricades.

He was right. It had been like dancing with someone
at a costume ball who went home without taking off her
mask. And, ironically, though he knew the intimate details of Toni's life, he knew less than nothing about the
woman herself. Indeed, when the time came for him to
go back to Boston, he could not resist venting his frustration with a farewell dig:

"Well, Toni, it's been nice *not* knowing you."

Naturally, he did not leave until the third blood tests
came through. They were—in Penrose's words—
"squeaky clean." He and Adam agreed that it was safe
to tell the patient that his recovery was certain.

Hartnell was overwhelmed. After spending an hour
with his beloved "Skipper," he summoned Adam for a
private conversation.

"Now you listen, Coopersmith, and listen good. I've
got a hell of a lot of influence, and thanks to your chief,
I'm going to be around to wield it for a long time. I
owe him. Now tell me, what would Max Rudolph want
most in the world?"

Adam moved closer to the bed and said almost in a
whisper, "The humanoid mouse is just one of Max's
many scientific achievements. I don't think anyone
alive deserves the Nobel Prize more."

"No problem," the Boss murmured.

5

ISABEL

ONCE MORE the demons had been awakened in Raymond da Costa. After his son had gone off to school and his wife to work, he was free to nurture his daughter's genius.

One of the advantages of his nonacademic appointment in the Physics Department was that he was not obliged to punch a time clock. Therefore, except for his obligatory presence during certain afternoon lab hours, he could build the apparatus for use by the physics professors even late at night if he wished. And, indeed, this freedom was an important aspect of the new regimen he began.

He was constantly testing Isabel, desperate to see how far the horizon of her intelligence stretched.

When they were on the floor playing with various blocks, he placed half a dozen of the red wooden cubes in a row, under which he placed another line with three white ones.

"Isabel, how many red boxes are there?"

She counted to six cheerfully.

"How many white ones?"

"Three."

"But how many are there altogether?"

She pondered for a moment and then answered, "Nine."

"I've read the books, honey," Raymond reported that evening to Muriel. "And the association of different

33

colored shapes as a group is a skill they expect from a seven-year-old."

Muriel smiled. "Are you sure you didn't coach her?"

"Don't be silly. I'll let you see for yourself."

Isabel had been playing in the living room when he summoned her, and placing a big leaf of drawing paper on the table, wrote:

$$6 + 5 =$$

She took the paper and immediately scribbled *11*.

Raymond glanced at his wife. "Well," he remarked with pride, "we have a budding Einstein, don't we?"

"No," she corrected him, "we have a flowering Isabel da Costa."

At first both of them took delight in Isabel's gift. Except now and then Muriel felt a twinge of guilt at the thought of her poor, sweet but ordinary Peter, who was sent off to school every morning like a package.

This time, having been blessed with a truly gifted child, Raymond intended to encourage her learning as much as possible. He resented having to surrender Isabel to some brainless nursery for three hours each morning. But since her mother insisted that she needed the playtime for her social development, Ray disguised his displeasure and rescheduled his afternoon commitments at the lab.

He reread Piaget, which made him passionately curious to learn when his daughter's mind would be capable of making the connection to abstract thought. He devised a simple test.

"Isabel, I'm picking a number, but I'm not going to tell you what it is. I'll call it *x*."

"Okay," she replied enthusiastically.

He took a piece of paper and scribbled:

$$x + 5 = 12$$

$$x = 12 - 5$$
$$x = 7$$

"Do you understand, darling?"

"Sure."

"Now I'll write a secret formula: $x + 7 = 4 + 11$"

"So—what does x stand for?"

The little girl pondered for a moment and then blithely announced, "Eight."

Raymond gaped. She had not merely crossed the threshold of abstract thought, but pirouetted through it like a ballerina.

From this apocalyptic moment onward, life in the da Costa household changed. Isabel became like a princess in a fairy tale—an almost divine creature guarded by a fierce dragon. And Raymond breathed fire on anyone who dared approach Isabel with the innocent hope of becoming her friend.

Muriel concurred that their daughter was a prodigy, but was determined that she would not become a freak. She tried to insulate Isabel's genius with as much normalcy as possible. This intensified her confrontations with Ray.

They were at loggerheads on the question of sending her to elementary school.

"Elementary school will just hold her back," he argued. "Don't you think that would be unfair to her?"

Yet, at this point, his wife had misgivings. "Raymond, I don't doubt that Isabel would learn more with you as a teacher. But what's she going to do about friends?"

"What do you mean?" he demanded.

"She needs playmates her own age. That is, if you expect her to grow up to be normal."

He did not, as she had feared, lose his temper.

"Look, honey," he reasoned quietly. " 'Normal' is simply not an adjective that applies to Isabel. There are no real precedents for someone with her ability. Believe me, she enjoys the time we spend together. In fact, her appetite is insatiable. She can't seem to learn enough."

Muriel did some painful soul-searching. Despite everything, she loved her husband and wanted to preserve their marriage. To continue disputing his every move would put an unnatural strain not only on them, but on both the children.

It was far from easy, but she realized there was no alternative. Though inwardly angry, she kept a stoic silence when Raymond took the inevitable step and informed the Board of Education that he would no longer send his daughter to school, but was himself assuming full responsibility for her education.

She simply stayed firm and, despite Ray's grumbling, enrolled Isabel in grammar school with her peers.

With the proviso—and with Ray there was always a proviso—that the moment Isabel came home from school, she would be under his exclusive tutelage. With no distractions.

Of course, Muriel took pride in her daughter's intelligence. But she was equally aware of Isabel's ability to relate to children of her own age. She could still discuss Winnie the Pooh with her nursery school classmates. There was only one difference: Isabel had read the book herself.

Two afternoons a week, Muriel would see pupils at home—children who were learning the rudiments of the violin—sometimes lending them Peter's long discarded quarter-size fiddle.

One day Muriel left the violin on the coffee table. And while Ray was grading lab papers and she was preparing dinner, Isabel picked it up. Copying the others she had seen taking lessons, she placed the instrument under her neck, grasped the bow, and scraped it across the strings.

The result was a raucous screech that brought Muriel

from the kitchen to the living room door. There she stopped to observe her daughter without being seen.

After a few more attempts, Isabel was able to bow an A string, which grew clearer with every stroke. She then began to explore the string with her first finger until she found a B. She did not, of course, know its name, but was satisfied that it sounded right.

It was not long before her experiments yielded a C-sharp—two steps higher.

At this point her mother could hide no longer. She entered the room and remarked as casually as she could, "That sounds lovely, dear. Now you can use just those three notes to play 'Frère Jacques.' Here, let me show you."

Muriel went to the piano and conducted and accompanied Isabel in her melodic debut.

She was too ecstatic to keep this discovery from Ray. Although he was excited, he was worried that Muriel might now try to seduce the girl into the realm of music.

"Gosh, that's fantastic, honey," he murmured. "Do you realize that she's not much older than Mozart was when he just picked up the violin and began to play?"

"I know," she responded, regretting his allusion.

"But did you know that he was also a mathematical genius? His father made the crucial decision that someone of his son's age could never have made."

"Which you are now making for Isabel?" she asked.

"Precisely."

"Don't you think that's a bit unfair—not to mention presumptuous?" she said, fighting back. "Who's to say that Isabel couldn't go further in—"

Her husband slammed the table and stood up. "I don't want to hear any more of this," he thundered. "The girl's a scientist, and maybe even—yes, I'll say it—another Einstein."

Muriel was incensed. "Did *you* know that Einstein was also a fine violinist?"

"Yes, darling," he answered facetiously. "But it was a hobby, a kind of recreation from his God-given task of explaining the universe."

"Am I hearing you right?" she asked, barely able to control herself. "Are you implying the Almighty has decreed that our daughter will become a scientist?"

"I'm not implying anything," Raymond shot back. "I'm simply saying that I won't let anything stand in the way of my daughter's development. That's it, Muriel, the discussion is closed."

August 10
There are two invisible people haunting our house, and the way my parents talk about them, you'd think they were members of the family.

One is "Albert Einstein," who's come to mean the same as genius (another word I keep hearing and which makes me very nervous).

I looked him up in the Encyclopedia Britannica and read that his ideas were so extraordinary that at first people refused to believe them. Dad did his best to explain them to me—apologizing that he himself had trouble understanding some of them.

But I feel very uncomfortable when he predicts that someday I'll make these kinds of discoveries.

Frankly—and I'm almost ashamed to admit this—I'd rather be compared to Brooke Shields.

If I could have my greatest dream come true, it would be to look like her. People say I already have her cheekbones, and now all I need is the rest.

Then, when I try to take refuge with Mom in the kitchen, she starts to "chat" about the music.

That's where the other ghost comes in. His name is Wolfgang Amadeus Mozart.

He lived in the eighteenth century and was—as people like to call me and make me cringe—a "prodigy."

Mom told me he played in a violin trio with grown-

ups when he was only my age (which makes me seem slow, thank God).

Dad goes crazy whenever Mom mentions Mozart. And he must have been listening because about half an hour later, when we were practicing Bach's Air on a G String, Dad came rushing in, all excited, carrying a very old book which describes Mozart covering all the furniture in his house with pieces of paper on which he had written his calculations.

Fortunately, Mom and Dad came to an agreement that I could do an hour of music a day and—as a special treat—two on the weekends.

Peter watched them fight without saying a word. Later, he came to my room and said, "Boy, am I glad I'm not smart."

By her ninth birthday Isabel was so well-grounded in mathematics that Ray could introduce her to the sacred temple in which he was merely a humble acolyte. He presented her with the same copy of *Physics for Students of Science and Engineering* by Resnick and Halliday that he himself had used in college.

She immediately began to read the first chapter.

"This is terrific, Dad. I wish you had given it to me sooner."

Though he was elated by Isabel's reaction and longed to plunge into physics with her, Ray had apparatus to build for Professor Stevenson that was due the next day. He never used to leave things to the last minute, but he had different priorities now. Recharging himself with black coffee, he set out for the university after the eleven P.M. news.

He returned on the fringe of morning and wearily turned the key in the lock. He could hear the sound of classical music emanating from the living room. And the lamps were still on.

Dammit, do they think I'm made of money? he thought to himself.

He entered irritably, only to find Isabel sprawled out on the living room floor, candy wrappers scattered everywhere. She had propped the textbook against the sofa and was working furiously with a pad and pencil.

"Hi, Dad," she called cheerfully. "How are things at the lab?"

"The same boring stuff," he replied. Then added, "Shouldn't you be asleep? It's almost time for the big bad wolf to knock on your door for morning studies."

"I don't care." She smiled. "I've been having a great time. The problems at the ends of the chapters are really neat."

Chapters? How many had she read? He sat down beside her on a hassock and asked, "Tell me what you've learned."

"Well, since I did the linear motion chapter, I know that acceleration is the first derivative of the velocity."

"And what's the derivative?"

"Well," she answered eagerly, "take for example a ball you throw into the air. Its initial speed greatly slows down when it leaves your hand because of gravity, and comes to a stop at the peak height of its path. Then gravity pulls it back down again faster and faster until it hits the ground."

Of course, Raymond thought to himself, she's a quick learner. He knew she had a photographic memory. But how much did she *understand*?

He probed carefully. "How come you have all these different speeds?"

"Oh well," she volleyed back. "At first the ball gets faster from your upward throw, and it takes time for gravity to determine its speed completely. So the acceleration is the rate of change of the velocity. And that, Dad, is the first derivative. Any questions?"

"No," he murmured barely audibly, "no questions."

April 20
Sometimes, when Dad is working really late at the uni-

versity, Peter taps on my door and we sneak down to the kitchen and raid the fridge. Then we sit and talk about all kinds of stuff.

He asks me if I miss the "outside world," so I sort of joke that I see it through a telescope when we do astronomy. But I know what he means.

He told me that he was going to a summer camp that specializes in soccer.

I know he's dying to make the school team, and I think our folks are just great to give him this chance to excel in something I can't do at all.

He's so excited at the prospect that every chance he gets he uses our garage door as a goal and kicks the ball against it. Unfortunately, Dad started to notice the scuff marks and really bawled him out.

I had a terrible nightmare last night, and when I woke from it, I couldn't get back to sleep. I dreamed that I forgot my multiplication tables. I mean I couldn't even do two times two. Dad got so angry that he made me pack and leave home.

I wonder what it means.

6
ADAM

AFTER HIS return from Washington, Adam had wondered whether to tell Max about that final conversation with Hartnell. But his mentor had already been upset to learn that the man for whom he had compromised his principles was not, after all, the President of the United

States. The fact that someone like the Boss had offered to help obtain him a Nobel, might stigmatize the prize forever in Max's scrupulous estimation.

In any case, whenever the Nobel had come up in casual conversation and someone suggested that Max had long ago earned it, he always commented dismissively, "Well, if it must come, let's hope it's not for a while. T. S. Eliot was right when he said, 'The Nobel is a ticket to your own funeral. No one's ever done anything after he got it.' "

"In that case," Lisl playfully called his bluff, "if the Karolinska Institute should telephone tomorrow, are you in or out?"

"Well," he continued to equivocate, "Did you know that some of their smorgasbords have more than twenty different kinds of herring? Not to mention smoked reindeer steak."

"Then by all means you have to accept," Adam interposed, "if only for gastronomic reasons."

That round was over. The trio exchanged silent smiles for a moment, then Max said earnestly, "Anyway, they'll never choose me—I don't go to conferences. I don't play the game."

Lisl beamed. At times like this he would only accept *her* reassurance. "Darling, granted you're not a politician, but on rare occasions simply being a genius is enough for the Nobel Prize."

The evening continued with small talk—although in the Rudolph household no talk was really "small." After a heated debate on the artistic virtues of Sarah Caldwell's revival of Monteverdi's *Orfeo*, Lisl brought out some more glasses of tea and asked casually, "Now that you've cured your mysterious patient, what are you whiz kids going to do for an encore?"

"Lisl," Max explained, "this lymphosarcoma was out of our line anyway. They were just borrowing our mice to test other people's research. After all, the sign on my door does say 'Immunology,' and there's no shortage of autoimmune diseases to investigate. And of course we still have the ongoing pernicious anemia project."

"I know," she countered. "But your lab is like a circus, and where you two choose to work is always the center ring."

"Don't worry," Max uttered with mock exasperation. "When we decide, you'll be the first to know."

"No," Max shouted, "I absolutely refuse—you're a sadist!"

"Come on, get in, it's good for you. Remember, I'm a doctor."

"No—it's insanity to make a normal person jump into freezing water at the crack of dawn."

Adam, treading water, continued to coax the distinguished professor to join him.

"Listen, you did your medicine back in the Stone Age. They didn't know that exercise was so important for your health."

"Very well," the older man capitulated, "but I'm coming down the ladder."

As Max—no picture of grace—huffed and puffed through the water, his self-appointed trainer swam in the adjacent lane shouting encouragement.

"Good going—the first ten laps are the hardest. How do you feel?"

"Like an old fish," he gasped as he struggled along.

"Great. You've never seen an overweight fish, have you?"

Afterward, as they sat in the locker room drying off, Max confessed, "I hate to admit it, but I actually feel wonderful. Now I only hope nobody from the lab saw me. I feel undignified without a tie."

"By all means bring one to the pool next time. Didn't you notice those two lab technicians who waved at us?"

"How could I tell what they were, they weren't wearing white coats."

"They certainly weren't," Adam grinned. "Still, they were sending very friendly smiles in our direction."

"*Your* direction. I've no illusions about my looks. But let's get upstairs. I want to talk to you about an important project."

"Something new? How long have you been hiding it from me?"

"Oh, about ten years." And there was something about Max's tone of voice that sounded as if he was not exaggerating.

Thirty minutes later they were locked within the glass-walled partitions of Max's office.

"This is very difficult for me to discuss," the older man began uneasily. "Tell me truthfully, have you come across any rumors about why Lisl and I didn't have children?"

"That's none of my damn business."

"Decency never slowed the circulation of juicy gossip, my boy. Do you mean to tell me that you've never heard it whispered in the corridors that I didn't have a family because it would distract me from my research?"

Adam looked his boss in the eye and said with conviction, "First of all, I've never heard it—and most of all, I don't believe it for a minute."

"I'm glad," Max responded, "The truth is, we both desperately wanted a baby. And in fact Lisl was pregnant at least fourteen times."

"Fourteen?"

"Well, a great number of them ended so early that only a doctor could have determined that she'd been pregnant at all. There didn't seem to be anybody in our illustrious OB/GYN Department who could shed light on the matter. So I took the investigation into my own hands.

"I soon discovered that there was a sizable number of women who go through this agony many times before giving up completely. It's a catastrophe that haunts them through their whole life. And a mystery which, to this day, remains unsolved." He looked up for a moment, his face flushed with emotion.

"Max, think of all the nights we've worked together in the lab, spilling out our hearts to each other. How come you never once mentioned this to me?"

"I didn't want to burden you with something that neither of us could do anything about. But I've been gathering data over nearly ten years."

"All that time behind my back?"

Max nodded. "I've been moonlighting in the Marblehead Gynecological Clinic, specializing in patients with repeated miscarriages." He patted his computer and said, "Everything's in here. All I need is the benefit of your brain."

"Okay, boss. But I still sense that if Batman's calling Robin, it means he's already on the trail of a solution."

"As a matter of fact, I am, Boy Wonder. Naturally, I'll give you the printouts, but I think you'll agree with my basic hypothesis: that these unexplained miscarriages might result from the woman rejecting the fetus as a foreign body, the way early transplant patients rejected hearts and kidneys.

"My experiments with mice have shown that certain females carry their own antigens, which are toxic to the baby." He lowered his head sadly and murmured, "I am afraid my little Lisl is that kind of mouse."

"You must have suffered a great deal," Adam whispered, unable to hide his sadness.

"No. She suffered—I just endured." And then, regaining his gruff tone of voice, he ordered, "Now, let's get to work, shall we? Your computer's already hooked to my database, so all you have to know is the password."

"Which is?"

"You don't have to be Sherlock Holmes to figure that one out."

" 'Blintzes'?"

"You have great scientific instinct."

"Thanks."

"What are you thanking me for, dear boy? I've just saddled you with a problem of enormous magnitude."

"I know," Adam conceded, "but it makes a difference to be working on an experiment and being able to visualize the human being involved." To which he added softly, "Even though it's too late for Lisl."

With the data, the technicians, and the mice already in place, it was relatively easy for Adam to move his investigation from the confines of Max's obsession to the open benches of Immunology Lab 808. Also, the information already gathered had given them leads with which to begin.

Moreover, there had been progress in other areas of the field, as Max explained. "I have it on good authority that researchers at Sandoz are well along the way with an immunosuppressant that will transform organ transplants into everyday occurrences."

"Great," Adam responded. "Now all *we* have to do is discover an analogy that would suppress the autoimmune reaction in pregnant females."

"Right." Max smiled. "And then we'll go for lunch."

Adam worked demonically. Whenever he was not seeing patients or delivering babies, he was in the lab.

Late one night, the lab phone rang, shrilly interrupting the quiet contemplation of those few still present and working.

"Hey, Adam, it's for you," called Cindy Po, a microbiologist from Hawaii. "Female—and very sexy."

So immersed was he in what he'd been studying, Adam did not at first react to someone "sexy" calling him at this time of night. He merely walked like a somnambulist to the phone and said, "This is Dr. Coopersmith."

"Hi, Doctor," came a cheery voice.

"Toni," he responded with pleasure. "It's nice to hear

from you. What made you call me at this ungodly hour?"

"The whole truth? I've been pining here, hoping you'd make a house call. Since it didn't look like it was going to happen, I phoned your apartment. When I got no answer, I decided to find out whether you were on a heavy date or buried in research. Is there someone else in your life yet?"

"Listen, now that you know where I am on a Saturday night, you must realize the only creatures I'm involved with are furry and have tails. It was you who was otherwise ... engaged."

"Actually, I wanted to talk to you about that. How about coming to Washington next weekend?"

He challenged her. "How about *you* coming to Boston?"

"Fine. Thanks for the invitation."

A few moments later Adam hung up and smiled broadly.

"Well, well, well," Cindy remarked from a proximity that left no doubt that she had overheard the entire conversation. "It looks like you've blown your cover."

"Meaning?"

"Your ostensible indifference to the female sex—at least the species that works in this lab."

"Cindy," he chided good-naturedly, "my private life is nobody's business."

"On the contrary, Prof, it's probably the best source of gossip we've ever had. You've been voted the cutest doctor every year I've been here."

"Come off it, Cindy. Go back to your amino acids."

"Yes *sir*," the young post-doc replied with playful deference, tossing off a final comment as she left. "We'll take a straw vote to see if she's worthy of you."

Max Rudolph lived by his own rules. And they included surprise visits to the lab. Late the next afternoon, he discovered his protégé hard at work. Eyeing him with disapproval, he demanded, "How many hours of sleep did you get last night?"

"A few."

" 'A few' is not a scientific answer," he admonished. "And did you take in a movie as you promised?"

"Actually, I got carried away and missed the last show."

The professor frowned. "I don't like disobedience on my staff. Even your great brain has to recharge. So finish what you're doing and we'll go out to Newton and get some decent food into you."

Adam was grateful for the invitation, and twenty minutes later they were in Max's vintage Volkswagen Beetle, sputtering along Commonwealth Avenue in the growing winter darkness.

As the older man failed to stop for the second red light in a row, Adam scolded, "Pay attention. Your mind's a million miles away. You shouldn't be driving at the best of times."

"At least *I* got some sleep last night," Max replied with mock sanctimony. "Now sit back and listen to the second movement of this Schubert." And with that he turned up the volume and hummed along.

Adam relented. At that instant he took his attention off the road—a lapse for which he would castigate himself the rest of his life. As they reached the crest of Heartbreak Hill on Commonwealth Avenue and began to hurtle downward, two teenagers on bikes suddenly appeared directly in the path of the car.

Max swerved to avoid them. Skidding on a patch of ice, he lost control and crashed violently into a tree.

The silence after the accident belied its gravity. There was the crumpling of thin metal. Then the sound of the driver's forehead striking the windshield.

And then total quiet.

For a moment Adam sat there motionless, in shock.

He listened intently but could not hear any sound of breathing. Reaching over to feel the old man's pulse, he knew this was merely a pretext to touch his mentor for the last time.

Slowly he was gripped by an agonizing awareness. *He's dead. My friend, my teacher—my father—he's dead. And it's all my fault.*

A cry emerged from him like the howl of a wounded animal.

He was still sobbing when the squad cars came.

The cyclists, though horrified, were able to give a more or less coherent account of what had transpired.

The senior police officer wanted to get his paperwork over with. "Do you know about next of kin?" he asked.

"His wife. Lisl. She only lives a few blocks away. I could walk right there."

"Would you like us to drive you?"

"No thank you, Sergeant. I need time to collect my thoughts."

Lisl took the news bravely. She murmured a few words about the folly of allowing her husband behind the wheel.

"He was so headstrong, my Max, I should never have let him drive."

She then realized how shaken Adam was and touched his hand gently.

"Stop blaming yourself. You have to accept that terrible things like this happen."

But why to Max? Adam grieved. Why to such a saintly human being?

Lisl called one of her close friends, with whom she had done her analytical studies. The woman was more than willing to sit with her while Adam went through the grim procedure of making the funeral arrangements—which, in case of accidental death, had to wait for the obligatory police autopsy.

At six P.M. Eli Cass, the press officer from Harvard,

telephoned for details of the accident to add to the release he was rushing to complete for the next morning's *Boston Globe* and the various wire services. Eli was pleased to speak to someone who could update the list of Max's awards.

"Dean Holmes said it was only a question of time before Max got the Nobel," Cass remarked.

"Yes," Adam replied numbly. "He was probably the leading immunologist in the world."

In the living room, Lisl had been joined by Maurice Oates, the Rudolphs' lawyer.

"I wouldn't be discussing Max's will so soon," he apologized. "Except that it's very emphatic about there being no speeches at his interment. In fact, no service of any kind. Otherwise the testament is straightforward." He paused, and then looked at the tall young doctor standing ashen-faced in the corner. "He wanted you to have his gold pocket watch."

"I'll get it," Lisl offered.

"No, no," Adam said. "There's plenty of time for that."

"Please," she overruled him. "If I don't give it to you tonight, you'll have nothing of Max's to go home with."

And now, suddenly, heedless of the others in the room, she fell into Adam's arms. And they both began to sob for the terrible loss of the noblest human being they would ever know.

Though it was nearly midnight when he left, Lisl was still surrounded by several friends and neighbors who had come to keep her company. In addition, the house was filled with palpable memories of Max: his office, his books, his clothes. His reading glasses placed neatly on the desk.

In contrast, all Adam had was the silent gold watch, a more poignant token since it had been given to Max by his own father when he'd received his M.D. It had now become a symbolic way of passing the torch. Adam held the cold metal to his cheek.

His phone rang. It was Toni.

"It was on the eleven o'clock news," she explained. "Are you okay?"

"Not really," he replied bitterly. "I should have been driving."

There was a silence. Toni did not know what to say. Finally she asked: "When's the funeral?"

"Tuesday morning. There's not going to be any ceremony—he specified no eulogy."

"That seems wrong," Toni objected, "there should at least be words—expressions of affection. Lisl may not realize how much she needs it too. You can't just walk away without saying *anything*. Would it be all right if I came?"

"But you didn't even know him."

"Funerals are for the living, not the dead."

"I realize that. But I have to look after Lisl."

"I know," she answered gently. "But somebody has to take care of you."

There was a momentary pause.

"Thanks, Toni," he whispered. "I'd appreciate that."

There were two dozen or so gathered around Max Rudolph's freshly dug grave: the dean, colleagues, their wives, his lab teams and students. And standing discreetly among them was Antonia Nielson from Washington.

The undertakers, experienced with "silent" funerals, had prepared cut flowers for the mourners to drop onto the lowered coffin as they passed by to pay their last respects.

Finally, only Adam and Lisl were left. And as he held his flower, unable to let go, words emerged from his throat unbidden.

It was the lines from Hamlet, which suddenly seemed so appropriate.

He was a man, take him for all-in-all,
I shall not look upon his like again.

Then, unwillingly, he let fall his flower.
And Lisl did the same.

7
SANDY

CURIOUSLY ENOUGH, Sandy Raven did not look back
on his formative years with any anger. For he was only
marginally aware of his parents' mutual hostility and he
always recalled childhood as a time of purest love. Not
anyone's for him, but his own secret passion for his
classmate, Rochelle Taubman. He burned for her with a
flame intense enough to vaporize diamonds.

Moreover, this was long before Rochelle became the
radiant goddess who graced the covers of *Vogue,*
Harper's Bazaar, and *Silver Screen.* In those days, she
was simply the belle of P.S. 161.

After all, she was slender and strikingly beautiful,
with high cheekbones, shiny auburn hair, and deliques-
cent eyes, while he was pudgy and bespectacled, with a
complexion reminiscent of oatmeal.

She barely knew he existed, except when finals approached and she cajoled him into helping her prepare
for their math and science exams. He did not feel the
slightest bit exploited.

The mere fact that she sweetened each tutorial session
with phrases like, "You're wonderful, Sandy," or "I'll
love you forever," was recompense enough. And yet

when the testing period ended, amnesia of the heart stepped in and she ignored him until the next semester's finals.

And in the interim Sandy would merely pine.

His father tried to cheer him up. "Don't take it to heart, sonny boy. Remember that even if she prefers the football captain, someday his jock will fade. And suddenly you'll find yourself alone with her on either side of Yankee Stadium with millions cheering as you walk toward each other in slow motion and embrace."

"God, Dad," Sandy exclaimed in wonderment, "where'd you get an image like that?"

Sidney beamed. "The movies, of course."

School was not yet over and Sandy still had time to boast of his father's new eminence in Hollywood. And he made absolutely certain to mention to Rochelle that his dad was now a junior executive at Twentieth Century-Fox.

Once again she remembered Sandy's existence, rushed to him and declared, "I don't know how I'll bear being without you. I mean, you'll be at Science and I'll be at Music and Art. When will we ever see each other?"

"There's always the telephone," he replied with a touch of sarcasm. But then he chivalrously volunteered, "Any night you need help with your homework, just call me up."

"I will, I will," she chirped. "I guess I never had a chance to tell you, but I was sorry to hear about your mom and dad splitting."

"Thanks," he replied. "I suppose it's better for all of us."

"But will you ever get to see your father?"

"Actually he's just sent me a bus ticket so I can spend the summer with him in Hollywood."

"Gosh, that sounds so exciting. I wish I could go too."

Oh Rochelle, he thought to himself, his heart drumming. If only I *could* take you with me.

"Be sure to send me a postcard." She smiled seductively. "That is if you still remember your old friends."

Sandy would never forget his first visit to California.

It was nearly lunchtime when Sid's Chevy arrived at the gate of the Twentieth Century-Fox studios on the corner of Pico and Avenue of the Stars.

The guard immediately recognized him, gave a kind of salute, and smiled. "Good morning, Mr. Raven. This is pretty late for *you*."

"Yeah, I had to pick up my boy at the station."

The guard waved them through with a cordial, "Hi there, young fellow. Welcome to Tinseltown."

Sid drove slowly to his parking place so that his son could drink in the sights of the studio. Indeed, for the first quarter mile they seemed to be in another era.

Huge swarms of stagehands were busy putting up an elevated railway track, while others were hammering and nailing what looked like a row of old-fashioned brownstones—the set for *Hello, Dolly*.

In the commissary, a cavernous dining hall whose facade served as one of the buildings in "Peyton Place," there was an elevated platform reserved for major moguls, a category for which his father did not yet qualify. The bigwigs would be joined by whichever stars were filming on the lot at that time. Today it was Charlton Heston, wearing an astronaut's gear.

Yet the most startling view was of the plebeians' eating area, which seemed to have been attacked by a legion of gorillas—who were sitting everywhere, casually munching sandwiches and swilling coffee.

Sid explained that these creatures were extras from an epic called *Planet of the Apes*, in which "a pack of overgrown monkeys chase Chuck Heston all over the map. It's a dynamite concept."

Everyone seemed to know and love his father. As

they ate their tuna on rye with pickle, Sidney was greeted by innumerable simians as well as other Hollywood animals. Sandy was awestruck.

"Musicals are in," Sidney declared to his son over that evening's chili, and went on to explain that *The Sound of Music* had struck a vein and the American people were waiting for more of the same.

"And I've got a notion for a blockbuster. Wait till you hear this, kiddo, it's a real winner."

"What is it Dad?"

"It's called 'Frankie'—a song and dance version of *Frankenstein.*"

"That sounds great. But hasn't that picture been done a lot of times?"

"Kiddo," his father pronounced, "in Hollywood there's a saying, 'If a thing's worth doing, it's worth doing again.' I've got five writers working on it already."

"Five? How do they all fit in the same room?"

Sidney laughed. "That sounds like the stateroom scene in *A Night at the Opera.* No, that's not how it's done out here. They're each working on separate versions. Then I get another writer to help me pick the best parts of each draft and stitch 'em together.

"Do you know why it's a guaranteed hit, sonny boy? Because it's one of the sure-fire stories of all time. For centuries men have dreamed of actually growing life in the laboratory. So all we need is a new twist—which is why I've got these five overpriced eggheads typing away on treatments."

He then inquired of his son, "Any ideas for a gimmick?"

"Well," Sandy said, proud of the opportunity to parade his learning, "as a matter of fact, I might. You could have Dr. Frankenstein be a genetic researcher building his monster with DNA."

"What's DNA?" his father asked.

"It's really the latest thing," Sandy said, waxing enthusiastic. "Back in 'fifty-three two guys in England named Watson and Crick deciphered the code of life—the genetic material we're all made of. DNA stands for deoxyribonucleic acid. It carries the instructions for making all living things in a simple code based on four chemicals. I mean, Dad, what makes your idea so brilliant is that it's right where science is at. I bet every guy in my school will see this movie twenty times."

"But kiddo, you gotta remember that in the great land called America, not everybody goes to Bronx High School of Science. I'm afraid your concept won't fly with Mr. Z."

Sandy felt embarrassed, thinking he had gone down in his father's estimation for having made so foolish a suggestion. He vowed to keep his big ideas to himself from now on.

The visit provided many an opportunity for heart-to-heart conversations, during which Sandy had revealed his unflagging passion for Rochelle. His father tried to be sympathetic, though platonic love was an emotion beyond his ken.

Sandy was relieved when the subject turned to one they could both comprehend: their aspirations for the future. On several occasions they had taken long walks by the ocean in Santa Monica, sharing the same cloud of fantasy.

The older man dreamed on a wide screen—of making big pictures with big stars for big money. And most of all, to have his work designated as "A Sidney Raven Production."

Biochemistry was the realm in which Sandy wanted to dominate—especially the genetic side. When he explained what this entailed, the elder Raven remarked warmly, "Well, in a way, we're both gonna be in the same business." He put his arm around the boy's shoulder. "You'll re-create life in a test tube, and I'll do it on the big screen." They understood each other.

And then, ever prone to rhapsodize, Sidney conceived of a time not too distant when—in a single year—he would win an Oscar and his son a Nobel Prize.

"You've got a vivid imagination, Dad," Sandy said affectionately.

"That's why I'm in the movie business, sonny boy."

Father and son had grown closer that summer than they ever had when they were living together 365 days a year.

Sandy returned from his first visit to the Coast tanned and confident. At least self-assured enough to put a dime in the slot and phone the lovely Miss Taubman "just to say hello."

She seemed less than overjoyed to hear from him until he reminded her with casual deliberation where he had spent his vacation. Her tone warmed and she suggested they meet for coffee.

At first he looked around for her in vain. Then, with a jolt, he realized that she had been waiting for him all the time at a booth near the jukebox.

She waved and he hurried to her table.

"Sorry, Rochelle, sorry," he apologized abjectly. "But I really didn't recognize you. I mean, you didn't tell me that you were a blond now. And that you . . ." He glanced at her face and was embarrassed to say it.

But she finished his thought. "I had it done last spring during Easter vacation. Didn't the doctor do a great job?" She showed him both sides of her new profile. "You'd never believe it wasn't my real nose."

Sandy felt genuinely saddened, for in truth he thought she had been far prettier with her original physiognomy.

And now he realized, to his growing chagrin, that he would never see that lovely face again. The operation had changed her from soulful madonna to Barbie Doll.

"Yeah, yeah, it looks great," he responded dutifully.

"Of course, I was against it at first," she explained. "But my agent insisted that I wouldn't have a chance in the movies without a more classic profile. Now, tell me all about Hollywood."

As he signaled to the waiter, she launched into a narrative that would have made Narcissus blush.

"Summer stock was unbelievable. I mean, not only did I get to do *Streetcar* and *Our Town*, but our final production was *Romeo and Juliet*. Joe Papp actually came backstage and spoke to me."

"Gosh, that's marvelous," Sandy remarked, but with a sense of unworthiness and loss. For he realized he was no longer in the same league as Rochelle Taubman. All summer he had merely watched, while she had *been* watched.

"Come on," she coaxed, "I'm waiting for your news. What's your father got on tap?"

He told her all about the studio, the apes. About "Frankie."

"And," he concluded, "it looks like 'Frankie' is a 'go' project."

"That sounds brilliant," she enthused. "Have they cast the female lead?"

"Actually, there isn't one in the story, that I know of."

"Really?" she responded. "But *Variety* says it's gonna be a musical. There's got to be a female lead. But what am I getting so excited about? It's bound to be Julie Andrews."

"I could always ask my father," Sandy offered generously.

"Oh, I wouldn't want to impose on you." She pounced like an amorous leopard. "All I'd ever accept is a screen test—the rest would be up to him."

Then she lowered her head and murmured apologetically, "I'm sorry, I really shouldn't be exploiting our friendship."

"No, no, no," he tried to dissuade her. "What else are friends for? I'll call him tonight."

"Oh, you really are a beautiful person," she added joyously. "Call me any time after you speak to him. I'll be sitting by the phone."

For the first time since they had met in kindergarten, Sandy Raven walked down the street with the unswerving certitude that of all possible telephone calls, Rochelle would be waiting most anxiously for *his*.

The news Sidney conveyed was bittersweet. Bitter for himself, but sweet for her.

It seemed the studio was retrenching and Mr. Z. had qualms about putting money into yet another big musical, even though he had loved the concept of "Frankie."

And yet, developing three other projects for Mr. Z., Sid was confident that he could arrange for Rochelle to audition for the Fox Players' School. This was less an academy than a collection of exquisitely beautiful, potential matinee idols and heartthrobs being groomed for stardom by the studio.

The next time they interviewed in New York, he would see to it that his son's inamorata would be auditioned.

She was unrestrained in her gratitude. "Oh Sandy," she gushed on the telephone, "I wish you were here—I'd throw my arms around you and give you a big kiss."

I can always come over, he thought. But he didn't say it.

Sid Raven was true to his word. That winter, when the scouts from Fox were next on the East Coast, they not only interviewed Rochelle, but gave her a screen test. They decided that "though she's a little skimpy in the boob department"—this was a confidential memo—she came across as an appealing personality, if not a convincing actress. But for her looks alone, she was certainly worth accepting for the studio's drama school on a three-year trial.

In her haste to depart for California, Rochelle somehow could not find time to contact Sandy. But when her jet had taken off and she had five hours to while away before she reached the land of the mirage merchants, she dashed off a note on TWA stationery, concluding, "For all the wonderful things you've done for me, I'll never forget you."

And yet, after alighting at Los Angeles Airport, she somehow neglected to mail the letter.

8

ADAM

THEY HAD called Toni's flight.

"Adam," she kept repeating like a litany, "if you want me to, I'll gladly stay."

"That's okay, Toni," he said, as if trying to prove his emotional independence. "I'll be all right on my own."

He missed her the moment he got back into his car. For he suddenly realized he couldn't go home. Not only was his apartment too full of Max, it was now bereft of Toni.

Instead, he went to the single place where he knew there would be fellow feeling and—what he needed most—talk of Max Rudolph.

His instinct proved correct. Not only had many of the staff chosen to go to the lab under the professional pretext of communing about Max, but by the time he arrived, they were all in a kind of forced good humor, remembering "the good old days," their boss's idiosyncrasies and gruffness.

Some had had a bit too much to drink, and Rob Weiner, a biochemist, spluttered, "If I know Max, wherever he is, he'll still make those surprise Sunday visits."

Adam then overheard a conversation he wished he hadn't.

"They've got to give it to Coopersmith," Cindy Po was saying. "I mean, that's what the old man would've wanted."

"I'm afraid you're still wet behind the ears," Clarissa Pryce, a veteran "mouse mother," retorted. "A person's ability to influence Harvard is limited to his lifetime. They'll choose whoever they want to run the lab. And, to be frank, Adam hasn't got the age or the publications to get the top job."

"Well I still say he deserves it," the younger woman insisted.

"Listen, honey, you may know your microbiology, but you have a lot to learn about academic politics. I'd say the biggest thing going against Adam—outside of sheer envy because a lot of the older men resent him—is that he was too close to Max."

At precisely midnight, his lab phone rang.

"Am I starting to haunt you?" Toni said, trying to sound casual.

"No, in fact I owe you an apology. Even during this 'wake'—and that's what it is, booze and all—while I'm missing Max, I'm missing you too."

"Thank you. I know that wasn't easy for you to say. If it means anything, I almost left the plane again before it took off."

"By the way, Lisl thought you were very nice."

"Oh," Toni said, unable to hide the satisfaction in her voice. "Give her my love."

It was in the evenings that Adam missed his teacher most. Especially since, after a decent period of mourning, only the night shift, the most introverted of all researchers, were at the benches.

The coldness of the Boston winters was intolerable without the warmth of Max Rudolph's intellect and friendship. Work was the only palliative, and Adam threw himself heart and soul into his mentor's last and most important project.

For Adam was now afire with an all-consuming dream—he wanted to complete this work so that he could mount the podium in Stockholm and tell the world, "This award belongs to Max Rudolph."

And yet the ache in his heart would still not go away.

When Harvard lured Ian Cavanagh from Oxford to take over Max Rudolph's chair and the directorship of the lab, the staff naturally transferred its wholehearted allegiance, closed ranks, and proceeded with research as usual.

Though Lisl urged him to be conciliatory—"even slightly sycophantic wouldn't be out of place," she said—Adam kept a cool distance. He had great difficulty bringing himself into the glass-walled office where the Englishman lorded it over the domain that had once been Max Rudolph's.

This was less deference than Cavanagh had expected from someone he still regarded as a junior man. It was immediately clear to everyone in the lab that he had set Adam in a special category. Whereas he called other members of staff by their first names, he always referred to his predecessor's favorite merely as Coopersmith.

Ignoring Lisl's protestations that he had better things to do, Adam insisted on taking her to dinner at least once a week. She was touched and flattered, and made every effort to succeed her husband as the young doctor's counselor.

"Have lunch with the man. Play the game. Cavanagh's first-rate and it won't take him long to recognize your abilities. But help him get to know you."

"I'm afraid it's too late for that," Adam replied dejectedly. "He dropped a little bombshell in my cubbyhole this morning. Apparently—because of 'financial restraints'—he's had to slash my next year's budget—and my salary—in half."

Lisl reacted angrily. "Excuse me while I revise my opinion of him. By cutting Max's most cherished project, he's just proved how petty he is. That money business isn't even a good lie. One of the reasons he got the job was his talent for grantsmanship, not to mention his ties with the biotech industry.

"He's probably intimidated by you, Adam. But you mustn't let him make you resign. Do some clinical work to bolster your income." She placed her hand firmly on his arm. "Just promise you won't give up."

"No, Lisl," he said with fervor. "I won't. This is something I've got to do for Max."

"No," she said emotionally. "You have to do it for *yourself.*"

Adam was determined to protect whatever little territory he still possessed in Max Rudolph's former laboratory. To make up the shortfall in his salary, he signed on as a supervisor in obstetrics at the Lying-In.

This meant the senior men could rest secure while the lowly residents handled the routine cases—with Adam close by to step in for the emergencies.

Moreover, since the terms of Adam's new employment required him merely to be in the medical school area, he could actually work in the lab, able to sprint to the delivery rooms of either the Lying-In or Brigham & Women's Hospital in less than five minutes. And whenever he was dejected by the enormity of his research, the part-time job gave him an emotional uplift.

His spirits were always buoyed by the sight of the

wriggling, wailing, red-faced newborn creatures destined to change the world of their new parents.

And perhaps even change the world.

And yet he found it hard to discuss this aspect of his work with Lisl. He felt that, if anything, Max's death had exacerbated the pain of her childlessness. But as the months passed, she had begun to come to terms with her loss. At least enough to realize that *he* had not.

"Trust me, Adam. Max wouldn't have wanted you to retreat from life. You're a young man. You should be thinking about your own babies, not just other people's."

Adam shrugged. "Give me a little time, Lisl," he replied evasively. "Cavanagh's still doing his best to make life difficult for me."

"Incidentally, how do things stand between you and that nice girl from Washington?"

Adam shrugged. "What can I say, I'm here, she's there. Geography just about sums it up."

"Why don't you see if you can dislodge her?"

Adam didn't wish to go into details about Toni's complicated social nexus. But he allowed Lisl's pressure to tip the scales in favor of his own inclinations. When he got home that night, he telephoned Washington and invited himself for the weekend. Toni did not hide her delight.

She met his flight. Something about her seemed different. Was he right in thinking she was more sedate? They sped off back across the Potomac in her car.

Though they had kissed perfunctorily at the airport, there was an uneasy silence for the first minute or so. After which she remarked, "Thank you."

"What exactly for?"

"For what you're thinking but are too shy to say— that you're glad to see me."

"What makes you so sure?" he asked.

"Most people don't smile when they're *un*happy."

* * *

In her apartment, Adam took off his jacket, donned an apron, and helped her prepare the salad. They worked like lab partners.

"Why are you so incredibly talkative?" she joked.

"I'm a scientist," he said as he patted the lettuce leaves dry. "I'm just trying to analyze the data."

"And what is your conclusion, Doctor?"

Adam turned and gave vent to the feelings of frustration that had seized him once again since he had entered her apartment.

"I'm confused, Toni," he said candidly. "I mean, you give off all kinds of different signals. On the one hand you have this incredible ability to make me feel like I'm the only man in the world. And yet we both know you have this commitment."

"To my job, Adam. To the Department of Justice. You, if anyone, should appreciate that."

"You mean your employer, don't you?"

Toni did not disguise her irritation.

"If you don't mind, I run my own show. Believe it or not, I employ two paralegals and two secretaries. How I spend my spare time is none of your business. I never asked what kind of involvements you have back in Boston."

"They're not married women, I assure you," he retorted.

"Well, good for you, Adam." She gave a sarcastic laugh. "You live in a town where the ratio of women to men isn't five to one. In case you haven't noticed, this village is not only our nation's capital—it's a political harem."

She paused for a moment and then commented, "Did you come all the way down from Boston just to bicker? You must be trying very hard not to like me."

"You're right," he admitted. "In my game I'd call it an 'autoimmune reaction.'"

Suddenly she put her hand gently on the back of his

neck and whispered, "It's all over with him, Adam. It's been over since the minute I got back from being with you in Boston. I was going to tell you but when Max died it hardly seemed the moment. I'd discovered the difference between a man wanting you and *needing* you. I hope it doesn't sound presumptuous, but I honestly felt I made a difference in your life."

"You did. You do. I only wish you'd told me sooner."

"Well, for once, the timing was right. Have I changed anything?" she asked hopefully.

"Yeah," he smiled. "I'd say it sort of changes everything."

The rest of that weekend was a kind of prologue to commitment. Toni finally felt secure enough to open her psyche as well as her heart.

Her childhood had been antithetical to his at almost every point. While he had climbed above his father by mounting the diving platform, she had viewed the world from the height of the pedestal on which Tom Hartnell had placed her.

He had divorced her mother and married twice more thereafter—being sure to synchronize one of his nuptials with his ambassadorship to Great Britain. He had two sons, but neither had the fire of his daughter Toni.

Buried somewhere in the Levittown of middle management at the Bank of America, there was even a Thomas Hartnell II. He had sorely disappointed his namesake by opting for the quiet life. Young Norton Hartnell was still more retiring than Tom Junior and had chosen an even quieter existence—teaching English as a second language in a Texas hamlet.

Understandably, Toni—or "Skipper" as her ex-Navy father loved to call her—was far and away his "favorite son."

Adam realized that her predilection for mature men was an inevitable continuation of her deep attachment to the Boss.

He understood what he was up against, but he was man enough to confess his qualms. "Look, Toni. Nobody knows better than I how close you are to your father. Do you think your relationship with him would allow you to forge another?"

"I don't know." She shrugged. "Why don't we try taking things one day at a time?"

"Well," he answered with a smile, "I was working within the parameters of 'the time being' and 'forever after.' Does that seem too onerous?"

"To be honest," she replied, "I can't even imagine being lucky in love."

"Actually, neither can I—which gives us yet another thing in common," he confessed. "Why don't we go on a honeymoon this summer? Take a house on Cape Cod maybe. Then, if we like it, we can get married."

"That's a novel idea," she said, her face radiant.

"Well," he smiled, "I am supposed to be a scientific innovator."

9

ISABEL

March 16

I picked up an old Latin textbook of Dad's the other day. It really opened a whole new window in my mind.

I discovered the origins of so many English words. Like "agriculture," for example, which comes from agricola, *meaning farmer, and "decimal" from* decimus, *meaning ten.*

I wondered what Dad's reaction would be when he

found out that I was spending some of my valuable time on a nonscientific subject. I was amazed when he told me I had terrific instincts. That not only was this so-called "dead language" a good exercise for keeping the mind sharp, but if I learned it well, I'd be able to "talk chemistry" in a single day—and immediately understand words as easy as "carbon" and "fermentation."

For once he was pleased that I was doing something extracurricular, probably because it turned out to be "curricular" after all.

Good news—Peter has just made the junior varsity team. Yay!

Just after turning eleven, Isabel passed the final high school equivalency exams, theoretically making her eligible to go directly to college, depending of course on how well she scored on the Scholastic Aptitude Tests.

One rainy Saturday morning in October 1983, Ray and Muriel—who was struggling to maintain a role, however minor, in the drama of her daughter's developing psyche—drove Isabel to the local high school. Here, alongside students five and even six years older than herself, she took the SATs that would evaluate her verbal and mathematical capacities. Then after a lunch break during which Ray fueled his daughter with brownies, she took three achievement tests: in physics, mathematics, and Latin.

On the first page of the questionnaire, she requested that her results be sent to the admissions departments of the University of California at San Diego and at Berkeley.

The second application, Ray explained, was just an exercise to see how she would be judged by the state's finest university. Obviously there was no question of her being sent away at so early an age.

At the end of the afternoon, she walked out as fresh as she had been early that morning.

Her good humor proved justified when the results arrived. Isabel scored a perfect 1600 on the two aptitude tests, and had done so well in the achievement tests that—although it was the last thing in the world she needed—both schools offered her advanced standing.

Yet no conscientious, self-respecting admissions committee could avoid taking the applicant's age into consideration. In fact, both directors wrote to the da Costas suggesting that Isabel wait a year or two—perhaps pick up a foreign language.

Undaunted, Ray even proposed driving all the way from San Diego to Berkeley for her interview.

"Isn't that a little beyond the limits of an exercise?" Muriel objected. "I mean, there's no point in going all that way when Isabel's not going to accept the place."

She looked into her husband's eyes and immediately understood his entire game plan. She took a deep breath and said firmly, "No, Ray. This is where I draw the line. We're not moving to Berkeley."

And then he shook her. "I've never said *we* were."

"Jesus," she exploded. "I don't think you're in your right mind. Do you imagine any court in the state would grant you custody of a twelve-year-old girl?"

Ray maintained a serene calm. "Who said a word about custody? We're not divorcing, Muriel. We're just doing what's best for our daughter."

"Do you regard taking her away from her mother at that terribly crucial age in a girl's life as best for her?"

"Intellectually, yes."

"That's all you care about, isn't it?" Muriel demanded furiously. "Well, I'm not going to let you twist her personality any further. I'll go to court and get an injunction."

Ray smiled with an unmistakable touch of cruelty. "No, you won't. Because if you meant what you said about wanting her to be happy, you know damn well that taking her away from *me* will have the opposite effect. Think about it, Muriel, think about it long and hard."

He paused and then added, "Meanwhile, I'll take Isabel to San Francisco."

The Berkeley dean of admissions had in his portfolio not merely ecstatic letters of recommendation, but also two confidential and somewhat disturbing communications. The first was from a high school examiner who had questioned Isabel orally. The second came from the girl's mother. Both warned in similar terms that there was "an unnaturally close relationship between the girl and her father."

These unhappy predictions were borne out the minute Dean Kendall opened his door and beckoned Isabel inside. He pulled up short when he noticed that Raymond was tagging along after her. Faced with a diplomatic crisis, he addressed Raymond in an unmistakably chilly tone. "Mr. da Costa, if you don't mind, I'd like to speak to your daughter alone."

"But—" Raymond began to protest before he realized the awkwardness of the situation.

"I'm sorry," the dean cut him off quietly. "But if she's old enough to be going to college, she should certainly be able to have this chat on her own."

"Uh, yes." Raymond mumbled, ill at ease. "You're quite right." And then to his daughter, "I'll be waiting right outside, darling."

Alone with the girl, Dean Kendall exercised supreme delicacy. The child was extraordinarily gifted but there was clearly a problem here. He did not specifically mention Raymond, but in an offhand manner asked, "If we were to admit you, Isabel, do you think you could live in dormitories with other girls, some of them twice your age?"

"No," she replied happily. "I'd be living with my father."

"Yes, yes," the dean murmured. "That would seem to make sense—at least for the first few years. But don't you think that would—how can I put it—inhibit your social life?"

The little girl smiled serenely, "Oh no. Besides, I'm not old enough to have a social life."

When they were gone, the dean had an inner argument with himself. She's far too young. She's immature. She should really go to a prep school till she's old enough.

But, goddammit, if *we* don't take her, those bastards at Harvard will.

Oscillating between guilt and avidity, he composed a letter of acceptance to Ms. Isabel da Costa, offering her a place in the freshman class of '88 in order to pursue her studies for a bachelor's degree in Physics.

In a pretense of fairness, Ray let Muriel have her say. She was barely able to control her anger.

"Ray, I hate your guts for what you've done to Isabel—*and* me. But you're right, the only reason I won't take you to court is because, unlike you, I genuinely care about what happens to her as a person. And also unlike you, I want her to grow up and be happy. I won't allow her to be the mutilated prize in a parental tug-of-war."

He listened silently, hoping that by fulminating, she would spend some of her rage. His tactics were successful, for in the end, Muriel had no alternative but to capitulate.

"Take her, if you must, but at least don't shut me out of her life."

He quickly accepted the terms of her truce—which were more like unconditional surrender. Suppressing his feelings of triumph, he responded softly, "Muriel, I swear, it's what Isabel wants. You can ask her. Berkeley's got one of the greatest Physics departments in the world. And we'll be home for every vacation, I promise you." He paused and asked, "Do we have a deal?"

"Yes," she answered acidly. "What we don't have is a marriage."

When they finally drove away from the house Isabel asked, "Oh Daddy, are you sure you packed my violin?"

He turned on her sternly, "As a matter of fact, I didn't—."

"Well then, let's go back right away."

"Darling, I did it deliberately. You're a college girl now and won't have time for recreational activities."

"But you know how much I love it . . ."

He did not reply. At last she spoke.

"Daddy, I know you think it somehow ties me to home. But I swear I want my fiddle for its own sake."

"Sure, sure," Raymond agreed all too quickly. "I'm sorry, it's all my fault. I'll arrange to have it sent up."

"Or Mom could bring it when she visits."

Raymond's expression was saturnine, but his voice held little conviction. "Yeah . . . sure."

August 24

For the first part of our journey I was excited and happy, like someone starting on a trip to an exotic place. But the closer we got to Berkeley, the more I began to feel afraid.

I mean, it's one thing to do college work with your father as the teacher. But it's a whole other thing when—as I imagined—I'd be sitting in a classroom with kids twice my age and maybe twice as smart.

Dad did his best to reassure me, and we even spent a lot of time going over the Berkeley catalog (he drove, I read) to be sure we had chosen the right courses.

Except for "Introduction to World Literature," which I insisted upon taking even though Dad swore that he could get me out of it, the rest of my subjects were from the upper division. We had to choose five units from physics courses like Quantum Mechanics, Electromagnetism and Optics, Particle or Solid State Physics.

We also planned on taking lots of Applied Math like Advanced Calculus, and Complex Variables.

I guess by restricting our conversation to academic subjects, we could somehow avoid confronting our feelings.

Anyway, by the time we reached Berkeley I was on the verge of panic. And when we got to this dinky little place Dad had rented on Piedmont Avenue, I was almost hysterical at the thought of having to move all the millions of books to the second floor.

Luckily there were three Berkeley jock types living on the ground floor, wearing sweatshirts that looked as if the sleeves had been cut off to show their biceps, and they helped us carry stuff up the stairs.

They acted embarrassed when Dad tried to tip them. All they really wanted was for us to join them for a beer(!)

Dad sort of promised that we might do it some other time. But as he whispered to me when they left, "They're definitely unsuitable characters and we don't want to set a precedent."

Since to my knowledge there aren't any other twelve-year-olds in the freshman class, that leaves the likelihood of my finding suitable friends pretty remote.

We unpacked—the books first, of course. Then Dad went out, bought a huge pizza, and we had the last meal before what he unreassuringly chose to call "the beginning of a whole new chapter" of my life.

I lay in bed a long time, tossing and turning.

Strangely enough, I wasn't worried about doing the course work. But I was scared about confronting the people. And Dad had failed to mention the surprise that was in store for me the next morning.

Then finally I realized what was keeping me awake. And it had nothing to do with what was going to happen tomorrow.

I crept out of bed, went over to my canvas duffel bag and pulled out my best friend in the whole world.

And the moment I was back in bed with Teddy in my arms, I fell fast asleep.

10

ADAM

ADAM AND Toni's solitude was highly populated, for the summer people who flock to the Cape are almost evenly divided between the Who's Who of Boston and the Who's What of Washington.

It was so atypical for both of them to steal even an afternoon off, that they had accumulated more weeks of vacation than they could possibly spend. But since, as Toni cheerfully put it, "when there isn't anything like a Watergate, Washington goes to sleep in August," she could close the door of her office with reasonable calm. Besides, she was amazed to discover that work did not seem to be the most important thing in her life at the moment.

They were both agreeably surprised how well each got along with the other's home team.

"I look at it this way," Adam mused lightheartedly. "The types I hang out with search for magic bullets, and the people you work with develop guided missiles."

Still, they found plenty of time to be alone. Whether it was an early morning jog on the beach or a late evening clambake, they enjoyed being together. And the lovemaking got better and better.

Toni's thirtieth birthday fell in August and her special request was curiously simple: lunch outdoors at the Sea Spray Spa & Resort in Chatham.

Adam was puzzled by her choice, until he saw the table she had booked. It was at the edge of the huge swimming pool.

She fixed him with her gaze and said affectionately, "Before we eat, I want my birthday present."

Adam knew what was coming when she raised her eyes to the diving platform at the far end.

"Did you bring your bathing suit?" she demanded.

"Yeah," he replied. "Matter of fact, I'm wearing it under my jeans."

She smiled. "Good. Now show me a glimpse of the old Adam Coopersmith. The boy who could fly through the air."

"Come on, Toni, it's been so many years—"

"I'll make allowances," she said happily. "So please get out there and fall for me."

Adam went to the locker rooms, changed quickly, and then, stopping once or twice to touch his toes and stretch, made his way nervously to the diving platform.

Climbing the steps, he took some comfort from the fact that it was only half the regulation height. As he stood poised at the summit, a sudden hush fell among the diners below, his grace and bearing hinting at what they could expect. He took a deep breath, stepped forward, and executed a respectable swan dive.

Emerging from the water, he looked over at Toni and called, "Satisfied?"

"No way." She was smiling. "I've got to see at least one somersault."

"Do you want me to break my neck?" he complained.

"No," she said, "I just want you to prove that the stories you told me aren't apocryphal."

He laughed, swam to the far corner of the pool,

placed his hands on the edge and, with a single action, propelled himself onto his feet.

When at last he was atop the platform again, even the waiters had stopped to watch. Adrenaline raced through his body and made his heart pound. He advanced quickly, sprang as high as he could, tucked in his legs, spun around and entered the water.

This time the observers applauded.

Proud of himself, Adam looked at Toni for a sign of approval. She was clapping enthusiastically.

"More," she called out like a teenager at a rock concert.

"No," he retorted. "Now it's *your* turn."

"Okay," she conceded, "let's have lunch."

As they drove back to their rented house that evening, Toni remarked, "You know, you're a different person on a diving board. I mean, for those seconds when you're literally flying in the air, you're the most beautiful thing I've ever seen in my life."

When they had "settled in," Lisl agreed to come and spend a few days with them in the guest cottage at the bottom of the garden.

The circumstances of the two women's second meeting were vastly different. At Max's funeral Toni had been a shy and sympathetic mourner. But now she clearly felt the enormous attachment between Adam and Lisl, and it awakened her instinctive feelings of rivalry.

Though she evinced a polite interest in Kleinian psychology, Toni was far from reticent about the importance of her own work in the Department of Justice.

She was unable to mask her feelings of power when describing a crisis in which she had to "send in the marshals" to safeguard the director of a Florida clinic who counseled pregnant women on their options.

This occasioned the only discordant exchange during the entire time she and Adam were together.

"I'm sorry you don't like Lisl more," he remarked as casually as possible when they were once again alone.

"What gave you that impression?"

"It was just a sense I got," he replied. "I mean, of all your exploits, did you have to boast about protecting the rights to abortion in front of a woman who couldn't have children?"

"Come on, Adam," she retorted. "If I was 'boasting,' I'm sorry. But Lisl lives in the real world, where most women can—and do—have children. You can't go through life as her psychic bodyguard."

"Hey, don't get me on *my* hobbyhorse about women having children. Let's just be a little more sensitive, okay?"

Toni knew when to change the melody. "That's what makes you such a man—you're an extraordinary combination of testosterone and sensitivity."

Her phraseology captivated him. And aroused his thoughts to other matters.

"Dr. Coopersmith, Dr. Coopersmith!"

A tanned, flaxen-haired woman in white shorts and a striped T-shirt, a cute four-year-old boy at her side, was waving frantically at Adam.

He turned and smiled. "Janice—it's nice to see you again."

The woman and her child hurried toward them. Before he could even introduce her to Toni, she pointed to the little boy and blurted, "Look, Dr. Coopersmith, this is your baby. Did you get the pictures?"

"Of course," Adam replied, and then stooped to shake the child's hand. "Hi there, young man. I'm the doctor who brought you into the world. You made a lot of people very happy."

His mother was bubbling over and immediately addressed Toni, "Oh, Mrs. Coopersmith, you don't know what a wonderful man your husband is . . ."

Toni was about to protest then saw that it would be

too great a disappointment to reveal that she was not Adam's wife.

". . . he took on Jeff and me when everybody had given up on us," Janice went on, "and as you can see from Larry, he gave us the greatest Christmas present of all time."

"It was all your doing, Janice," Adam said warmly. "I mean, I just rattled some test tubes. You were the one who had the courage to try yet another pregnancy."

"You're too modest, Doctor," she continued ardently. "I only wish Jeff were here, but his firm only gave him two weeks' vacation. He insisted that we stay on. We would've loved to have gotten together with you one evening."

"That would have been great," Adam responded. "Give him my best wishes." And then, addressing her son in a man-to-man tone, he said, "Take good care of your mother Larry. She's very special."

Moments later, as he and Toni were walking down the dock, Adam remarked, "Sorry about co-opting you as a wife."

"That's okay, Adam. I sort of enjoyed it. I only hope all your satisfied customers aren't that overenthusiastic."

The rest of the month raced by like an ever-accelerating cyclotron gathering its emotional energy by millions of electron volts.

On the final weekend they reached a crucial moment.

After an early morning walk on the beach, they found themselves placing their suitcases on opposite sides of the four-poster bed in the saltbox cottage that had sheltered such happiness for the past weeks. Without even pronouncing a word, they were having a passionate dialogue.

Then suddenly Adam murmured, half to himself, "I don't want this to end."

She gazed at him, the ache of imminent separation on her face, and echoed, "Me either."

Another awkward pause, then Adam said, "It doesn't have to, Toni."

"We'll only be an hour's flight away," she offered, knowing that this thought consoled neither of them.

"No," he insisted, "that's not good enough. We belong together."

There it was: the heart of the matter.

Toni gazed at him and asked, "Do you think you could live in Washington? The research facilities at NIH are as good as Harvard's."

"How about you? There are some very distinguished law offices in Boston."

"Adam, for me, Washington's a very special place. I mean, the dynamics of political power are something I can't put into words. My career's just taken off—and not only in government. Starting January, I'll be giving a weekly seminar in Con Law at Georgetown—which I find extremely flattering."

"Come on, Toni," he urged her gently. "There are plenty of good law schools up here—not least, the fairly famous one at Harvard."

She lowered her head and, barely in a whisper, said, "Shit, I knew it would boil down to this, but I didn't know how much it'd hurt. I mean, this is tearing me apart."

He was at her side now, wrapping her in his arms.

"Please, Toni," he implored, "I love you and I need you. Will you at least think about it?"

"What do you imagine I've obsessed about all month, Adam?"

"Hey look," he continued, "let's take our time."

She lowered her head again. "I can't."

He was taken aback. "You mean you'd rather end it?"

Toni looked at him, her eyes shining. "Yes."

"Yes, what?"

"Yes, I love you, I want to marry you. And if that means having to move to Boston—then I will."

Adam was overwhelmed. First by joy and then, a moment later, by a pang of remorse at having forced her to make the sacrifice.

They kissed and made love with such spontaneous passion that Toni missed her direct flight to Washington. That meant they would now have to drive all the way to Logan Airport in Boston. There were advantages. It gave them two and a half more hours together.

Vesuvius erupted.

"No way, Coopersmith. Not unless Hell freezes over!" Thomas Hartnell bellowed, pounding his desk for emphasis. "You're not dragging my daughter to that provincial mackerel-snapping, anemic excuse for a city."

"Dad, calm down, for God's sake."

"Skipper, you get lost so I can deal with this alone."

"No, dammit, it's my future you're discussing—or rather, tearing apart in a tug-of-war."

Toni stood her ground as the two men in her life battled. It was so acrimonious that she feared it might even come to blows.

"Will you listen to reason, Mr. Hartnell?" Adam demanded.

"Nothing you say is of interest to me, Dr. Coopersmith. And before you bring it up, yes—I do owe you my life. But I *don't* owe you my daughter— she's even more precious."

"I'm not taking her to Timbuktu, sir."

"As far as I'm concerned, anything beyond the Beltway is unacceptable. I mean for Christ's sake, Adam, I can pick up this phone and in ten seconds get you appointed to NIH at double your current salary. What's so damn special about staying at Harvard?"

"It's very difficult for me to explain," Adam said quietly. "But I suppose I can give you the answer in two words—Max Rudolph."

"But the man's dead. You could move all his research down here—and his wife, for that matter—lock, stock, and barrel."

Adam hesitated for a moment and then confessed, "I know this sounds crazy, but it wouldn't be the same. When I walk into that lab, he's still there. When I look through the glass walls of his office from the benches, I still see him at his desk. And when I ask him a question, he sometimes answers."

Toni was dizzy with admiration at the courage Adam displayed in standing up to her father's steamroller tactics. She had never heard anyone speak to the Boss like this.

"God, you're some kind of nut," Hartnell sneered.

Yet Adam, brave as he was, still could not bring himself to reveal his deepest motive: that he wanted to tear Toni away from her father's smothering sphere of influence.

Finally she cut the Gordian knot. "Dad, as far as I'm concerned, if Adam's in Boston, that's where I want to be too."

"But what about your goddamn career? Are you going to throw it all down the tubes for this white-coated creep?"

"Please try to see my side of it," she resisted. "I've had a career, but I've never had a relationship with a really good man—and to me that's more important."

"Skipper, trust me on this. You're an easy mark. You've been infatuated before—"

Adam objected. "This is not—"

Hartnell turned on him with ferocity. "I've had quite enough of your insolence, *boy*. Now I'm giving you exactly thirty seconds to about-face and march the hell out of my house."

"No, Dad," Toni overruled him. "We'd need at least an hour."

"W-What?" her father stammered furiously.

She nodded and said softly, "I'd have to pack. Because if he goes, I go with him."

Two months later Toni and Adam were married in St. John's Lafayette Square, the so-called "Church of the Presidents," directly across the park from the White House. The incumbent in the Oval Office was among the guests, no doubt a gesture of respect for the man who had done so much to help put him there.

And Thomas Hartnell managed to smile while giving away his only daughter.

At the reception, the Attorney General proposed the toast.

11

ADAM

DR. AND Mrs. Adam Coopersmith rented an apartment on the top floor of a Beacon Hill brownstone. Toni then dug in to cram for the Massachusetts bar exam.

Both were passionate about their careers, as well as each other. They would look back on this time as the happiest of their married life.

They worked till eleven, then joined the crowds of yuppies filling the many pubs and restaurants on Charles Street, transforming the whole area into a huge nightly block party.

When Toni began to hunt for jobs, there was no lack of Boston law firms eager to add a former Assistant Attorney General—for she had been promoted just before

she gave notice—to their roster. Osterreicher and
DeVane outbid them all in salary as well as prestige.

Meanwhile, Adam was making progress on the work
for which Max had so magisterially paved the way. His
new director had finally taken the time to examine the
official protocol for his study on idiopathic multiple
miscarriages.

Cavanagh was no fool, especially when it came to
sniffing out the value of a research project. And he now
realized the enormous potential of Adam's investigations.

Therefore, in a gesture of magnanimity, he restored
two of the post-docs he had removed from the team.

He also made a point of reminding Adam of the revised publishing etiquette for all work emanating from
what was now his lab.

"Max took a back seat," he explained with a thin
smile. "But I enjoy visibility. Since I'm chief, my name
naturally precedes all others."

It was a flagrantly unfair practice, but not uncom-
mon. Forcing himself to be pragmatic, Adam resentfully
acquiesced to what was an exploitative necessity. Yet he
was just concluding the outline he had been working on
with Max. Surely the Brit would never try to appropriate *this* as one of his publications? Unfortunately, the
man's ego was stronger than his conscience.

"Rules are rules, old chap, and we might as well start
on the right foot. Naturally, you'll have to put a
dagger—or whatever that mark is called—before Max's
name to indicate that he's passed on."

Thus the paper went out to the *International Journal
of Fertility* as being primarily the collaboration of an
Englishman and a dead man he had never met. Did
Cavanagh really think that the medical community
would accept this authorship as either credible or respectful?

Keeping a low profile, Adam continued his explorations. Meanwhile, Toni executed what she lightheartedly

referred to as a "double play." In the same week, she received positive results from the Massachusetts bar and her beta sub unit pregnancy test.

Excited by the prospect of fatherhood, Adam worked even harder, as though inspired by a subliminal creative rivalry. In the months that followed, he repeated the final experiments in Max Rudolph's half-filled lab book, using corticosteroids to suppress the embryotoxic reaction in pregnant white mice.

After much soul-searching—weighing the possible side effects of the steroids versus the good they might do—he reluctantly began to treat women whose tests revealed that they could not possibly have a child unless the killer toxins were somehow subdued.

As much as possible, he confined his scientific research and worrying to the daylight hours, so that he would not deny Toni her share of his emotional commitment.

Her drive to excel at everything extended to pregnancy as well. By sheer force of will she did not let morning sickness curtail her activities. She never once called Adam at the lab in panic, for she had read enough to be able to recognize Braxton-Hicks contractions as false alarms.

In her thirty-ninth week, Toni went into labor, and expertly breathed her way through the birth of six pound, eight ounce Heather Elizabeth Coopersmith.

Though not the first woman, Toni was, however, the first lawyer to avail herself of the firm's maternity leave. And then to take advantage of their excellent day-care facilities so she could return to work immediately.

Lisl, who took her job as godmother seriously, felt obliged to express her misgivings. "I know this practice is very much in vogue. But there really is no substitute for the mother in the early months of childhood," she observed diplomatically.

Toni took this advice as graciously as she could. "What if they have to work?"

"Well yes," Lisl conceded, "if they *have* to."

"Good," Toni replied pointedly, "because *I* have to."

Afterward Toni complained to Adam about what she regarded as Lisl's excessive interference.

"Next time you have one of your heart-to-hearts with that woman, tell her I agreed to her being a godmother, not a godmother-*in-law*."

"She's genuinely trying to help," Adam protested.

"She probably is," Toni acknowledged. "But I can't help her compensate for not having children of her own."

At the weekly meeting of his brown-bag staff luncheon, Adam was beaming with joy. He read the information from a computer printout and then crowed:

"We've smashed our own record—thanks to the steroids—seventy percent of our worst 'repeaters' have finally made it through their first trimester with the pregnancy intact. It's either a miracle, or we're geniuses. . . ."

Len Kutnik, a junior research fellow, grinned. "Can we vote on that, boss?"

"This lab isn't a democracy, Doctor," Adam rejoined. "I'll render my absolute judgment when I see real babies."

And he did. They then witnessed a surprising development: once these previously unsuccessful women had reached this point, almost all of them proceeded to deliver healthy children on schedule.

But what was the explanation for this happy phenomenon? Why did these patients who malfunctioned so early somehow outgrow their difficulty? The answer might provide a solution to the entire mystery.

As it was, the procedure was far from satisfactory. The pregnant mothers began to resent the side effects of taking steroids: the extra weight, swollen limbs, and bloated faces. Not to mention the risk—in rare cases, to be sure—of glaucoma, diabetes, and functional dependency on the drug. Max Rudolph would never have approved.

Meanwhile, Adam encountered his own unexpected fertility problem. As Heather neared her third birthday he began to rhapsodize about the possibilities of a second child.

"Heather's a handful already," Toni countered. "I don't honestly see how I could manage another little one and my legal practice."

"They're not little for long," he commented.

"I know," she said. "But I don't see the need for adding to the world's overpopulation crisis."

"This isn't China, Toni. Besides, it's a documented fact that only children tend to grow up with more problems."

"*I* was an only child," she reminded him. "I mean, I never lived with my brothers. And it didn't seem to do me any harm."

I wouldn't be so sure, Adam thought to himself. And then said aloud, "Toni, you can't imagine the heartache I encounter every day. I see women willing to go through the most agonizing procedures just for the *privilege*—and that's what it is—of having a kid. And here you are, in perfect health, abdicating the opportunity that other women would kill for. When I come home and little Heather runs to hug me, I feel incredibly blessed."

"Are you sure there's no ego involved?" she suggested. "Don't you maybe think your patients would get a psychological boost from knowing you had lots of children?"

"One child is not *lots*," he barked, losing his temper.

"Well, that's what you say now. But if we came up with another girl, I'm sure you'd want to keep trying until we had a boy."

"To be honest, maybe I would. It's hardly an unnatural urge."

"All right," she replied, on the verge of losing her temper. "While we're having this argument, let's get all the unpleasantness out in the open. I would never have let you call him Max. That's what you'd want, isn't it?"

"Not necessarily," he lied. And then added, tantalizing, "We could always call him Thomas—or even 'Little Boss.'"

To his surprise, she was not enticed.

"Well," Toni remarked with exasperation, "for once you and my father agree on something. But I refuse to be double-teamed. Whatever you'd call him—the baby still wouldn't sleep through the night for at least two years, and I'm not prepared to go through that again."

She was crushing his dreams with the recklessness of someone deliberately stamping on delicate glass.

Adam sat silent for a moment, inwardly bruised, then almost involuntarily murmured, "I never expected this."

"You mean you regret marrying me?" she asked bluntly.

"Of course not," he protested. "It's just going to become another dream I'll have to file under 'impossible'—along with my Olympic gold medal in the high board."

Toni saw the growing rift between them and, to counteract it, put her arms around him affectionately and stroked his ego.

"You forget something, darling. You're still a bit of a child yourself and you need a lot of mothering. I hitched my wagon to a star. I want to take good care of my boy genius so he can win the Nobel Prize. I promise you, we're doing the right thing."

As Heather grew older, her mother worked longer and longer hours, leaving Adam to make sure his daughter wasn't abandoned to the care of Toni's vast network of baby-sitters.

There were times when he simply could not bear to leave the house even when Heather was asleep, lest she wake up with a nightmare and be comforted—or worse, neglected—by a paid surrogate.

To his daughter's delight, he would put warm winter clothing over her pajamas and take her along to the lab, where she would nestle up on the couch with her Kermit the frog, covered in a blanket, and sleep peacefully until the awkward moment when he had to wake her up, and bring her home.

Adam actually grew to enjoy this routine, since it was far more inspiring to be able to look at his little daughter than wonder how she was.

There were, however, occasions when he was called out to emergencies and had to phone Toni and insist that she hurry home to take charge.

One evening she was in the midst of a crucial partners' meeting and was extremely reluctant to leave. "Adam," she complained when he phoned her. "When will you realize that you're not the only surgeon in the world? You could hand the job over to somebody else."

To which he retorted in a flash of anger, "And when will you realize that a *mother* can't?"

He joined the local country club and took Heather every Saturday morning to a class at the warm indoor pool where parents and their little children went into the water together to learn the intricacies of the doggie paddle.

She was an apt pupil, fiercely determined to show Daddy how well she could swim.

On the ride home she would discuss her future career plans, which, at the moment, involved being a doctor and a diver.

She already knew whom she wanted to marry, and Adam answered her proposal with what he hoped was artful evasion.

Meanwhile, there was an explosion in the lab that attracted world attention. Its antecedents had been such a well-kept secret that Adam and Toni only learned about it the morning all hell broke loose.

Ian Cavanagh had earned his reputation—and his fortune—primarily in the service of Hematics, a biotech company that had engaged him to test their new artificial blood substitute developed as a safer alternative for use by hemophiliacs.

His landmark paper demonstrating the efficacy of the drug elevated his standing in the scientific community—as well as the price of Hematics stock.

Yet subsequent attempts by other laboratories to repeat Cavanagh's experiment could not replicate his success. There were increasing demands to see his initial data. The Englishman's lame excuse that the original spreadsheets had "gone missing" convinced no one.

When the science editor of the *Boston Globe* caught wind of the brewing scandal, he blew the whistle, claiming in no uncertain terms that the eminent Professor Cavanagh had falsified his evidence. Every major wire service picked up the story.

Harvard was persuaded beyond doubt that he was guilty, and its terrible swift sword fell, instantly severing the scientist's connection with the university.

That morning, when Adam, still unaware, was approaching the lab's parking lot, a policeman waved him away, indicating that the road had been closed to all traffic.

"But I'm on the staff," Adam insisted.

"Look, Doctor, I have my orders. And besides, from what I hear, a lot of heads have rolled and your parking permit might have been revoked."

Finally, in an act of total frustration, he abandoned his car on Kirkland Street and raced back toward the lab.

Approaching the building, he was startled by the swarm of journalists, television crews—and the Law.

As he pushed his way through the crowd, Adam could see the officers berating what appeared to be graduate students who were trying to remove cartons of documents from the building and load them into the disgraced man's station wagon.

A Brooks Brothered university administrator was politely but very firmly informing a disheveled, unshaven Englishman—Adam had never seen him so unkempt—that he was no longer a member of the faculty. He could, therefore, remove nothing from his former office except demonstrably personal effects.

"And may I remind you, Dr. Cavanagh, that you've only got till noon before we change the locks."

All the while, newsmen were shouting a cacophony of questions which fell on deaf ears.

At the front door, there was yet another barrier to cross. Mel, the usual guard, stood helplessly by as a senior university policeman, holding a clipboard, preempted his authority.

Adam had a sudden attack of paranoia, thinking he too might be on what was clearly the blacklist. With some trepidation, he announced his name.

The officer glanced quickly at his documents, then nodded politely. "Go right ahead, Professor Coopersmith."

He reached the tenth floor, and went to his cubbyhole of an office to phone Toni that he had arrived safely through the tumult.

"You mean they didn't catch you?" she responded with surprise.

"Who?"

"The reporters, didn't they stop you downstairs?"

"Why should they?" Adam protested with irritation. "I'm not involved in this dirty con job."

"Of course not, darling," she replied sweetly. "But you are very much involved with the lab."

"I don't get it."

"The dean called a minute after you left, but it was impossible to reach you. I wish you'd listen to me and get a goddamn car phone."

"What's up?" Adam asked.

"You, my dear husband," she replied. "You are extremely up. Officially, as of 12:01 today, you're acting director of the whole shooting match. And their first three choices to succeed Cavanagh are you, you, and *you*."

Adam let out a whoop. "Hey, Toni, it was worth all the crap I had to take. Why not meet me at the Faculty Club? Maybe we'll even go wild and try the famous Harvard horse steak for lunch."

He hung up and, heart still racing, immediately dialed another number.

"Hello, Lisl, I've got some wonderful news," he said, his voice breaking. "I'm going to be in Max's chair after all."

The moment Adam's equipment was reinstated in an area adjacent to the big glass office, he expanded the staff by hiring three newly minted Ph.D.'s as research fellows: Derek Potter, from Cal Tech; Maria Suleiman, from MIT; and Carlo Pisani, from Venice, Italy.

At his first brown-bag lunch as director of the lab, each team member reported on his own area of inquiry, and then Adam threw open the floor for discussion. And offered his own critical summation at the end.

"I have this gut feeling that we're searching for a complicated answer and ignoring something obvious. Why don't we all demote ourselves to freshmen med students and carefully analyze the physiological changes of a normal pregnancy. Maybe we can pinpoint the moment our problem women no longer need steroids to sustain their pregnancies."

They all nodded, continuing the exercise with pencils in their right hands and sandwiches in their left. After painstakingly listing all the systemic changes in the course of a pregnant woman's first trimester, they turned the corner. The answer was staring them right in the face.

"Why didn't anybody think of this before?" Len Kutnik asked.

"Because we were working alone," Pisani candidly suggested. "And when Prof gathers us for lunch, our brains work overtime to try to impress him." He turned to Adam and inquired, "Right, *Professore*?"

"Right, Carlo," he answered, and then articulated their new insight.

"In the second trimester the placenta, which nourishes the fetus by admitting maternal blood and oxygen, also starts to work overtime as an endocrine organ producing estrogen and ... progesterone. Maybe in early pregnancy these multiple miscarriages needed more of the hormone to fight the mystery toxin that was keeping the fertilized egg from implanting."

"It makes sense," offered Maria Suleiman.

"Then why the hell don't we set up some trials?" Adam suggested. "To see if large localized doses of progesterone would protect the embryo till the placenta kicks in with its abundant supply? Any volunteers?"

All hands shot up. Everyone wanted to be on what looked more and more like a winning team.

There was no shortage of pregnant women willing to brave a blind trial. Moreover, the side effects were minimal compared to those of steroids.

It took several months to set up the protocol and find the subjects. By the middle of the second year, Adam had tangible results. The progesterone worked. But what exactly was it working *on*? He had the answer, yet did not fully understand the question.

The atmosphere at home, while cordial, was not loving.

Despite Adam's professional success, the most important thing in his life was his family. Toni, by contrast, seemed to derive most of her satisfaction from her career.

Quite unlike her husband, the goal of being an even better parent was not part of her ambitions. Adam had difficulty coming to terms with her attitude, but tried to convince himself that it was merely a phase from which they would both emerge, becoming closer and more loving than ever. He refused to see what was really happening.

They were simply running out of things to say to each other.

12

ISABEL

TWELVE-YEAR-OLD GIRL ENTERS BERKELEY

CHILD PRODIGY TO STUDY PHYSICS
(from the Associated Press)

SPROUL PLAZA, the forecourt to the University of California at Berkeley, always has a carnival air about it. But for several hours yesterday it took on the aura of a coronation.

It was registration day for new freshmen, and the entire spectrum of undergraduates—from the barefoot bohemians to the primmest of preppies—crowded at the rope barrier to catch a glimpse of the young lady who was about to make academic history.

Twelve-year-old Isabel da Costa from Clairemont Mesa seemed more composed than the incredulous spectators as she walked down the rope-lined corridor created by the campus police to register as the youngest freshman in its century-old history.

Accompanied by her father Raymond, a forty-six-year-old physics lab technician, Isabel was uncannily poised.

A gaggle of photographers tried to elbow their way for a

closer shot, shouting enticements like, "Look this way Isabel," and "Give us a smile, honey," as she walked serenely into Sproul to enroll as a member of the class of '88. . . .

Ironically, it was Raymond who had been unable to sleep the night before. As Isabel slumbered peacefully in the adjacent bedroom, he paced back and forth in the living room of their cramped apartment.

He could not understand why his emotions were so out of control.

What the hell am I so worried about? he asked himself. She's going into the record books. But that won't change our relationship at all.

Then he looked squarely at his innermost feelings and admitted, no, it's inevitable. Tomorrow's got to change something. Tonight she's all mine. In the morning, she'll belong to the world. He had somehow forgotten that he himself was responsible for the publicity extravaganza.

Dean Kendall was aware that a minor commotion was inevitable, and thus he vouchsafed the reporters a quarter of an hour—"and not a second more"—to interview the prodigy.

Just a few minutes before noon, Isabel stepped into the limelight as—uncharacteristically—Raymond hovered in the background.

"We've heard you're going to major in physics, Isabel. Can you tell us why you've chosen this subject?" asked Natalie Rose of United Press International.

"That's kind of hard to explain," the young girl responded amid the locust clicking of cameras. "But I've always been drawn to figuring out how things work. That's how I broke my cuckoo clock when I was three."

Appreciative laughter.

The *New York Times*: "What about your music? Will you be playing with the university orchestra?"

Isabel shot a quick glance at her father and then answered, "Only if *they* give me advanced standing too, and let me just play Spring and Summer of the Four Seasons."

More laughter. She had captivated all of them.

The articles that appeared the next day and indeed all through the week—for representatives of *Time* and *Newsweek* had also been present—were tailored to suit their respective audiences.

While the more serious papers emphasized her poise and intellect, the supermarket tabloids speculated on the possible Svengalilike role her father played.

Understandably, these far more emotive and insinuating stories upset Isabel.

"It's not fair, Daddy," she said, almost in tears. "One of those rags actually called you 'a diabolical ventriloquist.' "

"Take it easy, honey," he answered soothingly. "We know it's not true, and you shouldn't even read what the gutter press says. Their idea of news is things like who dyes Ronald Reagan's hair."

Isabel was not assuaged. "I know what you're saying, Dad, and I try not to let these things affect me. But couldn't you have arranged with Dean Kendall to have me registered in someplace private—like his office? I feel like a monkey in the San Diego Zoo."

"We discussed it," Raymond answered truthfully. And then, deftly crossing the frontier of mendacity, he added, "But he felt that if you were going to be treated like a normal student, gagging the press would only whet their appetite. This way, from now on the campus cops will be on the lookout for those parasites if they slink around your classrooms."

"Are you sure these accusations don't bother you?" she asked anxiously.

"Not at all," Raymond replied, "as long as we both know they're not true." His tone was convincing, since he had come to enjoy life in the center ring.

For, after all, when they trumpeted Isabel's genius, were they not also implicitly praising him?

Raymond had obtained an indefinite leave of absence from his post in the San Diego Physics lab, although Professor Kinoshita, head of the department, confided to his colleagues that in his view there was little likelihood that Raymond would ever return.

This left him without any visible means of support. Not only did he have to provide food and lodging for himself and Isabel, but, during a spasm of guilt, he had rashly promised Muriel to continue paying half the mortgage on the family home.

He could easily have pressured the Berkeley Physics Department to employ him in his experienced capacity as a lab engineer. For they, unlike Dean Kendall, had no qualms about welcoming his twelve-year-old prodigy to their midst. Talent is talent. But Raymond chose instead to put his tutorial skills to work.

With all the attendant publicity, he had become a kind of celebrity. The printed index cards he posted on bulletin boards in the department, offering to coach any student having difficulty with physics courses, brought more responses than he could accommodate, even at a fee of thirty dollars per session.

Indeed, when other perfectly bright students conveyed to their parents that Isabel da Costa's father was offering private pedagogy, they urged their offspring to seize the unique opportunity: perhaps Mr. da Costa could also work miracles for them.

To Raymond, this seemed to unearth a deeply held psychological secret; namely, that many parents cherished the notion that their children were geniuses—and lacked only the right conditions to develop them.

Prudently, he had scheduled his tutorials for Saturday mornings or weekday evenings between seven and ten P.M., hours when he knew that Isabel would be in the next room, hard at work.

Sundays were the exclusive property of father and daughter. Weather permitting, they would go on an excursion, or sometimes simply for a relaxing picnic across the bay in Golden Gate Park.

It was at moments like these that Isabel, who was beginning to experience the physiological transformation to womanhood, could not suppress pangs of longing for the little things in life that she was missing. She was struck, not merely by the couples young and old walking hand in hand through the park, but even by the numerous joggers breathing fresh air and chatting happily to each other as they passed down the tree-lined paths.

These were subjects that a young girl could quite naturally have discussed with her mother, but Isabel's thrice-weekly calls to Muriel were uneasy and awkward. Even had Raymond not been present in the room, she would have felt somehow disloyal by confiding private thoughts to her mother. And for her part, the best Muriel could do was to anticipate what might be preoccupying her daughter, and discuss it—almost as a monologue—from her end of the phone.

No matter how early Isabel awakened, Raymond would already be in the kitchen preparing a nourishing breakfast which was a scrupulous admixture of proteins for growth and carbohydrates for energy and brainpower. He had become something of an expert on nutrition, devouring not only the Harvard and Johns Hopkins medical newsletters, but also the wealth of material he could access through various computer databases.

Though he went to bed before midnight, he would leave his daughter hard at work—so dedicated, in fact, that she sometimes evaded his question as to when she had gone to sleep.

Though it seemed to outsiders that Isabel led a cloistered life, she was aware of the outside world through San Francisco's popular all-talk station. As soon as she heard her father snoring, she would reach into her bottom drawer, take out a cheap pair of earphones, plug them into her clock radio, and listen to callers-in discuss the popular controversies of the day.

This allowed her access to an unending cast of characters, some of whom would address burning political issues, like AIDS, women's rights, and Reagan's Star Wars. She also heard passionate—and sometimes ferocious—arguments on such topics as abortion. This was particularly vivid to her, since, as a developing adolescent, the entire subject of pregnancy and childbirth was inevitably on her mind.

As her thirteenth birthday approached, Isabel grew more and more unsettled by the changes in her body. Not that she didn't understand them *scientifically*, for she had long ago read books about human reproduction. She knew intellectually that the decrease in secretions of the pineal gland, simultaneous with the increase in the outpouring of adrenocortical hormones, accompanied by the appearance of hair in the genital area, signaled the onset of puberty.

It was quite another matter to cope with the reality of it.

February 25

I knew it would happen. I dreamed about it, worried about it, and was scared and eager all in one.

And still, when at last it came, I was totally unprepared.

It was late afternoon and I was in the midst of writing up a lab experiment, working like mad so I could get it out of the way by dinner.

But then I started sensing a kind of dull ache in my lower back. And I felt a kind of moistness. I escaped to the bathroom and hurriedly unzipped my jeans to take a look.

There were the stains.

I was having my first period.

Overwhelmed, I didn't know whether to laugh or cry.

Still, there was a more immediate problem. I had to get something which would absorb the blood.

For the time being I would make do with carefully-layered Kleenex. But this was only a temporary solution.

Though physically I felt better—and went back to typing my report—I found it almost impossible to concentrate.

I was preoccupied not with the "significance of it"— the way some of the teenage magazines that I read in the dentist's office make a big deal about "becoming a woman." It was something far different and more complex than any of those mags had ever broached: while I was sure I could handle it, I wondered what it would do to Dad.

Although Isabel did not want to tell her father, on a more profound level, she nonetheless wanted him to *know*, despite the fact that something irrational in her feared he might be angry.

But for now she had a pragmatic dilemma. Since Raymond rarely left her side—he appeared to have deemed only bookstores like Cody's as safe territory— she had to find some way to obtain what she needed each month.

She was determined to take action during their next trip to the Safeway on Shattuck Avenue.

The moment of revelation came as father and daughter were placing their items onto the black rubber treadmill at the checkout counter.

Ray looked mutely at the blue box of Kotex, then at his daughter, and asked, almost in a whisper, "Uh, do you need—uh, these things?"

She nodded.

Without another word, he turned and resumed emptying the wagon.

During the first few minutes of their ride home, he was silent. At last he said, as casually as possible,

"Why don't we stop off and have a good browse at Cody's?"

She clearly understood the subtext. "That's okay, Daddy, I don't need a book."

"Well, maybe you want to—you know," he said uneasily, "talk to someone."

"That's not necessary," she responded. And then, sensing the moment to be propitious, she added, "If I've got any questions, I can always call Mom, right?"

"Yes," he mumbled under his breath, "I think it would be a good idea if you spoke to her."

Understandably, Isabel was a frequent topic of campus conversation. It was not merely her genius and eloquence that continued to elicit interest, but gossip also focused on the fact that her father went with her to every class.

In an early press interview he had explained that this was merely to be sure that Isabel understood the material. So that, if necessary, he could help her later.

Wags joked that Isabel was so young, she needed him to help her cross the street. Others speculated darkly on the elder da Costa's own needs.

Consciously, at least, Ray did not want to suppress his daughter's emotional development. And so he attempted the impossible, trying to provide her with a social life while still remaining in firm paternal control.

Berkeley could justifiably claim to have pioneered the serious study of film as an art. After all, no less a cinematic heavyweight than Pauline Kael had spent her early career programming for the local arts theater.

Of course, Raymond wanted Isabel to see the Ingmar Bergman retrospective. So one Saturday afternoon the two of them sat through *The Seventh Seal* and *Wild Strawberries*.

"I haven't got the slightest idea what any of it was about," her father complained good-humoredly as they emerged bleary-eyed from the double feature.

"Yes," she remarked sympathetically, "the subtitles weren't very good."

"Well at least they—" He stopped himself, unsure of what she was saying. "You don't mean to tell me you understood the dialogue, Isabel?"

"Not all of it, of course," she replied ingenuously. "I guess you were in such a rush to pull out all the relevant books on Bergman that you didn't notice two of them were in Swedish."

Again Raymond da Costa was moved to wonder about the outer limits of his daughter's capacity for knowledge. If indeed there were any.

As a treat, he took her for a pizza at Nino's Brazilian, ordering a Coke for her and a pint of beer for himself.

A group of shaggy types were grooving to jukebox music. If nothing else, their squeals of laughter indicated that they were high—and not on Miller Lite.

Their apparent leader, motorcycle-jacketed and stubble-chinned, noticed father and daughter, pointed his finger and cried, "Look! There's Humbert Humbert and Lolita."

Raymond's face reddened. He had, of course, read Vladimir Nabokov's famous novel about an older man with a sexual penchant for nymphets, and the intimation was a thousand-volt shock.

Raymond lost his temper completely, bellowing, "You shut your dirty mouth."

This merely intensified their mocking laughter.

"Stay loose, Hummy-baby. I'm not dumping on you. I mean, everybody should be free to do their own thing, right?"

Now the arteries in Raymond's neck bulged, and as Isabel stared with mounting dread, her father pulled himself to his feet and started toward the antagonist.

"My daughter is not my *thing*, you little rodent," he snarled.

"Hey, mellow out." The scruffy youth held up his hands in what was at once a demonstrative and protective gesture. "I mean, I know you're not really screwing her."

Raymond exploded. He lunged at the younger man, who was, if not stronger, infinitely more agile and could step aside to avoid the blow.

To Isabel's alarm, her father swung, missed, then let out a strangled groan and fell to the floor.

"Holy shit!" the boy gasped in genuine horror at the havoc his offhand remark had wrought. "Somebody better call an ambulance. I think the old guy's cooled."

13

SANDY

ONE DAY Rochelle Taubman vanished forever.

Sandy Raven learned of this disappearance during a weekly phone conversation with his father. According to him, the studio did not believe that her original name had the celestial ring of stardom. So the Publicity Department performed some alchemy.

Taubman became "Tower," a word that not only rhymed with power, but also suggested the height for which she was destined. And, since there was no pizzazz to Rochelle, a name that one executive remarked "sounds like somebody's mother," they wove her a new identity out of pure iridescent neon.

Thus, Sandy had to reprogram his emotions. He was no longer worshipfully in love with Rochelle Taubman. The object of his affections had been metamorphosed into Kim Tower.

* * *

Sandy had also moved up in the world.

Those who believe that science is a religion regard the Massachusetts Institute of Technology as its Vatican, with the many Nobel Prize winners on its faculty as its College of Cardinals.

Situated in Cambridge, on the banks of the Charles River, the university is a short jog away from Harvard, with which it shares the unswerving belief that its students are the best and the brightest in the universe.

Both institutions would admit that they seek out a different sort of student. While Harvard takes pride in selecting the whole man or woman—athletic, charismatic, musical, artistic—MIT cares only about the candidate's brain.

What better proof than the simple fact that they do not even have a football team? How could they, when the average student's IQ is higher than his body weight?

In this academy, the fun aspects of college life were conspicuously absent. While in theory Tech students could go on dates during the weekend, this freedom was really illusory. For none of them would dare take time off from their slavery in the scientific salt mines.

So their joys were brief and vicarious. And pretty much boiled down to hamburgers and beer in the Kresge Grill. They lived in a kind of academic submarine, and their only brief glimpses of the outside world were through its electronic periscope—television.

It was here that Sandy was able to follow the progress of Rochelle's career. Though it had been a while since they had seen each other in person, he could still adore her on the tube. Thanks to the influence of the studio, she received fairly regular invitations to guest star on series being shot under their aegis.

Sidney alerted his son to the fact that Rochelle would assay her most challenging role yet as a deaf prostitute in a "Movie of the Week."

Sandy pinned the note on his bulletin board—as if he would forget. No doubt he unconsciously hoped that one of his neighbors would see "Kim, Tuesday 9 P.M." and think it was a real-life date.

He was already in a well-chosen seat in the student union by eight-thirty. The initial signs suggested that it would be an auspicious occasion—there was no wrangling among the guys about which channel they would watch: the title "Women of the Night" was too tantalizing to miss.

But Sandy had not reckoned on an unexpected factor—his classmates' hormones. For, while he had come to venerate, they had gathered to undress his beloved with their eyes. And Sandy marveled at how her breasts seemed to have developed.

"Wow, look at those tits!" drooled one sophisticate.

"Man, wouldn't you like to be her bra," grunted another.

"Shut up you assholes. She's a serious actress."

Sandy's unfortunate outburst shocked even him. All eyes turned to the slight, pimple-faced figure, perched anxiously on a chair in the back of the room. The object of his castigation growled, "Who the hell are you, Raven—her brother?"

"No," Sandy answered furiously. "She's just sort of an old girlfriend of mine."

"Like hell," his antagonist countered. "Why on earth would a piece like that go out with a wonk like you?"

"You don't understand," Sandy objected.

"You bet I do. You're bullshitting."

Just then Sandy's eyes returned to the screen. It was displaying a commercial for Kraft cheese.

"My God," he exploded. "What's happened to Rochelle?"

"You're a little slow on the draw, aren't you, Raven? The girl's name was Maisie and she's dead."

"Dead? But she just got on—I mean, who killed her?"

"Well, maybe if you shut up and let us watch the show, Telly Savalas will find out."

Sandy was crestfallen. And could not keep from crying on Sidney's shoulder when they spoke on the telephone later that night.

"But Dad, you said she had a big part."

"Kiddo, you gotta understand how the business works," his father reasoned. "This wasn't some afternoon soap. It was prime time, the major leagues. You have no idea how many households she died in. Frankly, I thought she was very . . . appealing. Particularly that fantastic blouse she wore—especially considering it was TV."

"Uh, yeah," Sandy agreed, remembering the garment that was the cause of his altercation. "Anyway, Dad, where does she go from here?"

"Well it's obvious, sonny boy—up."

"Do you really think so?" Sandy asked eagerly.

"Or down," his father added philosophically. "I mean, you never know in this business. Get what I mean?"

"Yeah, Dad. Do you ever see her?" he asked with a touch of self-pity.

"Across a crowded commissary, so to speak. Don't worry, I always give your love."

"And does she even remember me?"

"Are you kidding? Anyway, take care of yourself. Speak to you next week."

It was only when he had hung up that Sandy realized that his father had not directly answered his question.

College girls, however humble their respective academies, were not interested in MIT freshmen. Occasionally one of Sandy's classmates from the Boston area would show up with a date from his old high school. But even that was so rare an occurrence that when Barry Winnick of Malden, Massachusetts, his Kresge Hall neighbor, knocked on his door one Friday night, Sandy thought it nothing short of a miracle.

"Listen, Raven, you've gotta help me," he begged.

"What's the problem?" Sandy asked warily.

"I'm in trouble," his classmate replied. "I've got a date with the high school nymphomaniac."

"Nymphomaniac?"

"Yeah," Barry nodded. "Absolutely round heels."

"So what seems to be the trouble?" said Sandy, who had by now caught some of his classmate's rampant general anxiety.

"It's her cousin, dammit."

"She has a cousin?" Sandy asked eagerly.

"Yeah, in from Pennsylvania, or somewhere."

"Is she a nympho too?"

"How the hell do I know? It's not genetic—or is it?"

"They don't teach you that sort of thing, Winnick. Now, when do I get to meet the cousin?"

"You mean you'll do it?" Barry asked with astonishment and gratitude.

"Do what?"

"Take her off my hands. Distract her, or at least chew the fat with her in your room while I, uh, communicate with Ramona. Will you do it? Will you be a pal?"

"Sure," Sandy answered magnanimously, inwardly thinking, Is he kidding?

"Of course there's no guarantees," Barry cautioned. "I mean, just 'cause she's related to Ramona doesn't mean she's attractive—or that she'll put out. Or both—or either. You gotta be willing to suffer for the greater good."

"What greater good?"

"My getting laid, you schmuck."

There were four more days or ninety-six hours, or 5,760 minutes till the weekend, and Sandy scarcely drew breath during any of them. He, who had written down his lectures practically verbatim, found it hard to concentrate at all. If this kept up, it would be good-bye to the Dean's List.

Friday—eve of the big event—he laid out his clothes

and found his shirt collection wanting. The next day he blew ten bucks on a pink button-down item that he calculated would snow anyone. He spent practically the rest of the day grooming, and was dressed and ready for action before the sun went down.

Both in a highly tensile state, the two students waited for the girls to arrive by the change booth in the Central Square subway station.

Suddenly, Barry spied them out of the corner of his eye and whispered to Sandy, "I see them, Raven. Look cool and confident."

"That's very difficult," Sandy confessed.

"Don't fink out on me now," Barry snapped nervously. "This is my big chance."

Sandy tried to remain calm but could not resist taking a peek at what sensual delight might be undulating into his long-deprived life.

Even assuming Margie was the short and scrawny one, she didn't seem *that* bad. At least from thirty paces.

He was right. And for some reason, scrawny Margie could not keep her eyes off him. As her cousin made the introductions, she stared intently at Sandy.

Sandy was flattered and felt a surge of confidence. Then, a split second later, Margie whispered something to her cousin, who in turn called Barry aside and murmured something to him. The next thing Sandy knew, Barry was clearing his throat like a tic.

"Uh, Raven, we gotta talk," he hacked. "We gotta talk."

The two young men moved aside, and Barry muttered, "Sandy, I don't know how to tell you this."

"That's okay, Winnick. I can see she's a dog, but I said I'd do it, and I will. After all—"

"No," his friend cut him off sharply. "You don't get it."

"Well then, what?"

"She doesn't dig you."

"Huh?"

"I mean, I told her you were a great guy and everything, but Margie won't play ball unless I call in the second team."

"What are you talking about?"

"Roger Ingersoll—my backup. He's waiting by his phone."

"What?" Sandy exploded. "Ingersoll?"

A feeling of terrible hurt was beginning to overwhelm him.

"Raven, please," Barry implored. "This is my big chance with Ramona. Be magnanimous, Raven, and abdicate. I mean, go to the movies or something. I'll even pay."

Sandy glanced furiously at Margie and thought, You bitch. You heartless bitch. Am I that disgusting? Evidently, yes.

"Fine, Winnick," he mumbled, on the verge of tears. "I'm taking off."

And he walked sadly into the night, mourning the death of his confidence.

Later that night there was a feverish knocking on his door. Sandy opened it to find Barry resembling nothing so much as a Mexican jumping bean.

"Just to tell you not to worry, old pal. Everything worked out terrific. Ingersoll came through and Ramona delivered. Of course, Roger claims to have gotten to third base with Margie, but I think he's full of it. Anyway, I just didn't want you to worry."

"That's okay, Barry. I'm glad you told me."

Sandy pushed his door closed, muffling Barry's afterthought, "Oh yeah, Raven. Thanks a lot for understanding."

No, Barry, Sandy agonized. The truth is, I don't understand at all.

14
ADAM

IN THE four years since he had been made director of the lab, Adam Coopersmith was, metaphorically speaking, the father of nearly two hundred children. By treating multiple-miscarrying women with large dosages of natural progesterone, he had enabled 174 of them to carry their pregnancies to term.

Some of the couples were so overwhelmed at their miraculous change in luck that they went as far as to ascribe magical powers to Adam. And many women became so emotionally attached that they would allow only him to manage the rest of their pregnancies.

Dave and Celia Anthony drove all the way from Detroit to Boston two weeks before her due date, so that he could be the attending obstetrician. For they knew instinctively that their wonder-working doctor's reward was not his modest fee, but the enormous satisfaction he derived from sharing their own long-dreamed-of success.

The day he delivered their eight-pound little boy, the room was filled with tears of joy. No one was dry-eyed—although Adam tried not to show it.

"Isn't he beautiful?" Celia sighed. Her husband could merely nod mutely in agreement.

"What are you going to call him?" he asked.

"Well, Doc," Dave responded, gathering his courage. "If it's all right with you—I mean Celia and I have talked this over—we'd like to name him 'Adam.' It's the only way we have of thanking you."

His colleagues regularly sent Adam their "hopeless" cases, and he would prescribe a series of laboratory tests—especially those he himself had devised to determine if the women were producing embryotoxins.

Of course, not all women were suitable candidates for his hormone therapy, but his scientific intuition was often able to find clues to other little-known disorders that hindered their pregnancies. The end result, in any case, was happy mothers.

And yet, sadly, there were those whom even his vast knowledge and untiring effort could not help to become parents, and he felt their failure almost as keenly as they. Paradoxically, while he had trouble remembering all his successful patients, the faces of the sad ones haunted him forever.

Such a couple was Professor and Mrs. Dmitri Avilov, recent arrivals from the USSR.

Formerly a geneticist on the staff of the Soviet Academy, Avilov was so much in the avant-garde of the field that several Western countries had for many years been urging him to emigrate. No politics were involved, merely the prospect of unmatched facilities and lavish capitalistic salaries.

Finally, at an international congress in London, the two had bolted and sought sanctuary in the American embassy.

Avilov had already selected Harvard, not merely because of the generosity of their offer, which included a lab of his own, but also because of the med school's reputation for treating infertility. In more than five years of marriage, he and his wife had not been able to achieve a pregnancy.

Now, Adam sat across the desk from the tall, broad-shouldered Russian and his petite, full-breasted wife.

Anya Avilov was beautiful—but not by any conventional standard. She had large, deep-set brown eyes and a cherubic, heart-shaped face. But she obviously paid little attention to her appearance. Her short, dark hair fell carelessly onto her forehead, and she continually swept it back as a kind of nervous tic.

Adam's patients did not normally radiate optimism. All of them were battered survivors of unsuccessful consultations with other specialists, veterans of countless disappointments. His group was the last port of call before they would be set adrift on a sea of desperation.

But Anya was different. Despite the outward similarity of her history to that of the hundreds of unfortunate wives he had encountered, her expression did not emanate defeat. Anya's resilient, irrepressible cheerfulness seized his heart.

By contrast, her husband was dour and pompous, but Anya tried her best to mitigate this impression by telling lighthearted, mostly self-deprecating, jokes.

This levity made her husband frown.

"Don't act like child," he admonished in a loud whisper. "He is world-famous professor."

"I may be 'famous,'" Adam interposed, "but I'm not allergic to a laugh." It was his own quiet way of telling Avilov to stop leaning on his wife.

"You have lovely daughter, Dr. Coopersmith," the Russian woman said, looking at the silver-framed photograph behind Adam's desk. Her praise was genuine. As was the unmistakable tinge of longing in her voice.

"Thank you," he replied gently—and self-consciously. He had always debated whether to keep Heather's photo there, since for many patients it might be a painful reminder of what their own lives lacked.

"Look." Anya pointed to a portrait of Toni with Heather on a shelf behind the doctor's desk.

Avilov glanced briefly at it and turned scowling to his wife. "I think we should return to business," he said sternly. And then, turning to Adam, he demanded, "What do you think are the prospects, Professor?"

Uneasy, Adam shuffled some of the documents and began carefully. "From what I see here, Mrs. Avilov—"

"Actually," the husband interjected pedantically, "my wife is also *Doctor* Avilov."

"Really? What's your specialty?"

Somewhat embarrassed, Anya answered in English more broken than her husband's, "Is cruel joke of nature. But in Russia I was trained in *genekolog*."

"Oh, I didn't know I had so charming a colleague. Do you practice here?"

She shook her head. "Not yet. Dmitri does not see patients, so he did not have to take boards. But I have to pass exams for foreign medical graduates, and my English is still very . . ." She motioned with her hands as if trying to grasp an elusive word.

"Unpolished?" Adam offered tactfully.

Confused, she looked at her husband and asked, *"Shto eto?"*

"I think Professor Coopersmith is asking if you are Polish," Dmitri replied.

"No, no," Adam protested. "I read your records. I can see your wife was born in Siberia." And then, addressing Anya, he tried to steer the conversation back on course.

"Dr. Avilov, when was your last period?"

"I am sorry to say over six months," she replied, almost apologetically. And then smiled. "You do not have to be *genekolog* to know this is not very good sign."

"Well, I'll grant it isn't the best condition for someone trying to start a family. But, as you know, amenorrhea can be caused by several factors, some of which are reversible. I suggest you go along to see my colleague Dr. Rosenthal. Hopefully, the trials he'll run will help us pinpoint the problem."

"More tests?" Avilov asked irately. "This cannot be. I do not think any couple in the Soviet Union has been poked or prodded or squeezed more than Anya and myself."

At this point his wife scolded him gently, "Mitya, you know yourself doctors only trust their own labs." And then she won him over by suggesting, "And no doubt Harvard's methods are more advanced."

Avilov capitulated with a melodramatic sigh. "Very well," he said, standing up, "The eminence of your reputation persuades me, Professor Coopersmith."

Adam glanced admiringly at Anya and responded, "Your wife's a good soldier. You're a very lucky man."

"Thank you." She smiled, and turned to her husband. "I hope you remember what he has just told you—and give my opinions more respect."

Avilov obviously had a riposte for this, but one—it was clear—he would pronounce only after they left Adam's office.

"I'll be sure that Dr. Rosenthal sees you at the earliest possible moment. And you, Anya, good luck with your qualifying exams too."

"First things first," Dmitri interrupted, wagging an admonitory finger at Adam. "There is no hurry to practice medicine. We must quickly make family."

At eight o'clock on the evening he received the data, Adam telephoned the Avilovs at their Watertown apartment.

"Hi, Dmitri, this is Adam Coopersmith. Can you put Anya on the other phone?"

"Is not necessary, Professor. Besides," he added with pointed displeasure, "unlike our flat in Russia, we have only *one* telephone. They offered me a king's salary and lodged me in a proletarian dump. I have already complained. Anyway, please tell me your news."

"Well, Dr. Rosenthal will be calling you at the lab tomorrow, but knowing how anxious you two are, I thought I'd get you both started on the antibiotics right away. I've called in a prescription for doxycycline to the Charles Pharmacy—they're open all night."

"I don't understand," the Russian responded. "What is the infection we are being treated for?"

"The smear we did on Anya showed positive for mycoplasma," Adam explained. "Understandably, the same was found in your sperm."

"Oh." The Soviet scientist's tone suggested his surprise at being implicated. "So we have a urogenital infection. And will the treatment clear the path for everything, so to speak?"

"Well, it's too early to say," Adam hedged. "You two might have been walking around with this for quite a while."

"From my knowledge of your specialty," Dmitri said with disappointment, "that could have bad prognosis."

"But you've got a live-in expert in the field," Adam replied. "Why not consult with Anya on the ramifications of all this?"

At that moment Adam could overhear Anya Avilov's anxious voice. She was speaking Russian, but he could nonetheless intuit what she was asking in a pleading tone.

What's going on, Mitya, what did the doctor say?

And though he was no linguist, Adam did understand the one word Dmitri employed in response to his wife: *"Nichevo."*

Nothing.

Two weeks later the couple sat once again across from Adam. In the interim they had duly taken their antibiotics and been tested by Dr. Rosenthal's lab.

"I'm happy to say your mycoplasma is a thing of the past," Adam announced.

Anya was not totally reassured, although her husband beamed.

"Wonderful, wonderful. Do we therefore have, as you say, a 'tidy bill of health'?"

Adam continued slowly, "The X rays showed Anya's tubes were open and the uterus normal—"

"Well," Avilov interrupted, "how do you explain why she is not getting pregnant?" There was just a hint in his tone that Adam was not using his best efforts.

Knowing that the very name of her condition would be like a dagger in Anya's heart, he answered as gently as possible.

"As we already knew, your periods are extremely irregular. And the hormone tests they've done suggest that you're not ovulating. I'm afraid we're dealing with a case of premature ovarian failure."

"But she is so young," Dmitri protested.

Adam got the clear impression that the husband's ire was partially intended as a kind of reprimand for his wife. A suggestion that her unfortunate condition had somehow been a betrayal of him.

Anya covered her face and began to weep. At the same time, she was vaguely struggling to keep some professional distance.

"This happens, Dmitri," she said between sobs. "It is rare, but it happens. For reasons they do not understand, some of the follicles do not respond to stimulation from the pituitary gland. Therefore, there can be no eggs."

She looked at her husband, her glance clearly begging for a sign of reassurance. But he remained silent.

It took the Russian several more seconds to realize that Adam was staring angrily at him. Nothing could possibly have been lost in translation. His glare was so intense that it seemed to bear a warning: either you put your arms around her—or *I* will.

Anxious not to lose face with a colleague, Dmitri slowly turned and placed his hands on Anya's shoulders.

"Is all right, darling. We could adopt. Important thing is we have each other."

Though it was spoken in English, Adam did not believe a word.

And neither, it was clear, did Anya.

The barrel-chested Russian rose and his wife slowly followed him.

"I am sorry not to bring you good business," she said to Adam with a wan smile.

"I beg your pardon?" Adam asked.

"I speak as one *genekolog* to another. I shall have no babies for you to deliver."

"In any case, Professor Coopersmith," Dmitri interrupted manfully, "let me congratulate you on thorough work of diagnosis." He began to lead his wife toward the door.

"Wait," Adam protested. "You two should have some counseling. I'd like to—"

"With great respect, Professor," Dmitri cut him off, "I do not think such measures are indicated. We are scientists—all of us. We deal with facts and we accept them as they are." Then, turning to his wife, he declared, "We should go."

After they had left his office, Adam slumped back in his chair and began to brood about all the things that had been left unsaid.

And found himself whispering half aloud, "You arrogant shit, you don't deserve a woman like that."

15

ISABEL

RAYMOND DA COSTA was still on the floor of the restaurant when the paramedics arrived. The now-remorseful hippie whose taunts had been the cause of Raymond's agitation and collapse had placed his own leather jacket under the victim's head, while the restaurant owner had produced two tablecloths to cover him and keep him warm.

A police car had also responded to the call, and the officer volunteered to take Isabel to the hospital, but he did not press the matter when she insisted on riding in the ambulance with her father.

Trembling with fright, Isabel watched as they lifted Raymond onto a stretcher and began to carry him out. Suddenly, she felt a garment fall around her shoulders. It was the same coat that had provided her father with a pillow.

"Listen," the frightened young man pleaded. "I was only joking, I swear. You do believe me, don't you?"

"What difference would it make?" Isabel yelled at him.

Just then a calming male voice interrupted her. "Excuse me, miss, we want to get your Dad to the hospital as soon as we can."

Isabel nodded and quickly followed the paramedic out the door. Her shock was all the greater since she had temporarily lost the very person who had always cosseted and protected her from the harsh realities of ordinary life.

As the ambulance sped across the city, swerving wildly around corners, Raymond tried desperately to speak to her, but the attendants urged him not to upset himself any further and to breathe deeply of the oxygen they were administering.

Isabel tried hard to hold back her sobs, but the sight of her father, disabled, and now disfigured by the oxygen mask, brought her to the verge of panic.

The ambulance shrieked to a halt in front of the battered doors of the emergency room of Alta Bates Hospital on Ashley. From every direction disembodied hands reached out to transfer the ailing man onto a gurney and wheel him off.

Inside, the chief resident of the "Pit" rapidly fired orders to his staff. It was only when they were about to speed Raymond to Intensive Care that the doctor noticed Isabel, standing frozen and mute.

"Who's she?" he asked gruffly.

"The guy's daughter," the paramedic explained as he dashed out toward yet another emergency.

"Isn't there anyone to look after her?"

"Send her to Pediatrics and let her sit in the Outpatient Clinic," the resident commanded.

"No, no," Isabel protested, "I want to stay with my father."

Trying to restrain his own frayed emotions, the young doctor spoke as gently as possible. "Listen, kid, I've got my hands full running the Pit, and I wanna be able to concentrate on your old man. So please let someone take you up to Pediatrics, and I'll phone them when it's okay for you to come down. Now, let the nurse—"

"I can find my own way," Isabel asserted.

Though she did not realize it, this was the first time in her life she had expressed that conviction.

For nearly three hours, Isabel sat motionless in a whirlwind of coughing, squealing, and crying youngsters.

At last the chief resident appeared.

The moment she caught sight of him, Isabel lost her breath—preparing herself for the worst.

He walked over slowly and said gently, "Your dad's okay. I mean, he's had a cardiac incident—"

" 'Incident'?" she echoed angrily. "I'm not familiar with that term, Doctor. Can you be a bit more specific?"

"Look," he responded, "you're a little girl. I can't exactly go over the cardiogram with you. Let me just give you the salient, I mean, the main—"

"I know what 'salient' means," she shot back. "And I think I could even understand the cardiogram if you would deign to show it to me. But get to the important part—will he *live*?"

"Hell yeah," the doctor answered wearily. "He's had

a mild cardiac infarct, and at first glance there doesn't appear to be serious damage. Please forgive my temper, sweetie, but I've just finished a forty-eight-hour stint and I've got woodpeckers in my brain and cotton balls in my mouth—I'm really zonked. The cardiologist—lucky bastard who actually gets to sleep at night—will tell you everything you need to know."

In the elevator both were silent. He, speechless with fatigue, she with worry.

"I know how you must feel," she said at last, to fill the vacuum. "I mean, how can you tolerate what you're doing?"

He looked at her with a tiny smile. "Do you want to know something funny? I bitch a lot, but I actually like it. There's no greater high in the world than saving a person's life. Maybe you'll be a doctor when you grow up, huh?"

Isabel was too moved by the young man's kindness to retort that she already *was* grown up.

And yet had today's events not called that into doubt?

Though the doctors had assured her that her father was heavily sedated and would sleep for the next several hours, Isabel nonetheless remained by Ray's bedside and tried to comfort him with words he could not hear.

It was more than four hours later that he half woke and called out, "Isabel, where's Isabel?"

"I'm here, Dad," she whispered, taking his hand.

"Darling, I can't tell you how bad I feel about doing this to you."

"But, Dad, you were trying to protect me."

"Look at the mess I've made. What's gonna happen to you, Isabel?" Raymond said plaintively.

"I'll be all right, Dad."

"They say they want to keep me in for observation. Who's gonna look after you? Who'll cook—"

"Come on," she interrupted, "I'm not that out of

touch with reality. And if I'm too nerdish to defrost a dinner, it won't exactly be torture to eat pizza."

"No," Raymond suddenly exclaimed, terrified by what might occur in his absence. Namely, that by going into, say, a pizzeria, Isabel might strike up conversations with other customers. Or they with her.

She was too young, too inexperienced. Danger lurked at every corner.

And then he continued out loud, "Listen, darling, it's absolutely vital that you don't neglect your courses. I'm sure if I called Dean Kendall, he'd find a senior coed to take you to classes and back. And maybe I can talk them into letting you sleep here."

"That won't be necessary, Raymond," a female voice interposed.

Instantly, both turned their gaze toward the door.

Ray frowned but said nothing as Isabel leaped excitedly to her feet and rushed to embrace her mother.

"Gosh it's great to see you, Mom."

From Muriel's expression, the joy was clearly reciprocated. She then addressed her husband.

"How are you, Raymond?"

"I'll survive," he answered sullenly.

"I've sent Peter to Aunt Edna and rearranged my schedule so I can stay here as long as necessary." Then, gazing at her daughter, she remarked, "I'm really looking forward to it."

Raymond was too weak to protest. In truth, that part of him that loved Isabel unselfishly was glad she would be in safe hands.

"*I* called her, Dad," Isabel asserted, and then, anticipating a hostile response, continued, "Whatever you two feel about each other, it was the right thing to do." She precluded further altercation by adding, "I mean, for *me*."

The next morning, the cardiologist who had examined Raymond expressed optimism.

"I'm happy to say that the damage was only minimal. But it's a warning that should be heeded. I can tell from our conversation that Mr. da Costa's a classic self-driven type A personality. But from now on he's got to avoid stress, cut his cholesterol, and add three forty-minute sessions of aerobic exercise every week."

"How much longer will he have to stay in here?" Isabel asked.

"Well, I want him in for two or three more days of relaxation, even if I have to tie him to the bed."

One compensation for Raymond's illness was that Muriel would be living with Isabel till his release from the hospital.

Mother and daughter had so much to catch up on that they chatted endlessly.

"Are you enjoying your studies, sweetheart?"

"Yeah, it's really exciting. The Physics faculty has a lot of live wires."

"I'm glad," Muriel replied, masking her disappointment at having her worst fears confirmed. "I suppose you're too young to make friends with the undergraduates."

"Frankly," Isabel complained, "I'm really bugged by this age thing. I mean, on the one hand, according to my birth certificate I'm thirteen, and on the other, I'm taking a graduate seminar in astrophysics with people twice as old as I. Everyone on campus can drive, and I've still got to wait three years."

"Don't worry, darling, Nature has a way of making time catch up to you."

At which point Muriel's gaze was inexorably drawn to her daughter's budding breasts. There was no need to exchange words.

"Yes, Mom," Isabel confessed with relief, "and I've started having periods too."

"Were you frightened at first?" Muriel asked as she embraced her. "I remember *I* was."

"Yes," Isabel replied, enormously relieved at the opportunity to discuss her secret feelings and confusions.

"You should have told me on the phone."

"I wanted to, but Dad was in the room—and I was embarrassed."

Her mother's expression grew somber. "You mean, when we speak he's always there?"

"Well, it's a small apartment, Mom."

"But does he really have to come to every class with you?"

"How do you know that?"

"Isabel," Muriel replied, "there are always little snippets about you in the local paper. And if I don't see them myself, the other teachers at school keep me up-to-date."

She hesitated for a moment, and then added grimly, "They mean well, but their attitude is kind of one-dimensional. They think I should be proud."

"You mean you aren't?" Isabel asked with undisguised disappointment.

"Honey, to tell you the honest truth, I wish I could rewrite history. Then I'd still be driving you to junior high school instead of visiting you at college. Anyway, your dad and I had an understanding that we would spend all the vacations together as a family. But somehow, the two of you always seem to find reasons why you—"

"It's not me, Mom."

"Well, don't you miss me?" her mother persevered, beginning to reveal her hurt. "God knows my heart aches for you."

"Me too. Maybe we could try speaking to Dad together."

Sick at heart, Muriel looked at her daughter and said sadly, "I don't really think that would help."

She sat down, buried her face in her hands and began to sob quietly.

Isabel walked over and put her arms around her, murmuring, "Please don't, Mommy."

"I'm sorry, it's just that I miss you so much."

They hugged each other tightly.

Finally, knowing she had to regain control, Muriel said as convincingly as possible, "Everything will be all right." At which point she rose and went off to splash cold water on her face. When she returned, they both escaped into innocuous gossip.

"Tell me all about Peter," Isabel asked, attempting to sound lighthearted. "All he does is grunt when I try to talk to him."

"Well, he's a typical teenager—for better or for worse. He plays on the soccer team, doesn't do his homework, and talks endlessly to his pals on the phone about sexual conquests, real or imagined. But I know he carries condoms in his wallet."

"Mom, you don't mean you searched?"

"Of course not," she answered. "But we've talked about it."

Isabel could not suppress a pang of jealousy. Peter had the luxury of living at home, even confiding in a parent—and, most of all, enjoying friends and having fun.

Yet she did not want to give the impression that in its own way her life was less happy than Peter's.

"Berkeley's a neat place, Mom. I'll give you a tour tomorrow."

"I'd like that very much, darling."

"I've got courses till noon and a lab at two-thirty. But we could have a quick bite and I'll show you around."

"I guess it'll be a funny feeling," Muriel remarked. "I mean, going to classes on your own, without Dad to explain things."

"Well, he doesn't really have to explain—" She pulled herself up short. "I mean, you're right, I guess I will miss him."

Muriel read her daughter's face and saw profound ambivalence.

But sensing that she might be pressing too hard on this delicate subject, she switched gears. "I've got a surprise for you," she said cheerily, bounding from the chair.

She hurried into Raymond's room, which she had temporarily appropriated for herself, and came back with—

"My fiddle!" Isabel cried with delight. "Thanks, Mom, I've really missed it."

"And I've brought you lots of music." Her mother smiled. "Actually, you'll discover, as I did, that being good at an instrument can improve your social life."

"Meaning?"

"Well, besides going to orchestra practice, I've been taking advanced classes with Edmundo. And when the Physics Quartet needed a second violin, they stretched a point and asked me to join. It's been wonderful— traveling, meeting new people. I even enjoy the squabbles we have about tempo. Why aren't you playing with the Berkeley orchestra?"

"When would I find time?" Isabel grinned mischievously. "I mean, I am only thirteen years old."

"That means you'll really like my other surprise," Muriel responded. She reached into her handbag and pulled out an audio casette.

"This is from a fun series called *Music Minus One*. They give you a concerto with only the orchestral backing, so anybody can play the solo part with a genuine philharmonic."

"That's neat!" Isabel enthused.

Muriel was pleased. "I thought you might like to start with the Mendelssohn E-Minor. If you like, we can attack it together, and I'll try to help you over some of the rough bits."

"That would be great, Mom. There's only one problem. . . ."

"I can't believe it," Muriel uttered. "You don't have a cassette player?"

Isabel shook her head.

Muriel winced. "But you always loved working to music."

"Yeah, only Dad thinks it's bad for my concentration."

"Do you do *everything* he tells you?" she asked, trying to make light of what she inwardly regarded as a serious matter. "At your age, you should be rebelling like mad."

"Okay, Mom," Isabel joked, "I'll join a few street marches. Now, can *I* ask *you* a question—what's gonna happen to you and Dad?"

"I can't answer that," Muriel replied in a muted voice.

"Why not?"

"I don't know how I feel anymore."

"About what?"

"Ray." Before her daughter could react to this bombshell, Muriel deftly shifted gears. "Now, can I make us something to eat?"

"Great." Her daughter's face brightened. "Dad's a terrible cook."

Thank God for that, Muriel thought to herself.

Shopping for ingredients liberated them from the tense atmosphere of the apartment, as well as giving Muriel the chance to engage in another activity for which her husband was unsuited.

She broached the subject as delicately as possible.

"I know the Berkeley fashion is for women to let it all hang out, so to speak. But don't you think you could do with a training bra?"

"Sure, Mom. Thanks for asking."

After helping Isabel to locate the appropriate item, Muriel left her trying on some bright new spring blouses and darted across the street to buy an inexpensive cassette player. When she returned, she was delighted at the change in her daughter's mood. The two of them began to giggle, and Isabel was in absolutely no hurry to leave the store.

Unfortunately, when they returned home, Ray's spirit was still hovering in every corner. Yet the conversations earlier in the day had equipped Muriel with an inner radar that kept her from striking shoals of dangerous topics.

After dinner, they went back to the hospital. Raymond had now been moved out of Intensive Care. Mother and daughter spent an hour making small talk, competing for his attention with a basketball game on television. When they had come to the mutual conclusion that Raymond would be just as happy on his own watching the college hoopsters slam dunk, Isabel kissed him good night and they returned to the apartment.

It was a rare moment of equilibrium for Isabel. She seemed to be resting precisely at the midpoint of the magnetic force between her father and mother. Muriel knew this was a propitious time to produce the cassette player, which Isabel greeted with excitement.

"Oh, Mom, you should visit more often."

Her mother smiled. "Try and keep me away. Now, shall we try the Mendelssohn?"

"Why not?" her daughter responded.

Muriel immediately went to her luggage, withdrew her own violin and tuning fork, and the two of them savored the unique experience of playing a violin solo as a duet.

The next day, Isabel took her mother to classes with her.

Muriel enjoyed Professor Rosenmeyer's lecture on Greek tragedy, but was lost in "Introduction to Physical Chemistry."

Moreover, she could not fail to notice that Isabel's presence was unique not only for her age. She was one of only two girls taking the course.

As they were leaving the lecture hall, one of Isabel's classmates called out, "Hey, da Costa, your new bodyguard's a lot cuter than your old one."

After an alfresco lunch followed by another cheerful shopping expedition, they returned to the apartment to find Raymond leafing through a copy of *Science*.

"My, I was beginning to wonder if something had happened to you," he remarked with a perceptible edge of disapproval.

There was an uneasy silence. Muriel knew full well that the halcyon days were over.

"I'm glad you're feeling better, Ray," she remarked with as much conviction as she could muster.

"Yeah," he replied, "I checked myself out. Actually, I'm fit as a fiddle."

"Was that intended to be a pun?" Muriel asked wearily.

Raymond glanced at the sheet music propped up against a pile of books on the dining table.

"No," he answered somberly. "It was more like a slip of the tongue."

Muriel suddenly had an awkward realization. "I guess I'd better call and see about flights this evening," she volunteered.

"Can't you stay, Mom?" Isabel asked with genuine disappointment. "We could all have dinner." A further thought tumbled out. "Like the good old days."

"By all means," Raymond added, "Isabel would really enjoy that."

"But then I'd have to stay over," Muriel explained as delicately as possible. "And you don't seem to have a guest room."

"There's always the couch," Raymond suggested.

Was he aware, she wondered, of how cruel he sounded?

"No, I'm afraid I've never been a very good camper," she said, declining with a smile. "It'll only take me a few seconds to pack. I know I can get a flight to San Diego without any problem."

By the time she was in the taxi, speeding along Route 101 to the airport, Muriel was shaking with rage.

Had Ray been totally insensitive to the horrendous example of a married couple they had presented to their daughter?

With this precedent, Isabel could never hope to form a normal relationship in her later life.

But then, maybe that was precisely what Ray wanted.

March 27
Why are they making me choose between them?

16
SANDY

"ARE YOU still a virgin, kid?"

Sidney Raven's question caught his son off guard. Sandy did not know how to reply. Although he wanted to stand high in his father's esteem, he was desperate to surrender his celibacy.

He hesitated. "Gee, Dad, that's a tough one."

"No, sonny boy, it's easy. And you've just answered it. And that's why I've booked a table for you and Gloria at Scandia."

"Who's Gloria?" Sandy asked, confused.

"Your date," Sidney responded with a mischievous wink. "She's a nice kid—anxious to break into movies, and who happens also to be friendly—and generous with her body."

"Oh," Sandy said, suddenly growing nervous. "And who am I supposed to be?"

"Just who you are," his father stated, with a touch of pride. "Sidney Raven's son. I think you'll like her. She's got a college degree in something or other. When the bill comes at the restaurant, all you have to do is add a fifteen percent tip and sign my name. I've got an account there."

"What about Gloria?"

"What about her?"

"How do I—settle with her?"

"Are you kidding?" Sidney reacted with mock indignation. "She's not a hooker or anything. She's a clean-cut kid like yourself."

Sandy was at a complete loss. "But, Dad," he confessed, "I haven't got the vaguest idea what to do."

"Don't worry, son, leave it all to her."

For the rest of the afternoon, Sandy was stricken with high anxiety. Suppose—like the fastidious Margie—Gloria found him unappealing? The wound from that terrible rejection was still fresh and painful.

And even if the girl were commercially bound to grin and bear him, he wondered nervously if he would have the courage to initiate the action—or whatever it was called out here in L.A.

To optimize his appearance, he spent four hours in the sun, hoping a tan would make his face look a little less like the surface of the moon. After cutting himself three times shaving, he was so nervous that he had to take another shower. He spent eternities going through his father's wardrobe, trying to decide which tie he should wear.

Sidney was still sitting by the pool sipping a martini as the late afternoon sun filtered through the huge fir trees casting long ithyphallic—or so it seemed to Sandy—shadows on the lawn.

"Have a good time, sonny boy," the elder Raven called. "Be sure to try the *gravlaks*, it's great."

Sandy nodded, went out into the crescent courtyard and climbed into his father's leased Jaguar XJ 12. He cruised down Stone Canyon and turned east at Sunset Boulevard.

To say the least, Sandy was driving below the speed limit, cautioning himself that the police were severe with speeders. In fact, all day long he had been reminding himself to be cool and casual in everything he did.

Sunset Boulevard was precisely as it appeared on film. The vast lawns of the mansions he passed seemed as if they had been trimmed that morning with cuticle scissors by legions of Disney dwarves.

In addition to his panic, Sandy was vertiginous with a sense of déjà vu. It felt as if he had been there a million times. And yet at this moment he felt like a stranger from another planet.

In less than five minutes he was pulling up at Scandia and a red-vested, blond and tanned parking valet hurried to relieve him of his car.

Sandy somehow felt naked without the four walls of automotive metal that had been insulating him from the dreamlike realities of Hollywood.

When he entered the restaurant, he marveled at its elegant decor and the strangely mellifluous hum of its sedate diners.

The moment Sandy gave his name, the head waiter replied with unctuous deference, "Ah yes, Mr. Raven. I've already shown your guest to the table."

First they moved through the luxuriantly carpeted cocktail area, and then into a bright, cheery dining room.

Preoccupied though he was, Sandy could not keep from staring at a titian-haired young woman in a light tan suit and frilly white blouse, sitting all alone. As they drew closer, he had the uncanny feeling that she was smiling at him.

Surely this could not be Gloria. It was an angel-faced Aurora, Goddess of the Dawn.

"Hello, Sandy." She smiled, politely offering her hand. "It's nice to meet you." Her accent was East Coast posh.

As he sat down in the deep-cushioned chair, all he could manage as a response was, "Uh, it's nice to meet you too."

The maitre d' bowed and offered them menus, at the same time asking Sandy, "Aperitif?"

"I've taken the liberty of ordering a Kir Royale," Gloria said, with what seemed like respectful deference.

Why did she seem so in awe of him?

"Then I'll have the same," Sandy responded.

The captain nodded and evanesced.

Now at last, Sandy thought, a legitimate topic of conversation. He looked straight at Gloria, trying to overcome his bedazzlement at her natural beauty: "What exactly did I order?"

"Champagne and cassis," she said with a smile.

"Oh, I know a lot about champagne," he volunteered, leaping with enthusiasm on a topic he knew something about. "Mostly from a scientific standpoint. I guess it would bore you."

"On the contrary." The young woman reached over to touch his hand. "I'm fascinated by science, even though I only had to take one course for distribution at Radcliffe."

Jesus, Sandy thought to himself, this ... professional went to Harvard! And then he responded out loud, "Uh, what did you major in?"

"Art history," she replied. "In fact, I'm just finishing a master's thesis at UCLA on the engravings of Albrecht Dürer."

Sandy breathed an inward sigh of relief: she's doing this to support her education. I'm actually helping subsidize her studies. The fact that she was so widely educated was a great relief. He had wondered how they would pass the time before the critical moment.

When the moment came to order, Gloria proved

knowledgeable about the restaurant's Scandinavian fare. And, when the wine waiter came, she did not usurp his initiative, but merely whispered, "Try number one hundred twelve. But be sure it's very chilled."

Sandy relayed her suggestion in a louder voice, and after noting it was an excellent choice, the sommelier retreated.

Suddenly Sandy's jaw went slack. His eyes bulged.

Gloria's instinct made her think that he had just seen someone he was dodging. She came to the logical conclusion and whispered, "Is it your wife?"

Sandy shook his head wordlessly.

Gloria turned discreetly to follow the direction of his gaze. His attention seemed to have been caught by a table in the far corner which, to the best of her knowledge, at least, was currently being peopled by a quartet of nonentities—three men and a woman.

"You've got Hollywooditis," she whispered solicitously.

"What do you mean?"

"Well, it's a kind of delusion you suffer from during the first few days you're here. I had it when I arrived. You sort of hallucinate that everyone you see—the butcher, the baker, the candlestick maker—is actually someone like Robert Redford or Jane Fonda. The truth is, the major plebeian preoccupation out here is *trying* to look like the real thing."

"No," Sandy protested, still in a semitrance. "I'm sure I know this person. We went to grade school together."

Gloria took another discreet look.

"Surely you don't mean Kim Tower?" she asked disparagingly.

"Yes," Sandy insisted. "But I know her, I really do."

"That's nothing unusual," she answered dismissively. "I mean, everybody in the town does."

Sandy deliberately chose to ignore Gloria's remark.

He asked, as a child would a parent, "Do you think it would be all right if I went over and said hello?"

"If it'll make you any happier," Gloria answered. "But in your parlance, I'd say she has a molecule for a brain."

Sandy's defense was instinctive. "She's very smart, actually," he said sternly.

"Well," Gloria surrendered sweetly, "I guess clever women have to keep their minds in check. In any case, she does a good job hiding it."

Unaffected by Gloria's derision, Sandy rose, still in the semitrance that had been induced by the appearance of his personal goddess. He tentatively approached Rochelle's table.

The closer he came, the more refulgent his idol seemed—flawless skin, perfect teeth, sparkling everything. When he was as near as he dared, he said shyly, "Hello, Rochelle, fancy meeting you here."

A look of puzzlement crossed her face. Simultaneously, her three escorts whirled around to deal with what they assumed was some out-of-town autograph seeker.

Her sudden smile deterred them.

"It's not Sandy, is it?"

"For a moment, I thought you had forgotten me," he confessed.

"How could I?" she answered with a flourish. She stood and held out her arms. "Come here, so I can give you a big hug."

He complied, and before his senses were benumbed enough to appreciate it, was pecked on either cheek.

But this was merely an overture to his twenty-one gun salute. For she then proceeded to recite a florid introduction to her trio of attendants.

"Guys, I'd like you to meet my dearest childhood friend, and probably one of America's greatest scientific geniuses. And, by coincidence, Sidney Raven's son. Sandy, this is Harvey Madison, my agent; Ned Gordon, my business manager; and Matt Humphries, my publicist."

All three men rose and shook Sandy's hand with bone-breaking vigor, while Rochelle rushed on to say, "I'm really sorry I can't ask you to join us, but we're having a business meeting. My contract's coming up for renewal and we're working on a game plan."

"That's okay," Sandy replied, a bit of confidence returning, "I'm with a friend, in any case."

"Oh, really?" Kim inquired with a hint of genuine curiosity.

"Yes," Sandy acknowledged proudly. "She's over there."

Four pairs of eyes scrutinized Gloria from afar.

"Lovely lady," Harvey Madison pronounced. "Is she in the business?"

For a split second Sandy thought the agent's remark was intended to demean his date. "No," he replied with a tinge of sanctimony, "she's an art historian. It was nice meeting you, but I have to go back. Please excuse me."

As he moved away, Rochelle called out cheerfully, "Don't forget to give me a ring before you leave. We'll have some eats and catch up on old times."

"Sure, sure," Sandy mumbled.

He weaved his way along the serpentine route back to his own table and addressed Gloria as he sat down. "Sorry, but she's an old friend from back East."

Gloria simply nodded. "You've got lipstick smudges on your cheeks."

Their food arrived then, and the waiter's bustling enabled Sandy to make a detailed study of Gloria's face. Apart from a touch of mascara, Gloria did not seem to be wearing any makeup at all, in sharp contrast to Rochelle.

His unexpected encounter with a group of what he imagined to be the "in" crowd had emboldened Sandy.

"Uh, I understand you're interested in making movies," he remarked.

"As a matter of fact, I am. I think it's about time that women got their fair share in this town, don't you?"

"Well, Barbra Streisand does okay. Don't you think?"

"But who the hell would want to be an actress?" Gloria sneered. "I have no desire to be gawked at. I'm already working part-time in the Paramount Editing Lab. If I'm good enough, someday you'll see my name in lights—as a director."

"I'll drink to that." Sandy raised a goblet of the Chablis she had chosen.

Gloria then declared, "Now it's my turn to toast: 'May you fall out of love with Kim Tower as soon as possible.' "

He was stupefied. "Why on earth did you say that?"

"Because, Sandy, she's plastic, and you're the real thing."

Later that evening at her apartment, after they had made love well into the night, Sandy whispered in a moment of sensual intoxication, "Gloria, what if I told you I think I'm falling in love with you?"

"I would talk you out of it, darling. I'm not nice enough for you either."

When he pulled the Jag up to his father's front door, it was nearly four in the morning. Entering the house as quietly as he could, Sandy was surprised to see a streak of light from the study spilling across the carpet.

He peeked into his father's office and saw the elder Raven, clad in a silk bathrobe, feet up on a chair, piles of scripts on either side, swiftly leafing through what was clearly a scenario.

"Dad?" he whispered.

"Oh, sonny boy, you gave me a start. I didn't expect you home so early."

"Do you always stay up this late?" Sandy inquired.

"That's what you gotta do if you want to get ahead in

the movies, kiddo. In a few minutes the calls'll start coming in from Spain, where I'm shooting an Italian western. Meanwhile, I took some submissions home to see if there are any worthwhile properties."

"When do you sleep?"

"What is this," his father asked good-humoredly, "twenty questions? I should be asking you. You've got a strange look on your face, Sandy. Did everything go okay?"

"That depends on how you interpret the data, Dad."

"Well, let's get to the important part. Did you enjoy yourself with Gloria?"

"She's a terrific person. Really bright and—"

"Son, I'm not asking you for a character reference. To mince no bones, did you have a good time horizontally?"

"Are you kidding? Thanks for the fix-up. I hope I can get to see her again before I go back East."

"You can count on it," his father answered with enthusiasm. "But how come you're not beaming from ear to ear?"

Sandy flopped down on the easy chair, then leaned forward, elbows propped on his knees, and inquired, "Dad, would you level with me if I asked you a really intimate question?"

The elder Raven was puzzled. "Sure, fire away."

Sandy gathered up his courage. "Is Rochelle Taubman like Gloria?"

"I don't understand. You're talking apples and oranges."

"No, I'm not—I'm talking about two ambitious girls who are desperate to get to the top in movies."

"Okay, I get it. Yeah, from that point you might say they're both oranges."

"Then does Rochelle have to sleep with anybody her producer tells her to?"

"I'm not her boss," Sidney replied, in a tone wavering enigmatically between sincerity and evasiveness.

"Come on, Dad, you're on contract to the studio. I bet everybody at those top tables knows who's screwing whom and whether it's for love or . . . advancement."

"These things are not mutually exclusive, sonny boy. But I still can't figure out why, after I orchestrated what I hope was the most memorable night of your life, you're acting like this was the *Caine Mutiny* court-martial."

"Dad, did you know that she would be at Scandia tonight?"

"Of course not. We don't ask our players to sign out with their dinner destinations. Anyway, I hope she gave you a warm welcome. I mean, she owes you a lot careerwise."

Sandy was growing more upset, and asked nervously, "In your estimation, would her debt be as large as a roll in the hay?"

"Oh, at least," his father replied matter-of-factly.

"Jesus!" Sandy exclaimed, rising to his feet. "Doesn't anything in your business ever get done without screwing?"

"Listen, Sandy, it's too late at night to discuss philosophy. Let me just tell you that a certain amount of humping is a useful lubricant that makes the movie machine run smoothly."

"That's immoral," his son complained.

"What is this?" Sidney retorted. "Now, you're doing a Burt Lancaster in *Elmer Gantry*."

Without another word Sandy stormed upstairs to his room, tore off his clothes, and fell back onto the bed.

For that evening in the land of impossible dreams, he had seen his own private fantasies shattered. Worse, it was with an arrogant hypocrisy that pretended its skewed morality was the way of the world.

And as he lay there, still feeling the warmth of Gloria's caresses, Sandy berated himself for not having the guts to bring the conversation to its ultimate conclusion.

He had missed an opportunity that might never occur

again. To ask his father if *he* had slept with Rochelle
Taubman.

17
ISABEL

DESPITE HIS vigorous protestations, Raymond da Costa
had been deeply shaken by his heart attack. He could
take no comfort from the pious platitudes mouthed by
Dr. Gorman or even from reading the articles on which
the cardiologist based his optimistic prognosis that, with
a healthier lifestyle, he "could live to be a hundred."

One afternoon as they were walking home from
classes, father and daughter stopped in at the university
store, where he bought track suits and shoes for both of
them. While he chose the least ostentatious for himself,
he gave Isabel free rein, and she opted for a slightly
bolder outfit emblazoned with U.C. BERKELEY.

Thereafter, he would set his alarm for five-thirty A.M.
and wake Isabel so the two of them could jog incon-
spicuously on the track at nearby Edwards Field. He
was damned if he'd let himself die without seeing his
cherished daughter mount the podium in Stockholm.

While rummaging through the Medical Reference Library on his computer database, he had come across an
article asserting the theory that regular physical activity
could raise a child's IQ between five and ten percent.
Imagine how high that would put his Isabel! He made
sure that she never missed a day.

Isabel was painfully stiff during that first week, and
was so out of shape that she could not do more than one

lap without slowing down to walk and catch her breath. At last she was hooked and began to feel the high that running brings. It was not long before she could go two miles without stopping.

Yet she never tried to progress beyond this point, because it seemed to be the limit of her father's ability.

Early one morning several weeks after their exercise routine had begun, Raymond emerged in his track suit to find Isabel seated at the dining table, still in the jeans and sweater she had been wearing the night before.

"Hey," he said with mock severity, "how come you're not ready for our pre-Olympic workout?"

She glanced with surprise at her watch and exclaimed "Ohmigod, is it morning already?"

"You mean you haven't been to bed?"

"No—I got addicted to the fiendish problems in this book. They're like Cracker Jacks—once you start, you can't stop. I was so involved that I guess I didn't notice the time."

"Really?" Raymond remarked with satisfaction. "For what course?"

"None," she replied, showing him the cover of J. D. Jackson's *Electrodynamics*.

"But you're not taking Electricity and Magnetism this term," Raymond objected. "What's the rush?"

"It's just for fun," she explained. "Karl told me that most of his Ph.D. candidates couldn't do half the questions, and I was so intrigued that I begged him to lend me his copy."

"Who's Karl?" her father asked suspiciously.

"Professor Pracht, my new adviser."

"Since when?" Raymond demanded uneasily. "What happened to Tanner?"

"Well, Elliott's going on his last sabbatical next year," Isabel replied matter-of-factly. "And, as he put it, he wanted to leave me with a good baby-sitter."

The chairman's phraseology did not reassure Raymond. "Why didn't you tell me yesterday?" he asked, trying to mask his apprehension.

"Well, when I got home last night, you were speaking to that reporter from Sacramento, and then your first pupil came. Besides, it's hardly headline news."

"That's not the point," Raymond objected. "He's much too young. I mean—"

She laughed. "Dad, I'm all of fourteen, and Karl's nearly your age. Besides, he's really with it. He's a specialist in particle physics."

Raymond forced himself to smile and then prudently changed the subject. "Coming to work out?"

"I don't think I could go one lap." She yawned. "I'll have breakfast ready when you come back."

"Are you sure you're not going to use the time sitting over another of those problems?"

"Well," she grinned, "I might—if you run long enough."

Raymond nodded and left for his workout.

Jogging seemed especially difficult for Raymond today. Perhaps, he thought, because he was still in a state of shock. The sight of Isabel playing with that text had been traumatic, for though he had never confided this secret even to Muriel, electromagnetic theory was one of the fields he had flunked on his own Ph.D. qualifying exam.

He himself had deliberately ignored Jackson's book, knowing the problems at the ends of each chapter were far beyond his abilities.

The moment Ray had been dreading for years had finally arrived. His daughter had transcended the limits of his own intellectual capacity. How could he now justify his role as her mentor?

Ray trembled at the prospect of his daughter forming a relationship with a greater mind than his.

In a strange way, it was not unlike a mother having to let go of her child at the nursery school gate.

Except that Raymond da Costa was determined to postpone *their* separation as long as possible.

"I object, Professor Tanner. I most strenuously object."

"On what grounds?" asked the grandfatherly chairman of the Physics Department.

"Well, with due respect, compared to some of the world-class scientists on your faculty, Pracht's too young and inexperienced."

The chairman was bemused. "Surely I don't have to tell you, Mr. da Costa, that math and physics prodigies bloom early."

"Well, maybe. But, to put it mildly, my daughter is a rather special student, wouldn't you agree?"

Tanner leaned across his desk for emphasis. "Mr. da Costa, all of us share the same respect for Isabel's intellectual gifts—and that's precisely why I thought Pracht would be the perfect choice. He's so well-regarded that we almost lost him twice last year, and only kept him by giving him the highest raise we could. But what's most important, he and Isabel get on like a house afire."

Raymond was satisfied. But not happy.

Toward the end of Isabel's second trimester at Berkeley, Raymond received a letter from the Dean's office, acknowledging his request that, based on Isabel's advanced standing in the Scholastic Achievement Tests, she could, by remaining at Berkeley for the summer sessions, attain her Bachelor of Science degree in two and a half years.

Yet the dean added a personal note, imploring Raymond to dissuade Isabel from undertaking this acceleration. In his view, it would once again call attention to her precocity and bring the swarming journalists out of their hives.

Weary of such homilies, Ray took the advice with a grain of salt. When he picked Isabel up at Le Conte

Hall that afternoon, he conveyed only the good news, without the cautionary addendum.

She was pleased—mostly because it made *him* so happy.

In mid-June 1986 father and daughter drove back to San Diego for Peter's high school graduation. He urged his daughter not to reveal their plans for the summer. "We don't want your mother to talk you out of it," he said as lightly as he could.

Isabel was more concerned with how Peter would react to seeing her, especially since she was so far ahead of him academically.

Yet all her anxiety dissipated as they drove up to the house and her brother ran out to the car to embrace her, carrying a "Welcome Home" balloon.

Isabel felt happy to be home, to be sleeping in her own bed surrounded by the dolls and furry animals she had been obliged to leave behind. There was a special kind of happiness just being in that room.

She lay awake trying to imagine how her life would have been had she never left, but gone to junior high school instead. Yet there was no use dreaming—she had already traveled too far on a different road. And there was no turning back.

The graduation exercises took place the next morning in the high school stadium. Although there was hearty applause as he came up to the podium, Peter's brief moment of glory was dimmed when the spectators suddenly realized that, if he was on the rostrum, his celebrity sister would surely be somewhere nearby.

Dozens of eyes scanned the audience and discovered the famous prodigy. So enthusiastic were they to see her in the flesh, they did not even wait for the ceremony to conclude.

Several of those seated nearest to her badgered Isabel to autograph their programs. She was caught off guard, and did not know what sort of reaction would least detract from a day that rightfully belonged to her older brother.

At the outdoor picnic that followed, Peter did not seem resentful. He merely kissed his family and ran off to join his classmates, who, it was rumored, had smuggled in a case of beer.

That night, elegantly dressed and painstakingly groomed, and smelling as if he had splashed the latest macho cologne on every inch of his body, Peter set off.

Muriel had loaned him her car so that he could pick up the girl he referred to as "my woman" and drive her in style to the graduation dance at the gym.

When he returned in the early hours of the morning, he headed to the kitchen and was surprised to find his young sister still awake, leafing through a copy of *Cosmopolitan*, of all things.

"My God, Isabel," he joked, "I never imagined you'd read stuff like that. Are you sure you're not using it just to hide some highbrow physics journal?" He reached into the fridge and withdrew a can of beer.

"Come on, Peter, I'm not a complete freak," she answered amiably. "Don't you think I have any fun at Berkeley?"

Her brother sat down and, irreverently placing his feet on the table, pulled open the beer tab and replied, "No. From what I see about you in the papers, you devote every minute of your life to the pursuit of knowledge."

"Well, you should never believe what you read."

"And what exactly do you do for recreation?" he asked.

"Go to the movies a couple of times a week."

"On dates?" her brother probed gently.

"Of course not. I'm just fourteen years old."

"Well, that shouldn't stop you from having a sixteen-year-old boyfriend."

"Gosh, you seem to view the world as one big dating game."

"Well, at your age that should at least be part of it."

Isabel was confused. She could not tell if he was mocking her or—as she increasingly hoped—offering her a chance to open up and vent her feelings.

"Look, Peter," she explained, as much to convince herself as to persuade him, "I'm taking graduate seminars. I love the work, but there's a heck of a lot of it."

He took another sip of suds and asked point-blank: "Does Dad have a social life?"

The question stunned Isabel—and embarrassed her. "Of course not, he's married to Mom."

"Are you serious? It's more like a long term cease-fire. Actually, I'm happy *she* doesn't sit home and mope."

"You mean Mom goes out with other men?" Isabel asked, upset by the thought.

"In a word, yes. Now, I can't tell whether they're platonic relationships or not. But she's definitely not letting herself wither on the vine."

"Uh, is there somebody special?"

"Well, she goes to a lot of the musical evenings with Edmundo."

"Isn't he married?" Isabel asked.

"My God, what planet do you live on, Isabel? This is California—divorce is more popular than baseball. But actually, even though they haven't seen each other for years, Edmundo's wife is very Catholic and still refuses to give him a divorce. Mom likes him and they have a lot in common."

"I don't know whether I want to hear any more of this," Isabel complained, uncomfortable with her brother's matter-of-fact description of their mother's private life. "Do you think Dad and Mom are going to, you know, break up?" she asked apprehensively.

"Well, they're hardly together now, are they?"

She was silent for a moment. Peter removed his feet from the table, stood up and put his arm around her.

"Listen, Isabel, I'm not saying any of this to freak

you out. But what are brothers and sisters for? Besides, you're the only person in the world I can talk to about this."

Isabel was moved. She looked at him with affection and whispered, "You know, I didn't realize how much I missed you until tonight."

"I'm glad." He responded with a quick hug. "I'm really looking forward to this summer, when we'll be together. Mom's booked a cabin in Yellowstone and—" Peter suddenly realized that Isabel had stopped smiling. "Shoot, you don't mean to tell me that you're finking out?"

She nodded but could not look him in the face.

"No," he muttered through clenched teeth. "He couldn't do that to you. I was looking forward to—"

"So was I, Peter," she said plaintively. "But the department granted my request to get an early B.S."

"You mean *his* request, don't you?"

"Peter, it doesn't matter who wrote the letter. We both agreed that it was the right thing to do."

Her brother's face reddened with anger and disappointment. "Isabel, if you'll allow my plebeian comparison, you're going to be like the bear who climbed over the mountain. Only after you get your Ph.D.—which no doubt will take a mere four to five weeks—there won't *be* any more mountains."

"There will, Peter. The sooner I finish my courses and get my degrees, the sooner I'll be able to do my own research."

"Sis, he doesn't really love you for yourself. He's only using you to compensate for—"

Isabel rose to her feet. "I'd prefer not to discuss this any more," she said firmly.

"Why, are you afraid you'll believe it?" She had begun to march off when Peter called gently, "Isabel, let me say one more thing."

She stopped and turned to him. "What?"

"Someday you're gonna open your eyes and realize

how unhappy you are. I just want you to know that whenever that happens—at any time of the day or night—I'll be at the other end of the phone."

Peter knew she could not answer in words. To do so would be to acknowledge that he was right. But he could tell from her eyes that she was touched.

Isabel grew increasingly anxious in the days that followed, knowing that her parents were headed on a collision course. But when the terrible moment came, it was uncannily silent—like an emotional implosion, for her mother had resolved that she would not let anything imperil her already tenuous relationship with Isabel.

Two days later, as her daughter was packing to leave, Muriel came in and tried to broach the subject casually.

"Need any help?" she asked.

"No thanks, Mom, I didn't bring much down."

"Listen, darling," Muriel began softly. "Your father's told me of the new supersonic academic plans. I've given up trying to reason with him. He's dealing from a position of strength. He knows that—even though I'm dead set against it—I'd never try to take you away from your studies."

Isabel looked at her mother's anguished expression and was at a loss for words. The best she could manage was a simple but sincere, "Thanks, Mom."

But there was more to say. "On the other hand," Muriel continued, "Your father and I have our own business to settle, and we've come to the conclusion that we might as well ring down the curtain on what isn't really a marriage anymore. We're going to file for divorce."

Isabel was rocked. For though the rational—scientific—part of her had observed the outward dissolution of her parents' marital bonds, she had nevertheless taken wishful comfort in the illusion that they had maintained for her benefit.

Yet now that it had been brutally shattered, she felt

compelled to confess, "Oh, gosh, Mom I'm so sorry. I mean, I know it's all my fault."

"What are you talking about, darling?" Muriel asked.

"Wherever I go I seem to mess things up."

"I don't know why, Isabel, but I somehow suspected you'd want to take the blame. That's the crazy thing about divorce. Even the most aggrieved party feels guilty. But as strange as this may sound," she continued more softly, "one of the most important reasons I wanted to put an end to the unspoken tension is that—at least for the time being—you're the only thing keeping Ray alive."

18

ADAM

ADAM STILL hoped to reawaken Toni's maternal instincts. He persuaded her that to have a real home, they needed a real house.

By now Heather was old enough to need a large garden, and so they became suburbanites, moving to a rambling three-story white house with traditional green shutters, occupying a corner plot in Wellesley Hills.

Toni converted one of the smaller bedrooms into an office for herself, hooking up a computer not only to the firm's mainframe and to Lexis, the database of the legal profession, but to her father as well.

Adam concentrated on making the garden a child's paradise. The old oak in the back had its thick sturdy arms outstretched enough to attach a swing, and in a rare display of practical craftsmanship, Adam actually succeeded in building a climbing frame.

These facilities he correctly calculated would immensely enhance his daughter's social life, for the neighboring children were immediately attracted by the play area.

From the moment Heather was born, Adam had sworn an inner oath that he would never take her for granted. And to be sure that her world was circumscribed with love, he would make a point of coming home for dinner every night, then reading a good-night story—or two or three.

When Heather was at last comfortably asleep, he would return to the lab for peaceful, unhassled, scientific quality time.

His research was soon earning not only professional recognition, but also the coveted prizes that would normally accrue to his gray-haired seniors. And all that glittered very often *was* gold. Even relatively minor prizes carried with them rewards in the $25,000 to $50,000 category. And these honors created a momentum of their own.

One evening at dinner, Lisl predicted that Adam was advancing so swiftly, it would not be more than three years before he received the Lasker Award.

"Isn't that pretty much the stepping-stone to Stockholm?" Toni asked with uncharacteristic interest.

"Yes," Lisl answered. "The prize after that comes with a handshake from the King of Sweden."

"And a cool million dollars," Toni added.

"Not so fast, honey," Adam admonished her jocularly. "That's only if I don't have to share it."

"That's okay, I wouldn't object," Toni said. "It would still give us enough to buy the house we rented on the Cape this summer."

"From the pictures, it looks divine," Lisl remarked. "Did Heather like it?"

"Absolutely adored it," Adam replied. "She and I got

up every morning, packed sandwiches, took a long walk
down the beach and had a picnic, with only sea gulls
for company."

Lisl sighed. "That sounds idyllic."

"Except that Heather's going to have a hell of a time
finding a husband to match her father," Toni commented. "In fact, I sometimes feel jealous. Every
woman in the world seems to want him for something.
The minute they came back from their walk, Adam was
on the phone for hours with patients all over the country
in various stages of pregnancy."

"Shame on you," Lisl scolded. "Are you becoming a
workaholic?"

"That's a fine one, coming from Max Rudolph's
wife," Adam chided. He had never been able to say the
word "widow." "Did Max ever go anywhere that wasn't
within driving distance of the lab?"

"Listen," Toni said, "when it comes to workaholics,
nobody in this room can throw the first stone. In fact I
have to disappear upstairs to bone up for this damn dep-
osition tomorrow morning. Would you excuse me,
Lisl?"

"Of course, dear."

Although this was not the first time his wife had retreated to her office, Adam was uncomfortable, especially considering the guest Toni had abandoned.

He looked apologetically at his guest.

"That's okay," Lisl said, patting his hand. "I have a
tendency to be a nudge."

"Come on, you know that's not true," Adam objected, and then added *sotto voce*, "Lately, I think I've
been getting on her nerves myself."

"I'm afraid nothing in Boston can match what Toni
had in Washington," Lisl observed. "And she's probably
feeling professionally nostalgic."

"I'd say resentful is more like it," Adam asserted, instantly regretting having been so candid, even with such
a good friend.

"Does she still speak to her father so often?"

"Not really," Adam answered dryly. "I mean, rarely more than two or three times a day."

"Oh, that doesn't sound ideal. But in any case, she should never let her . . . attachment . . . affect her parenting," Lisl insisted.

"*You* tell her that," Adam remarked with frustration. "The problem is that Heather's too bright for her own good. I'm sure she can tell that her mother's just going through the motions."

"Well, if it's a consolation, I honestly don't think Toni would be any different if you lived in Washington."

Adam put his head in his hands. "Damn," he murmured. "How could I have known when we were getting involved that she had an allergy to motherhood?" It hurt him to say it.

"Darling, you were madly in love. Would anything have dissuaded you?" Lisl said lovingly, trying to soothe his conscience.

He pondered for a moment and answered, "Frankly, yes." Then added, "Meanwhile, I'm trying to work fewer hours at the lab, just so I can compensate for some of her parental shortcomings."

"That's good for Heather," Lisl said approvingly, "but it's also unfair to you. After all, as I well know, research can't be a nine-to-five job."

"You know something?" he commented. "That's exactly what Toni tells me about her law practice."

Lisl hesitated for a moment and then ventured, "So it's not just Heather who's getting short shrift. May I ask a very nosy question?"

"I've got no secrets from you."

"Has she mentioned boarding school?"

"That's out of the question, Lisl. I mean, you don't bring children into the world and then farm them out and expect them to show up on your doorstep as well-adjusted adults—ready to go off again to college. After all, look what living at school did to Toni."

"How much of this does Heather sense?"

"Well," Adam responded, "I'd say she's got a good idea of where she stands in her mother's priorities."

"Then I'm going to shake you with a bit of radical advice," Lisl said, rising to get her coat. "In your case, boarding school might be Heather's salvation."

"No," Adam protested. "I couldn't bear that."

It was nearly nine o'clock in the evening. The Indian summer heat had been so intense that the asphalt still felt like melting licorice beneath the feet of the pedestrians crossing Longwood Avenue.

Adam had left the lab and was walking toward his car when, out of the corner of his eye, he spied what he thought was a familiar figure. A young woman was standing by the curb, right hand covering her face, her body shaking.

As he drew nearer he recognized Anya Avilov, the unfortunate Russian to whom he had given such bad news several months earlier.

"Anya, is something the matter?" he asked.

She looked up, startled, her face wet with tears. "Oh, Dr. Coopersmith. Is nothing," she replied unconvincingly.

"Please tell me what's wrong. Come on, I'll buy you a drink and we can chat."

"No, I am all right," she again protested. "Besides, you have more urgent things to do."

Before she could object further, he took her by the arm and swept her toward the coffee shop at the motel next to Children's Hospital.

Adam ordered a beer for himself. But at that moment it was all he could do to convince Anya that she was worthy of a cup of coffee.

His attempts at small talk were in vain. He could elicit only monosyllables to banal questions, like how was she adjusting to life in Boston, or the progress she was making with her English lessons. She answered with polite platitudes.

"And how is Dmitri?"

She shrugged. "I suppose he is all right."

"Suppose?"

"He has left me," she said abruptly, yet still trying to sound nonchalant.

Adam was tempted to say, Good riddance, he was unworthy of you. But he kept his counsel and let her thoughts cascade.

"He has found, so to say, a better deal."

"Oh?"

"Yes, he has fallen in love and moved in with a woman."

I knew it, Adam thought. He had sensed that day in the office that Dmitri was on his way out of her life.

"And you're all on your own?"

She could only nod.

"How do you live? I mean, pay the bills and that sort of thing?"

"He gives me money. And besides, I still work in his laboratory."

"When did this happen?"

"Not long after we saw you."

"I wish you had gotten in contact with me, I would have—"

"There was no professional reason," she said self-consciously. "Anyway, I was managing to cope." She paused, and then continued, "Yet, it was easier to accept the idea of a woman I did not know. But just now I actually saw them walking arm in arm across the street. I cannot honestly say they are an attractive couple."

"Well, she can't possibly be as beautiful as you," Adam offered, hoping to reassure her.

"No," she explained mischievously, "*she* is pretty enough. It is he who makes any couple unappealing. I wish I had been wearing my glasses when he asked me to marry him."

Adam laughed. "Well, at least your sense of humor's intact," he said.

"It would have to be," she answered pointedly. "The woman is pregnant."

Adam was stunned. "Are you sure?"

"Yes, that was one of the first things he told me. I think he wanted to punish me."

"What a bastard! Too bad you have to see him every day."

"That was one reason I think he informed me. I am sure he would be more comfortable if I found another job."

"I agree."

She gazed at him and gestured hopelessly. "But I have not yet qualified, where could I go?"

"I have a lab," he replied impulsively. "I wouldn't ask you for a diploma."

"That is very kind," she answered. "You are such a good man, Dr. Coopersmith. So I will tell you what a nasty person I really am. I want desperately to hurt him for what he did. And I do. Now he comes in every morning and has to look me straight in the face. And begin the day with an upset stomach."

"Frankly, if I saw you first thing in the morning, it would make my day."

She blushed. "You flatter me, Doctor."

"First of all, I want you to call me Adam," he countered. "And secondly, I'm not flattering you. And third of all, I want you to take my offer seriously. I mean, take all the time you want, but promise me you will at least think about it."

She smiled. "I promise."

"Good. I'm flying to a conference in San Francisco tomorrow morning, but I'll try to call you to make sure you're all right."

19

ISABEL

MURIEL'S OUTWARD calm belied her inner turbulence. Her apparent serenity was in great measure due to the strong tranquilizers prescribed by the therapist she had been seeing. To safeguard any future relationship with Isabel, it was best that in the short term she seem to be in agreement with the revised plans. Though she deeply resented Ray's perfidy, a pitched battle would only make things worse. For it was abundantly clear that however strongly she held on, Ray would only pull harder. And Isabel would inevitably be torn to pieces.

Without emotion she wished Ray a safe journey. It was only when she embraced her daughter that she could not hold back the tears. Peter bit his lip as he in turn hugged his sister, then tried not to reveal his intense loathing as he perfunctorily shook hands with the man who had refused to be his father.

Isabel napped as Ray drove demonically through the night. He was intent on lifting her mood by reaching San Francisco at the magical moment when dawn and darkness met, driving further north than necessary so that they could turn onto Route 80, along the eastern side of the bay, and contemplate the first rays of the morning sun beaming over the Berkeley Hills and illuminating the Golden Gate bridge in the distance. The side lamps of the majestic span still burned as the first beams of sunlight brushed the cables strung between the

huge arches, making them glow like the filaments of a
giant light bulb.

"Ah," he remarked, "home sweet home."

Isabel pretended to be asleep. But in her heart she
still thought of the house they had left behind as her
"home."

When they reached their apartment on Piedmont Avenue, Raymond had to push open the door, since the
floor inside was piled high with mail.

"Anything for me?" she asked hopefully. As a rule,
Isabel never received letters at the apartment, since Ray
had arranged with the University to withhold all personal information, including their address and phone
number. Any correspondence that came for her was
directed to the Physics Department. It consisted mostly
of requests for autographs.

It all embarrassed her. Isabel did not want to be
treated like a pop star. Nor did she relish the notion of
being held up as a shining example to female children.

Raymond was busy tearing open envelopes, grumbling to himself, "I can't believe this electric bill, you'd
think we were running Cape Canaveral in here."

And then he noticed it. "This is your lucky day, Isabel. There's actually something for you." He felt comfortable passing the letter on to her since he had already
seen that its provenance was the Physics Department.

She opened the envelope, stared at the card inside for
a moment, and then smiled broadly.

"Hey, this is really neat. Karl's invited me—I mean
us—to a party."

"Who'll be there?" her father inquired, suspicion immediately surfacing.

"Oh, just physics types," Isabel replied. "For some
reason most of them are loners. It comes with the territory, I guess, since they live so much inside their own
heads. But Karl sweeps them out of the lab one day a
year to get some fresh air."

"That sounds very hospitable." Raymond averred,

knowing from his own experience that his daughter was right. But it was not really Isabel he worried about, but himself—concerned with the disquieting possibility that he might not be able to hold his own in conversation.

But at least it would give him a chance to size up this Pracht fellow.

The professor's home was, appropriately enough, on Panoramic Way in the Berkeley Hills, straight above the university and in the area to the east of the Cyclotron and the Bevatron, a high-energy, multibillion-volt proton accelerator. It was definitely an up-market neighborhood, its lavish homes giving architectural testimony to the fact that their owners were the most highly prized, and therefore most highly priced, members of the Berkeley science faculties. Raymond looked around him with satisfaction. It was common knowledge that MIT had been wooing Pracht with a lucrative offer which Berkeley, a state university, could not possibly match. Judging from his house, the professor liked to live well; maybe he would, in fact, be lured to Boston.

Karl Pracht himself answered the door. He was lean and stoop-shouldered, with a prematurely receding hairline, and was undeniably attractive, especially when he smiled. Raymond disliked him instantly.

Pracht welcomed Isabel warmly and introduced himself to her father. "Glad you could come, Mr. da Costa."

Feeling defensive, Raymond interpreted this greeting as a bit of subtle irony, criticizing his constant presence as Isabel's shadow.

"Come out into the back garden," Pracht continued. "Isabel can introduce you to just about everybody. But I warn you, they're not all as bubbly as your daughter. It takes two or three drinks to make them let down their hair."

As they walked through the back of the house, Raymond glanced at the guests' faces. This was an ideal opportunity to check out the cast of characters

Isabel worked with during her labs, where he could not find a plausible excuse for being present.

It was a typical Berkeley summer evening, just cool and refreshing enough so that most of the guests wore sweaters—at least tied around their necks.

He was not surprised to find that most of them were male. The few women present, wives of the graduate students, were especially thrilled at the sight of Isabel, the departmental celebrity.

The young scientists were indeed, as Ray whispered to her, "all cut from the same cloth"—Isabel had smiled and quipped, "Yes, wet blankets." It was no wonder she shone like a Roman candle in their midst.

They greeted Raymond with a respect he had not anticipated. His confidence returned until a sudden thought struck him. He whispered to his daughter, "Isn't there a Mrs. Pracht?"

"There is, yes, but they're in the process of splitting."

"Oh," Raymond said. Paradoxically, even though he himself was divorcing, he counted Pracht's dubious marital status as a point against him.

Raymond felt more at ease with the professors than with the graduate students. While the junior physicists were so involved with their doctoral projects that they could speak of nothing else, the senior guests were happy to take a night off from talking shop. They preferred gossip . . . like who might get the Nobel this year.

Two young boys, roughly sixteen and thirteen respectively, were grilling vegetarian hot dogs and burgers when father and daughter reached them with their empty plates. The elder chef, sinewy and bronzed, greeted Isabel jauntily.

"Hey, you must be Ms. Einstein."

Ray frowned. "Come on, Isabel," he chided her with surly impatience. "We're holding up the line."

"On the contrary," the boy dissented. "*I'm* holding it up so I can get acquainted with God's gift to physics and—regardless of age and mental capacity—the cutest

thing to happen in science since the apple that hit Newton on the head."

"Just who do you think you're talking to?" Ray
demanded.

"Have I caused offense in some way, Mr. da Costa—
or is it 'Doctor'? I know you're in the game too."

Raymond took this to be a not-too-subtle put-down.
Surely everyone in the department knew he had no doctorate, and this young upstart was deliberately trying to
humiliate him.

"May I introduce myself?" the boy continued.

"That isn't strictly necessary," Ray replied acer-
bically.

"Yeah, I guess you're right," he agreed. "I'm just the
backward boy with the forehand, sometimes known as
the forward boy with the backhand."

"What?" Isabel exclaimed.

"Did that get you?" he asked, his eyes twinkling. "I
rehearsed it on my kid brother all afternoon, didn't I,
Dink?"

The younger chef, now burdened with double duty,
nodded obediently. "Yeah, my brother's an amazing
pain in the ass."

"Isabel," her father urged, "I see a free table over
there on top of that slope. We could—"

Totally without precedent, Isabel ignored her father
and refused to move, captivated by this manic icono-
clast.

"Is your brother's name really Dink?" she asked—
simply to make conversation.

"Not officially. He got saddled with 'George,' but I
gave him something more colorful and onomatopoetic.
Which reminds me—I'm Jerry, Karl's punishment for
being too smart. I mean, how else would I have gotten
into this highbrow party—right?"

Then, turning to his assistant, he commanded,
"Dinko, take over the food while I show these V.I.P.'s
to a table."

"There's no need for that," Ray began to protest. But by now he had been caught up by this teenage equivalent of a gale-force wind.

The young man scooped up their paper plates and led them across the lawn, calling irreverently en route to various professors to "make way for the princess."

They reached a table on the little ridge, which Isabel now noticed had a hand-scrawled place card with "Reserved" on it.

"Yeah," Jerry acknowledged without being asked. "I personally saved it for you guys—and you don't even have to tip me."

Then, balancing the two plates on one arm, he flicked his towel to remove any crumbs and elegantly placed the food down.

"Thank you," Ray said in dismissal, hoping he could cut further dialogue between his daughter and this juvenile delinquent.

"Mind if I join you?" Clearly, Jerry regarded the question as rhetorical, because he sat down before either of them could answer.

Though fuming inwardly, Ray had to keep tight control of his temper. After all, he kept reminding himself, this was the son of his daughter's adviser.

"I've seen your picture on Karl's desk," Isabel remarked.

"For use as a dartboard, no doubt," Jerry retorted. "I suppose he told you I'm not exactly a microchip off the old block."

"Actually, he told me you were rebelling at the moment," Isabel responded. "But that you're very brilliant."

"No, I used to be. But I gave it up when I quit school to take up tennis full-time."

"Why are you so anxious to be thought of as stupid?" she asked with genuine interest.

"Truth?" he answered somberly, in stark contrast to his previous frenetic behavior. "Let me tell you a cautionary tale. It might some day influence your choice of a husband."

How much more of this could he tolerate? Ray wondered.

Jerry launched into his narrative. "Until you came along, Karl Pracht had been the youngest person ever admitted to the Berkeley physics program—"

"I never knew that," Isabel interrupted.

"Yep." The young man nodded. "You took his crown. Anyway, if that wasn't bad enough, at an all too precocious age he married a supersonic math graduate student. The result of this genetic overkill is yours truly—cursed with an IQ around the Fahrenheit boiling point of water."

At this moment, Ray's interest was awakened. He found himself intrigued by this young man's lineage and the staggering intellectual potential it bespoke.

Isabel instantly knew she had met someone who would understand why she sometimes felt like a freak. And what's more, he'd been brave enough to escape from the monkey house of genius.

"But think of how much you could learn about the world," Raymond offered in the first civilized words he had exchanged with Jerry Pracht.

"I'm not exactly knocked out by the world, Mr. da Costa. It's a polluted, overpopulated suburb of the universe. I'm more into space."

He certainly is, Ray grumbled to himself.

"In fact, as my dad won't let me forget, the first question I ever asked was, 'Why do stars shine?' "

"Really?" Isabel remarked, thinking of her own childhood curiosity and feeling an uncanny kinship. She could not help noticing how the sun had bleached his blond hair nearly white, making his eyes seem all the bluer.

"How old were you?" Ray inquired. There was an unmistakable competitive edge to his voice.

"Oh, I don't know," Jerry mused jocularly. "I guess I

began stargazing and asking questions when they changed my diapers."

"Well, you had the right parents to ask," Isabel offered.

"So did you," Jerry said, returning the compliment, his instinct telling him that flattery in this area would get him very far indeed.

"Did your mother and father tutor you?" Ray inquired.

"Endlessly," Jerry answered, "bordering on child abuse. I had to beg them to send me to school to get away from the academic pressure." He grinned. "Of course, it was a school for 'special' children. I hesitate to use the word 'gifted' in reference to myself, but I bluffed my way in. I was motivated because at least they had tennis courts.

"Anyway," he continued, "that's where I met my future pal Darius, who, like me, was crazy about the stars. We built a telescope, even ground a perfect twelve-inch F6.0 mirror. I did most of the glass work, and Darius figured out how to use a laser to check the curvature. He actually made the interferometer.

"It took us a couple of months until the mirror was absolutely perfect. As you might have guessed, Dad wanted us to write it up for *Sky and Telescope*, but Darrie and I both nixed the idea. Our technological triumph's currently mounted on the other side of the garden in a handmade plywood shell with a dome that can actually swivel. I'd be happy to show you if you have the slightest interest."

"I would—" Isabel responded instantly.

"Not at night," Ray interdicted, with such urgency that only after he'd spoken did he realize the absurdity of his objection. "I mean, some other time," he quickly corrected himself.

"Great," Jerry enthused. "I regard that as a firm commitment. Anyway, now that I've made an indelible impression on you, could I hear more about Isa?"

Raymond cringed at the barbarous mutilation of his daughter's name.

"I'm afraid I live a very dull life compared to you."

"I wouldn't say that," her father pouted.

"Well, it's true, Dad. You're too nice to rebel against—even for a game of tennis."

"What?" Jerry exclaimed histrionically. "You mean you don't play?"

"She's not interested," Raymond quickly answered.

"Actually, Dad, I really don't know because I've never tried."

"It's a game," Raymond declared categorically. "*Life* isn't a game."

"Negative, negative." Jerry Pracht dissented passionately. "That's the one thing that makes me happier than all the eggheads at this party. My horizon ends at the baseline, and nothing in the world brings me more joy than crushing a forehand winner to a corner. How many other people here would settle for less than a new Theory of Relativity? By the way, would you like some lessons, Isa? I'm not much at physics, but I'm one hell of a tennis teacher."

"Gee, that would be nice. I mean—" She glanced instinctively at her father for guidance.

"Isabel's got a punishing schedule, Jerry. I really don't know how she could manage it."

"No one appreciates that more than I, Mr. da Costa, but you'd be surprised how much I could accomplish on a Saturday morning while you're teaching."

Stymied once again, Raymond wondered fleetingly how the minutiae of his activities were such public knowledge. And then he instantly remembered the many notices he had put up on bulletin boards near the Physics Department, offering his tutorial services and indicating when he was free.

Jerry turned to Isabel. "Why don't I come by this Saturday around ten? I'll bring an extra racket, and I'll pillage my attic to see if I can find a pair of shoes the right size."

Isabel knew what she felt, but she did not know how her father wanted her to feel.

Before she could answer, Jerry suddenly glanced over his shoulder and quickly excused himself. "Hey guys, my poorly coordinated brother's causing havoc back at the grill. I'd better shoot over there and bail him out. See you Saturday morning, Isa," he called as he dashed off.

"My God," Ray observed the moment Jerry was out of earshot. "Pracht must be brokenhearted."

"What do you mean, Dad?"

"That boy is obviously very disturbed."

"He seemed okay to me," Isabel remarked innocently.

Ray frowned at his daughter's naïveté. "There's no way I'll let you play tennis with somebody like him."

"Why not?" Isabel countered. "I'd really like to learn."

"Then I'll get you a qualified tutor," Ray insisted.

"But that's just the point! He *is* qualified."

Ray felt uneasy disputing this in Pracht's home territory. "We'll discuss it later."

"There's nothing to discuss, Dad. You're letting me go."

"What makes you say that?" he inquired with surprise.

"Because I know you, and you'd never deny me something I really wanted."

Raymond's jaw tightened. This was the first hint of disobedience his daughter had ever displayed.

No, that was too mild a word for it. It bordered on revolution.

20

ADAM

MEDICAL CONVENTIONS are complex phenomena—at once serene encounters of Olympian minds and convivial occasions like high school reunions. And yet there is also a great deal of time spent in bad-mouthing, backstabbing, and mutual denigration.

That first September evening in San Francisco, his official duties discharged, Adam was enjoying a drink at the Top of the Mark with several West Coast colleagues. One of them, Al Redding of USC, looking across the room, caught sight of an approaching interloper, shielded his mouth and whispered, "Hope you've got your parachute, Coopersmith. Red Robinson's heading our way faster than a speeding bullet."

"Too late," Adam responded with a melodramatic sigh. "But you guys stay here in case he attacks me with a swizzle stick."

Professor Whitney "Red" Robinson of the Louisiana State Medical School was a southerner from tip to toe. He even managed to project aggression with excruciating politeness.

"Why, Professor Coopersmith, how very fine to see you here."

"Likewise," Adam replied, lobbing the ball back.

"Would I be intruding if I joined y'all?"

"Of course not, Professor Robinson. I'm sure those present who know you by your writings would be fas-

164

cinated to meet you in the flesh," Adam said, adding mischievously, "As long as you'll buy a round."

Adam's coterie had difficulty suppressing their smiles. Robinson was a notorious tightwad who, after the introductions, settled in for a long evening's free-loading.

"I must say you know how to hurt a man, Professor Coopersmith," he drawled. "Don't you think your paper in last month's *Journal* went a bit overboard in discounting my theories about embryotoxins? After all, you saw my statistics."

"I did indeed. And I didn't believe a single one of them. You seem to be the only scientist in history who claims a hundred percent success rate. I mean, pretty soon you'll be curing more patients than you treat."

Robinson would not be roused to anger. The idea in medical politics was not to burn bridges, but to gather allies.

"Coopersmith," the professor cajoled, "though our views are not the same, can't you allow the possibility that my techniques—while different—might also be efficacious?"

Adam wondered how to handle this. It was late. But Robinson was such a crawler, he could not resist.

"Red, this isn't like the wave and particle theories of light, which can coexist. Either you go my way—and fight an allogenic reaction by immunosuppression—or yours, which involves, to employ a cruder metaphor, using a hand grenade as a suppository."

Robinson, sensing that he was rapidly losing ground, rose and bade his distinguished colleagues good night.

When Red was out of earshot, Al Redding addressed Adam. "Why the hell did you let him off so easy?"

"I couldn't help it," Adam answered. "He's a prize asshole, but he's incredibly sincere." He changed the subject. "Why don't we have one last drink? And just for a gag we could sign Robinson's name on the check."

"Better not," one of the other doctors offered sheepishly. "He talked me into letting him stay in my room."

As Adam fumbled with the key to his door, he could hear the telephone ringing persistently from within. It was Toni.

"My God," he mumbled, slightly inebriated. "It must be nearly morning in Boston."

"It isn't exactly early in San Francisco either. Where the hell have you been? I've been trying to get you for the past three hours."

"Is something wrong?"

"Your daughter's in rather hot water at school," she replied.

"How hot?" he inquired.

"Well, to give you some indication, Miss Maynard the headmistress actually made a house call this evening. It seems Heather and two friends were caught smoking in the girls' room."

"God," Adam reacted angrily. "What kind of students do they have at that school?"

For a moment Toni did not reply. "That's not the worst part," she said somberly. "It's true she was the youngest smoker, but Miss Maynard claims that Heather provided the cigarettes."

He glanced at his watch. "Hey, listen, honey," he said hastily, "these damn meetings go on for another day. Can you hold the fort till then?"

"Yes—I just don't know if I can hold my temper."

"Well, keep calm and get some sleep. Call me in the morning and we'll talk again."

Adam sat wearily on the bed, trying to decipher the enigma of Heather's behavior. It couldn't be coincidence that she picked the one day he was out of town to cry out for attention. He felt like calling her right now and saying he loved her.

He suppressed the urge, sensibly concluding that it

would probably be more destructive to wake her at this hour.

And then, after a few minutes, he began to see the positive side to this event. Their daughter's misbehavior would be the ideal pretext to get some family counseling for all of them.

Lisl had long campaigned for this, believing that it would force Toni to confront her inadequacies as a mother.

And yet a part of Adam doubted that anyone could force her to do anything.

As he was brushing his teeth, he suddenly remembered his promise to call Anya. He knew she rose early, and as he started to dial he glanced at his watch. It was half past six in Boston—and she did not answer the phone.

Toni hit the roof.

"I bet that childless old witch put this into your head. I don't want any shrinks butting into our lives," she shouted. "We're perfectly capable of dealing with Heather on our own—I am, anyway."

Adam was taken aback by the vehemence of Toni's reaction, which convinced him—if nothing had before—that their relationship needed, to put it mildly, fine-tuning.

Wisely, he waited a day and called her at the office, where—again buffered by the telephone—he convinced her that they owed it to their daughter at least to go through the motions of consulting a psychologist.

By now, having had time to reflect, Toni was more receptive to the idea. But under one condition—that the recommendation come from a full professor of psychology and not "that woman."

Adam gladly accepted the compromise.

"Hello?" Her voice was toneless.

"Anya? It's me—I mean, it's Adam Coopersmith. I—"

"Oh, Doctor," she replied, her mood immediately brightening. "It is nice of you to call."

"I hope you didn't think I forgot. But I tried you this morning and you weren't in."

"Yes, I like to schedule my hours to avoid Dmitri—so I went to work at dawn."

Adam felt relieved that her reasons were professional and not personal. "Still, I'm late and I apologize."

"That's all right, a friendly voice is never late."

"Siberian proverb?"

"No," she answered playfully. "I just made it up myself."

There was a sudden awkward silence, which Adam finally broke.

"I think we should have another chat as soon as possible. I don't know my exact schedule, but may I phone you at your lab?"

"Of course."

"Do I ask for 'Dr. Avilov'?"

"No. Dmitri insists that because I am, for the moment, only a technician, I should merely be called Anya." She was silent for a second, then added, with another display of levity, "At least in this case it has an advantage—there is no chance you will reach him by mistake."

Adam laughed sympathetically. "You're right. That's a blessing. And, in any case, it might be prudent if I just referred to myself as 'a friend.' I mean, we wouldn't want people to misunderstand."

"No," she agreed. "We certainly would not."

For Heather's sake, Adam forced himself to sit on the other side of the desk and accept the criticisms, as he viewed them, of Malcolm Schonberg, M.D.

After the initial interview, the psychiatrist deemed a weekly meeting essential, "to reestablish the lines of communication among all the parties."

Ever the lawyer, Toni came to these sessions with a case already prepared in her own defense.

"I can't help it, Doctor," she pleaded. "I can't fight the Oedipus complex. My daughter insists on Adam driving her to school."

"Because *he* talks to me," Heather shouted at Schonberg. "*He* actually asks me what I think about things."

"But darling," Toni addressed her, "I take just as keen an interest."

"That's bull, Mom. I admit you talk—that is, your lips move—but you interrogate me like a witness. I sometimes think you're warming up for court."

Again Toni turned to the arbiter. "You see, Doctor, how can I compete with this? I'm up against a perfect father."

"He's not perfect," Heather acknowledged. "But at least he tries. I mean, he actually listens to what I say. I hate it when you ask me things like what all my 'little friends' think about the Republicans' chances. I don't give two screws about politics. Maybe things'll be better if you take that Georgetown offer."

"What Georgetown offer?" Adam interrupted, glaring at his wife.

Caught by surprise, Toni answered defensively, "It's just come up. Heather happened to walk into the room while they were sounding me out on the phone—"

"Hey, you guys," Heather exploded. "Why don't you fight this out later? Right now you're supposed to be concentrating on *me*."

Both Adam and Toni were suddenly shame-faced, casting self-conscious glances at Dr. Schonberg.

Heather burst into tears.

As she continued to sob uncontrollably, Adam embraced her and glared at Toni.

They drove home in glacial silence. In addition to the humiliation, Adam was furious at having to learn so indirectly that Toni had been making important plans be-

hind his back. But he would deal with that later. For the
moment, he had to make things better for his daughter.

"Hey, guys," he said jauntily. "I just had a terrific
idea. I know it's a little while away, but why don't we
plan to go skiing during the Christmas vacation?"

Toni began to defrost. "That's great."

"And listen to this," Adam continued, enormously relieved that his gesture of conciliation had garnered at
least one vote. "I've heard about a terrific place in Canada, near Lake Huron. It has lots of cabins and a great
indoor pool. It would be a long haul, but I'm willing.
What about you, Heather? I could give you those diving
lessons I've been promising."

From the back of the car the sound of his daughter's
voice suggested that she was Daddy's girl again.

"Oh," she said with artless gratification, "I'd really
love that, Dad."

Adam had no illusions that his other problem would
be so easily resolved.

Emotionally exhausted, Heather barely picked at her
food, then went up to her room to prepare for bed.

Adam walked into the kitchen and confronted Toni.
"What the hell is this Georgetown business?"

"It's pretty flattering, really," she replied, trying to
gloss over the fact that she had kept it from him. "A
visiting lecturer in Con Law just finked out on them,
until the end of next term. I *was* going to talk it over
with you tonight."

"What do you mean 'talk it over'? You've obviously
decided yourself."

"As a matter of fact I have. I could do the whole
thing in a single day and be back the same night. I think
I deserve a chance to spread my wings a little bit, don't
you? Especially since I could revive some of my flag-
ging Washington contacts."

"But what about Heather?" he asked, furious.

"I've got a lead on a fabulous nanny who's willing to come in on her day off," Toni replied.

"Nanny? I thought we agreed not to be parents by proxy."

"Okay," she said firmly, "then you can stay home every Wednesday."

"Come on, you know that's impossible," he protested. "I've got a lab to run and patients who have unscheduled emergencies."

"Well, she's *our* child, you offer another solution."

Adam paused for a moment, and then, smoldering, backed down. "Maybe we should see if this nanny's any good."

Mrs. Edwina Mallory turned out to be such a pleasant and efficient woman that it sometimes seemed as if their daughter actually looked forward to her Wednesday visits.

By the time Toni returned at ten-thirty P.M., the grayhaired nanny would have served dinner, the kitchen would be immaculate, and Heather would be fast asleep having—rare occurrence—done all her homework.

Toni's weekly absence afforded Adam the opportunity to have regular phone conversations with Anya. He was able to monitor her mood—and lift it when necessary.

He was sometimes tempted to propose a meeting. But then, he did not trust his feelings. Or, more accurately, he did not want to surrender to them.

One Wednesday evening in mid-October, when Mrs. Mallory was still tidying the kitchen, Toni phoned to say that she had missed the last flight back to Boston.

Irritated, Adam glanced at his watch and frowned. "Don't tell me you gave a six-hour seminar."

"Not a chance," she replied good-humoredly. "But I dropped in on a cocktail party for a special guest and sort of lost track of time. I'll stay at the Marriott and take the first plane tomorrow. With luck I'll be there to see Heather before she leaves for school."

She paused and then added quietly, "Hey, I'm sorry about this."

"Listen, these things happen," he commented without much conviction.

Moments after he hung up, a thought suddenly struck him. Wasn't Toni's one-time patron, the former Attorney General, now a professor at Georgetown Law School?

At first he blamed himself for even entertaining such untrusting fantasies. After all, he had never cheated during his own solo journeys.

Nonetheless, a half hour later he found himself dialing the number of the Marriott Hotel at National Airport.

"Hello." Toni's voice sounded surprised.

Adam was relieved. "I'm just calling to say I miss you," he said, in what he hoped was a convincing tone.

"Thanks, Adam," she replied. "I'm really glad you did."

"Anyway, I hope you won't make a habit of this," he cautioned. "Have you had a good dinner?"

She laughed. "Stop talking like a mother. Yes, I had soup and a sandwich in my room."

They chatted idly for a few more minutes, then exchanging endearments, bade each other good night.

After he hung up, Adam could not help thinking that there was still the possibility that someone else might have been with her. And in a curious way, the notion suited him. For now he dialed Anya to propose a change in their plans.

"Hello," she said. "I'm so happy it's Wednesday night."

"Me too. I was just wondering—if I can get Mrs. Mallory to stay, I might be able to come over and pay a personal visit. Does that sound all right to you?"

"Do you even have to ask?" she replied.

21
SANDY

DURING HIS first three undergraduate years at MIT, Sandy Raven's social pleasures were—to be precise—nonexistent. During summer vacations he redressed this imbalance by dedicated hedonism on the West Coast. But by the time he was a senior, he had made up his mind that he would no longer be a winter monk and a summer satyr.

What seemed to be holding back his social life in Cambridge? The conclusion was all too painfully clear. Here, being the son of a Hollywood producer was no big deal. He was neither tall, nor dark, nor handsome. But he resolved to change as much of that as he could.

To expand his physique he bought a set of weights, although—to his embarrassment—he had to enlist the help of two other undergraduates to haul the equipment up to his room from the lobby, where it had been delivered. Meticulous scientist that he was, he studied the exercises recommended in the pamphlet and embarked on a program that he supplemented with ingestion of protein powder, to speed muscle growth.

They were an odd fraternity, those MIT boys—fiercely competitive, yet tolerant of one another's idiosyncrasies. Barry Winnick not only endured the bizarre grunting and groaning emanating from Sandy's cubicle in the wee hours of the morning, but even agreed to serve as a safety man when Sandy lay on his back to do bench presses.

"I tell you, Raven," Barry commented as he supervised his neighbor's exertions, "if this works for you, I'll try it too. I haven't been that lucky with girls myself. I can see where you're getting stronger. But how exactly do you intend to achieve the triple goal you outlined to me? Especially the tall part. Are you going to try and stretch yourself by hanging for hours in your doorway?"

"Winnick," Sandy protested, "do I look that stupid to you? Anyway, even though my plan's classified, you've been such a good pal that I'll let you in on it. The dark and handsome part is going to come from a sun lamp I'm buying at Lechmere. These weight exercises will increase my shirt size, which'll add to the impression of power. But the real secret will be if Dr. Li heeds my appeal."

"You mean Professor Cho Hao Li from San Francisco?"

"Yes, the one who's used recombinant DNA techniques to synthesize the human growth hormone—"

"Right, hGH—otherwise known as somatotrophin. It's a single polypeptide with 191 amino acids. Anyway, it's for curing dwarfism in children. What good could it possibly do for you?"

Sandy sat up and wiped his face with a towel. "I've written to Li, making an appeal to inject me on compassionate grounds."

"*What* 'compassionate grounds'? You're average height, about five-foot-nine."

"Yeah," Sandy acknowledged, "when I stand up straight. But that's nowhere enough. I've asked the professor if he can get me as close to six feet as possible."

"My God, that much hGH might kill you. Why the hell do you want to be so tall?"

Sandy looked at Barry and shook his head as if to say, You ignorant asshole, isn't it obvious? He needed no words to reply. He simply pointed to the many pictures of Rochelle pasted around the room, by now so numerous they almost qualified as wallpaper.

"Jeez, are you *still* hung up on her? I'd have thought you'd gotten over her by now."

"I don't wanna get *over* her," Sandy replied. "I wanna *get* her. And I've read in the gossip columns that she goes for hunk Hollywood types."

Barry looked at his classmate for a moment and muttered, "Gosh, Raven, I used to think you were normal—I mean, relative to the other weirdos around here. But now I think you're really off your tree."

"I'll remember you said that," Sandy countered. "Don't expect an invitation to the wedding."

"I never did," Barry retorted. "I'm not tall enough."

Sandy waited impatiently for Dr. Li's reply. When the second week passed and his mailbox remained empty, he gathered his courage and called San Francisco. He actually got through to the great man himself.

"Yes, I received your letter," the professor acknowledged in a kindly tone of voice. "But I couldn't possibly reply to the immense number of appeals I get, even from genuinely serious cases. Besides, as far as we know now, the drug is only really effective if administered before puberty. And I assume if you're at MIT . . ."

"Yes, Doctor, I am. I understand. Thanks for your time."

That night he shared the bad news with Barry.

"Well, at least it's over," his neighbor consoled him. "So you can start thinking about other more important things."

"Yeah," Sandy replied, "like learning enough genetic engineering to make a *super* hGH."

Unfortunately, Sandy was not able to become hunk enough for Rochelle—at least this time. In the checkout line at the supermarket the following week, he flicked through one of the tabloids and found the announcement of her forthcoming marriage to Lex Federicks, one of her classmates at the Fox Academy who had graduated to feature roles and become something of a teenage idol.

Predictably, the wedding was an outdoor affair at Malibu. Before a crowd of the ritziest and the glitziest, the couple exchanged vows, kissed, and then ran into the water.

The news broke the day Sandy received word he had been accepted into the MIT doctoral program in biochemistry. Otherwise his spirits might have sunk even lower and he might have contemplated hurling himself into the Charles.

His summers in Hollywood had made him aware that Lex was not only a dimwit, but the owner of a nasty temper whose physical expression did not even respect the female gender.

During the weekly telephone call with his son, Sidney made a Herculean effort to cheer the boy up.

"Hey kiddo," he commented, "I know how much you liked her. But believe me, marrying an actress is like jumping out of a plane without a parachute. It's exhilarating for the first few minutes, but pretty quick you're gonna hit the ground with an awful thud."

"I know how stupid it sounds," Sandy confessed openly for the first time. "And she's used me for a doormat since we were kids, but I love her. It's—how can I put it, Dad? Like some sort of disease."

"Just wait awhile, son," his father reassured him. "I promise you your time will come. A starlet is like the Roman Empire. Sooner or later everything falls. The boobs. The ass. The ratings. In the long run the broads who once took your breath away let the plastic surgeons take their dough away."

Sandy may have been a step or two behind in the Hollywood social rat race, but he was a front-runner in his choice of speciality, for arguably the most important achievement in the late twentieth century study of the body was the discovery and cataloging of the genes that composed it. As James Watson, the DNA pioneer, stated, "If you're young, there's really no option but to be a molecular biologist."

There were already genetic tests that could reveal the absence of abnormalities in a growing fetus. On the far but visible horizon was the possibility of discovering which chromosome carried which diseases—the different cancers, brain tumors, even Alzheimer's.

If the specific gene were found, its defects could be studied and, with time, scientists could build the equivalent of a better mousetrap—a new, improved gene, that, like an unmanned spaceship, would automatically do its repair work inside the body.

Just how far these studies could be carried was a matter of heated debate. There were still many who believed genetic engineering was mere science fiction. But in laboratories all over the world medical researchers were busy transforming fiction into fact.

As usual, Hollywood both exploited and trivialized the medical trend. *The Six Million Dollar Man* may have been a potboiler, but its basic thesis—that various replacement parts of the human apparatus could be manufactured to order—was, at the laboratory level at least, truer than its creators could have imagined.

And in this real-life drama Sandy Raven was determined to become a hero.

The MIT graduation day was doubly festive for Sidney Raven. Not only was his son receiving a Bachelor of Science degree with Honors, but his latest release of the soon to be legendary *Godzilla Meets David and Goliath* was in its sixth week among the top twenty grossers around the world.

Sandy was allowed to book any restaurant for his celebratory lunch. Without hesitation he chose Jack and

Marian's in Brookline, which served gargantuan sandwiches for gargantuan appetites.

It took only a few outsized bites before the conversation got around to Rochelle.

"She's going to be huge, Dad, isn't she?"

Sidney replied with evasion, "Mmmmm . . ." feigning a full mouth.

But Sandy waited.

"Listen kiddo, let's not spoil the day. . . ."

"What do you mean? Is something wrong with Rochelle?"

"No—she's fine." He paused and then added, "It's just that her career's dead. The studio didn't pick up her contract."

"But why? I don't get it," Sandy asked, heartbroken. "She had so much going for her."

"Yeah, maybe," his father acknowledged. "But she did lack one small thing—talent."

"Isn't there any way you can help her, Dad?"

"Listen, I've already gone out on a limb for her lots of times. You gotta realize one thing—Hollywood isn't a charitable institution. But if it'll make you happy, I'll see if I can get her some kind of job with the studio."

"Oh, thanks Dad, thanks," Sandy whispered affectionately.

"No problem," Sidney murmured, and then asked cautiously, "What exactly is it with you and Rochelle, Sandy? I mean, you've been in Hollywood. There are broads just as beautiful as her serving hamburgers on roller skates. I could understand it when you were just a wet-eared kid, but you're a big boy—good-looking in your way—and there's all kinds of women who'd be tickled to know you. So what the hell's so special about this gal?"

Sandy shook his head. "I don't know, Dad."

The elder man was silent for a moment, and then asked tactfully, "Isn't part of it that she never gave you the time of day?"

"Yeah, I guess that's most of it."

A week later Sidney telephoned his son in Boston. "Okay, sonny boy," he announced. "I moved heaven and earth, called in all my markers, made all kinds of promises I shouldn't have—but your secret love won't be booted off the lot after all. Starting Monday, she's an assistant editor in the story department."

"Oh," Sandy said. "You're really terrific, Dad. How did Rochelle take the news?"

"Well, she took the job like a shot. She's got a lot of spunk, that girl. As we were walking out of the interview, she swore to me that in a year she'd be *running* the whole department."

"Gosh," Sandy rhapsodized. "That's wonderful. Uh, did she, um, mention me at all?"

"Sure, sure," Sidney replied as convincingly as he could. "She sends her . . . love."

22

ADAM

ANYA'S DRIVING instructions had not been precise, and Adam had some difficulty in locating her house after going through Watertown Square. At last he found it, and for once agreed with an opinion of academician Avilov's: if the peeling paint on the wooden porch was any indication, the place indeed qualified as "a dump."

It had occurred to him that the canny Russian scientist might have already planned on leaving Anya and deliberately remained in this wretched place so he could conveniently bequeath it to her as their home.

In any case, Dmitri had done his real estate shopping well in advance of his announced departure. He was already established with the future mother of his child in a comfortable apartment in Charles River Park.

Adam climbed up to the porch and rang the bell to the upstairs flat. Anya buzzed, and he entered to find a cold and narrow stairway.

To his astonishment, when she opened the door she was wearing a parka.

"Are you planning to go out at this hour?"

"On the contrary," she answered. "I am intending to stay in, and, as you will soon see, it is much colder in here than outside. You had better keep your coat on as well."

The apartment was spare. The only source of real warmth seemed to be an electric heater—and Anya's personality. What furniture there was looked old and tired. The single new item was a metal bookshelf—conspicuously empty.

"They were all his?" Adam asked.

"Yes," she conceded with quiet resignation. "We were going to a Genetics Congress in London. Dmitri thought the authorities might get suspicious if they saw . . . too many obstetrical books."

As he flopped into the chair, the springs twanged like ruptured banjos, making them both laugh.

"Well," Adam observed, "I must admit that this apartment is even shabbier than you described. Doesn't it depress you?"

"It's not that much worse than the Russian medical school dormitories. But to what do I owe the honor of this personal visit?"

"I just wanted to look straight into your eyes. It's the only way I can tell if you're really happy."

"I am really happy." She beamed. And both of them understood that she meant it was because he was there.

They spent the next few minutes in idle chatter about their respective laboratory activities. Then Adam took the opportunity to find out more about his Russian friend.

"I know this is a stupid question," he began. "But how did a nice girl like you ever get mixed up with an oaf like Avilov?"

"Do you insist on all the gory details?"

"I'm fascinated by gory details," Adam replied.

"Then I had better open a bottle of wine—or two— it's a long story."

As he filled the glasses she had placed on the coffee table, she recounted, "It all started in Siberia. . . ."

"You met him there?"

"You want to hear every single chapter," she said lightheartedly. "So I begin at the beginning—Siberia, where I was born. My father was a doctor who had the dubious pleasure of being one of Stalin's last deportees to the land of polar bears and prisons."

"What was his alleged offense?"

"He was guilty of being Jewish. Toward the end of Stalin's life, he had the paranoid fantasy that a cabal of Jewish doctors were planning to poison him. So he had many arrested.

"Fortunately, my father had been decorated for bravery during the Second World War, or else he would not have been honored with mere exile. In fact, we were assigned to one of the most famous forced labor camps in the whole of the Gulag system. It was named Second River. Have you heard of it?"

"Frankly, no. It sounds like the name of a John Wayne movie."

"Actually, it was a uniquely Russian institution called a *sharashka*. It was part prison and part research institute, a mixture of Alcatraz and Princeton. Its clientele were known as *zeks* in Russian slang. They were scientists and engineers who were too dangerous to keep in circulation but too valuable to kill. Especially those who could do research of military importance. So in some buildings they had cells and in others the most sophisticated laboratories you could imagine.

"For a while, one of our neighbors was Sergei Korolev, who—with the wave of a wand, so to say—was transformed from prisoner to chief designer of the Soviet space program.

"My father was assigned to be the prison doctor, and so we had a little flat of our own."

"Did you have any playmates?"

"At first only my imagination. But as soon as I could talk, I would visit the laboratories where the *zeks* kind of 'adopted' me.

"When one of my favorite 'uncles' was rehabilitated, he got permission from the authorities for me to go to school outside the camp. After all, in Siberia it was not very likely that I would run away. Besides, Primary School Number Six was not really freedom. It was just a new kind of prison.

"Because my family name was Litvinov, even the provincial children of Vladivostok shipbuilders knew I was a *zhidhovka*, a 'Yid.'

"Ironically, I didn't really know what being Jewish meant. I asked my father to explain it to me, and all he answered was, 'bruises in the schoolyard, insults in the army, invitations to Siberia.' "

"Is that what it was for you too?" Adam asked sympathetically, struck by the prism of good humor through which she viewed the most distressing events.

"No," she answered, her pained expression belying her words. "For me it was mostly the endless game of quotas. For example, I know I did well on the entrance exam for the scientific *gimnaziya*. But I was only placed on the waiting list. Later in the summer my father received a note from the principal with the happy news that the parents of one of their Jewish students had been recalled from exile, which meant there was now a place for my humble, stigmatized self."

"Were you bitter?" Adam inquired.

"On the contrary, I was delighted. *In* is *in*. Because then came the good part. I finally had a weapon to fight back with—my brain."

She smiled. "Their 'friendliness' made me work like a crazy person, and my greatest joy was when they posted the grades. My fellow students never congratulated me—but I enjoyed hearing the sound of their teeth grind."

"So you beat the quota system after all," Adam said, raising a half-filled glass of wine in a congratulatory toast.

"Inspired by my *gulagniks*, I wanted to go into pure science. Of course, since it was all a kind of game to me, I was aiming even beyond the university at Vladivostok. I wanted to go to the top of the mountain—Moscow."

"Brava," he cheered.

"Why are you so joyous?" she asked with mock surprise. "It didn't do me any good, getting the top grades. I was barely accepted by the local university—and even then I was demoted. They offered me a place not in pure science, but at the Institute of Medicine."

"What's so bad about that?"

She smiled. "My dear friend, in the Soviet Union the profession of medicine is so lowly regarded that most of its practitioners are women. Few men could raise a family on a doctor's salary, since it was less than the monthly wage of a factory worker. Anyway, I obviously accepted the place and went through the head-breaking memorization of biochemistry and other such tortures.

"But the moment I began clinical work, everything changed. I loved the contact with other human beings, even if it was simply taking a pulse or blood pressure. The healing process was so ... inspiring."

Her description intensified Adam's admiration for her. Indeed, from the moment he had first met Anya, he had been struck by the kindness she emanated.

In a very real sense, she was the most maternal person he had ever met. Although this was something he could never tell her.

"Naturally," she continued, "among my irritations was the emergency room. As you know, Vladivostok is Russia's 'Wild Far East,' and with so many sailors in port, their drunkenness produced horrific accidents. The worst part was having to sew up some of the same people every Saturday night. But even this had an advantage."

"Anya, with you, everything seems to have an up side," Adam remarked with admiration.

She nodded. "Yes, when others did the sewing, *I* got to deliver the babies. It made me think of obstetrics as a speciality. So once again I applied to Moscow."

"You're a glutton for punishment, aren't you?" he observed good-naturedly.

"Yes, but this time they really tricked me—I was accepted. And at the university clinic, no less. Don't you believe that if you never give up trying, sooner or later you will get what you want?"

Adam reflected for a moment, and wondered in his heart of hearts if she still cherished the vain hope of having a child.

"Anyway," she continued, "the night before I left, the commander of Second River allowed us to use the main hall for a farewell party. I never laughed and cried so much in my entire life."

"Why so much of both?"

"Because I am Russian, and that is how we behave. I was happy to be getting out of that horrible place. But I was also sad to be leaving my parents. Finally, I enjoyed the look on my teachers' faces when they met the eminent prisoners who were ten times more qualified than they were."

Suddenly, her voice grew soft. "My father was allowed to take me to the airport," she continued, her eyes filling with tears. "He too was overflowing with sadness and happiness, and I shall never forget his part-

ing words to me. He embraced me and whispered,
'Annoushka, do everything you can—never to come
back here.' "

And now she was crying. She was not the legendary
Russian admixture of happy and sad. She was racked
with painful memories. He longed to take her in his
arms and comfort her.

And finally he did.

Her lips were so warm, her hands so loving. Anya
had so much to give, and she held nothing back. It was
a fiercer passion than anything he had ever known. The
whole experience was like seeing his first rainbow. He
had always known that the colors were there, but he had
never seen them with his own eyes.

To him, Anya had, until this moment, been beauty in
the abstract. Now she was real to him, and he sensed for
the first time an expansion in his own emotional spectrum. To the outside world it might have seemed that
she needed him. But what he now realized—to his gratification and his fright—was that he more than simply
needed her. He could not live without her.

23
ISABEL

JERRY PRACHT was the cause of Ray and Isabel's first
serious argument.

Her father was not disposed to allow her to see "that
unbalanced dropout," even in the most benign of circumstances. "I'm completely baffled by what you can

find of the slightest interest in this character," he told her.

"He's lively," she stated emphatically. "And independent. Anyway, when I spoke to Mom last night, she said that learning tennis would be a great thing. It's a very social sport. And besides, he's the first person I've ever met with an IQ higher than mine."

Ray was wide-eyed. "What makes you believe a thing like that?"

"Well," Isabel confessed, with a touch of embarrassment, "I asked Karl straight out."

The doorbell rang then, and Ray glanced at his watch. It was precisely ten A.M. The boy was nothing if not punctual. They could hear him bounding up the stairs. A moment later the alleged genius manqué was standing there in a blue track suit, dangling a pair of tennis shoes that had obviously known better days.

"I think these'll fit," he said cheerfully. "And what's more, they're golden. My brother wore them when I coached him to the Bay Area twelve-and-under singles title. Anyway, try 'em on. If you need to, you can maybe put on an extra pair of socks."

It was also clear that Jerry had reconsidered his behavior toward Ray and decided on a more diplomatic approach.

"How do you find the Berkeley undergraduates, Mr. D.?" he inquired politely as Isabel sat on a hassock and tried on the shoes.

"I only get to see the dim ones," Ray answered, "so it's hard to tell."

"Well, sir, at least you can console yourself that you're spared the worst—you don't have to tutor me," he said, then turned to his own pupil. "Hey, Isa, we'd better make it snappy. I only booked the court for an hour and a half."

"That long?" Raymond asked in a disapproving tone. "It'll absolutely exhaust her. And she's got a load of work to do this afternoon."

"Please," Jerry declared. "When it comes to the pedagogy of tennis, your daughter is in the hands of a master. If she gets really bushed we can take a break, and go for a little drive."

"A what?" Raymond's voice registered dismay. "Do you mean to tell me *you're* driving her?"

"Don't sweat, Mr. da Costa. That was one of the few courses I aced in high school. I'll be extra careful. I know how much you love your daughter—and how much my father loves his car."

Realizing with frustration that had he broached the subject of transportation earlier, he could have had adequate grounds for canceling the entire encounter, Ray capitulated and hoped for the best.

"Now, I want you to be sure to be back by noon. I've got a whole afternoon planned for her."

"Oh, that's a shame. Is it definite?" the young man commented, and then addressed Isabel. "I thought we'd be able to have lunch at the club. I get a staff discount, and their hamburgers'll blow your mind."

"Well, I'm sorry," Raymond overruled him. "You'll just have to 'blow my daughter's mind' another time."

The buzzer sounded again, heralding the arrival of Raymond's first student.

Sensing the moment propitious, Jerry signaled Isabel with a nod and they both headed for the door, where he turned to reassure the overprotective father. "Stay loose, Mr. D. I'll bring her back in mint condition."

Isabel was far from a genius at tennis.

As she missed shot after shot she grew increasingly embarrassed, and could not seem to benefit from Jerry's tutelage. Also, after little more than half an hour she was bushed.

"I think we should knock off early, Isa. Remember this was just your debut and you're a little out of shape."

"I can't understand it," she puffed. "I jog almost every morning."

"Don't let it worry you. Maybe you're not running fast enough. In a few more weeks—especially when I teach you my atomic serve—you'll probably make mincemeat out of me."

At five minutes to twelve he checked his watch and proposed, "Listen, champ, why don't we use our last precious moments to have some iced tea?"

Isabel smiled wearily. "I was hoping you'd ask."

"I know you enjoy the shock effect of masquerading as an idiot," she remarked as they sat down at a table on the terrace. "But just what exactly do you plan to do when you grow up?"

"That's the whole point, Isa," he insisted. "I *am* grown up. Paco Rodriguez, my coach, thinks if I work hard, in another couple of months I should be ready for the pro tour. I don't suppose you ever read *California Tennis*, but they did a piece on my winning the national sixteen-and-under championship last summer. I mean, I may not be able to do much yet, but even getting mangled by the big boys could be an educational experience."

"What about your astronomy?" Isabel asked. "Don't you want to pick it up again?"

"Hey, I've never dropped it. Just because I'm not enrolled in school doesn't mean I don't devour every issue of *Sky and Telescope*. Or visit the Exploratorium or the Morrison Planetarium. And sometimes I sit up all night at my 'scope, watching the fireworks of the universe."

"With your friend Darius?" she asked, anxious to show she remembered every word of his at their previous meeting.

A strange expression crossed Jerry's face. His eyes grew unfocused and he mumbled quietly, "No. Not with Darius."

"But I thought—"

"It's a long story—and I'm not so sure you'd enjoy hearing it."

"Try me."

The moment he began, it was clear Jerry had been longing to tell her.

"Darius Miller was a year ahead of me at the Manchester School for so-called Gifted Children. He was a mathematical genius—had his first paper accepted by *Random Structures and Algorithms* when he was barely twelve. And even while it was being set in type, he gave a piano recital at the Arts Center in Walnut Creek.

"Would you believe a 'scout' from the Hollywood Bowl invited him to play at one of their summer concerts? But his parents, who were also academics, didn't like the idea of him wasting time on rehearsals."

Jerry grew increasingly agitated as he continued. "*Wasting time,* Isa. Can you imagine such a concept when you're just twelve years old?

"I was his only friend—and had no illusions why I got through the barbed wire of his parents' disapproval. Not only was my dad who he is, I was such an astronomy freak, they knew we'd sit around discussing blue dwarfs and red giants instead of—God forbid—*wasting time* talking about girls or baseball.

"Only I was also wild—and hooked on sports. Obviously I couldn't play tennis with Darius. Still, one day when he was at my house I introduced him to roller skating. He wasn't exactly an athlete, but he loved it—got so carried away that he fell and broke an arm.

"You can imagine his parents' reaction. They were so ticked off they forbade him to play with me again—even at his house.

"Anyway, I'm not saying it was all my fault—though God knows I do feel guilty—but six weeks before his fifteenth birthday, Darius killed himself." Jerry smiled sadly. "I guess he couldn't bear the thought of growing old."

Isabel shuddered. Not only at the tale itself, but at the pain in his eyes as he told it.

"You must have been devastated," she whispered.

He nodded. "And angry—very angry. They held a memorial service for him at the school. All the teachers eulogized his brilliance—what a loss it was to science and all that crap. Foolishly, they asked me to speak too.

"Admittedly, I was absolutely out of control, but at least I told the truth. I said that wherever he was now, Darius might be the one thing he never was when he was alive—*carefree*. I wanted to say 'happy,' but Karl—who'd gone over the speech with me before-hand—thought that was going too far. After all, Dr. and Mrs. Miller were really hurting."

He stopped, visibly shaken by the summoning up of nightmares past. For a moment it seemed as if he would burst into tears.

"I'm sorry, Isa," he muttered. "I guess I shouldn't have told you—"

"No—I understand why. The shoe almost fits," she conceded, "but not quite."

"But I was also trying to explain myself. I want us to be friends, and we can't be if you think I'm a senseless weirdo. It's just that right after . . . what happened to Darius, I dropped out."

"How did your mom and dad feel?"

"They weren't exactly jumping for joy. But I guess they figured it was better for me to leave school than leave them. So I became a tennis bum. It got my mind off things.

"I banged the ball all day long—and watched the stars all night. Anything but serve the system that had crushed Darrie." He paused, worked up the courage and added, "He left me the telescope. It's in my dad's back-yard."

Isabel was consumed with sadness—both for Darius and Jerry.

Suddenly they were interrupted.

"Isabel, do you know what time it is?"

Both youngsters were shocked. They had lost all track of time, and it was, as Raymond's presence now attested, well past her curfew.

Totally nonplussed by Ray's unexpected appearance, Isabel could not help admiring Jerry's poise.

"I'm terribly sorry, Mr. da Costa," he said contritely, rising to his feet. "It's all my fault. May I expiate by asking you both to join me for a quick lunch?"

Isabel cast an imploring glance at Ray. But he had other ideas.

"I'm sorry," he declared sternly. "We've had enough frivolity for one weekend. Isabel's got a full schedule of homework—including a very important seminar paper."

Jerry was nothing if not resilient. "If you're thinking of her report for my dad, she delivered it last week."

"Oh," Raymond remarked icily, "does your father always discuss the details of his courses with you?"

"No," the young man conceded. "Especially since I'm usually bored to tears by the theoretical stuff he teaches. But he admired Isa's paper so much he mentioned the possibility of getting it published." And then, congratulating his tennis pupil, he said, "By the way, nice going, Isa."

"Published?" Ray murmured half to himself. He turned to his daughter. "How come you didn't tell me?"

"Because this is the first I've heard of it. Isn't it exciting?"

"I'm sure there'll be many others," Jerry interposed. A glance at Raymond's stern face stopped him from saying more. "Well, I don't want to stand in the way of scientific progress," he announced, beginning to retreat. And then, looking at Isabel, he added nervously, "Maybe you can stay for lunch next week, huh?"

"Thanks Jerry," she said noncommittally. "I had a really good time."

"I'm glad. I only hope our conversation wasn't too much of a downer."

Raymond turned and began to lead the way toward the parking lot.

"What was that conversation he referred to?" he asked as they were driving home.

"I understand Jerry better now. I mean, why he dropped out."

"What do you mean?"

"His best friend committed suicide."

"Any particular reason?"

Isabel hesitated for a moment, and then said quietly, "Because he was a genius."

June 28

Today I had what I guess was my first real "date." I mean it wasn't anything passionate like Romeo and Juliet. But it was a few hours in the company of a boy who's a high school dropout—and light years smarter than I.

And we didn't even have a chaperone. At least not till the very end.

Dad and I spend so much time together I can almost read his mind.

He was very taciturn on the way home. For some crazy reason, he thought that Jerry's telling me about Darius was an oblique way of criticizing him. I hope I convinced him that it really was Jerry's own way of explaining himself.

Then, out of the clear blue, he asked, "Did he behave?"

I knew that it was his awkward way of asking whether Jerry had tried to make a pass or something. Part of me wanted to scream, "That's a stupid question, Dad!" I did my best to brush it off and answer calmly, "Of course."

Yet as I was taking my shower, I remembered vividly—that Jerry had (in a way) "touched" me. That is, in showing me how to follow through with my backhand, he stood behind me and moved my arms to dem-

onstrate the motion. And though I'm one hundred percent sure that he was simply being a serious tennis coach, my back did rub slightly against his chest a few times.

That was all there was. And I'm sure for him it was no different from any other lessons he gives.

Anyway, it's not likely to happen again in this century. Because I knew from Dad's cranky behavior that there was no point whatever in even asking whether I can play with Jerry again.

Especially since, for the rest of the weekend, I had so much trouble concentrating on my schoolwork.

July 7

Jerry hasn't called yet.

July 12

Jerry still hasn't called.

July 19

Jerry's never going to call.

July 26

Good news and bad news. Dad let slip that Jerry had in fact called, two days after our first date.

But he made him promise not to ask me out till I finished my exams.

It's bad enough that he chased him away.

I wish he had at least told me.

24

SANDY

Sandy Raven was in the right scientific specialty. At the right time. At the right place.

Neighbors in the MIT lab where he was toiling for his Ph.D. included both once and future Nobelists in Medicine or Physiology. They had been drawn, through various detours, from the four corners of the earth, and included Salvador Luria, originally from Torino, Italy, as well as Har Grobind Khorana from Raipur, India. Not to mention a few local prodigies.

By the mid-1970s, scientific information was proliferating at the astonishing rate of two and a half million articles a year. Not even the most brilliant minds could absorb it all. Teamwork became essential, and lab groups would hold weekly meetings during which, munching on sandwiches, they would listen to colleagues reporting in depth on projects in their particular fields of interest.

Moreover, these groups were remarkably heterogeneous—a patchwork quilt of personalities. To begin with—and this was something the older and exclusively male faculty especially noticed—there were now almost as many women as men. And a veritable crazy salad of nationalities, united by their passion.

The natural world suddenly became a great treasure hunt with secrets buried everywhere. The search sometimes required expensive hardware, and the quest an infinite supply of patience.

194

"Can you imagine," Sandy remarked to Kanya Wansiri, a cell biologist from Thailand. "You can get the stuff of life delivered right to your door. They even have 800-numbers you can dial."

He picked up a telephone and mimicked an order: "Hi there, guys. We're going to need 350 micrograms of pure genomic DNA, ten blood maxikits, and the usual Proteinase K reagents and buffers. Then how about a few flavors of actual DNA—a kilo each of bovine, chicken, mouse, and human. Also, while you're at it," he grinned, "two pastramis on rye."

He hung up, looked at her and commented, "Who'd have believed we'd see the day when we had 'take-out life'? Wild, huh?"

"Yeah, absolutely," she agreed. "By the way, what's 'pastrami'?"

Sandy was so dedicated that he did not mind associating himself with a figure generally respected as a "good loser" in the scientific community.

To his credit, Gregory Morgenstern did not share the allergy to students that characterizes most scientific giants. Everybody seemed to want him as a thesis adviser.

His lifelong project had been a search for a genetic means of defeating cancer of the liver, a disease that is more extensive in Southeast Asia than in the industrial world. And it is the most common type of cancer among men in huge areas of tropical Africa. These were not potential markets that aroused much enthusiasm among the large pharmaceutical companies.

Morgenstern was therefore obliged to be a constant commuter from Boston to Washington, hat in hand to seek federal funding. Meanwhile, nearly every team in his lab was investigating different aspects of the problem.

During the weekly report meetings of the various groups, Sandy caught his attention, for what the profes-

sor could only describe as "pathological altruism." The
Raven boy reminded Morgenstern of himself at the
same age—seeking not recognition or advancement, but
answers. The young man's appetite to learn was insatiable.

Sandy's horizons were broadening both intellectually
and socially.

Instead of remaining in the dormitory, he accepted his
lab partner Vic Newman's invitation to join him and
two others in sharing an apartment near Central Square.
What startled Sandy at first was Vic's casual description
of their potential roommates as "a couple of girl grad
students from Penn."

Girls? Females? Members—whatever their elevated
credentials—of the opposite sex? The very idea of living in close proximity to a nubile woman made Sandy
weak at the knees.

"How do you manage it, Vic?" he asked, both frightened and excited. "I mean, suppose they walk around in
their underwear or something?"

Newman laughed. "I guess you're not a man of the
world, Raven. There's nothing like living twenty-four
hours a day with girls to turn *off* your hormones. I
mean, after the first few minutes they seem just like
guys—except that Stella and Louise are incredibly
bright. The only thing that'll excite you is their brains.
Otherwise, it's strictly brother-and-sister time."

"Okay, I'm game," Sandy responded, not without
some inner qualms.

"Oh, by the way," Vic asked casually, "can you
cook?"

"No—an egg maybe. But what's that got to do with
it?"

"Well, I already agreed that would be our share of the
chores. So I suggest you hasten to the Coop and digest
a few health food cookbooks. Oh, I knew there was
something I forgot to tell you—the girls are vegetari-
ans."

They also turned out to be astonishingly adept electrical engineers. For since the night skies not only teemed with stars, but also man-made satellites, their choice of televised entertainment had increased vastly. Although commercial firms could have done so for a fee, no self-respecting MIT type would stoop to pay for what his or her ingenuity could obtain gratis.

The very day Sandy moved in, the two women were fiddling on the roof, adding the last touches to the antenna they had assembled from inexpensive secondhand components. Apparently there was no broadcast code they couldn't unscramble. Their TV bill of fare was enriched enormously—except on those occasions when Stella and Louise wanted to watch a fight and the guys were more eager to see a movie.

At first it was hard for Sandy and Vic to hold up their side of the bargain. But it was even harder for the ladies—who actually had to eat the stuff the men rustled up.

Within a month the dinners were getting—in Stella's judgment—marginally tolerable.

Vic Newman was the closest thing to a pal that Sandy had ever had. He was bright, tenacious, and hardworking. Yet what made these initially antisocial traits acceptable was his infectious sense of humor.

Naturally, there were house rules. If, for whatever reason, the door to any of their rooms was closed, this was to be respected in every instance except a three-alarm fire.

But since these were all serious graduate students, they never had to bar their gates when they were studying. Indeed, one of the nicest aspects of this think tank—as Vic referred to it flatteringly—was that any of them could seek the other's advice on matters scientific.

Vic's sociological observation had been correct to an extent. Living in such mundane, close quarters, men and women somehow did not develop erotic thoughts about each other.

And yet, if you are a red-blooded American boy taking a shower, grabbing for a towel and finding instead a brassiere—albeit an empty one—the testosterone does not remain totally quiescent.

Also, summer was coming to Boston. And since graduate students did not enjoy the luxury of a vacation, for the first time in five years Sandy would not visit the Coast, where the likes of Gloria were annually replenished. (Where the old ones went, he never knew.)

But by now the rise in ambient temperature evoked a corresponding Pavlovian rise in Sandy's libido.

He would have to fend for himself that summer.

And he was determined to do so.

The first naked woman Sandy saw that summer was the last he expected to see.

Cruising down a row of periodicals in the Coop, his glance fell casually on *Playboy*, whose cover enticed potential readers with the promise of "Exclusive Photos—Hollywood's Hottest Newcomer."

The rest was masked by the barrier of publications displayed on the shelf below. Sandy quickly grabbed a copy. His worst fears were confirmed: silver letters proclaimed that the Playmate of the Month was—Kim Tower.

He suddenly felt dizzy and needed fresh air fast. Rushing to the cashier's desk, he bought the magazine and bolted outside.

Finding shelter behind a column, he hurriedly turned the pages. The double-length centerfold tumbled out— and there she was: artfully careless blond tresses, unique turquoise eyes, dazzling smile and flawlessly even teeth.

And yes, her breasts. Perfectly formed, exquisite— and bare.

He sprinted all the way back to the apartment, the erotic publication bouncing in his bag.

When he arrived, Vic Newman was sprawled across

the couch, working on his astrophysics. He looked up. "What's the matter, Raven?"

Too upset to speak, Sandy tossed the bag at Vic, who took out the *Playboy* and examined it with pleasure. "Hey, terrific. I've always wanted to see what she . . . looked like."

Sandy snatched it back and agonized, "I don't understand it. Why the hell would a nice girl from a decent family do something so gross?"

"Are you serious, Raven? This is about the greatest publicity a starlet could get."

"But she's not an actress anymore."

"Come on, Sandy," Vic chided. "People never give up acting—only vice versa—and they never stop dreaming. Who knows, this might even get her started again. I'll bet every able-bodied guy in the country's ogling her right this minute."

Indeed, this was the very thought tearing Sandy apart. She was public property now.

Disconsolate, he retreated to his room, sat on the bed and stared at the photographs.

Is this the woman I've worshiped all my life? he asked himself.

Gradually he realized his dominant emotion was not shock, nor outrage, but embarrassment.

And profound sadness.

25

ADAM

As CHRISTMAS neared, the level of excitement in the Coopersmith household intensified. Adam took Heather to pre-ski exercise classes at the local gym, and Toni awoke fifteen minutes earlier each morning to perform some of the routines in the Royal Canadian Air Force book.

Since it would be a long drive, Adam proposed that they invite Charlie Rosenthal, his colleague from the fertility clinic, to join them. Toni liked his wife, Joyce, and Heather was midway in age between their two sons—which gave her two near-contemporary playmates.

The two husbands took turns at the wheel of the Rosenthals' station wagon. They were inspired in great measure to press on because of the intolerable rap music their offspring insisted on blasting through the car's loudspeakers.

Late in the afternoon of Christmas Eve, tired but exhilarated, they reached the resort hotel at the tip of Georgian Bay.

The families separated, each to their own bungalow, and agreed to meet in the main lodge for dinner at seven. Eager for winter action, the young Rosenthals and Heather stayed outside to build a snow person—as politically correct Heather insisted it be called.

By the time Heather condescended to go into the cabin, she was thoroughly soaked—and freezing. She

willingly dumped herself into the Jacuzzi bathtub and
then put on the new plaid skirt and blue blazer Toni had
bought her for the holiday. Later they all donned boots
and hiked off to the main dining room with high spirits
and large appetites.

Charlie and Joyce and the Rosenthal boys were waiting by the gigantic stone fireplace, each with a glass of
eggnog, although the youngsters' drinks were rum-free.

"This place is great," Joyce enthused. "If you guys
are game, I've signed us up for tobogganing tomorrow
morning."

"Why not?" Charlie joked. "We're doctors, we can
set each other's legs. Come on, let's go in before all the
turkey's gone."

The noise level in the dining room was high and the
alcohol level even higher.

A string quartet of college students from Toronto was
playing pseudoclassical versions of popular Christmas
chestnuts, like "Rudolph the Red-Nosed Reindeer" in
the style of Bach—a concept that delighted the diners
young and old and added to the magic of the atmosphere.

Sitting between the two Rosenthal boys, Heather was
radiating hints of grown-up beauty that tugged at
Adam's heartstrings.

Charlie could always be counted on for some new
jokes, and he did not disappoint on this occasion either,
while his sons, who had heard them all before, moaned,
"not that one again, Dad."

After the feast, as they were waiting for the baked
Alaska, the concierge suddenly arrived and whispered
something in Adam's ear. Nodding, he rose and addressed the others.

"Hey, guys, be sure they save me a slice. I've got a
phone call."

"Look at this, Joyce," Charlie announced histrionically. "I have a monstrous full-time practice and nobody bothers me. Coopersmith probably has a measly

six private patients and they can't get along without him. They even chase him across the frontier. Should I feel lucky—or jealous?"

"Hold your fire till we see who's hassling me," Adam retorted good-naturedly as he headed for the phone booths, wondering what on earth could be the matter.

"This is Dr. Coopersmith."

"Doctor, this is Marvin Bergman. I'm the senior resident at Mass. Mental. Sorry to bother you, but it's about Mrs. Avilov."

Adam suddenly went cold. "What about her?"

"She attempted suicide, ingested about thirty diazapam fives. Then had second thoughts and called your service, which contacted us."

"My God," Adam said in shock. "Is she all right?"

"No problem," Bergman replied. "We got there in plenty of time and pumped her stomach. She'll have a nice long sleep. And wake up alive." He paused, and then continued, "Well, sir, obviously you're her OB/GYN. Do you know her psychiatrist?"

"She doesn't have one. Did she, uh, ask for me?"

"She did mention you by first name a couple of times," Bergman reported in a nonjudgmental tone. "But she's completely out of danger, so there's no real need to disturb your vacation."

"That's okay. I'll call Toronto and see if I can still get a plane. If by some chance she should wake, be sure to tell her I'm on my way. Is that clear, Dr. Bergman?"

"Yes, sir. Although depending on when you get here, I may be off duty."

"Well, then make damn sure your replacement remembers to tell her," Adam barked. Realizing he may have betrayed his emotional involvement, he calmed himself and said, "Uh, thank you, Doctor, I know Christmas Eve is a rotten assignment, but I'm grateful for your concern."

Adam hurried to the front desk to see if there was

still another flight to Boston that evening. There was one he could catch if he was willing to risk a wild taxi ride. He asked them to book both and went back to the dining room very slowly—to face the daunting task of extricating himself.

His return was cheered by all those at his table, though his own expression remained grim.

He bent over and whispered to Toni, "Could we talk outside for a moment?"

A worried look crossed her face as she stood up and followed him to the lobby. "Tell me quickly, Adam, is something wrong?" she asked anxiously. "Is it my father?"

"No, no. He's fine. But there's a problem and I've got to go back."

"What?" she nearly shouted. "The biggest emergencies you ever have are miscarriages, and there are plenty of people in Boston who can deal with them."

"This is a hell of a lot more serious." Adam persisted. "Remember Mrs. Avilov?"

"The Russian?"

"Yes. She tried to commit suicide."

"God, that's awful." Toni's response was instinctive, then she abruptly realized there was something fundamentally wrong with all this. "Isn't that a little out of your area? I mean," she said carefully, "you're not a shrink."

"I know, I know. But it's complicated to explain. I'm her only friend. She's—how can I put it?—illogically dependent on me."

"Well, darling, you happen to be on vacation with people who are very *logically* dependent on you. Why don't you let the Psych Department handle this and come back to the party?" She took him by the hand, yet he remained rooted to the spot.

"Toni, I haven't got time to explain. Can I ask you to simply accept that I have to make this trip?"

"Adam," she said with a scowl, "you're not keeping

your word. I sacrificed our being at Clifton with Dad so
we could take this vacation. I mean, I've got all the
sympathy in the world for this Avilov person. But practically every patient you see is a walking tragedy. What
makes her so different? Is there something going on between you two?"

"For God's sake," Adam replied with exasperation,
"I just want to be certain that she's properly taken care
of. I mean, you can't imagine what kind of junior people are on duty over Christmas."

They stared at each other, suddenly aware of how
fragile their relationship had become.

"All right," Toni said with a sigh, stoically suppressing her own outrage. "How long will you be
gone?"

"A day—two, at the most."

"What about your daughter?" she demanded angrily.
"This was supposed to be our big rapprochement."

"I don't know, dammit. But can't we just say that
I've had an emergency?"

"*We* aren't going to tell her anything. *You're* the one
who has to face not only Heather, but the other members of the jury. And Adam," she said tartly, "try to be
a little more convincing with them than you've been
with me."

He spoke to his daughter alone.

"I know this is lousy luck, honey. But you've got to
understand that I'm a doctor and this patient needs me
very badly."

"So do I," Heather murmured half under her breath,
and then pleaded, "Can I come with you? I don't want
to stay here by myself."

Adam was uneasy. "Sweetie, this is just going to be
a quick turnaround. I'll go to the hospital and come
right back. Do me a favor and take care of Mom while
I'm gone."

Puzzled and disappointed, his daughter looked at him and muttered, "You must be kidding, Dad."

26

ISABEL

RAYMOND HAD scarcely anything more to give her. His storehouse of knowledge was almost depleted. The best he could offer was constant support and encouragement—and protection from external distractions. In other words, he had subtly been relegated from coach to cheerleader.

Yet Ray never relinquished the responsibility for Isabel's inner equilibrium. After ascertaining that she was more than ready for the next day's World Lit. exam, he suggested that they loosen up by going to the Holiday Bowl and getting a little exercise.

The cavernous bowladrome echoed with the clatter of tumbling pins and the cacophonous shouts of the spectators. As father and daughter sat on a bench lacing up their well-worn rented shoes, Raymond looked off into the distance and a sudden flash of anger crossed his face.

"What the hell is he doing here?"

"Who, Dad?"

"Your 'swain,' Mister Won't-take-no-for-an-answer Pracht."

Isabel's eyes widened. "Is Jerry here?" she asked excitedly.

Ironically, Isabel had spent most of the lonely summer trying to come to terms with the fact that she would never see Jerry again. And yet now, unexpectedly, he was scarcely a hundred feet away, ever joyful and ebullient, the obvious leader of his small pack. She could barely endure the tension. But before she could act, Raymond was back at her side, holding two large plastic cups.

The da Costa party was second in line and had at most five minutes to wait.

Jerry was in lane nine, and the groups in six and twelve seemed to be concluding their games. Either way, Isabel calculated, they had the chance of getting close enough to have him notice her. And if he did, Dad could not be rude to her adviser's son in public.

Jerry was standing in the approach area, holding the ball next to his cheek, poised to let fly. His eyes were fixed intently on the head pin at the far end of the lane. Then he strode forward, firing the ball at the foul line as he pivoted gracefully to stop his motion. His follow-through was perfect, and instantly all the pins were scattered. It was a strike. His comrades cheered.

"Beautiful, Jerry!" "Way to go!"

Isabel, who had been captivated by his agility and skill, involuntarily cried out, "Great going, number one nine four."

The hero of the moment looked up, spotted Isabel, and called enthusiastically, "Hey there, long time no see." He started toward her. "How come you know my number?"

"I spent a dollar and bought the magazine. Sancho must be very pleased, because you're right on schedule—over a hundred places higher."

Isabel could feel her father smoldering as he demanded, "What's all this nonsense?"

"Jerry's taken a giant leap in the tennis rankings," she explained as the subject of their conversation reached them.

"Hi, Mr. da Costa," Jerry said breezily, offering his hand.

Raymond was too sensible to make a fuss, especially before so large an audience. He merely shook Jerry's hand and said affably, "Hello, Jerry. That was quite a shot you made there."

"Thanks," the young man replied. "I didn't know you guys were into bowling."

That's a minor miracle, Raymond thought sarcastically. It was about the only thing except ballooning that he hadn't invited Isabel to do with him.

Just then a fresh-faced Japanese-American girl in a red-and-white-striped blouse called out, "Lane twelve ready for da Costa."

Nudging his daughter slightly, Raymond tossed off a "Nice seeing you" to Jerry and began to move away.

"Me too. In fact we've just wrapped up ourselves. Would you mind if I watched?"

"That would be great," Isabel interposed before her father could think of a politic refusal. "Maybe you could give me some tips."

"Cool." He smiled and signaled to the rest of his friends. "Take it easy guys, I'll be there in a couple of secs."

Raymond was so flustered that his first shot fell into the right gutter and rolled impotently to the pit.

"Tough luck, Mr. D.," Jerry commiserated, "but I think you let go a little too soon."

Still fighting to control his temper, Raymond acknowledged this unsolicited counsel with a barely civil, "Yeah. Right. I guess I'm just a little out of practice."

"If you don't mind my saying," Jerry continued, "you'd probably do better with a lighter ball."

Raymond deliberately ignored this advice and then fired his second shot with such effort that it curved swiftly into the *left* gutter.

Now it was Isabel's turn. Without overtly acknowledging it, she took Jerry's suggestion and chose the lightest ball she could find. Yet she did no better than walk awkwardly to the foul line and let go of it. Unlike her father's, it at least stayed on the lane, and when it finally arrived, knocked over three pins.

She looked at Jerry.

"Not bad," he said with encouragement. "It's just a typical beginner's error, stopping short just before you release the ball. As a scientist you should've realized that this dissipates all the momentum you've built up in the approach. The whole point of the run up is to give more power when you let go."

"Gosh," Isabel remarked, "you talk like a physicist yourself."

"I sure as hell hope not," Jerry remarked, "but I guess I've been a little brainwashed."

Suddenly they were interrupted by the appearance of an attractive blonde about Jerry's age.

"Come on, Pracht, we can't wait forever," she called seductively. "Some of us have eleven o'clock curfews, you know." Jerry nodded and then turned to the da Costas.

"Sorry about this, but I've got the only car, and I can't mess up my buddies' evening. Maybe some other time, huh?"

"Sure," Isabel responded, masking her disappointment.

She and her father were left to bowl in their mutually inept way, although—after a while—they were at least able to laugh about it.

On the way home, Raymond felt that enough time had elapsed for him to make a cautionary comment.

"Well, Isabel, I guess now you see why I don't want you hanging around with young people of that ilk."

"I don't know what you mean, Dad," she said, genuinely baffled.

"Simple mathematics," he replied. "Since that nubile creature had an eleven o'clock curfew, and it's only twenty past nine, we can imagine what sort of mischief they'll get into."

Isabel understood only too well that Ray's remark was another attempt to discredit Jerry Pracht.

Yet all she could think of was how much she would like to have been that other girl.

27

ANYA

As SHE lay semiconscious in her hospital bed, Anya's thoughts took refuge in the past.

It was lifetimes ago, and a million miles away.

To young Anya Litvinova, Moscow was the destination of a dream. All through her childhood, her mother and father had made it sound like some kind of earthly paradise. As she rode the bus and subway from Sheremetyevo Airport to the city, she was too exhausted to notice the gray blandness of postwar apartment blocks lining the road.

By a stroke of good fortune—or in the opinion of some, bad luck—she had managed to secure a place in the overcrowded dormitory at the university clinic.

She soon found out why the bed was available. It was the upper half of a bunk in a cubicle occupied by a bad-tempered future eye surgeon.

Olga Petrovna Dashkevich was so magnificently unpleasant that she had frightened off no fewer than six previous roommates in her very first year of residency. Anya had been warned, but she was still not prepared for her new companion's opening salvo.

"What happened to your nose, Litvinova?"

Anya put her hand to her face, thinking she had inadvertently scratched it.

But Olga quickly elucidated, "I mean, it almost looks normal. I thought all Semites had oversized beaks."

Anya tried to take even this with equanimity, and responded with a smile. "Olga Petrovna, can you explain why a Jew-hater like you chose Professor Schwartz to be your supervisor for Ophthalmic Surgery?"

"Sweetheart," Olga retorted with a knowing grin, "I've never said you people weren't clever."

If Anya had learned nothing else in this obstacle course that had been her life, it was that for her, salvation came only from perseverance. Good humor could be a weapon strong enough to erode even wills of steel. The gift of seeing the best in everyone was ingrained in her nature, and she resolved, paradoxically, to help Olga with a problem that was obviously born of her own personal unhappiness.

The girl was not attractive. Nor, compared to the other med students, was she particularly bright. Until Anya came along, she'd had no friends of either sex. And, to top it all, she smoked like an aggressive chimney.

"Have you ever seen the lungs of a cadaver who died of cancer?" Anya coughed through the fumes.

"Don't lecture me, Anya. I know it's medically unwise to smoke," she conceded. "But I intend to continue until I'm fully qualified."

"Thanks," Anya remarked sarcastically.

"What does it matter to you? You'll move out next term anyway."

"What makes you so sure?"

"Everybody does."

"You needn't worry," Anya countered cheerfully. "However hard you try, I'm going to learn to like you."

A month into the term, Olga came down with a terrible flu and was forced to remain in bed. Not only did

Anya bring her soup from the refectory, but even volunteered to take notes at a lecture she would be missing.

"I don't understand you, Litvinova," Olga commented bluntly. "I'm beginning to think you actually want to be my friend."

"I do."

"But why?"

"Frankly," Anya laughed, "I already have enough enemies."

Although the Soviet Revolution successfully abolished Christmas, even the most tyrannical regimes could not suppress the spirit of the holiday.

Its universally attractive traditions were merely channeled into the celebration of Novy God—New Year's Eve—a "secular" occasion for decking the halls with boughs of fir, trimming the tree, and exchanging gifts.

Naturally, good Socialists did not believe in Santa Claus. But curiously enough, on the night before New Year's they awaited the arrival of Grandfather Frost, who comes laden with presents for the children.

This year, for the first time in her life, Olga was bringing a friend home for the holiday celebration.

As their subway train passed through a succession of gleaming marble stations, Olga casually remarked, "I think you'll enjoy meeting my uncle Dmitri. He works in genetics. In fact, he's an academician."

Anya was amazed. "You mean you're related to a member of the Soviet Academy of Science and never mentioned it?"

"How else do you think I got into the surgery program?" Olga answered with a touch of self-mockery. "I'm not as clever as you—I needed *protektsiya*. As a matter of fact, Dmitri is such a genius that he was elected when he was only thirty."

In proudly disclosing the existence of her illustrious uncle, Olga neglected to mention that he was, if not classically handsome, certainly vibrant and virile—and a bachelor.

As Anya respectfully shook his hand she could barely muster the polite words, "It's an honor to meet you, Professor Avilov."

"Please, please," the tall, wide-shouldered man insisted. "You must call me Dmitri Petrovich. Also, I don't think it's such an honor." He paused for a moment and then added with a grin, "But I do hope you'll consider it a pleasure."

The entire house was permeated with the smell of walnuts and tangerines as they sat down to dinner. There was Olga, her younger sister, her parents, her maternal grandmother, Anya, and Dmitri.

The meal was sumptuous and, by Russian standards, something of a fairy tale. There were no fewer than twelve cold appetizers, including the rarest of treats, fresh tomatoes and cucumbers, all highly salted and spiced. Vodka was torrential.

As they were eating the main dish, Olga's mother announced to the gathering, "For this marvelous salmon, we have Dmitri Petrovich to thank."

The grateful diners raised a toast to their benefactor, *"Na zdorovie."*

As if to the spotlight born, the professor held forth on the relative beauties of various cities of the world—with particular attention to Paris, where he had just delivered a paper, and Stockholm, which he visited each summer at the invitation of the Swedish Academy of Medicine.

Had she been more cosmopolitan, Anya might well have found him arrogant. But as an exile returned in body, though not yet in spirit, she was totally captivated.

Later that evening, after they had welcomed the new year with goblets of champagne, Anya was helping Olga and her mother clear the table when she suddenly found her way blocked by the large frame of academician Avilov.

He gazed down at her, an unmistakable glint of mischief in his eyes, and whispered, "And you, my little dove, why have you said nothing of yourself?"

Anya felt awkward, and sputtered, "What could I possibly say that would interest a personage like you?"

"I am not a personage," he responded. "I'm just a person who finds you enchantingly attractive. Furthermore," he continued, "You're not a Muscovite. . . ."

"Is it so obvious?" she inquired.

"Yes—you didn't even ask me what car I drive. Which is yet another reason I find you irresistible." He smiled broadly.

Irresistible? During her childhood and teenage years Anya had been variously praised by her parents and the other inmates at Second River as "cute," "sweet," and "charming." But the notion that she might be an attractive woman had never entered her mind.

"May I have the honor of driving you home, Anya Alexandrovna?"

"Oh," she replied, instantly relieved. "Olga and I would enjoy that very much."

"I'm sure she would," her friend's uncle replied. "But she's staying overnight with her parents. And besides, there are only two seats in my car."

"In that case, I must respectfully decline," Anya responded bravely.

Avilov looked puzzled—and impressed.

And thus Anya shivered in the cold December night waiting for a taxi that would transport her back to the safety of the hospital dormitory.

The next time, Avilov caught her at her own game, inviting both Anya and Olga—her "chaperone" as he joked in his otherwise formal letter—to hear him lecture at the academy on the genetic aspects of Huntington's disease.

Anya could not refuse, for the simplest of reasons: she wanted to go.

Dmitri was a brilliant speaker, with a rare gift of being able to make himself intelligible even to nonexperts in his field—although Anya was, after all, a qualified medical doctor.

After the lecture there was a small reception in the elegant high-ceilinged room adjoining the amphitheater.

Both Anya and Olga stood awkwardly on the sidelines watching noted scientists fawning about the guest of honor. It was clear, even from their distant vantage point, that Avilov was enjoying the energetic flattery.

"I feel silly," Olga confessed. "I mean, nobody wants to talk to us. Why don't we get the hell out of here and have something to eat? Maybe we could meet some guys."

"Uh, not yet," Anya demurred. "Guys" were the furthest thing from her mind. "I mean—I mean, it's sort of interesting to watch."

"Then I'm getting another vodka," Olga countered, and went off to fetch it.

Anya was inexperienced but not naive. She knew that in accepting Dmitri Petrovich's invitation, she would not this time go home alone. And yet she wondered how he would disencumber himself from his niece's presence. But Anya had underestimated her admirer's resourcefulness.

At precisely nine-thirty Ivan, an attractive, crew-cut, scholarly young man introduced himself as academician Avilov's chief research assistant. He recited what was obviously a prepared speech to the effect that, although he knew that Anya would have to return to the hospital and study, he hoped that Olga would come along with a few of the younger staff to listen to jazz in a terrific place on Novy Arbat.

Olga was too delighted to realize it was a ploy. Either that, thought Anya, or she was a consummate actress.

For a moment Anya feared she had been genuinely abandoned. She was about to fetch her coat when

Avilov glided up to her and whispered, "We will meet in Seventh Heaven."

"What?" For a moment she was totally baffled.

"That's the restaurant on top of the television tower. I've booked a table for ten o'clock."

She spent nearly an hour walking around Red Square to avoid the embarrassment of arriving early and having to sit self-consciously alone in a sophisticated place where she would feel inadequately dressed.

Rising skyward nearly two thousand feet, the Ostankino Television Tower was perhaps the ultimate expression of the Soviet obsession with phallic monuments. Seventh Heaven rotated slowly, giving the distinguished diners the opportunity to see the entire city between cocktails and dessert.

Since its service was similar to that of all Russian eating establishments—slow, slovenly, and surly—most guests usually traveled the 360-degree circuit at least twice.

Anya had never in her life seen anything like it—the guests were elegantly garbed, and there was a glint of what looked like real silver on the tables.

Avilov was already seated and rose to greet her, smiling.

"You didn't have to walk around in circles, you know. I was here on the dot of ten."

Anya hoped she was not blushing. Had he seen her meandering? Or could he simply read her mind? Nor could she hide her uneasiness when he ordered their meal.

"What is the matter, little one—do you not like cutlets à la Kiev?"

"No," she stumbled, "it's just that—"

Avilov nodded. "I understand, Annoushka. It cannot have been frequently on the bill of fare at a place like Second River."

"You know about my family?" She felt more nervous than ever.

He nodded and replied gently, "I was still in primary school at the time, but I remember that last spasm of Stalin's paranoia. No one spoke up in those physicians' defense, and our principal lectured us about being wary of certain kinds of doctors who poisoned their patients."

"Did you believe it?" she asked.

"To be quite honest, I wished I was already a doctor so I could poison the principal."

Anya laughed.

"What I can't understand," he continued, his voice now softly serious, "is why your father never got recalled. I have at least half a dozen friends in the academy who are graduates of the Gulag system."

"I guess he didn't have any friends in the academy," she replied, touched by what seemed like genuine compassion in his voice.

"He has now," Avilov replied, putting his large hand on hers. "Don't worry, I have got plenty of vitamin P—*protektsiya*." He looked into her eyes and understood that she was too moved to speak.

Finally, her lips parted and let forth a single syllable. "Why?"

"Why what?"

"You don't strike me as someone who makes quarrels with the system. Why should you want to help them?"

"You're right," he conceded. "I'm the most selfish person I know. But if I do something for them, perhaps I can make you like me."

"I already like you," she whispered.

"Enough to marry me?"

For a moment Anya was too incredulous to believe what she had heard. Only then did her face become a mask of total shock.

"Why?" she repeated.

"You are so full of questions," Dmitri reprimanded. "Even Lenin didn't try to abolish love at first sight."

She shook her head in dismay. "I just don't understand it. You could have any girl you wanted—"

"But, Anya, you're not 'any girl.' You're someone very special. You have a gift of happiness that's almost magical."

She mustered the courage to defend herself against her own emotional impulses. "How many times have you said that to a woman, Dmitri Petrovich?"

"Never," he insisted. "Never in my life."

At twenty minutes to one he opened the car door for her. As she brushed by him to sit down, she had the fleeting impression that he was about to embrace her. But he did not.

When he started the motor and put Charles Aznavour on his cassette player, Anya was certain they would be driving to his apartment.

There too she was wrong.

And when Dmitri dropped her at the hospital and did not even attempt a perfunctory good-night kiss, she was convinced she had made a gauche fool of herself.

Only when the roses arrived the next morning—and with them a formal note requesting her to marry him— did she know she had been wrong about everything.

Except the fact that he really loved her.

October 21, 1982, was the happiest day of Anya's life. Now she was not only a diplomate in obstetrics, but at the Matrimonial Department of City Hall she became the bride of academician Professor Dmitri Avilov. Her new husband had arranged a sumptuous reception at what would be their apartment on a high floor of one of the giant blocks bordering the Moskva River.

Anya felt like a princess in a fairy tale. For among the many well-wishers were the two dearest people in her life.

Her mother and father.

But that was lifetimes ago and a million miles away.

28

ISABEL

PROPELLED BY her dazzlingly creative work in the two graduate seminars, Isabel da Costa achieved her goal—or more accurately, Raymond's—and in the late summer of 1986 became the youngest graduate in the history of Berkeley. Summa cum laude in physics, with a shining gold Phi Beta Kappa key hanging around her neck.

Once again the press was out in force, and once again Muriel and Peter reenacted their familiar roles of loving mother and admiring brother. Though some of the reporters were anxious to get photos of father and daughter, whom one of them had dubbed "the thermodynamic duo," Raymond had outmaneuvered them and made certain that they were only photographed as a complete family.

Though the TV cameras concentrated almost exclusively on close-ups of Isabel, when she graciously thanked her family for their support, they intercut to close-ups of Ray, the man she singled out as "still the best teacher I ever had."

Back in June, during her brief visit home for Peter's graduation, she and her brother had forged a relationship that continued to strengthen, even when Peter—himself entering college that fall—was consigned to the status of wallpaper.

They went to dinner at the Heidelberg, and continued

to talk about their futures as if they were on the same level of magnitude.

Peter told her that he was thinking of majoring in physical education. "What's next for you, sis?" he asked, although he already knew the answer. His generous nature enabled him to admire Isabel without envying her.

"Do you have any suggestions?" she asked playfully.

"Actually, I do," he replied. "I mean, my advice would be to take a trip around the world."

"What for?"

"God, can't you even guess? You know all the formulas that govern the movement of the universe but you've never even seen your own planet. A couple of buddies and I are using the money we earned washing cars on weekends to go backpacking in France. I'd invite you to come along, but I already know what Dad would say."

"Gosh, I'd love to go, but it's urgent that I start on my master's thesis with Pracht right away."

"Isn't that a little bit premature, even for you?" Peter asked. "I mean, you haven't even done the course work—or," he said with a fond smile, "did you finish it all last night while I was sleeping?"

"I know it sounds strange," she explained. "This is strictly between us—do you know anything about the Theory of Forces?"

"Only what I remember from *Star Wars*," he joked. "Can you put it in language that a half-wit can understand?"

"Okay," she began, "It's like this. Conventional physics recognizes four different forces in nature. Most everybody is familiar with gravity and electrodynamics—they operate over large distances. But then there is a 'strong' force, which works over a short range and holds atomic nuclei together, and a 'weak' force—which is associated with the decay of neutrons outside the nucleus. Are you with me so far?"

"Let's just say I believe you—but I wouldn't like to take a test on it. Go on, I'll keep straining my brain muscles."

"Well, ever since Newton, physicists have made about a zillion attempts to develop things called G.U.T.'s, or Grand Unified Theories—some way of encompassing all four forces. Einstein tried, but even he couldn't find an answer. Twenty years ago, a guy named Stephen Weinberg made the best unifying attempt so far by using a mathematical technique known as gauge symmetry. I won't bore you with the details."

"Thanks." Her brother laughed.

"Lately, theoretical physics is evolving G.U.T.'s using principles of symmetry, but there's still no definitive answer."

"Which is where you come in—right?"

"Not yet." She smiled. "Don't be so anxious to get me onstage."

"I can't help it, I'm rooting for you to get there first."

"Well, there're a couple of guys still ahead of me on the track, including Karl. He's collaborating with a team in Cambridge and one in Germany. They're all gathering data in the field of high-energy physics which can only be explained by the existence of a *fifth* force. That might be the key to the whole picture. I've read their article in draft—and obviously so have the heads of a lot of Physics departments.

"If he's right, it's a mega-breakthrough, and that'll mean mind-boggling job offers not only from MIT, but the other go-go schools who recruit potential Nobelists like trophies on a shelf."

"But where do you come in?" Peter smiled.

"Your patience is rewarded. Here I am—really trying to get into this whole question. And since nobody is closer to the material than Karl, maybe you can understand why I want to start this while he's still in our backyard."

Peter nodded and said with affection, "Isabel, for

once I find myself agreeing with you. Go for it. And may the fifth force be with you."

Muriel had been a good trouper. But this was to be her last appearance as perfect wife and mother.

Her final conversation with Ray was strangely poignant. They sat at the round, dark wood table of the rathskeller, its surface etched with generations of initials of lovers and vandals.

"So this is it?" Raymond sighed.

To his own surprise, he was painfully reliving the early part of their marriage, the birth of the children, each christened with hope of increased happiness.

At this moment he took no joy in his victory. Perhaps it was the beer. Perhaps a moment of unguarded honesty in which he realized what a generous human being Muriel was.

He looked at her and whispered, "I'm very sorry it had to happen this way."

"So am I," she answered quietly.

"I mean, we've lived this sham so long, I can't understand why it couldn't have gone on a little longer until the kids were a bit older."

"They're both strong enough to find their way in this world. On the other hand, at my age a second chance for happiness doesn't come along that often."

"What do you mean?" Raymond asked, already sensing that the reply would destroy the gentle empathy of the moment.

She looked at him and murmured almost apologetically, "I want to get married again."

He hesitated for a moment. Perhaps in his acute selfishness he had expected her to wait for him, like Patience on a monument.

"Anyone I might know?" he asked.

"I thought it was obvious," she responded. "Edmundo and I have grown very close. Maybe it's because we're both cripples in a way, him physically, me emotionally. But at least we can listen to music and communicate without the need for any words."

"Well," Raymond remarked, trying to mask the feelings of jealousy that had gripped him by surprise. "I guess you've been in love with him for years."

Muriel lowered her head. "I suppose so," she conceded. "But never the way I loved you."

When she heard that her mother was remarrying, Isabel burst into tears.

Peter tried to reason with her. "Isabel, you're not being fair. Mom's been alone for so long—and everybody needs a partner in life."

He was suddenly self-conscious, realizing that his unpartnered father was present and might take offense.

But Raymond simply inquired phlegmatically, "Isn't there already a Mrs. Zimmer?"

"Up till a few months ago," Muriel replied. "Then *she* found love, with of all people, the church organist. And actually badgered Edmundo for a divorce."

Then Muriel said softly, "Naturally, I want Isabel at the wedding."

"I'm sorry," Raymond objected civilly, "but don't you think she's a bit too young to ride the bus—or even a plane—by herself?"

Muriel smiled bitterly. "That's an irony, Ray, and you do have a point. But Peter's got his license now, and if you don't mind the idea of his driving Isabel all the way down—"

"I can make it in one day easily," Peter interrupted with a touch of pride, "and I mean sticking to the speed limits too."

Now all eyes were focused on Ray, who sensibly realized that he had to accommodate the majority's wish. It was clear even to him that Isabel wanted to go.

"Uh, what time is the, uh . . . ceremony?"

"Well," Muriel replied, "we're just going to go to the courthouse and have a few friends over for a drink. If it'll make you feel any better, we could schedule it for mid-morning. Then Isabel could fly down on the first plane—"

"Yes, yes, of course," Ray conceded. "There's an eight o'clock flight from Oakland, and I'll be glad to drive her to the airport. She can easily be back by dinnertime."

Isabel herself was about to interject that she might want to spend the evening and even the night with the rest of the family.

But she could try and persuade her father later.

Maybe.

Upon her return to San Diego, Muriel wasted no time arranging the wedding. Two weeks later Isabel, in a frilly pink dress that she and her mother had bought in Berkeley, stood to one side with Peter as a magistrate formally decreed that henceforth their mother would be Mrs. Edmundo Zimmer.

Another pair of siblings stood on the groom's side, a sister in her early thirties and a brother older still. Both Dorotea and Francisco had flown up from Argentina to honor their father as well as to serve as legal witnesses.

After the brief ceremony, all six of them repaired to a private room at the faculty club for drinks and a small but elegant nuptial meal.

Both Muriel and Edmundo were in buoyant spirits, and they seemed especially touched that Isabel had come. After the glasses were raised to them, Edmundo in turn proposed a toast to "the famously brilliant young lady who has traveled a long way to be here with us."

Isabel was self-conscious, especially since Edmundo's children had flown much farther. But she was soon completely won over by the conductor's charm and the genuine affection radiating from his eyes.

There was a larger reception planned for that evening, at which various members of the orchestra would be playing solos, trios, and even a wind quintet.

"I really wish you could stay for it," Edmundo remarked sincerely. "I was so looking forward to hearing you play the violin."

"You won't be missing much. I haven't had a lot of time to practice lately."

"Don't be so modest," he protested gallantly. "Muriel tells me you make your instrument sing. I want you to promise me that you'll bring it down at Christmas."

Isabel was so enchanted by Edmundo that she resolved to duke it out with Raymond if he tried to object to her visiting again at Christmas.

Her plane landed at Oakland just after nine P.M. And as she walked toward her loving father's outstretched arms, Isabel felt an inexplicable sadness.

He was everything to her. Or almost everything.

But there was no music in Raymond da Costa's life.

29

ADAM

TWENTY MINUTES before midnight on Christmas Eve, Adam pushed open the door of Room 608 at the Massachusetts Mental Health Hospital. A matronly Hispanic nurse was gently trying to lull a female patient into slumber.

At first he was unsure of what to do. Although he knew that Anya desperately needed to sleep it off, he was anxious to reassure himself that she was all right.

Yet even though he was silent, she sensed his presence and called out weakly, "Adam, is that you?"

"Take it easy, Anya. Try not to upset yourself."

"That is funny joke," she remarked, her words slurring. "After all the terrible things I have done." She was able to turn her head slowly and face him. "You should not have come," she murmured.

"I had to," he countered. "And you wanted me to."

She did not reply, either to protest or to acknowledge his claim.

Uneasily, Adam said to the nurse, "It's all right, I'm one of her physicians."

"Very well, Doctor." The woman nodded and made a discreet exit.

Adam immediately sat in her chair beside Anya's bed.

"I'm so sorry," she repeated hoarsely. "I have such talent for failure, I could not even do a good job of killing myself."

He shook his head in consternation. "Why the hell did you do such a stupid thing? I thought we were so happy together."

"That was precisely why, Adam. It was Christmas—I was all alone. I missed you so terribly, and I realized we could never be together."

"Why not?" he inquired softly.

"You are married," she responded slowly. And then added even more emphatically, "You have a child. In fact your entire life would have been happier if we had never met."

"No," he objected. "You're the most wonderful thing that has ever happened to me, Anya. All I want in this world is to be with you."

"It's wrong," she persisted.

"Since when did love behave by a rule book? For God's sake, stop being so hard on yourself."

"You cannot love me," she whispered.

"What the hell do you mean by that?" he demanded.

She answered with a sad smile, "Because nothing that good has ever happened to me in my entire life."

He wanted to sweep her into his arms and reassure her, but she was tired, and ill. And this was a hospital. And he was a doctor.

"Let's turn on your TV," he suggested. "We can just catch Midnight Mass from St. Patrick's."

"If you would like," she answered softly.

He switched on the set and they began to watch. Every so often he would glance at Anya, and was gratified to see that his instinct was correct. She was in some way distracted by the tranquility of the service.

Afterward he shut off the television and with soothing words tried to loosen her tenacious grip on wakefulness. Remarkably, she resisted. For it was clear that her desire to talk to him surmounted any physiological need to sleep.

Morning was fast approaching. The nine o'clock flight to Toronto was one of the few operating on Christmas Day, and Adam knew he had to be on it.

"Listen, my Russian friend," he said, clasping Anya's hand tightly. "I've really got to go now. I promise I'll call every morning if you promise to start believing that I'm going to work things out."

"I will try." She smiled. It was just a slight upturn of her lips, yet nonetheless an affirmation of life.

"That's my girl," he said encouragingly, and kissed her on the forehead.

"Thank you, Adam." Her smile widened. "Thank you for coming."

"Anya, darling," he whispered, "the next time you need to see me, try the telephone—it's less expensive."

Their eyes exchanged smiles.

"Daddy!"

Heather had been playing with the Rosenthal brothers in the snow in front of the cabin when she caught sight of her father approaching.

He greeted her with a loving hug. "Gosh, I missed you. I must have screwed up your Christmas, huh?"

"Not exactly," she said, but pouted. "I got my presents anyway."

"Where's Mom?" Adam inquired, trying to be nonchalant.

"With Charlie and Joyce taking a ski lesson."

"Well," he replied, "I'll just change my clothes and surprise them at the bottom of the slopes."

As he started inside, Heather called after him, "Don't hurry, Dad."

Adam turned and asked, "Why not?"

"You really did screw up *her* Christmas."

As if this were not sufficiently bad news, she added the final punctuation to his welcome by hurling a snowball—which landed square in the middle of his back.

God, he thought to himself, what the hell have I done?

Toni zoomed down the slope as if aiming straight at him and, in a flurry of snow, braked to a halt scarcely ten feet away.

For an instant neither spoke.

Finally Adam managed, "I'm back."

"I've noticed," she answered curtly.

"Did you also notice that I wasn't gone very long?"

"I was aware that you were gone," she said enigmatically, leaving him to draw his own conclusions.

"Well, the crisis is over," he announced uneasily.

She looked at him with an eyebrow raised. "Is it?"

"Toni, for God's sake, I was making what I thought was a humanitarian gesture."

"All night? I called home every half hour. So unless you booked into the Hilton, I can only conclude you were holding her hand."

"Come on," he said, raising his voice in exasperation.

"Are you crazy enough to imply what I think you're implying?"

She stopped and faced him and her words came out in tiny puffs of air.

"Adam, you don't have to physically sleep with another woman to qualify as being unfaithful."

Adam's heart began to beat faster.

She pointed a ski pole at him and pronounced, "Let's just say you're on probation."

In the following days they kept up appearances for the sake of Heather and the Rosenthals. But the tension was palpable enough to be felt by all.

However hard he tried, he could not expel Anya from his mind—even for a moment.

On the morning of their departure he woke early, hurried to the main lodge and settled their hotel bill. For if Toni paid it, she would surely see the heavy charges for long-distance phone calls to a single number in Boston.

At noon they clambered aboard Charlie's station wagon, the Rosenthals radiating health and good spirits, the Coopersmiths each in his own way knowing that somehow their lives would never be the same.

30

SANDY

THE SOCIAL high point of the year for the drones—as they were fond of calling themselves—who worked in Gregory Morgenstern's lab was the chief's Fourth of July barbecue. It was a doubly patriotic occasion, since the professor and his family lived in the town immortalized by Emerson, where the courageous American farmers "fired the shot heard 'round the world."

First they watched a re-creation of the famous Battle of Lexington, in which the younger villagers preferred to play the defeated British because of the flashy red costumes. Then all would repair to the prof's domain where, for one exceptional day, the scientists would disregard their own warnings against the cholesterol content of marbled steaks cooked over a carcinogenic charcoal fire.

Though their female roommates preferred to commemorate the original revolution by flaunting their own independence and working in the lab, Stella generously lent Vic and Sandy her four-door "shitbox."

In the huge Morgenstern garden the shots fired were strictly from the lips to the throat. After the evening fireworks, Gregory let down his rapidly receding hair and led his guests in songs from the modern American folk repertoire.

His pièce de résistance was Bob Dylan's "Blowin' in the Wind." In his inebriated state, the professor claimed that Dylan was a closet quantum physicist and the "answer, my friend," was subatomic particles.

Exacting a promise from Sandy to drive them home, Vic then proceeded on a concentrated quest to juice and seduce, giving his friend a final bit of advice: "The best place to find pliant ladies is in the satellites surrounding Judy Morgenstern."

"The Old Man's daughter?"

"Bingo," he replied. "Anyway, she's a senior at Bennington—and you know about those types."

Poor, introverted Sandy really did not know what his worldly companion was talking about. But he had an inkling.

And he found himself drawn to a circle of young people seated in the shade of an oak tree, listening to a very pretty freckle-faced guitarist with a reddish-brown ponytail. She was wearing denim cutoffs and a Beethoven T-shirt.

Gosh, Sandy thought to himself. I never imagined that a daughter of Greg Morgenstern's could be so good-looking. It almost casts doubt on genetics. I mean, if Rochelle was a goddess, this creature certainly qualified as a nymph. Too bad I don't have the guts to talk to her.

At that point the singer coughed histrionically and uttered, "Will somebody please have some pity and get this poor girl a beer?"

The normally reticent Sandy heard a cue and pounced on it.

"I'll get it," he called out.

"Thanks. Be sure to take it from the bottom, where they're really cold."

He jogged over to the refreshment area, plunged his hand into the metal garbage can that was today serving as an oversized ice bucket, withdrew a bottle of Miller Lite, and hurried back to the parched performer.

"Thanks," she murmured smiling. "You saved my life. Where's yours?"

"Oh, I forgot," he confessed with embarrassment.

Quickly offering him a sip, she suggested, "Why don't you finish mine and get us both another."

Yes, Vic's prediction had been accurate. There were several attractive girls encircling the troubadour—at least half of them unattended. But Sandy was mesmerized by the singer, not the song.

After his third trip to the watering hole, he had swallowed enough liquid courage to sit down next to her and introduce himself.

He even emulated his father's style. "Hi there. Raven's the name, Chem's the game."

"Well, Raven," she responded gaily, "do you have any requests?"

"To begin with," Sandy remarked, "it would be nice to know *your* name."

"I'm the Princess Judy," she replied. "At least of these five acres. Greg's my Dad—and even though I'm not into science, I'm still his best pal."

"I don't blame him," Sandy remarked, calling upon his prodigious memory for ancient films. "As Bogart said to Claude Rains, 'I think this is the beginning of a beautiful friendship.' "

"Oh," she said her face brightening, "are you a *Casablanca* freak too?"

"I'm afraid I'm worse than that. I'm a movie loony. My dad's in the business."

"Just what does he do?"

"He's a producer."

"What's he produced?"

"Me, for one thing." Sandy grinned. "The rest is stuff on celluloid. Actually, if I didn't want to make such a good impression on you, I'd confess that his greatest hit so far is *Godzilla Meets Hercules*."

Her jaw dropped. "You're kidding—that's my favorite bad film." And then, quickly reining herself in, she added, "I hope I didn't offend you."

"On the contrary," Sandy replied. "As my dad says, 'Put-downs are as good as Valentines, as long as you buy a ticket.' "

"I bet that helps you meet a lot of girls," she offered.

"What?"

"I guess lots of girls play up to you to get an introduction to your father."

"I wouldn't mind if *you* did," he responded.

"Not a chance." Judy strummed an angry chord. "The only thing I want to be less than a scientist is a movie star."

Sandy was thrilled. Yet suddenly feeling his confidence waning, he proposed they walk over together and get another beer.

"Suits me." She smiled, climbing to her feet. "I'm not driving."

"Me either," Sandy lied, thinking: If this girl likes me, I can *fly* home without a car.

The Morgensterns' barbecues were renowned for their liveliness and longevity. It had been late afternoon when Sandy met Judy, but all time had dissolved after that.

They chatted endlessly about movies, until it became clear that guests were finally starting to leave.

It was almost midnight as Sandy made his way toward Professor and Mrs. Morgenstern to bid them good night.

Judy took his hand and whispered, "Will I hear from you or is this just a one-night stand?"

"Who's standing?" he rejoined. "As Elizabeth Taylor said to Montgomery Clift in *A Place in the Sun*, 'Every time you leave me for a minute, it's like good-bye.' "

"Wow, you've got an unbelievable memory, Sandy. By the way, who's driving you home?"

"I am—that is, if I can find my car. In fact, I'm supposed to be taking Vic Newman."

"Not in that state, you're not," Greg Morgenstern reprimanded as they approached him.

"Yeah, I suppose you're right, Prof," Sandy conceded, his words slightly slurred. "Guess Vic'll have to drive."

"Have you seen him?" Morgenstern asked. "He's under a tree—out cold."

"I could drive them both, Dad," Judy volunteered. "I switched to coffee about two hours ago."

"But darling, you're not a good driver at the best of times," her mother interposed.

"Look at it this way," Judy explained, "I'm the only one sober enough to do the job."

"You'll be careful?" Mrs. Morgenstern insisted.

"Stay loose, Mom. In Boston people drive the same—drunk or sober. I'm used to it."

By the time they reached the house in Central

Square, Vic was ambulatory, and tactful enough to get out of the car and disappear inside.

As she turned to Sandy in the passenger seat, Judy whispered, "You're really cute, did you know that?"

"No," he replied. "I'm usually regarded as wall-flower material."

"Well, then you're an attractive wall," she responded playfully. "Anyway, stop being shy and tell me if we're going to see each other again."

"Hey, lady, this is only the first reel," Sandy answered. "We'll kiss gently and look forward to the ulti-mate clinch."

And that was precisely what they did.

The next morning, Stella was outraged by what she deemed Sandy's "sexist co-opting" of her vehicle.

"Stay loose, Stella. I'll take care of everything."

"Since when have you ever taken care of anything?" she said angrily.

Sandy did not wish to pursue this secondary matter, and proceeded to dial the Morgenstern household.

Like a nervous schoolboy—which, in a way, he was—he rehearsed his conversation, even going as far as jotting a few choice phrases on an index card.

Unfortunately, it was the prof's wife who picked up the phone: Why had he not prepared for this even-tuality! Quickly regaining his balance, he thanked her for her bounteous hospitality, and then, as casually as possible, asked, "Uh, is Judy around?"

"Yes. She's sleeping."

"Oh, in that case—"

"No," Mrs. Morgenstern cut short his demurral. "She said to wake her if you called."

Ohmigod. Then it wasn't wishful thinking, Sandy re-alized. Maybe she really *does* like me.

A moment later Judy was on the phone, her voice still slightly husky with sleep.

"Hi," she murmured.

"Hi," Sandy echoed. "I'm, uh, just calling to be sure you got back all right."

"Well, as you see, I did," she answered.

Feeling somewhat fuzzy-headed, Sandy was temporarily released from his normal inhibitions. "Judy, I had the craziest dream last night. . . ."

"Tell me," she urged. "I'm majoring in psych, so maybe I can interpret it for you."

"I had this ridiculous fantasy that I kissed you," Sandy joked. "But I guess I was imagining it, huh?"

"I'm sorry, Sandy," she responded with a pseudo-Teutonic Freudian accent. "But I must know whether this vas a pleasant experience."

"To be frank, Judy—it was wonderful. I was sorry to wake up."

"I'm glad," she responded. "By sheer coincidence, I thought of you a lot too. Only I know it wasn't a dream, 'cause I couldn't fall asleep until nearly four."

Sandy was suddenly short of breath. Never, in his twenty-two years of life, had he savoured the sublime experience of reciprocated affection.

He tried to disguise the fact that his heart was doing somersaults, and remarked matter-of-factly, "I'm afraid I have to talk business, Judy. I mean my roommate's on my back about the car and I've got to return it to her before she goes through the ozone layer. I was thinking I might bike out to your place."

"No. Actually, I planned to bring the car in and pick you up so we could have lunch."

"That sounds fine to me," Sandy responded with enthusiasm. "What time would be good for you?"

"Well," she answered, "unless you want me to drive naked, I'd better put on some clothes, and have a cup of coffee first. Is an hour okay with you?"

"Great." To which he quickly added a remark that surprised him: "And you don't have to put on clothes on my account."

* * *

She was even more attractive than Sandy remembered. Instead of ragged jeans and T-shirt, she wore a sleeveless, off-the-shoulder summer dress that plunged boldly.

They bought colossal submarine sandwiches and picnicked on the banks of the Charles.

They had scarcely been sitting for a quarter of an hour when he blurted, "When do you have to go back to school?"

She laughed. "Are you trying to get rid of me already?"

"On the contrary," he declared, "I just want to know how much time I have to snow you."

"What makes you think you haven't snowed me already?"

"Well, frankly," he confessed, "I'm not exactly Robert Redford—"

"Why are you so obsessed with external beauty?" she chided.

"Is there any other kind?"

"Maybe not in Hollywood, but there is where I come from. I mean, even if I hadn't heard my father mention you a couple of dozen times this summer, just talking to you for a few hours last night convinced me that you're smart as hell. And, if you must know . . ." She leaned closer and whispered, "I really think the sexiest part of a man is his brain."

Incredulous, Sandy thought, Jesus, I might even stand a real chance with this girl.

The sleek, white, stretch Lincoln Continental glided up to the Beverly-Wilshire Hotel. Seated in the back, wearing an ermine coat and glistening with jewels, was Kim Tower. The chauffeur hurried around and bowed as he let her out. As she walked gracefully toward the portals, the doorman greeted her with a deferential salute.

Suddenly, a pair of menacing figures appeared, each brandishing Magnum .38 revolvers.

"Okay, lady," growled the larger of the two. "This'll teach you not to play in the big leagues."

Kim had just enough time to register shock and cry out, "No! No!"

In the next instant both assassins fired. Struck in the neck and chest, Kim recoiled and fell back onto the sidewalk, rivulets of blood staining her white coat.

"My God, Sandy," Gregory Morgenstern cried out in astonishment. "They've just killed your old girlfriend."

Sprinting so fast that most of the coffee in the paper cups he was carrying splashed onto the floor, Sandy raced toward the lab table where the television, normally reserved for athletic events, had been turned to a "Movie of the Week."

"That's impossible," he protested. "They were just showing the titles when I left."

"I'm sorry," Greg commiserated. "It doesn't look like she had a very big role."

"Did she at least get to say something?" Sandy asked with disappointment.

"Just a couple of words," Morgenstern answered. "And then a kind of last gasp before she hit the deck."

"That's all? Just a lousy walk-on?"

"Well," his teacher jested amiably, "*I'd* call it more of a 'die-on.' But I tell you, she looked like a million bucks."

"Damn it," Sandy railed. "She must have gotten typecast. I mean it always looked like whenever they had a part where someone croaked they gave it to her. I'm telling you, *that's* what killed her career before she had a chance to prove herself."

"Well, show business isn't my area of expertise," the scientist replied. "Why don't we get the electrophoresis under way and then call your father on the university's penny?"

Sandy nodded, and the two men used pipettes to place droplets of silver-stained gel into the small squares at the end of what looked like a miniature, clear plastic bowling-alley. They then placed the closed tray into a small tank and turned on the electrodes, which activated the migration of particles.

"Mind if I join you, Sandy?" Morgenstern asked. "I'd like to take five on the couch. I promise I won't listen."

"Well, Greg," Sandy retorted with a grin, "it's only your office, so I guess you're entitled."

Morgenstern kicked off his shoes and stretched out on the couch, opening the latest issue of *Cell* and placing it over his face as Sandy dialed Hollywood.

"Good to hear from you, sonny boy," Sidney Raven chimed. "How's life in the lab?"

"Fine, Dad. I—"

"Hey," his father interrupted, "I just looked at the time. It's late as hell back East. Why aren't you in bed—alone or otherwise?"

Sandy blushed inwardly and prayed that Gregory Morgenstern was really napping. Having long since acquired the techniques of Hollywood hype, Sidney always shouted on the phone for emphasis.

"Dad, I've just watched the CBS 'Movie of the Week'—"

"Yeah," his father commented, "that South American drug caper. We passed on it."

"Did you know that Rochelle was one of the guest stars?"

"Of course, I read *Variety* every day. That was the last picture she made before her contract ended."

"Well, how come her part was so small?"

"Jeez, you're starting to talk like her agent. But to give you an answer in a nutshell, her Q-ratings were lower than the Dead Sea."

"God, that's terrible, Dad."

"On the contrary, kiddo. She retired before rigor mortis set in," Sidney consoled him. "Anyway, I wouldn't worry about that young lady. Not only is she taking

over the Story Department, just as she predicted, but
she's also dating Elliot Victor, the head of Paragon.

"It looks like her next career move will be a quickie
Mexican divorce from Lex—and another trip to the al-
tar. Now tell me about you. Have you got a girlfriend
yet?"

Sandy glanced furtively over at the couch where
Morgenstern appeared sound asleep.

"I can't talk now," he said as softly as possible. "But
I think I'm in love."

"Great," his father cheered. "Now maybe you'll get
your mind off Ms. Tower and have a normal relationship.
Tell me about her."

"Dad," his son replied, "she's so nice, I can't understand why she would settle for a guy like me."

"Hey," his father chastened, "where's your confidence? As Clark said to Vivien in *Gone With the Wind*,
'With enough courage, you can do without a reputation.' How far do you want to go with this girl?"

"I don't know what you mean," Sandy answered,
hoping his father did not mean what he feared he
meant.

"Is it someone you're serious about?"

"Could be. It's fairly possible."

"Then marry her before she gets away."

"Don't you think I'm a bit young for that?"

"You're never too young if it's the right woman,"
Sidney counseled. "Then you've got to reach for the
brass ring and grab it. Otherwise," he finished wistfully,
"you'll end up like me."

31

ADAM

THE DOCTORS were anxious to discharge Anya Avilov—not least because her medical insurance was running out.

From the second of January, Adam had visited her every day during his lunch break. Though he agreed that she was strong enough to cope with the outside world, he had misgivings about letting her go back alone to the dingy, cramped apartment in Watertown.

The psychiatrists overruled him. But at least he convinced them to delay her release until Saturday—which enabled him to take her home.

The Coopersmiths were having Sunday brunch with the Rosenthals. As Joyce and Toni studied the new fashions in the magazine section of the *New York Times* and *Boston Globe*, and the kids were in the den watching "The Mark of Zorro" on TV, Charlie convinced Adam to go out for a walk.

The moment the two men were alone, Rosenthal demanded, "What the hell's wrong with you?"

"Nothing, nothing," Adam insisted. Yet his feelings about Anya were raging within him, and he had to tell someone for the sake of his sanity.

"Listen, you know I'm not bullshitting when I tell you that in all the years Toni and I've been married, I never so much as looked at another woman."

"I know, I know," his friend cut him off. "But have you done anything more than look at Anya Avilov?"

"Who told you—"

"Schmuck!" His friend exploded. "Have you forgotten I'm the guy you referred her to? The second day we were back from Canada, I had a patient in prodromal at the Lying-In. Since I had a couple of hours to kill, I walked down the block to visit Anya. She was in surprisingly good humor, and it only took me about three seconds to realize that it wasn't the effect of the medication, but a visit from you at lunchtime."

Adam felt trapped, but he was anxious to know more. "What exactly did she say?"

"Oh, nothing compromising," his colleague answered with an amused smile. "She just wouldn't stop talking about you. I mean, she thinks you're a combination of Dr. Schweitzer and Warren Beatty."

"Don't joke," Adam responded with annoyance. "I'm serious."

"You don't seem serious to me," Charlie countered with disapproval. "I mean this isn't teen time, baby. You're an adult with grown-up responsibilities."

"I know, I know," Adam said, his voice full of pain. "Honest to God, Charlie, I adore Heather—and I still love Toni. It's only that . . ."

"You love Anya more," his friend concluded sarcastically.

Adam looked helplessly at Charlie, asking without words what his friend thought he should do.

"Well, Coopersmith, you might go to Saudi Arabia and become a Moslem, which would even give you two more conjugal slots to fill. Or you can take the only decent way out."

There was a sanctimonious tone in Charlie's voice that began to irritate Adam. "What makes this whole complicated mess so simple to you?" he lashed back in annoyance.

Charlie replied with quiet sympathy. "For the very

reason that I'm *not* involved. I can look at this objectively. And it's clear that you don't have any real choice."

"How can you say that? Dammit, Rosenthal, don't you see I've got to choose between two women?"

His friend stopped walking and grabbed him by the shoulders. "Two women, yes," he acknowledged. "But only *one* kid. You've got to think about Heather."

"Do you seriously imagine that I don't? The very thought of leaving her breaks my heart."

"So de-infatuate yourself with this Russian woman."

"It's not that easy. What's supposed to happen to Anya?"

"Whatever would have happened if you hadn't gotten involved. She's not the first decent woman to get a raw deal from a lousy husband. But from what I know of her as a patient, there's an inner core of real strength. She'll brush up her English and pass the damn qualifying exams." His voice grew louder, as if competing with the cold, harsh wind that was now blowing in their faces. "She'll be all right, Coopersmith."

"Can't I make you understand?" Adam said in desperation, "I'm in love with her."

"No, dammit," Charlie shouted back. "You *pity* her. That's not the same."

Adam was furious. "Just for a minute, suppose this were happening to you—"

"But it *wouldn't*," Charlie said cutting him off. "It *couldn't*. For the simple reason that no matter how beautiful the woman was, how terrible her circumstances, I have my priorities. My job is bringing kids into the world. I know how fragile they are. If I had it my way, this sort of behavior would be classified as a crime."

Then the two were silent, gusts chilling them as they stood there unmoving.

Finally, Adam asked helplessly, "What if I can't break it off?"

"I'll help you."

"What if I still can't?"

Charlie paused and then stated categorically, "In that case, I *won't* help you."

By now, the compulsion to see her was so great that Adam sped to Watertown just to be with her for a few minutes, his behavior bordering on recklessness.

In the mere twenty-four hours since he had last seen her, Anya looked as if she had begun to grasp the tiller of her life. Charlie was right. The young Russian woman had enormous resilience.

Wearing jeans and a maroon turtleneck, she was busily cleaning the house when he arrived. To his amazement, there were even half a dozen books on the shelf that earlier had been totally empty. They ranged from a biochemistry text to English for foreigners, and from Julia Child to a campus love story.

"Where did you get these?" Adam asked.

"As usual, I was up at dawn," she answered with a smile. "Maybe it is a good thing there are no curtains yet, because the sun awakened me. I had tea and walked all the way to Harvard Square. It is a wonderful place—nothing ever closes. Musicians were playing and the bookstores were full of people."

"Good for you," Adam said with admiration.

"On the way home I went into Star Market and bought croissants . . . in case you came. Would you like one now with a cup of coffee?"

"Yeah, that'd be nice."

As he sat down in the armchair, he noticed a Russian periodical on the weather-beaten table by the couch.

"What's the paper?" he called out.

"*Pravda,*" she replied from inside the kitchen. "I was surprised to find such a recent issue."

"Did it make you homesick?"

"No," Anya declared as she reappeared carrying a tray. "In fact it cheered me up immensely. Here in

America newspapers also do not tell the truth, but at least you have a choice of liars."

She sat down on the far side of the sofa, placing the food on the low table.

As he reached for a pastry, Adam could not help but notice the color in her cheeks.

"I'm glad to see you in such a good mood," he commented. Then, at a loss for neutral topics to discuss, he inquired, "Have you thought of going back to work—when you're ready, I mean?"

"Oh, I'm a little tired, but I feel I'm psychologically ready now. The only problem is . . ." She did not have to finish the phrase.

Adam voiced her thoughts. "Surely you still can't want to go back to Dmitri's lab."

"Yes," she replied, her anger rising. "I want him to see that he is not so all-powerful that he could make me disappear."

"To what purpose?" Adam asked. "Hatred is such an unproductive feeling."

She sighed. "I suppose you are right. But what else can I do? It was only Dmitri's influence that got me a job in the first place."

"Well, I've got a little influence of my own. And I'd like you to come and work in our lab."

"But I know nothing about immunology," she protested, trying to mask her elation.

"You're a medical doctor. You already know the basics. It's just a question of diving in at the deep end of the pool. It'd take guts, but we both know you've got plenty of that."

Her eyes were now sparkling. She broke into what was indisputably a smile as he concluded, "And, of course, if you get into trouble, I'll always be there to keep you afloat. Now, how does that sound?"

"It sounds lovely." Her dark eyes radiated affection.

"Good. When do you think you'll feel strong enough to begin?"

"I know you would want me to say tomorrow, and that is what my heart says too. But I do not want to look like an idiot before your colleagues. So if you could possibly give me a week—and some proper textbooks . . ."

"Done," Adam agreed, and then fought the urge to put his arms around her.

It would be wrong now, when she was still weak and groggy.

"I'm afraid it's getting late," he murmured lamely. "I mean, I have a family."

"Yes," she agreed, "it is good that we both remember that."

32
ISABEL

ISABEL WAS making such splendid progress on her master's thesis that Raymond paroled her for a brief Christmas return to San Diego. To her elation, she was able to get home in time to watch Edmundo conduct Handel's *Messiah* with the University Orchestra and Chorus.

Perhaps it was an illusion created by the gray December weather, but to Isabel her stepfather seemed somewhat pale.

"It's just fatigue," Muriel explained when mother and daughter were talking at breakfast the next morning. "Edmundo has gone through hell with this production. Two weeks before the performance, the baritone soloist left to sing *The Marriage of Figaro* in Chicago. If Edmundo hadn't been able to cajole José Mauro to come out of retirement and fly in from Argentina, we'd probably have had to cancel the whole concert."

Since Muriel had badgered her to remember her promise, Isabel diligently brought her violin and, on Christmas Eve, the Zimmers had a real soirée musicale. Francisco Zimmer, while not a professional, had become a fairly accomplished pianist. And Dorotea bravely took up the cello, having for a time played in the Buenos Aires Symphony.

Despite his handicap, Edmundo could, as he put it, "at least make a tolerable noise" on all of the stringed instruments. Now that Isabel had joined them, the happy family gathered around the Christmas table as a piano quintet—with one spectator.

As Peter joked, "When I was growing up, a conspicuous failure at every instrument, Mom taught me that *somebody* has to be in the audience. I've developed my claps and bravos to a virtuoso standard."

Indeed, the evening was so joyful that it made Isabel feel pangs of sadness that Raymond had been left to celebrate on his own.

December 28
Naturally, I would never tell Dad that this was the happiest Christmas I ever spent in my life. Though I had some intermittent qualms about him being on his own, I rationalized that he was being well looked after by the Prachts, who had invited him over.

When I asked him on the way home from the airport how their celebration had been, he confessed that he had called Karl and canceled at the last moment. He mumbled something about having felt under the weather when he woke up that morning.

But I think he was afraid to face Jerry, who might have given him some subtle—or maybe not so subtle— heat about "keeping his little bird locked in her cage," as he once said on the phone.

But then of course there was the chance that Dad's

*illness really wasn't psychosomatic. He's been kind of
lax on the jogging lately, and he's put on weight. Most
mornings he just walks me to the track and waits while
I do my laps.*

*I can't help feeling guilty at not having been there.
Yet I somehow sense there was a part of him that
wanted me to feel that way.*

Isabel's remorse for having abandoned her father during
the holidays was magnified when she learned that he
had spent the time cleaning up her computer—
organizing the interim results of some of the experiments she was doing on the Fifth Force.

Ray tried to downplay his sacrifice, lightheartedly
insisting, "That's my job." Indeed, he seemed to have
slaved nonstop, for he had also spent hours in the library, photocopying everything he could find on Lóránt
Eötvös's publications.

"Gosh, Dad," she said gratefully, "in return for all
you've done, I'm going to wash all the dishes myself
for the next year."

"Come on, Isabel, I was just a simple gofer. All these
theoretical physics types based their work on the experiments of this unpronounceable Hungarian. But there's
no question that the guy was a major figure at the beginning of this century. His work on gravity provided
one of the major principles of Einstein's General Theory of Relativity."

"Well, he's certainly the flavor of the month—at least
in our lab," Isabel agreed. "Everybody seems to be getting on the bandwagon—although I think Karl has a
definite game plan. He agrees with Eötvös's argument
that the gravitational force depends on the baryon
number of the material. Now, if that's true—and Karl is
pretty sure it is at short distances—that really cuts the
grass from under Einstein's principle of equivalency."

Just watching his extraordinary daughter walk

surefootedly through the labyrinth of complex thought made Raymond beam.

"I don't know if Karl is helping me, or vice versa," Isabel rushed on, "I mean, he's given me some of those experiments to repeat. And of course if my data matches his, that will make him the king of the hill."

"It's called paying your dues," Raymond commented sagely. "You'll do his spade work, he'll get the credit, and then—if I'm any judge of the man at all—he'll find a way to pay you back."

"Just working next to him is reward enough," she replied with equanimity. "Besides, I'm not the only player on his team. The key to the whole theory is to prove that gravitational force isn't constant.

"So would you believe that Karl has gotten two of his graduate students working down a mine in Montana? And another two taking the same measurements on top of the Transamerica Pyramid in San Francisco? Their results ought to come through any day now. Karl can hardly wait."

"Yes," Raymond allowed. "And I bet those miners didn't stop work for Christmas."

Isabel felt a stab of remorse. "You know something?" she confessed. "I'm feeling so bad about it that I wish I could go to the lab right now."

"Why not?" Ray reacted eagerly. "I'll drive you over. After all, science never sleeps, so why should scientists?"

December 29

By the time I'd spent two hours with Dad, the sparkling colors I thought I had perceived in Mom's house had faded into a monochrome gray memory.

There's no greater joy than a carnival of intellect, and I spent the hours of last night and all today in the lab, running new experiments that I worked out to test the Fifth Force hypothesis.

The Prachts had never been known as party-givers, so, when they decided to throw a big New Year's open house, tongues began to wag. The corridors buzzed with rumors that MIT had finally signed him up and his gathering was, as one wag put it, a "fête accompli." This conjecture was certainly supported by the professor's extraordinarily high spirits.

Ray had misgivings about their attending the celebration. It would be difficult, if not impossible, to keep young Jerry from at least a minimal social contact with his daughter.

Jerry himself was in a state of anticipatory ecstasy, oblivious to the dozens of guests already present, his eyes fixed unswervingly on the front door, waiting for Isabel to arrive. The moment he caught sight of her, he moved through the crowd like a broken field runner.

The elder Pracht started the New Year with an act of paternal complicity. He locked Raymond in conversation, keeping him a prisoner of politeness while his tennis-playing son attempted to pursue his infatuation with the pretty scientific genius.

"Hey, Isa, you can't imagine how desperate I am to see you. D'you know what number I am now?"

"As a matter of fact, I do." She smiled. "In less than half a year you've broken into the top fifty. . . ."

"And if I make the quarter finals tomorrow, which is the only reason I'm staying sober, I'll jump thirty places. *And* if you come and watch me play, I might even be inspired to win."

"Come on Jerry, you know I have . . . previous commitments."

The young man sighed in frustration. "God, Isa. You're going to slow down my career, do you know that?"

"What do you mean?"

"I mean I'll have to wait till you're eighteen so I can take you to watch me play at Wimbledon. And you've got to tell me before your father interrupts this conversation whether you'll come if I wait."

A strange new thought for New Year's Eve—one that had never struck Isabel before. The notion of being grown-up and an adult, free to follow her emotions instead of just her curriculum.

"Say, do you think your dad would go ballistic if we took a walk in the garden to look at the view? It's absolutely breathtaking."

Isabel surprised even herself by answering, "Why don't we go before he can stop us?"

To her right she noticed the outline of a wooden shack, with a long, conical shape protruding from its roof.

"Is that your observatory?" she asked.

"Yeah," he answered. "It's now known as the Darius Miller Memorial Planetarium. I want you to spend the night with me there sometime—with your dad, of course. But before he can find us . . ."

Isabel glanced over her shoulder and saw Raymond still deep in conversation with Karl Pracht.

Suddenly, Jerry's fingers were enlaced with hers, which caused a little tingle at the back of her neck. She walked quickly with him to the edge of the garden, and they stood there, gazing down at the lights of San Francisco.

"Isn't it terrific?" Jerry exclaimed. "Look, you can even see the harbor, way over there."

For all her mighty vocabulary, the best Isabel could respond with was a monosyllabic, "Wow."

"I think Karl is crazy to give all this up for MIT, don't you?" Jerry whispered.

"You mean it's definite?" Isabel asked, unable to conceal her feeling of disappointment at the possible departure of the Pracht family.

Ignoring her question, Jerry turned to face her and murmured, "Isa, I can't wait any longer. I'm going to kiss you."

She remained silent and motionless.

"Thank you," he said gently.

"What for?" she asked.

"For trusting me enough not to run away."

Thus, at twenty-five minutes before midnight on the last day of the year, Isabel da Costa let Jerry Pracht take her into his arms and press his lips to hers.

She so enjoyed it that she lost all sense of time. For all she knew, it might have been several minutes. And a little tingle became a full-fledged shiver down her spine.

"What's wrong?" Jerry murmured.

Isabel wanted to say nothing was wrong. Feeling as though she was about to drown in emotion, she reached out and grasped onto reality to save herself. "Jerry, we've got to stop. My father will find us."

"So?" he murmured with defiance. "What we're doing is perfectly innocent. *Not* doing it would be abnormal."

Instinctively, Isabel knew he was right. But she was suddenly afraid. She was not sure whether it was fear of being discovered by her father, or her own growing ambivalence about her cloistered life.

She tried to break away, and he let go of her. As she hurried toward the house, he addressed her from a few paces behind.

"May I call you?"

"No," she said without turning.

"Will you call me?" he persisted.

For a moment she did not reply, and then, for an instant, she stopped, looked over her shoulder, and answered, "Yes."

33

SANDY

IN THE history of champagne, the most unusual bottles ever used were those reportedly made of genuine crystal and supplied to Czar Alexander II by his French purveyor, Louis Roederer. That is until the fall of 1975, when torrents of fine champagne were served in large laboratory flagons to the crowd of well-wishers gathered in David Baltimore's lab at MIT to celebrate the announcement that he had just won the Nobel Prize for discoveries concerning the interaction between tumor viruses and the genetic material of the cell.

Naturally, all the teams from the neighboring labs were invited to join the festivities.

As one would have expected, the moment the prize was announced on the radio, Greg Morgenstern immediately sprang into action. He phoned Sandy to meet him at Martignetti's Wine Store to help schlep the bubbly—a magnum of which he paid for out of his own pocket.

He also outsped all the other famous MIT professors, including the many Nobelists, and was the first visitor to congratulate the thirty-seven-year-old wunderkind.

After the celebration, as they were walking back to their own domain, Sandy remarked to Morgenstern, "I bet we'll be drinking to you someday soon."

"No," the older man replied. "Not a chance."

"But Greg, you're close as hell to synthesizing that

protein. Take my word for it, you'll be in the history books too."

"Sandy," his mentor responded, "I wish you'd stop referring to me as a one-man band. If I hadn't been lucky enough to find the other young Turks—especially you—I'd still be miles away."

Though he had not revealed it, Sandy had been deeply affected by his father's inability to establish a suitable new relationship. Neither of his parents, he sometimes reflected, would have qualified for passage on Noah's Ark. Even Sidney, who was a professional success, had been a personal failure. He would love to have a woman of his own, but unfortunately it was never the same one. And Sandy was convinced that he had confused his priorities.

True, Greg was not a giant in his profession, at least not yet. But he had a devoted family who worshiped him like a hero. Wasn't this the most important aspect of life?

Thus Sandy fell in love not merely with the Morgensterns' daughter, but with their values. Their sense of togetherness.

It was a heady new experience for him to join a happy cohesive family for occasions like Thanksgiving dinner, Christmas punch, and New Year's Eve. All of them—Greg, his wife Ruth, as well as Judy—opened their home and their hearts to him.

It took Sandy much longer to realize that Judy's feelings were, to an enormous extent, influenced by her father's admiration for him. Greg Morgenstern had never felt so strongly, spoken so rhapsodically, of a scientific mind—even a senior colleague's. It was never mentioned specifically, but it was clear beyond any doubt that the greatest gift she could give her father was Sandy Raven as a son-in-law.

Independence Day became a double celebration on their calendar: not only the declaration of American autonomy, but the anniversary of the first meeting of Sandy and Judy, who by this time were living together in Cambridge without benefit of clergy.

At first, when they discussed the possible housing arrangement, Sandy was worried about the effect it might have on his professional relationship with Greg. But she reassured him.

"The other day he told me he loved you so much, that if we hadn't gotten together, he would have adopted you."

If Gregory Morgenstern possessed a flaw, it seemed to be an almost fanatic sense of honesty. When a high-powered biotech company lured away his second-in-command, he insisted upon going through an elaborate selection process—even soliciting letters from other faculty members—so he could make the choice with his head, not merely his heart.

When Sandy finally received the seal of approval, he felt at once honored and exasperated. Greg was so maddeningly egalitarian that every paper coming out of their lab listed its authors not in order of rank, but alphabetically. It was almost as if Morgenstern had an aversion to eminence.

Sandy theorized that this was what drew Greg to the urgent yet scientifically unpopular scourge of liver cancer: he would be left alone.

The liver is the largest—and the busiest—organ in the human body. Not only does it metabolize carbohydrates, fats, and proteins, it also detoxifies the blood, filters its impurities, produces helpful clotting factors, and destroys exhausted red blood cells. Clearly, since it does so much, if it should be impaired, the body would be in grave danger.

There were many theoretical "cures" for hepatic cancer, the most obvious being transplants. But this was obviously impossible on a large scale, especially in areas where the disease had reached epidemic proportions.

Greg was leading a biochemical quest into uncharted territory. Since cancers occur when the usual checks and balances of cell growth cease to function, he hoped to produce an artificial protein that would restore the damaged gene to normal functioning.

Their "patients" were mice. More specifically, humanoid rodents developed in Max Rudolph's laboratory at Harvard.

"Dad never explained to me why you guys always use little Mickeys and Minnies instead of more grown-up species," Judy remarked over dinner.

"I know it doesn't seem to make sense," Sandy replied. "But a quirk of nature made those creatures' systems more like ours than some primates'. By contrast, guinea pigs are completely different. Did you know that if they had been chosen for the first penicillin tests, we might never have had antibiotics? Because—for some strange reason—at certain times of the year, even small doses can simply *kill* them."

"Wow," Judy reacted. "That was a close call. Now, how about you guys—is it a state secret or are you near anything resembling paydirt?"

"It's funny, I'm so close to the stuff, I find that question impossible to answer. But if it's any indication, a film crew from 'Nova' is visiting the lab tomorrow. Maybe they're getting some vibes."

"Super, be sure to wear your lenses. Would it be okay if I came and watched? I really like the way Dad fields all those difficult questions and explains them so ordinary people can understand. And I can be sure your hair's properly combed."

"Great," Sandy enthused. "You could even do my part of the interview, since you're so much better-looking."

By the time Judy arrived the next morning, a large WGBH van was parked in front of the lab, two wheels up on the sidewalk, its cables reaching through the front door like electronic tentacles.

Inside, separate film crews were at work. One camera was set up in Morgenstern's office, interviewing Greg as he spoke of his altruistic motives in attacking the liver cancer problem. Meanwhile, Sandy was leading the other camera on a tour of the rest of the plant, introducing the teams and the technology.

As he spoke, various techs could be seen in the background, performing different tasks like loading up the PCR machine, a device that "photocopied" individual segments of DNA in a heated test tube, and scurrying to and fro to check the contents of petri dishes under the various microscopes.

Though he too had an office, Sandy preferred to sit at a desk where the action was. "I like to be as close as possible to my hardware." He smiled to the lens.

From off camera the producer, a frizzy-haired girl in jeans, fed him questions.

Sandy first tried to explain to the lay audience how DNA carries the genetic code. Then how they were working with it.

"There's also a particular protein that acts something like a traffic cop. It supervises the cell division, and if something begins to go wrong, it can stop it immediately.

"Now, little mutations happen all the time, but they're usually not dangerous. The one thing we worry about is if the duplication goes crazy and starts to grow cancer cells."

"What exactly are you and Dr. Morgenstern doing?" she asked.

"We've analyzed tissue from different cases of liver carcinoma and found that in every instance a specific area of this protein was damaged. Obviously, if we can fix it, we might repair the disease."

"You make it sound so easy, Doctor."

"Oh, there's nothing radical about the *theory*—it's the actual realization that's so tough. We have to evolve a drug that will cause the 'folded' parts to flip back so the cell can resume its normal shape and function."

At this point, he had reached a large computer monitor at the SUN computer work station. The camera zoomed to a close shot of the screen as Sandy continued to explain.

"Our X-ray crystallography unit is helping us to determine the makeup of the protein. We have a multiwire proportional chamber that sends the structure pattern straight to the computer. Someday we may get our solution quite literally on television."

"Are you optimistic, Dr. Raven?" the producer asked.

"Let's put it this way. When you're searching for a molecule in a mountain, you've either got to be very optimistic—or very crazy. I'd say I was a little of both."

"You were cool," Judy declared when the filming was complete and they were walking arm in arm to lunch. "And I'm really happy Dad's finally getting some recognition for all his unsung labor."

"Yeah," Sandy agreed. "And if this thing pays off, I'm afraid Greg will be inflicted with honors, probably even a Nobel. Do you think he'd like that?"

She looked at him with a gleam in her eye. "Not as much as the other project you've helped develop."

"What are you talking about?"

"I'm talking about being pregnant." She smiled. "By the way, does that make you happy?"

"Yes and no," Sandy answered, his cheeks flushed. "I mean, I love babies—but I don't believe in unwed mothers. Are you willing to do something about it?"

"Oh, what the hell," she replied blithely. "I'll bow to convention and go legal. What about high noon tomorrow at City Hall? That'll give us time to get the blood tests."

"As a matter of principle, your father never takes a lunch break," Sandy warned.

"Yeah," Judy acknowledged, "but I somehow think in this case he'll make an exception."

34
ADAM

IN THE past, Adam had always succeeded in discharging his duties as a parent by tearing himself away from the lab to be at home for dinner. There, he showed a genuine interest in his daughter's homework and waited until she was planted at her computer—and a telephone—before returning to work.

Knowing Toni would herself be buried in her upstairs office at least until the eleven o'clock news, it had long been Adam's practice to call about ten-thirty to give her some indication of whether he was running out of strength, or had been sufficiently inspired to spend an all-nighter.

Lately his inspiration seemed to be in high gear. Not only did Adam stay out till dawn, he was sometimes too carried away to phone and forewarn his wife.

Charlie Rosenthal, the innocent if concerned bystander, thought Adam was "living like an ostrich."

Adam lowered his head. "Maybe," he murmured. "I just need time to work things out."

"Come on, I think you've been living on borrowed time already. Do you honestly believe Toni doesn't suspect? I mean, suppose she suddenly dropped into the lab and saw Anya working there?"

"She's never seen Anya," Adam interrupted quickly.

"Well, considering the girl hangs around you like a

necklace, it wouldn't take her more than fifteen seconds to figure out what was going on. Besides, Adam, you've never screwed around before. Adultery just isn't your scene. Something in you wants this to come out in the open." Charlie's voice took on an almost conspiratorial tone. "Have you got any contacts in Hawaii?"

"What?"

"I'm serious. Let's get a copy of the *Medical Directory* and see if we can come up with somebody who might give Anya Avilov a job."

"But why?" Adam protested, trying a new strategy to evoke his friend's sympathy. "Have you ever thought of *her* feelings?"

"Yes," Rosenthal admitted. "But when you consider that one of your options will definitely mess up at least three people's lives—and since I know how crazy you are about your daughter—I'd say you have to go for the greater good."

"You're talking like a cold-blooded scientist," Adam snapped.

"And you, my dear professor, are talking like a hotheaded moron. Of all the times in your life, this is when you should be most objective and analytic. *Let Avilov go.* Let her go where she really has a shot at starting over."

He paused and then, with a tinge of suspicion, added, "Or are you also starting to feel possessive about her research talents?"

"Don't be ridiculous."

"Come on—you yourself told me she's learning immunology like a whiz kid. Even coming up with ideas of her own. If you didn't keep leaning on her to work in the lab, she'd have more time to study and requalify as the doctor she already is."

"Dammit, you're implying that I'm a selfish shit."

"You are," Charlie stated curtly. "And you're on the slippery slope to disaster."

* * *

Adam had been jolted by Charlie Rosenthal's blunt admonitions. During the weeks that followed, he exercised superhuman self-restraint. Though they resumed their Wednesday night telephone conversations, he did not visit Anya. He did not even invite himself along when she went with other members of the staff to the cafeteria for a quick lunch. And yet he sensed that with every look at her, his resistance was eroding.

Anya, herself consumed with guilt, was convinced that she deserved no more. And accepted that though her moments of intimacy with Adam had been the happiest of her life, they were now definitely at an end.

It had been nearly two months since Anya Avilov had begun working in Adam Coopersmith's immunology lab. Naturally, she had started with tasks as menial as washing test tubes, preparing animals, and the like. But she was a quick study and assimilated scientific material at an astonishing pace. In less than a month she was promoted to the data section, collating the results of various experiments on a computer that would thereafter be hers alone.

It was nearly seven o'clock on a Wednesday evening, in the depth of winter darkness, when Adam noticed her closing up for the day, shuffling papers into a folder to work on that night. In an instant he was at her side, his own coat draped over his arm.

"How are you getting home, Anya?" he asked as casually as he could.

"The usual way," she replied. "Number sixty-six to Harvard Square, and then the seventy-one, which takes me practically to my doorstep."

"That sounds worse than a forced march to me," Adam remarked. "Why don't you let me give you a lift? It's practically on my way. Besides, it's dark and cold and the streets are icy."

She pondered for a moment and then smiled. "I'd be very grateful."

He was silent during the first part of the ride, stealing

occasional glances at his passenger. She seemed shy and reticent, but more beautiful and desirable than ever. He knew he could not simply drop her off.

As they were nearing Watertown Square, he inquired, "Have you got time for a quick bite?"

She hesitated for a moment and then asked deliberately, "Have you?"

"Uh, yes. My wife's in Washington today."

Anya made one further halfhearted attempt to discourage him. "That means your daughter must eat—"

He tried not to think of Heather, for whom Wednesday dinner was special since she had him to herself. Suppressing his qualms, he responded, "I can just give the housekeeper a call ... she's used to my coming home from the lab at all hours."

Anya smiled. "In that case, why don't we go by the market and I will buy a few things and make something simple."

The apartment seemed to have undergone a metamorphosis, with new living room wallpaper matching new curtains. There was a large, cheery Miró poster, its bright colors clearly reflecting the purchaser's change of mood.

And the bookshelf was nearly full.

Since there was still a shortage of furniture, they were forced to sit cross-legged on the floor and eat from the coffee table.

At first conversation was awkward.

"How's your work going?"

"I love it." She smiled. "Your main project is very exciting. How could anyone have ever imagined that simple progesterone could have such immunosuppressive effects?"

"Actually, the drug's been around for so long, the medical community's kind of taken it for granted," Adam commented. "Back in 'seventy-three, a Paraguayan doctor named Csapo ran a pretty cruel experiment. He had removed the ovaries from women at various stages of pregnancy, and demonstrated that those who had them taken out after nine weeks could still carry their babies to term—though unfortunately for the last time."

"That's terrible," she sympathized. "But it does prove why your progesterone therapy is only needed for the first trimester."

"Maybe," he acknowledged. "But there is still the remote possibility of side effects. So I won't be home free until I synthesize it—then maybe rearrange the molecules. I hope the work they've given you isn't boring."

"On the contrary," she countered with fervor, "It's an education just being in a room with so many creative people. Even the brief time I spent with Dmitri's colleagues in the academy taught me to distinguish a mind that's not merely good, but great. And you, Adam, are the most brilliant person I've ever met."

He smiled. "Well, while we're dishing out compliments, even though we've only worked together for a few weeks, I can tell you have wonderful scientific intuition."

She blushed. "You flatter me."

"It's still true," he insisted. "And another thing," he continued, moving closer to her, locking her eyes with his own gaze. "I love you, Anya."

"And I love you," she responded. "But what can we do about it?"

"We can give in to our feelings. We've been apart too long—I can't bear it anymore."

She did not try to move away as he took her in his arms, though there was a split second during which she had to let down the last of her defenses.

The hours they spent together in the tiny Watertown apartment were the most blissful Adam had ever experienced. It was not only that he filled a desperate void in her life, but he was also enthralled by her indescribable maternal quality, which satisfied a need he had never acknowledged before.

He had now crossed the Rubicon.

Late one Sunday afternoon, he reluctantly left Anya's embrace and, as he dressed himself, murmured, "I can't go on like this."

"Adam," she whispered, "believe me, I understand. If you told me this was the last time we would see each other, I would grieve. But I would accept it."

He turned and said passionately, "No, Anya, it's just the opposite. My life has boiled down to a single desire—to spend the rest of it with you."

As he walked slowly down the porch steps, the icy weather awakened both the inner and the outer man. It made him realize that he was a moral coward. Counterbalancing the resolve he had so bravely displayed before Anya was the fear of hurting his family. And saying what now had to be said.

As he was putting his key in the lock of his car door, Adam heard the persistent ringing of his cellular telephone. He clambered in and grabbed it.

"This is Dr. Coopersmith," he gasped, lungs burning from the cold.

"Where in God's name are you?"

It was Toni, in a fury.

He stalled for time by saying, "Take it easy, I'm on my way back."

Toni ignored his reply and fulminated. "Heather waited in the cold for nearly an hour."

"Heather?"

"Yes, Adam. You may remember taking your daughter to ice-skate this afternoon. You were supposed to meet her outside the Watson Rink at four. I don't know what time zone you're in, buddy, but my watch says nearly six o'clock. You claimed you were going to the lab while she skated," Toni went on. "I called but nobody had even seen you. So I got into the car and picked her up myself.

"Don't try to fabricate an excuse. Tell me the truth. It can't be worse than what I'm thinking. What the hell have you been doing?"

This jolted him into breaking silence. "Toni," he mumbled hoarsely, "we've got to talk."

"Okay, talk."

"No—not like this. Face-to-face."

"Adam, don't take me for a total fool," she stormed. "I know there's someone else in your life. And since she seems to have such a hold on you that you'd let your own daughter freeze to death, you'd better stay away."

Her sudden silence puzzled him, until he could discern her weeping softly. At last she managed to say, "Just tell me where to send it."

"Send wh-what?" he asked with a slight stammer.

"The subpoena, dammit," she raged through her tears. "I'm calling the best divorce lawyer in our firm to have him nail you to the wall."

"Don't I even get a chance to speak in my own defense?"

"Of course, Adam," she replied bitterly. "As soon as the court fixes a date."

He hung up in a state of shock, swept off his feet by the cyclone of Toni's justifiable anger. And yet he also felt a curious relief, because he would no longer be preoccupied in trying to find the courage to tell his wife.

But now something terrible overwhelmed all other thoughts: Oh God, Heather. How could I do this to you?

35

ISABEL

January 1

Jerry kissed me.

I confess it's something I had often dreamed about but never thought would really happen. For a second I was so scared I was kind of dumb. I could scarcely feel the pressure—I should say gentle touching—of his lips.

All the time I was so terrified that Dad might see us that I couldn't react at all. Jerry must have thought I was a total innocent.

Actually I am, because no one's ever taught me how to kiss. And yet after another moment, I realized that if your feelings about the person are strong, the rest comes naturally. And though our whole embrace might have taken thirty milliseconds—or even nanoseconds—by the end of it I was no longer a neophyte.

I suddenly ceased worrying about my father and kissed Jerry back. It was the loveliest moment of my life. I only wonder when I'll ever get a chance to repeat it.

As we quickly walked back toward the house, I saw Dad standing outside the back door and waved casually at him.

Still, for all my efforts to hide my emotions, I wondered if my face would show any telltale signs of what had happened. Would he notice that I was just a tiny bit unsteady on my feet?

But he didn't seem annoyed or anything. He just mut-

*tered very calmly, "I think Pracht is trying to talk me to
death. Let's get out of here."*

And we left . . .

For the first time, Isabel was unable to focus like a laser
on her studies. Her mind wandered. She daydreamed of
Jerry. Perhaps her father noticed, but he misinterpreted
what he saw. Scientists also let their minds roam in
search of ideas.

Even at his most paranoid, Raymond would never
imagine that thoughts of Jerry Pracht could possibly
take precedence over his daughter's research.

Since she was taking only graduate seminars now,
there was no possible pretext for Raymond to be present
in the small classrooms. He merely escorted her to Le
Conte Hall, and would be waiting like a stage-door
Johnny when she emerged.

It did not take her long to ferret out the most secluded public phone in the building. As soon as she was
sure that Ray was well on his way home, she would call
Jerry. Knowing how limited her pocket money was, he
would call her right back and they would chat until it
was time for him to get ready to leave for the club.

A sure sign of their deepening relationship was the
fact that they could talk endlessly about everything—
and nothing. She would tell him about what she was
studying, and he went to great lengths to protest that it
was all too far above his head. Yet by the time she had
explained things to him in broad strokes, she was sure
he understood.

The study of theoretical physics follows no timetable.
The activity goes on as long as the brain holds out.

Isabel's afternoon sessions exploring the theoretical
possibilities for her master's dissertation began to
stretch out later and later into the evening. Since going
out to eat might break the momentum of her thoughts,
she would bring sandwiches with her so she could stay
in her carrel and keep concentrating.

"The most important issue in high-energy physics deals with certain properties of a particle called the kaon," she explained to Jerry. "For some of the latest thinkers, this calls into question Einstein's principle of equivalence."

"God, poor Albert," he lamented. "They use the old guy like a football, don't they? What are they doing to him now?"

"Well," Isabel expounded, "the classic example is of a man riding in an elevator mounted on top of a rocket, smoothly accelerating into outer space. Despite the speed of the rocket, the man inside—"

"Let's call him the elevatornaut," he joked.

"Fine. A real 'nautcase,' " Isabel countered with a grin. "Anyway, as the elevator is climbing, the guy is somehow still rooted to the floor. According to Uncle Albert, that's because the force of gravity and the acceleration are indistinguishable."

"In other words, if my brilliant dad and his brilliant protégé are right," Jerry interjected, "then Einstein takes it on the chin, right?"

"Right. In fact, this information can actually be traced back to Newton." She glanced at her watch. "Ohmigod, I have a meeting with your father in about four minutes, and he's going to want to hear what I've come up with."

"I'll give you something really novel," Jerry suggested. "Tell him you want to take a sabbatical and come with me on the indoor tour."

"Come on," she protested. "If you keep bugging me about that, I'll encourage him to pressure you into going back and taking your high school exams."

He reacted in mock horror. "Anything but that! Now, when am I going to see you in person?"

"I don't know," she answered earnestly. "I'm trying to figure something out."

"Well hurry the hell up," he urged. "Take a look at my father's forehead. The men in our family lose their hair early. Don't you want to know me before I'm bald?"

By mid-February, Isabel was putting in so many hours in the library after dinner that she looked haggard and on the verge of exhaustion. Uncharacteristically, even Raymond began to plead with her to ease up, but her only reply was, "I can't yet, Dad, I'm into something really important and I've got to finish it as soon as possible."

"Any little hints for your poor old father?" he asked with mock pathos.

"Sorry, Mr. da Costa." She smiled mischievously. "This item is still strictly classified."

Raymond was disappointed but did not press the issue, though this was the first time she did not share the totality of her thoughts with him. She had never before been secretive with any of her projects—and yet she had never been so deeply involved as she was now.

He consoled himself with the thought that she was nearing a breakthrough that would bring her recognition transcending the now tired journalistic superlatives like "child prodigy" or "girl genius." They would simply trumpet, "Isabel da Costa, the renowned physicist, today announced . . ."

One evening just after nine P.M., while Ray was finishing a session with one of his pupils, the phone rang. He assumed it was one of his students, pestering him about something trivial.

He could not have been more wrong.

"Dad, come to the back of Le Conte and pick me up right away. I've got to talk to you."

Her tone was urgent. There was even a touch of fear in her voice.

"What is it?" he asked anxiously. "Are you all right?"

"I can't talk on the phone. Please hurry."

Terrified, Ray summarily dismissed the pupil he was teaching, and rushed for the car.

During the short drive to the campus, a worried Raymond tried to imagine what might be wrong. He could only conclude that his daughter was truly ill. All the way to the Physics building he berated himself for not heeding the signs of her fatigue.

The moment she saw the car, she rushed out laden with a pile of lab notebooks. Far from being pale, her face was flushed, and, with an air of what seemed like apprehension, she demanded, "Quick, Dad, open the trunk and put this stuff inside."

He obeyed wordlessly as Isabel climbed into the car.

"Let's get out of here," she urged like an escaping prisoner.

"Relax, honey," Ray said gently. "We'll be home in a minute—"

"No," she interrupted. "Let's go someplace where we can speak really privately."

"What's wrong with home?"

"Dad, you don't understand. This is something really top secret."

"Well, for heaven's sake, we're not being bugged or anything," he countered. And then, looking at her frightened expression, he relented. "Okay, I'll think of something."

Ray racked his brains and finally decided on Oscar's Den in Oakland, which was usually not student turf.

They sat down at one of the booths, separated from its neighbors by tall wooden partitions.

"Now, Isabel, I insist you order something to eat." He was genuinely concerned, since lately her appetite seemed to have vanished.

"No thanks. I'm not hungry."

"Hey, listen, I humored you, now you humor me by at least having a hamburger."

"Okay, Dad," she said with exasperation. "And a cup of black coffee. I just want to talk."

Raymond quickly ordered. The moment the waitress bustled off, he leaned toward her and whispered urgently, "Now, what the heck is all this about?"

She replied with a single enigmatic syllable. "Karl."

"I don't get it," he said. "Has Pracht done anything . . . improper?"

"No, no, it's nothing like that."

"Then for God's sake, what's the matter?"

Isabel's face revealed the gravity of what she was divulging and the pain it had caused her.

"He's wrong," she said quietly.

"What?"

"Karl's off base. His theory doesn't wash. I've gone over all his calculations again and again, and they don't jibe with his conclusions."

"But he's a world-class figure in the field," Raymond protested.

Isabel slapped the table. "Dad, I don't deny he's got a great mind. And he's already done important work that justifies his reputation. But this time he's wrong— dead wrong."

Raymond shook his head, worried—and confused. It was the first time he'd ever doubted his daughter's abilities. For he was concerned that she had made an error in her *own* computations.

He tried to be calm and objective. "Isabel, why is this so important to you? Isn't it Pracht's problem?" He looked at her squarely and could see she was clearly hiding something more.

"Dad," she murmured, "I've come up with some ideas of my own, and I think my data argues conclusively against the existence of *any* Fifth Force."

Raymond was silent for a moment, aware—as perhaps she was not—of the potential danger in what she was saying.

"Do you realize what you're doing?" he finally asked. "Instead of taking a leap into uncharted territory, you're throwing a firebomb into a roomful of some of the most important scientists in the world."

She nodded. "I know, Dad, I know. But I've never in my life been more sure of what I'm saying. I mean, the refutation isn't complex—its greatest strength is its simplicity."

Raymond da Costa was gradually finding the courage of his daughter's convictions. After all, she had never been wrong before. "Who else knows about this?"

"No one, of course. That's why I wanted to speak to you so desperately."

"Where's your proof?"

"In my notebooks in the trunk of your car. But if you want to see it boiled down into the basic formula, take a look at this."

She reached into the pocket of her flannel shirt and handed him a piece of paper that had been folded many times. As he quickly scanned the data, Raymond found his anxiety rapidly transmuting into intense euphoria.

"Jesus," he murmured half to himself. "This is unbelievable."

"Trust me, Dad, I'm right. My theory will stand up to the most minute scrutiny."

"I know, Isabel. That's why I'm so knocked out. Just imagine what an impact this will have. What a debut—"

She lowered her head.

"What's the matter?" Ray asked.

"You don't get it! Can you imagine what would happen if I refuted my very own thesis adviser?"

Yes, Raymond thought to himself. That will really make headlines.

Isabel shook her head. "God, this is so painful. I don't think I can do it to him."

Raymond had his work cut out for him. He launched into a homily. "Isabel, scientific truth is no respecter of rank or eminence. Its only criterion is integrity. You've got to publish your findings."

"I know—but it doesn't have to be right away."

"What're you talking about?"

"If I let the deadline for this year's conference go by, then there's no way of endangering Karl's appointment at MIT. I mean, what's my rush?"

"Isabel, you owe the man absolutely nothing."

"That's not true. He's a great teacher. He's been more than generous to me."

"Come on," he remonstrated. "If Pracht were in your place, would he withhold publication of something that would be so important to him?"

Isabel reflected for a split second and then answered quietly, "I think he would. I honestly think he would."

Ray shifted gears. "It's getting late, and you're incredibly wired. Why don't you get some rest and we can discuss it again when our minds are fresh?"

"Okay, Dad," she replied, inwardly grateful to postpone the moment of decision.

They drove home in total silence.

Knowing his daughter as well as he did, Ray could easily sense her sadness and disappointment. But then, he convinced himself, that was why he had continued to remain by her side.

Once more he was playing the central role in her life.

36

ADAM

For Adam Coopersmith the process of divorce was more agonizing than anything he could have imagined.

Three days after their telephone conversation, Toni had gathered her emotional resources sufficiently to invite him back to the house that evening, so they could both tell Heather.

The experience was all the more difficult because everyone involved felt wronged or guilty—or both.

There had even been initial periods when Toni suffered fleeting pangs about not having been a good enough wife and mother, perhaps concentrating too much on her work to be what her family needed.

Yet she convinced herself that this was not a case of her own negligence, but rather Adam's unilateral withdrawal of the love he had pledged at their wedding and had now transferred to another woman.

Heather's reaction shook both her parents. Surprisingly, upon learning that he was leaving, she had burst into tears, thinking Adam was abandoning her for a nicer family.

Her anger, curiously, was aimed at Toni.

"You did this, Mom. You're so caught up in your goddamn career. You blab about it so much, you never pay any attention to him."

She then turned to her father and, lapsing from prosecutor to wounded child, implored, "You'll let me live with you, Dad, won't you?"

Adam melted with remorse.

During this entire conversation he was unable to look Toni in the eye. Yet she herself uttered not a single syllable in rancor. That is, not in front of their daughter.

Finally the wounded girl went upstairs to telephone her best friend, who had gone through the very ordeal Heather had just begun to suffer.

Adam was now alone with Toni, who did not raise her voice, but nonetheless spoke barbed words. "Just don't let her farewell speech give you any ideas, Dr. Coopersmith."

"What do you mean?"

"She's got as much chance of living with you and Mata Hari as a snowball in Hell."

"Wait a minute—" Adam protested.

Toni continued and all but ignored him as she spoke with what sounded like a computerized voice. "The court always finds in the child's best interests, and whatever you think of me, I'm still the primary parent. That woman's not going to get near my child."

Adam was baffled. "Toni, can you be honest with me—and yourself? Heather's never been at the center of your life. Why are you so insistent on custody?"

"I'm her mother, dammit. Do I have to say anything more?"

"Yes. You could say you love her."

"That goes without saying."

"No, Toni. In your case, I don't think it does. You regard her as a possession, and you're hanging on to her just to spite me."

She hesitated for a moment and then conceded quietly, "That's part of it. But frankly, is it in Heather's best interest to live with some Russian *babushka* she doesn't even know?"

"Anya's a caring person," Adam protested. "She'd be good to Heather."

"Does she have any experience with children?" Toni asked with an edge of cruelty in her voice.

"Do you?" he lashed back in anger.

His unexpected hostility was actually making it easy for Toni, hardening her resolve. "Don't push me too far, Adam. You can't win."

"I'll call character witnesses."

"If it comes to that, the Boss will call everybody from the man in the Oval Office to the Pope himself. But you'll end up damaging Heather more. And I know you'd never want to do that."

Adam paused to weigh what she had said. She sensed she'd stopped his assault, and now began a velvet-gloved counterattack of her own. "Adam, believe me, the mere act of having people testify to our respective unfitness—which is what it all boils down to—will be a worse trauma than settling this privately. Because, even if it's only in his chambers, the judge is going to make Heather choose between us in our presence."

"Why are you being so vindictive?"

"Can't you see, Adam? Can't you even see that *I'm* the real injured party in this? My father was right after all. I should never have left Washington. And yet, do you know something? I've never had a moment's regret . . . until now."

Adam shrugged. "I guess you've got every reason to hate my guts."

"Oh no, that's putting it too mildly. All that's stopping me from murdering you is that Heather still needs you to be a part-time father. And let me tell you, buster, if you step out of line, I'll come at you with guns blazing."

He gathered the strength for wrath that he did not have for apology. "Wait a minute! There are norms for parental visitation, and I expect us to go by the book."

"Don't count on it," she replied in a whirlwind of hatred. "You may not have respected me as a lawyer up till now, but when you see what you're left with after this litigation, you'll be sorry we ever met."

Adam slowly climbed the stairs carrying two old suitcases he had dusted off and brought up from the cellar. He shuddered as he passed Heather's closed door, through which he could hear muffled sobs. And hated himself for what he was doing to her.

He knocked. There was no reply.

He knocked louder and called, "Anybody home?" And heard Heather's hysterical voice: "Nobody important."

"There's you, darling," Adam said affectionately.

"And nobody gives a damn about me."

"I do. May I come in?"

"No. You can go to hell."

Adam spoke quietly but firmly. "Listen, Heather, I'll be leaving soon, and I want to talk to you before I go.

I'll be back in fifteen minutes and I expect you to open this door."

In the quarter of an hour he was gone, she washed her face, combed her hair, and heroically pulled herself together. Her door was open.

Adam sat down next to her on the bed. "Hey, kid, I know it may sound terrible and self-serving, but this is going to turn out to be the right thing. Your mother and I were making each other very unhappy."

"That was no secret," his daughter muttered. "I wasn't exactly overjoyed either."

"Well, I guess we'll all have to start to rebuild our lives."

"Are you already involved with someone?" Heather asked. It was clear she dreaded the answer.

He hesitated and then said softly, "She's a very good person. I think you'll like her."

"Is it that Russian woman I heard you and Mommy fighting about?"

Adam nodded.

"Why is she so important that you have to abandon us?"

"But I'm not disappearing from your life, honey. On the contrary, I'm going to put up the best custody fight I can, because Anya really wants you to come and live with us too."

"Really?" she asked. "Why?"

"Well, I've told her so much about you that she almost feels she knows you. Trust me, Heather. She's a lovely, gentle, caring woman."

There was a pause. Finally, Heather found the courage to ask, "Tell me, Dad. Why did you marry Mom in the first place?"

He hesitated for a moment, and then answered, "To have you."

Suddenly they were embracing, Heather in tears, he crying inwardly.

"Please, Daddy, don't leave me," she begged. "I'll be good, I swear. I won't make any trouble for anybody."

Adam felt as though he had been kicked in the stomach. For a moment he even thought of capitulating and remaining. Anything that would not hurt his daughter more. But then he thought of Anya and the words exchanged with Toni, which could never be taken back.

After a final moment, he closed his eyes and hugged her. He could feel her heart pounding.

Half an hour later he came down the stairs with new resolve. Toni was in the living room, reading. She looked up as he entered.

"Well?" she said calmly. It was clear she had regained some mastery over her emotions.

"I'll see you in court," he answered.

Toni was true to her word. In the negotiations with her lawyers—no doubt quarterbacked by the Boss—Adam was almost skinned alive.

Naively, he had chosen an old friend, Peter Chandler, to represent him, unaware that compassion and sentiment are not positive traits in divorce lawyers. Adam had testified as expert witness for Peter in two malpractice suits. This very fact should have warned him that the attorney's specialty was fighting on behalf of patients who had been maimed, crippled, and killed—the victims.

Adam's only instruction to him was to ensure his visitation rights. For many reasons, he wanted Toni to have everything.

"Let her keep the house, the cars—I don't give a damn. I'm pretty sure the court won't give her alimony since she earns more than I do. But I'll pay Heather's tuition and some child support—as long as it doesn't break my back."

"Hold it, Adam," Chandler intervened. "I don't want to make you into a monster, but I have to negotiate with her people. If you walk in and surrender everything right off the bat, they'll take that as a starting point and we'll get hit for even more."

"I don't believe it, Pete. I mean, Toni's a reasonable person. She'll see that I'm being decent."

"Decent? Since when did the law have anything to do with decency? You're just laying yourself wide open to be raped and pillaged."

"Listen," Adam answered emphatically, "I'm completely in the wrong. If you must know the truth, I'd feel relieved if Toni did take me to the cleaners."

"Maybe," Peter commented. "But Boston winters can be awfully cold if you haven't got a shirt on."

His attorney proved to have a keen insight into the implacable anger of the injured. For not only did Toni petition the court for complete custody of their daughter, ownership of the house, and massive child support, she even sued for loss of earnings.

Two senior partners from the law firm in Washington that represented the Boss testified that had she stayed in the nation's capital, her income would have been more than twice what it was in Boston.

Peter objected. He protested. He argued himself dizzy. But the court upheld the relevance of the testimony, and ultimately, its validity.

But the most egregious injustice was when the magistrate openly asked Heather which parent she would prefer to live with, and after she explicitly responded, "Dad and Anya," granted full custody to Toni, on the grounds, however antiquated, that an adolescent girl was far better off with her mother.

Battered and bruised, Adam was granted merely one weekend a month with Heather and only four weeks during the summer vacation. No Christmas. No Thanksgiving. No Easter.

Hearing the verdict, Adam gasped audibly. "Jesus, I bet an axe murderer would have done better."

"We could appeal," Peter offered tentatively.

Adam grimaced. "No. All I've got left is my balls, and I'd probably lose those in a rematch."

Heather was devastated. "I don't understand it, Dad," she sobbed. "You're a much better parent."

"Yeah," Adam replied, smoldering. "But your mother's a much better lawyer."

Adam's suffering was far from over.

The night their divorce decree was granted, he received a savage telephone call. It was from Thomas Hartnell.

Adam had long dreaded this moment. In fact, he sensed that it was part of his former father-in-law's strategy to wait until the last possible moment to add his boot to the others that had already kicked him.

The Boss spoke with an icy calm. "Dr. Coopersmith, you have lived up to my worst expectations. You have caused irreparable harm to the two things I love best in the world—my daughter and granddaughter. I intend to make absolutely sure that you regret your actions. Now, I have not as yet decided how, but I assure you that from this time forward, I will be concentrating my life on finding a suitable vengeance. Do you read me?"

"Yes, sir."

"Remember this, you heartless bastard. Even if you don't hear from me for a long while, never draw breath and imagine I've forgotten that we have unfinished business. Now you go back to that Russian gal, and I hope she gives you all you deserve."

37
SANDY

SCIENCE HAS known many multifaceted geniuses. Leonardo da Vinci made his mark in art, anatomy, and aerodynamics. Isaac Newton excelled in optics, astronomy, physics, and mathematics; Albert Einstein in physics, cosmology, and music.

By the late twentieth century, Harvard's Walter Gilbert—a molecular biologist who, in a spectacular display of versatility, won the Nobel Prize for chemistry after having trained as a physicist—was more the norm than the exception.

Gilbert even followed Sir Isaac Newton in another domain. Whereas the good Sir Isaac ended his polymorphous career in the lucrative position of Master of the Royal Mint, the Harvard professor also made a mint as Chief Executive Officer and a major stockholder in Biogen Incorporated.

Yet throughout history, the combination found least often in a scientific thinker was that of devotion to his family as much as to his work.

Most "civilians" balk at working more than forty hours a week, and their union leaders militate for reductions. Yet serious scientific investigators of their own free will think nothing of working night and day, including weekends. This is wonderful for the progress of mankind, but not salubrious for marriage and raising children.

Even Sandy Raven, who had exchanged vows of

matrimony with the deepest of passion and the loftiest of intentions, became increasingly involved in the race against time, and against other laboratories, to find a cure for hepatic carcinoma.

Admittedly, Sandy had no role models for parenthood. And he was so dedicated to his work that he had no time to read up on the phenomenon. Still, being a scientist's daughter, Judy fell easily into the pattern of being a scientist's wife.

She knew from her own childhood that if she wanted her daughter Olivia to see anything of Sandy, she would have to bring her to the lab. Which she did. At all hours of the day and night—even breast-feeding the baby in her father's office.

Greg was especially delighted to see his grandchild, and proposed setting up a playpen in the coffee area. This gave Judy a further idea.

A few weeks later when Sandy returned home for dinner, he found their living room completely redecorated.

"My God," he exclaimed, "it looks like a great big kindergarten."

"That's exactly what it is, pal," Judy chirped. "A couple of the lab widows and I have decided to set up a play group. I'll be the music teacher, of course."

"What a great idea," Sandy marveled. "It kills two birds with one stone."

"What birds were you thinking of?"

"You and Olivia," he said, hugging them both. "I mean, you know life has got to be this way till we finish the job. But at least I won't feel so guilty about leaving you guys for so long at a stretch."

Every Sunday night, the family came up for air. They chose some ethnic eatery, most often Joyce Chen on Fresh Pond Parkway, and tried to talk about something other than science.

One weekend they were joined by Sidney Raven,

who had come East for the major city premieres of his latest blockbuster, a seasonal offering called *Godzilla Meets Santa*. After all, as he declared, why mess with a winner?

If she could have talked, Olivia would have told her other relatives that Grandpa Sidney was the only one who knew how to communicate with children. He dandled her on his knee and told her story after story.

"This is a cutie," he pronounced. "This is a real superstar."

By sheer coincidence, Sandy caught a glimpse of Judy's face out of the corner of his eye. For some unfathomable reason it registered disapproval.

"What's the news from Hollywood, Dad?" Sandy inquired, anxious to give his beloved father the floor.

"I think you can cover that by asking what's new with Kim Tower," Judy said, revealing to Sidney that she knew of her husband's obsession.

"Well," Sidney obliged, "the news on the Rochelle front is that Elliot Victor is on his way out of Paragon. And rightly too, I might add. His brief reign produced so many dogs that the boys in the trade refer to him as 'One Hundred and One Dalmatians.' "

"Gosh, that's too bad," Sandy offered.

"Yeah, there's a twisteroo in this plot, sonny boy. It's a last-reel shaker. Guess who's succeeding him?"

Sandy looked at his father wide-eyed, "No, Dad. You don't mean it? Rochelle is going to be the head of the studio?"

"Yep. And she deserves it. The three pictures she produced personally made more money than the ninety-nine losers that Victor supervised."

"That's fan-tas-tic! But won't it be a bit of a strain on their marriage?"

"Not at all," Sidney replied. "It goes without saying they'll get a divorce. I mean, it's a hell of a lot easier to get a husband than a studio."

* * *

Early the next evening, Sandy was alone in the lab. Taking an unprecedented liberty, he barricaded himself in Greg Morgenstern's office and breathlessly dialed Paragon Studios.

After talking his way past three assistants in ascending order of importance, he was granted the honor of being put on hold and, while waiting his turn, being entertained by several of Paragon Records' latest chart busters.

Finally, the senior assistant came on again and said, "Are you still there, Mr. Raven?"

I'm really *Professor* Raven, he thought, but what the hell. The important thing is, Rochelle will speak to me. "Yes," he said. "I'm here."

A few seconds later her voice—ever mellifluous, now more turbocharged—uttered a colorful salutation.

"Raven, you old fart. I thought you'd croaked with the dinosaurs. To what do I owe the honor of this call?"

Sandy was thrown completely.

"Rochelle," he managed to reply. "It's me, Sandy."

She burst into gales of laughter and remarked, "My God, Sandy, it's *you*. My scatterbrained assistants must have thought it was your dad. How the hell are you?"

In the fleeting instant before he replied, Sandy wondered if Rochelle had been joking. Would she have genuinely addressed a man of his father's age and reputation in so condescending—not to say cruel—a manner?

"I'm fine," Sandy replied, suddenly tongue-tied. "I'm a professor at MIT, actually."

"That's great," she remarked. "God, if I only had your brain, I'd be . . ."

Her voice trailed off. In fact she was so quick to invoke hyperbole that she had no idea how Sandy's, or anyone's, brain could make her any better than she already was.

He tried to concentrate on the remarks he had prepared. "Rochelle, I've just heard about your promotion.

I was so happy for you, I just had to call and say congratulations."

"Sandy," she said with fervor, "you're a truly beautiful person. Would you believe me if I told you that I miss you more than ever? I mean, there's nobody like you out here."

Even when distilled from the exaggerated idiom of Hollywood, he thought, the essence of her message remained an expression of, at the very least, amicable feelings toward him.

"How does it feel to be on the top of the mountain?"

"Ineffably inexpressible, Sandy. I actually wonder why I ever dreamed of being a movie star when making movies includes holding the fate of practically every actor in the business in the palm of my hand." Then, a sudden shift. "Are you married, Sandy?" she asked.

My God, he thought to himself, this can't be possible. The woman is about to be single again, and she asks me point-blank about my ... eligibility. Why did she wait so long?

"Yes," he replied. "And I've got the most wonderful daughter."

"Oh, how I envy you." She sighed theatrically. "I'd give up the keys to the kingdom—even the keys to the studio—to have a darling little girl like yours."

"Well," Sandy responded, as he reveled in the attention she was paying him, "it won't be easy, but you're bound to find somebody worthy of you. You must be under a lot of stress at the moment," he offered.

"How extremely sensitive and considerate of you to say that, Sandy. You're right. I'm in a great deal of mental anguish. It's wonderful to be able to talk to someone who goes as far back as you do. I mean, there are no real friendships here in Hollywood. Only alliances of expediency."

Gosh, she has a lovely turn of phrase, Sandy thought to himself, not realizing that her words were apt as a description of her own behavior.

There was an abrupt silence. Then Sandy heard some voices in the background.

She returned apologetically to their conversation. "Sandy, listen. Redford's just burst in demanding to see me about script changes. I've got to cut this marvelous conversation short. Why don't we talk again?"

"Sure, sure, any time," Sandy responded, the only lapdog with tenure in physics at a major university.

"I'll put you on to my assistant, Michael, who'll take your numbers. Thanks again for calling—and loads of love to your wife and lovely daughter."

Sandy thought it best not to give Michael his home phone number, but indicated that, especially as he spent most of his life in the lab, he could be reached there.

"Gee, Mr. Raven," Michael remarked deferentially, "how does it feel to be saving mankind the way you are?"

The question had never been put to Sandy in quite that way, but he owed this respectful humanitarian a confirmation of his commitment to science. "It's rough, Michael, but the job's got to be done."

"Amen, Mr. Raven. Oh, by the way, I'm terribly sorry I confused you with that clown of a producer."

Sandy could take it from Rochelle, but he saw no reason not to inform this underling with quiet irony, "That's okay. He's only my father."

Sandy was so upset afterward that, defying the dictates of the Cambridge police, not to mention ordinary common sense—he went out and walked on the moonlit banks of the Charles River.

What had begun as a spontaneous gesture of greetings for old times' sake had concluded with an enormous emotional upheaval.

Though he felt he had put Michael in his place, he was still terribly hurt by the way the arrogant young creep had spoken about Sidney.

And though Rochelle had acted enormously affectionate during their phone conversation, he had no illusions that their relationship was anything more than platonic. Still, it was obviously not something he could discuss with Judy. For then he would have to admit that just hearing Rochelle's voice could still evoke in him pangs of regret.

38

ISABEL

"EXCUSE ME, Professor."

Karl Pracht peeked over a copy of *Science*, removed his feet from the desk and acknowledged his unexpected visitor.

"Ah, the good Mr. da Costa. Nice to see you. Where's Isabel?"

"In the library," Ray answered cautiously. "Why do you ask?"

"Oh, just being cordial. I mean, the two of you are inseparable, so I assumed . . ."

He's putting me down, Raymond thought darkly. He's one of those bozos who think all I am is an intellectual parasite.

"Come in for God's sake," Pracht urged affably, motioning him toward a chair.

"Actually, I'd prefer to stand, if you don't mind."

Ray's veiled hostility somewhat baffled Karl. "To what do I owe the honor of this visit?" he inquired.

"You mean you have no idea?" Raymond asked sarcastically as he closed the door.

"Frankly, no," Pracht answered. "Unless you're finally accepting my offer to be a development engineer in our department."

Ray's suspicions were confirmed. The arrogant bastard was trying to buy him off.

"I've always thought you were hiding your light under a bushel," Karl went on, pleasantly. "From everything I've heard from my colleagues in San Diego, you really livened up the place."

"Thank you." Ray brushed off the compliment like an unwanted thread from his shoulder. "But that's not why I'm here. Can we talk man-to-man?"

Pracht smiled. "Well, the Women's Studies department would prefer we say 'person-to-person.' But we can chat in confidence. Is this about Isabel? I've noticed she's been looking a little peaked and frazzled lately."

Ray stared at the professor, unblinking. "Just tell me one thing, Karl," he said, deliberately savoring what he regarded as disrespectful use of the man's first name. "Has Isabel kept you up-to-date on her research?"

"Of course. I'm her adviser. Why—"

"Then you know," Raymond interrupted.

Karl Pracht leaned across his desk with a look of bemusement on his face.

"For God's sake, da Costa, can you stop speaking in half-baked innuendos and tell me what you're driving at?"

"Well, we could begin with the four forces and Einstein's theory of equivalence."

At this point he had expected Pracht to interject and mention the so-called Fifth Force—and his own contribution to the field. But the physicist was clearly playing cat and mouse. Perhaps to find out how much Raymond knew.

"Fine," he agreed, "let's start there."

"According to your reputation," Ray continued, "you're of the school that believes in the existence of a Fifth Force."

"I've published a few papers on the subject," Pracht conceded.

"But never a fully blown exposition, never a complete soup-to-nuts discussion of the whole question . . ."

It wasn't what Raymond was saying, but the bizarrely intense manner in which he was saying it, that caused Pracht—a normally placid individual—to lose his temper.

"You know, Ray," he said, fast reaching the boiling point, "I've done my best to try to like you—and it hasn't been easy. Because, frankly, I find you untrusting, unpleasant, and uptight."

Good, Ray thought, we're going to get to the nittygritty. "You're entitled to your exalted opinion," he commented, for the first time ever addressing the scientist in an arrogant tone. "And while we exchange home truths, I've never been very fond of you either. Even less so of that hoodlum you call a son."

"You leave Jerry out of this," Pracht snapped angrily. And then a thought struck him. "Or is he what this is all about?"

"Well, I can't say I was overjoyed by his interest in my daughter."

"I'm sorry you feel that way," the physicist answered. "I thought the two youngsters were well-suited to one another."

"I can't agree with you. In fact, if you must know, I've forbidden Isabel to speak to him."

"I've inferred as much," Pracht answered. "And now that I know you're not here to discuss your daughter's dowry, why don't we get down to brass tacks. Just what is it you want of me, Mr. da Costa?"

"I want you to publish my daughter's paper," Ray demanded.

"I'm not the editor of a journal." The physicist smiled ingenuously.

"Stop playing the innocent," Ray demanded. "If you were to recommend an essay of Isabel's, it would be guaranteed publication anywhere. We both know that, Karl. And we both know you'd do everything in your power to suppress the masterful demolition job she's done on your cockeyed theory."

"Are you sure?" he asked with a slight grin.

"You don't seem like a hara-kiri type to me. And what university would want you after Isabel's essay blows you out of the water?"

"I think I'll survive, Ray," Pracht allowed quietly, with a look of disdain.

"You mean MIT would still want you?" Ray asked bluntly.

Fed up with this pussyfooting around, the professor lost his temper, rose quickly, reached into his middle drawer, pulled out a letter and slapped it onto the table.

"Read this, you sick bastard. It's my appointment at MIT as of July first, 1988—no strings attached. That means if I forget how much two and two are between now and then, I'll still be the Winthrop Professor of Physics."

"A pretty empty title when Isabel's paper comes out, don't you think?"

Pracht did not comment. Ray was sure he had him cornered. He played his trump card. "Listen, Karl, I'm willing to make a deal."

"A 'deal'?" Pracht's tone was more curious than offended. "Who gets what?"

"You get six months' grace ..." Ray began.

"And you?"

"We get rid of your cub when you take him to Boston."

"No way. Besides, why should I disturb his life? Jerry's his own man, and seems to be finding his way out here. He's got a good job and a good coaching relationship with Paco. I feel bad enough that I messed up his childhood with my academic bullying. I'm not about to make the same mistake again." Pracht then added, with a tone of contempt, "Anyway, I'd never do anything like that for you."

"But you might do it for yourself," Ray responded sarcastically. "My deal is still on the table. He goes to Boston with you, and you get another six months on the top rung of the profession. Now, what do you think?"

Pracht studied Ray's expression like an ornithologist looking at an odd bird.

"Mister, what I think is that you belong in a loony bin. I only hope some day Isabel discovers what a creep you are."

"You're ducking the question," Raymond continued aggressively. "Do we have a deal or not?"

For a split second there was silence, during which Pracht's gaze burned into Raymond's brain. "No, sir, we do not."

"Did I hear you right?" Ray demanded with astonishment.

"I think so. And since that winds up all we have to say to one another, I'd be grateful if you'd get the hell out of my office."

Ray regathered his forces and repeated his menace. "Okay, buster. I'm going to personally fax Isabel's data to every major scientific publication in the world. You can't possibly have a lock on everyone. Some editor somewhere will realize that it's solid gold and print it immediately."

By now Pracht had grown sick and tired of this fencing. "Don't waste your money, da Costa. It'll only make you more of a laughingstock than you already are. For your information, the minute I saw her calculations I called up Dudley Evans, the editor of *The Physical Review*. He accepted Isabel's paper on my word alone."

Raymond was speechless.

"You see," the professor explained, "the first concern of a real physicist is to learn more about the universe. It's great if he can be a pioneer in discovering new knowledge, but that's secondary. The point is, we're all richer for what Isabel has done," Karl Pracht stated passionately, "*even* you—you selfish, bungling bastard."

39
ADAM

FORTUNATELY, THERE was one financial resource that Adam had not reckoned on. Anya's modest salary as a lab employee suddenly gained significance. Moreover, thanks to Dmitri's perverse "generosity," they had a roof over their heads. Leaky, but a roof nonetheless.

Still, for Adam the emotional compensation more than justified his financial loss. Now he could be with Anya openly, walk over to her station in the lab at any time and give her a hug.

He had always known that she was intelligent, but now he could appreciate her scientific acumen to the fullest. And whatever she had not absorbed from her omnivorous reading, he could fill in.

Heather was their house guest the next weekend. For some inexplicable reason, she adored their rickety apartment and enjoyed sleeping on the new convertible sofa they had purchased to replace the sagging couch.

She had liked Anya instantly. Among other things, Anya had an unerring instinct for talking to younger people. Far from making Heather feel like a child, she soon had her feeling like a friend and equal.

"Your father's a great teacher," Anya enthused to Heather.

"No," he told his daughter, "Anya's a great pupil."

Heather laughed. "Well, at least you both agree that the other's 'great.' "

There was something satisfying—even reassuring—to Heather in the way her father and Anya so obviously cared for one another.

"I was just thinking," Heather offered. "Wouldn't it be amazing if I could move in with you guys? Can you imagine how I'd do in my science homework?"

Adam smiled warmly. "Well, honey, you know how Anya feels. And how hard I've tried."

"Yeah," Heather acknowledged, unable to mask her disappointment. "Do you think maybe the court would reconsider if you were married?"

Anya turned to Adam, her eyes sparkling. "Did you put her up to saying that?"

"Not at all, darling. You know Heather well enough to realize that nobody puts words into her mouth."

"Absolutely," his daughter concurred. "And speaking as a Boston bluestocking, I want to express my official disapproval of your unofficial shacking up. In fact, I was going to ask you for a CD player for my birthday. But I'll drop that request and settle for a quiet wedding."

At this point Adam addressed Anya melodramatically. "Darling, for the sake of my daughter's sensitive psyche, would you consider marrying me?"

She smiled happily. "Yes, my love, I'll think about it."

"When will you make up your mind?" Heather asked enthusiastically.

"Now. I've thought about it. And I will."

But the honeymoon would have to wait, for professionally they were making progress at a feverish pace. Other medical centers throughout the world had been helping them by running identical trials on similarly afflicted women. Results were now beginning to come in from the larger scale studies in Minnesota, Bonn, and at the University of Nice. These statistics were so astonishingly alike that, in his wildest dreams, Adam would never have dared to imagine them.

Oh Christ, Max, he thought, I wish you could have lived to see these printouts. The trials selected women who had had five or more unexplained miscarriages in the first trimester of pregnancy and divided them into groups. In subsequent pregnancies, one-third were treated with cortisone. Another third were given large doses of natural progesterone in vaginal suppositories, with the rest merely used as controls.

To the elation of Adam and his team, more than seventy-five percent of groups A and B carried their babies successfully to term. This meant that, if he could convince the medical community, doctors would be able to replace steroid treatment with natural progesterone and risk far fewer side effects.

Now the scouts for the pharmaceutical companies caught wind of the profit potential in Adam's work and approached him. Clarke-Albertson, the most enthusiastic of them, was anxious to buy into his research.

After wining and dining the two Coopersmiths at the Colonnade, their vice-president for public relations, Prescott Mason, a patricianly tweeded Boston Brahmin with an upper-class accent, was somewhat nonplused to find Anya the reluctant party.

"With due respect, Mr. Mason," she argued, "I personally can't see a reason for making a pharmaceutical commitment now. Adam's pretty well fixed to do his work. We not only have research money from the Harvard endowment, but NIH has responded generously to our proposals."

"All the more reason to let us on board—I mean, for your own protection," Prescott Mason countered. "It's pretty certain they're backing a winning horse. And my company has always seen to it that the jockeys get their share of the purse."

He turned deliberately to Adam and remarked, "A little extra pocket money never hurt anybody, did it, Dr. Coopersmith?"

Adam wondered whether this was mere salesman's banter or if Mason had done his research and was making a thinly veiled allusion to his punishing monthly matrimonial debt.

Clarke-Albertson's man was a trained scientist and could discourse on every potential use that might arise from Adam's research.

"Our people are not only interested in the cure you're searching for, but the exact identity of the villain. Imagine what benefits could accrue if we ever reproduced the antibody you're trying to tame. I mean, right now, the women you're treating object to the negative effects it has on their pregnancies.

"To look at it from the opposite perspective, it could be the perfect medium for birth control. I mean, there's been such a fuss because the French RU-486 is, technically speaking, an early abortion pill. But since your ultimate product is a natural hormone, the fact that it can also prevent conception would pose no moral dilemma at all."

"That's a good point, Mr. Mason," Anya interposed, "I can imagine a range of possibilities in developing countries with population problems—India, for example."

"Quite," Mason agreed, unable to evince much enthusiasm for the profit potential from a third-world country.

But then, in a cadenza to his pitch, he added, "And, of course, there's the ultimate side effect. If your research succeeds, you will inevitably attract the attention of the Swedish Academy."

Anya's face was glowing as she turned to her husband. "Haven't I always told you that, darling?"

"Come on, it's a real rat race," Adam protested.

"I agree," the executive said, "but Clarke-Albertson not only has resources to subsidize and ultimately market your work, we've also got plenty of influence in the Nobel situation. Actually, we've already stage-managed two prizes—and one near-miss. The fellow died on me."

"I'm surprised," Anya commented, "I'd have thought that was the last morally unspoiled domain."

"Oh, let me assure you," Mason responded. "They don't give the award to undeserving people. They'll pick you sooner or later. But wouldn't it be nice if the recognition came sooner?"

"Mr. Mason, there's something I want you to understand," Adam responded. "I am—quite literally—the heir to a wealth of research and insight that should have brought Max Rudolph the Nobel. Frankly, if recognition came 'sooner,' there'd be a better chance that his wife would be around to see it."

"I hope, if anything, that strengthens our appeal to you," Mason commented.

"Let me be absolutely candid with you, Mr. Mason. There's only one appeal to me in any of this—time. This is one instance in which money can buy time, and that's the one thing I can't give my patients. They need answers as soon as possible, and if what you're proposing brings them even a day closer, then I'm morally bound to accept the best offer possible."

"I appreciate that, Dr. Coopersmith," Mason said with genuine admiration. He quickly added, "Only promise me that if any of our competitors get to you with something concrete, you'll give us a chance to beat it."

They sat up for the rest of the night discussing the matter. They quickly realized that the opportunity was too attractive to let pass.

"Adam, let me speak as a woman for a moment," Anya said with emotion. "This cure couldn't help me, but I know how others would feel. Right now they're walking around thinking themselves inadequate, with their own personal rain clouds darkening their lives."

"Yes," he agreed. "A lot of my patients are in their early forties—which is adding to the agony. For their sake, we shouldn't keep him waiting. I think we'd be derelict not to say yes right away."

Adam refrained from telling her how much he had been moved by her altruism. He still regretted that he could do nothing to help her own pain. Perhaps she would take some consolation from helping others.

The next morning he phoned Prescott Mason. Who, in turn, phoned his legal department. Who, in turn, phoned Harvard's legal department. And at the end of politely tenacious bargaining, each side came out thinking that its deal had bettered the other.

Now, in a very literal sense, Adam and Anya were in business.

40

ADAM

ADAM AND Anya Coopersmith had become relentless hunters in the dark jungle of the immune system, and slowly but surely they were nearing their prey. Somewhere, among the benign and benevolent cells that whirled through the body, lurked a secret predator whose sole savage purpose was the destruction of the human fetus growing peacefully inside the womb.

It was the final act, and, in true Agatha Christie fashion, the killer was about to be exposed. Thus far it had left certain clues. But the evidence was merely circumstantial and not sufficient to make a definitive identification.

Moreover, to further complicate the plot, the interferons—three clusters of proteins code-named somewhat unimaginatively alpha, beta, and gamma— were like an army that guarded against viruses. The alpha squad was produced by white blood cells; the beta, by cells of connective and other tissues; and the gamma, by T-lymphocytes, which are the natural killer cells in the normal immune response against disease-causing viruses.

Here the skills of chemist Giancarlo Pisani came into play. And together, in assay after assay, sometimes painstakingly changing the parameters by a mere .01 percent, they were seeking traces of the invisible. A hint of a shape. Anything distinctive that could be placed on a laboratory Wanted poster.

After testing with various pore sizes, they established the molecular weight of the unidentified killer at between ten and thirty thousand kilodaltons.

Coincidentally, the same as gamma interferon.

They put the mystery substance through more elaborate tests, including an affinity column containing microscopic plastic beads coupled with antibodies to the suspected toxin. After passage through the column, toxic activity was removed from the solution and bound by the bead, again suggesting that gamma interferon was the culprit.

A final series of multimedia investigations left no further doubt: gamma interferon was indeed a double agent—immensely useful against many diseases, but lethal for healthy pregnancies.

The question now was how to destroy the would-be enemy while preserving the victim it tenaciously stalked.

It was doubly appropriate that the breakthrough should occur on their anniversary. They were hard at work in the lab, testing Anya's hypothesis that there might be a very subtle structural rearrangement of the specific atoms comprising the gamma molecule in the reproductive area.

With the help of crystallographer Simon Hillman, they visualized the conventional molecule on a 3-D video screen and superimposed it on fetal tissue.

Wearily pressing the enter key on her computer, Anya glanced perfunctorily at the screen, which she expected to show her bleary eyes yet another near-miss.

What she saw, however, made her blink into focus, move closer to the screen and finally let out a squeal.

Adam, who was just unpacking their millionth Chinese takeout, dropped the carton and ran over, thinking perhaps she had hurt herself.

"Look, Adam. Look."

He just stared at the screen. His jaw dropped.

"Jesus Christ," he murmured. "You were right. I never thought I'd live to see this moment. The receptor molecules are different—subtly different—but enough to cause all the damage we've been trying to prevent."

She nodded mutely.

He was dizzy. "After all this time, I'm suddenly at a loss for something to do."

Anya beamed. "We just wait for the ultimate scientific reaction—the telegram from Stockholm."

The final step was almost anticlimactic. It would be a matter of pharmacological trial and error to develop a receptor uniquely designed to protect nature's treasured prize.

At this point the pair recruited every team in the lab, ordering that all other research be tabled so that the finish line could be reached at the greatest possible speed.

By late fall they had created a drug—dubbed MR-Alpha to commemorate the still-vivid memory of the man who had started Adam on this quest so long ago.

Clarke-Albertson put the drug on their fastest track for commercial development and FDA sanction, while

Adam's and Anya's moods oscillated between ecstasy and frustration.

"How long does it take to get government approval?" Anya asked.

"That depends on the circumstances," Adam replied, thinking briefly of a moment long ago when he had helped administer an unapproved drug to save the life of a man who was now his sworn enemy, and whose threatened vengeance still hung over him like the sword of Damocles.

"Approval can take two months or two years," Prescott Mason commented.

"Well," Adam warned, "if they don't make it snappy, I'm gonna pull a John Rock."

"Who is this 'Rock' person?" Anya asked.

"He's a legend, and the story's absolutely true," Adam replied. "He was a central figure in the creation of the first oral contraceptive, which he duly submitted for FDA approval. But after a while he grew impatient with the bureaucratic road blocks. So one morning he simply showed up at the agency's headquarters and announced to the receptionist that he had come to receive approval for his pill.

"After she made a number of nervous phone calls, she politely explained to Rock that he would be hearing from the agency very soon. The good doctor chose to interpret this literally. So he sat down on a little chair, pulled out a sandwich and said, 'In that case, I'll just wait.' I guess it was the first sit-in in the history of the FDA."

"And what was so amazing," Mason jumped in, "was the old boy succeeded. Somehow his presence galvanized the authorities into approval that very afternoon."

"Well, I'm willing to go to Washington," Anya offered cheerily.

"Don't worry," Mason reassured her. "They're finally starting to clear up the logjam. And besides, we've got two full-time lobbyists doing a slightly subtler imitation of John Rock. Anyway, this won't be a very controversial call—"

"And more important," Adam interrupted, "Anya's going to sit down and study for her qualifying exams. I've always wanted to be married to a doctor."

It took six months for Mason to achieve Washington's blessing, and by then Anya had already passed her examination.

Thus, when the good news was phoned through by one of Clarke-Albertson's "men on the spot," the toasts could be raised to "Dr. Coopersmith and Dr. Coopersmith."

Before they had even received their first advance from Clarke-Albertson, Adam and Anya decided to spend it on a house.

They purchased one of the stateliest homes on Brattle Street, a stone's throw from the poet Longfellow's house. Clarke-Albertson provided the down payment and guaranteed the mortgage.

Unfortunately, the plumbing and electricity were as venerable as the building itself. And since vintage pipes and wires do not improve with age, they had to engage a specialist architect to perform, as Adam jokingly put it, "a circuit transplant."

Anya, with irrepressible optimism, insisted upon designating a room for Heather, and planned to have Adam invite her over to choose the color scheme.

They also spent many hours in the kitchen. The original pretext was that Anya could teach the young girl Russian cooking. But the recipes just gave them something to do with their hands while they conversed in increasingly intimate terms. Exchanging their feelings about life, love, marriage, Adam, and—inevitably—Toni.

"You know, I'm not trying to take your mother's place," Anya commented affectionately, "but I want you to feel that this is your home too. And you needn't wait for your allotted time to come over." She paused. "In fact, Adam and I thought you might like to have this."

She reached into her apron pocket and withdrew a newly made front-door key. Offering it, she added, "You don't even have to call to say you're coming."

The young girl was deeply touched. "I'd like very much to give you a big hug," she said shyly.

"Darling," the older woman answered lovingly, "the feeling is mutual."

But not long after the Coopersmiths had bought their mansion, Adam shocked his wife and himself by proposing that they take a sabbatical.

"And do what, Adam?" Anya asked. "The lab is your life."

"That's exactly the problem," he replied. "Why don't we actually take that long holiday we've been promising ourselves?"

"Where would you like to go?" she asked, delighted at Adam's rush of enthusiasm.

"Actually, a distant star would be perfect," he replied with a smile. "But since we're not qualified astronauts, would you settle for a trip around the world?"

"That would be wonderful," she enthused. "Do you want to start westward or eastward?"

"I was thinking of west," Adam answered. "We could stop in California and see some of our colleagues. Then Hawaii. After that, we'll play it by ear. I've got some long-standing invitations to lecture down under, and that might even make it tax deductible for Uncle Sam. But in any case, we'll definitely visit your parents on the way home."

Anya was thrilled. And they embraced warmly.

"Tell me," he asked, "aren't we the happiest couple in the world?"

"I think so," she murmured. "But we could find out empirically when we travel."

* * *

Unselfishly, Heather encouraged them. "You guys deserve some time by yourselves. I mean, even old people go on honeymoons, don't they?"

Adam and Anya laughed at what they hoped was meant to be a joke, and then he asked seriously, "But if we go, what'll happen to you on our weekends?"

"Well, something tells me Mom'll let you make up the time when you get back. And if she's so horny that she has to go to Washington while you're gone, I can always stay with Auntie Lisl."

"From what I understand," Anya remarked, "I don't think Toni likes her very much."

"Yeah, most of the time," Heather conceded. "But when it comes to a place to dump me, I'm sure she'll make an exception."

41

SANDY

GREG MORGENSTERN'S laboratory staff had burgeoned to thirty and was subdivided into groups working on different aspects of the problem. But, of course, he placed his highest hopes on Sandy, whose capacity to solve the mysteries of cellular behavior was the greatest he had ever seen.

As they came closer and closer to finding the long-elusive protein that would provide the ultimate solution, both men verged on the monomaniacal. Greg did not even take into account that many of the hours Sandy spent in the lab were the rightful property of Judy and little Olivia. Neither had been the best of family men.

Yet Sandy Raven's personal loss was his professional gain.

Late one night when he was all alone in the lab, he discovered the golden fleece—the molecular structure of the anticancer virus that he, Greg, and their teams of biologists and crystallographers had spent years seeking to replicate. And it was there in glorious Technicolor on his monitor.

Sandy was ecstatic—at once elated and exhausted. And yet, for some inexplicable reason, before broadcasting the news to the world he wanted to savor the delicious taste of being the only man on earth to know one of God's secrets.

He walked into the deserted coffee lounge, opened the Frigidaire, pulled out a small green Perrier bottle, twisted the cap, and poured the liquid into a glass.

Giddy with excitement compounded by his solitude, he toasted himself out loud: "To Sandy Raven, the first man in his Bronx Science class to win a Nobel Prize."

"Amen," said a voice.

Startled, Sandy whirled around. It was his father-in-law.

"My God, Greg, I thought you'd be asleep at this hour."

"No," his mentor answered. "I had this uncanny feeling that we were getting close. I woke up and was drawn back here like a magnet."

"We've done it!" Sandy suddenly exploded. "I've got the answer right here."

Morgenstern was thunderstruck. He seemed temporarily paralyzed by the shock. Then, finally, he managed a breathless, "Show me."

They raced to Sandy's lab station, where the computer still glimmered with its victorious construct and his lab book lay open at the page when the writing had come to a complete, unexpected, and triumphal end.

For a minute or so the older man was speechless, his eyes darting frantically from the page to the screen and back again.

The two men embraced.

"I can't believe it, I can't believe it," Greg murmured. He turned to his son-in-law and said, "Go home and wake Judy. I'll just read through these last few days of notes and call Ruth." Tears welled up in his eyes. "Oh Sandy, you can't imagine how I've dreamed of this moment."

"I can, Greg. I can. This is like being on top of Mount Everest."

The rest of the day dissolved into a blur. After waking Judy and, as an inevitable result, three-year-old Olivia, Sandy was too excited to go to sleep. His wife was so elated she opened her heart and said everything this victory meant to her.

"Oh God, I'm so happy about Daddy. My whole life, people have told me that he was the smartest guy they'd ever met, but that his only fault was being too noble to fight for all the recognition he deserved. And now, like it or lump it, he's going to be famous."

"Hey," Sandy protested, "what about me? I wasn't exactly the office boy in all this."

"Oh, you're *my* special prize," Judy bubbled affectionately. "Now we'll get you back. It's like the end of a long, hard war. The troops—even generals like you and Daddy—come marching home to their families."

"Yeah, you're right," Sandy acknowledged. "I've been sort of delinquent. But as soon as we tie up the loose ends, we'll go away for a while."

The long evening of festivities began at five P.M. as champagne corks popped in Gregory Morgenstern's lab. This time some of the neighboring dignitaries came to drink to *him*. Professor Baltimore was there, as well as

Har Grobind Khorana. And the long-emeritus Salvador Luria.

Greg was forced to make a speech. But with characteristic modesty, he downplayed his own role.

"This is a team effort," he began, "and a team victory. And if it means the beginning of the end of one of the cruelest diseases ever to afflict man, then all of you should feel as gratified as I."

Then it was down to the waiting taxi that sped them, with Judy and Ruth, to the Ritz-Carlton to continue the effervescence *en famille*.

The aristocratic diners could not fathom the cause for the loud laughter and jubilation. They simply came to the most obvious conclusion—that these plebeians were from out of town.

"And now my fellow inebriates," Greg announced, with a perceptible slur in his voice, "I'm gonna share with you—and *only* you—the cherry on the sundae." He put his finger melodramatically to his lips and uttered in a stage whisper, "Shh!"

They all leaned forward as he murmured confidentially, "Guess when the news is being published?"

"Oh, that's an easy one," Sandy volunteered, also mumbling slightly. "It'll take us about two hours to write it up—"

"Two hours?" Judy queried with astonishment. "Is that all?"

"Yeah, honey," Sandy smiled. "It's a piece of cake it's so simple. The computer can practically do it on its own. The hard part was all the years that came before. Anyway, as soon as we knock off the draft, we'll call the editors of *Cell*, *Science*, and *Nature* and see who begs the most. I'd say the best offer is gonna be less than three weeks to publication."

"An excellent hypothesis, Dr. Raven," Greg pontificated tipsily. "That's what would've happened in the normal run of things. But my special surprise is . . ." He took a dramatic pause and concluded, ". . . the paper's already in the press."

Naturally the others did not take this literally. But something about Greg's tone made Sandy uneasy.

"What do you mean?" he asked.

"Well," Greg responded grandiosely, "you would all agree that *Nature* is the most prestigious journal in our profession. Watson and Crick used it to announce the cracking of the genetic code. And, as you know, it's published weekly in London.

"What's more, Marcus Williams, the current editor, happens to be one of my former research fellows. When I called him this morning, he was in his office going over the latest proofs. But he was so happy for me—for all of us—that he held everything while I scribbled out a few pages and faxed them. He not only dispensed with the normal refereeing, but rammed it into *this week's* issue. It'll be in every lab in America by Wednesday."

"Wrong," Sandy interrupted. "In every lab in the *world*."

In the days that followed, Sandy walked on air.

On Wednesday morning he fell to earth with a thud.

Arriving at the lab earlier than he had since the Great Breakthrough, Sandy was not surprised to find a cluster of staffers crowded around what he assumed to be a copy of *Nature*. The huddle was so large, it was impossible for him to see.

Just then Rudi Reinhardt, one of their star biochemists from Munich, noticed him and called out, "Hey, Sandy, can you believe this?"

"What're you talking about?"

The German's expression abruptly changed to one of concern. "You mean, you don't get your own copy of *Nature*?"

"Sure," Sandy replied. "I was just gonna amble over

to my mailbox and see what's new in the world of science."

"Then prepare yourself for a shock," Rudi answered sympathetically, holding out the publication to him. "It turns out that our humble prof is a closet egomaniac."

Sandy suddenly grew cold and the hairs on the back of his neck began to bristle. He grabbed the magazine, which was already turned to "An Antibody for Some Hepatic Oncogenes."

The listed author was Gregory Morgenstern, Department of Microbiology, Massachusetts Institute of Technology.

He was the *only* author.

All the usual collaborators' names were relegated to the first footnote and prefaced by the demeaning platitude, "I owe my deepest thanks to . . ."

At first Sandy thought it was a bad dream. It was tantamount to discovering that the saintly Albert Schweitzer was a werewolf.

In a move without precedent, Gregory the fair, Gregory the altruist, Gregory the self-effacing, had taken sole and unique credit for what should not even have been called a team effort, but was really the fruits of Sandy's own sweat and brains.

He suddenly felt dizzy and then desperately sick. He barely made it to the men's room in time.

Fifteen minutes later, having composed himself sufficiently, he appeared chalk-faced in front of Greg's secretary. "Where is he?" Sandy mumbled.

"I don't know," the woman replied, attempting to be offhand, but without sufficient conviction.

"Marie-Louise—you don't have any experience at lying." Sandy slammed her desk and demanded, "Now, tell me where he is."

Frightened, she stammered, "He and Ruth are going to Florida for a few days. That's all he told me."

Sandy's temper was swiftly reaching boiling point. "When? What airline?" he asked, browbeating her. "I know you must have made the reservations. You always do."

Marie-Louise glanced downward, partly to avoid his gaze and partly to check her watch.

"Delta at noon. He's probably on his way there," she answered, still unable to look at him.

Sandy checked his own watch, raced out the door, down the steps, and into the parking lot.

It was just after eleven, and the Callahan Tunnel was relatively quiet. He drove like a demon.

When he reached the Delta terminal, he simply abandoned his car and ran inside.

As Greg Morgenstern and his wife were arriving to join the other first-class passengers to board, he spied a figure hurtling toward them down the corridor.

He tried to hurry Ruth into the passageway.

Suddenly, a hand grabbed his shoulder and spun him around.

"Greg, you thieving sonovabitch," Sandy cried out.

"What the hell are you doing here?" Morgenstern responded, cowering.

Sandy had never before lost his temper. But now he was so consumed with anger that he was shaking the older man and shouting, "You stole it. You stole my work."

As airline personnel and a police officer rushed toward them, Sandy held him tightly and continued to demand, "Why, Gregory? Why?"

"Please try and understand," Morgenstern pleaded. "It was like a stroke of madness. I've been playing second fiddle my whole life. And Sandy, whatever you may think, this project *was* my life. All I could see was the chance of getting honor, respect—instead of all those condescending backhanded compliments I've heard for thirty years. You're young, Sandy, your time will come—"

This facile consolation cut the last thread of Sandy's

self-control. "My time is *now*," he insisted. "You should have given me credit."

"Oh, shut up, will you," Greg countered, matching fury for fury.

Then Sandy shocked even himself by unleashing a blow aimed at Greg's head. Fortunately, it was deflected by a large policeman. Instantly, they were surrounded by uniformed figures.

"Now, what seems to be the trouble here?" the cop demanded in a Boston-Irish accent.

Sandy and Greg glared silently at one another. In the end, it was Ruth who rescued them.

"It's just a family argument, officer," she said, her voice strained. "My husband and I are on our way to Florida. This other gentleman is our son-in-law and . . ." Her verbal powers failed her.

She grasped her husband by the arm and led him off down the gangway toward the airplane.

Sandy stood rooted to the spot. Then he realized that he had been left in the "custody" of the various officials. He took a deep breath, scanned their faces and capitulated. "Like the lady said, it was just a family argument."

Though he would not have believed it, the worst part of Sandy's day was yet to come.

Judy's reaction was the coup de grâce.

Indeed, the most painful discovery was the fact that, first and foremost, she was not really his *wife* as much as Greg's *daughter*.

She was furious at him. "You struck my father," she repeated in a hysterical litany. "How could you dare even touch him?"

Sandy could not explain his own loss of control. Indeed, a very small part of him was ashamed of his behavior. But his greatest preoccupation was with the low blow that Greg had just dealt him.

"He stole what was rightfully mine," Sandy insisted.

"You presumptuous bastard," Judy shrieked. "Whatever you did was nothing compared to the years my father put in."

"Jesus Christ, this has nothing to do with time. It has to do with brainwork. I 'owned' the best ideas—the ones that led to the solution. But even so, I would never have dreamed of not sharing the credit with him. He's as much a common thief as a guy who mugs an old lady."

"Stop it! Stop it!" she screamed. "I won't let you talk about him that way!"

The fires of Sandy's own temper were being stoked by indignation—and incredulity.

"I don't believe this. You're actually defending his dishonesty—his theft of my solution?"

"For God's sake, Sandy," she shouted back, "he earned it! I mean, he deserves recognition."

"Dammit, I do too. Judy, there was room for another name on that article. What Greg did was patent an invention that was not completely his. I mean, the courts recognize intellectual property—and your father's just robbed me of mine. . . ."

They fumed in silence for a moment, each waiting for the other to lash out.

Sandy was gradually coming to an agonizing realization.

He suddenly did not recognize the woman he had married.

"I'll tell you one more thing," he said quietly. "You can't have it both ways anymore. You can't be *his* daughter and *my* wife."

"Good. I agree," she hurled back.

"What the hell's that supposed to mean?" he demanded.

"Isn't it clear?" she answered, softly but sternly. "After what you did today, I don't want to be married to you, Sandy."

42

ISABEL

Isabel da Costa woke up one morning to find herself living face-to-face with harsh reality.

Throughout the first sixteen years of her life, Raymond had succeeded in cocooning her from intrusions and distractions. Indeed, that was the source of his greatest pride.

To the best of his knowledge she had never known pain, denigration, or hostility of any sort, although, to a large extent the secret talisman had been her precocity. But it was no protection from attacks on her intellect.

As Raymond rightly expected, the publication of her article on the Fifth Force had created a storm. But however magisterial her argument, it did not convince those scientists who had spent their working lives trying to prove precisely what she had demolished.

Pracht kept a respectful silence, but colleagues in universities all over the world did not feel any such noblesse oblige. If the girl was old enough to attack, she was old enough to *be* attacked.

For young Isabel, the articles published in the *International Journal of Physics* as well as in other distinguished periodicals were tantamount to hate mail. It was not merely that her adversaries were trying to refute her conclusions, it was the style in which she herself was referred to.

Some of the essays reeked bile. One went as far as to

sneer, "But what can one expect from a mind so young? She has not had time to learn her physics properly."

Naturally she would be accorded space by the editors of these various publications to defend herself. But who could assist her?

Raymond could not really be of any help. In fact, unwittingly, he increased her tension by voicing his worries. And Karl Pracht, who had so magnanimously allowed her to dig his scientific grave, could not be expected to help pour earth on it as well. Besides, he and his family were caught up in the complexities of moving their household across the American continent.

She felt isolated, except for what moral support Jerry—who was away at a tournament—could give her by telephone.

At the outset, the newspapers had once again trotted out the old stories about the Berkeley Child Prodigy and updated them. But this time they were not all patting a bright little girl on the head. Her antagonists had their own conduits to the press, who were more than willing to quote them when they spoke daggers.

Isabel was so busy formulating her counterattacks that she decided not to attend the ceremony to receive her master's degree and thereby risk exposure to the media.

Indeed, the storm dissolved Isabel's aura of infallibility and replaced it with one of controversy. She was now perceived as such an enfant terrible that some members of the Physics Department let it be known that under no circumstances would they supervise her doctoral dissertation.

But of course not all the reaction was negative. A good many scientists wrote to congratulate her on her achievement, and the journals printed many replies from distinguished physicists who were won over by her arguments.

Just prior to his departure for Boston, Karl Pracht invited Isabel to lunch at the faculty club. He could not

hide his astonishment—nor mask his displeasure—
when he saw that Raymond had come along as well.

"With due respect, Mr. da Costa," he said with exaggerated politeness, "this was supposed to be a meal for
a student and her adviser."

It suddenly dawned on Pracht that Raymond was desperately anxious to make sure that he did not divulge to
Isabel anything of the unpleasant altercation that had
taken place between the two of them. And realizing that
he could never dislodge the adhesive father, Karl relented and asked his nemesis to join them.

The conversation was friendly, though delicately
avoiding any mention of the Fifth Force debate. Over
coffee, Karl revealed the principal purpose of his invitation.

"Isabel, I have a gut feeling that you're going to find
Berkeley a little less congenial from now on. Obviously,
I'm pitching for my new team now, but I really think
you should let me arrange that fellowship for you at
MIT. I promise you'll find somebody world-class to direct your thesis, or failing that, humble has-been that I
am, I'll do the job myself."

Raymond listened in contemplative silence. Yet he
could see on his daughter's face a certain unmistakable
reluctance, and knew when she told Pracht "We'll think
about it," it was something she definitely did not want.

His instinct was confirmed when they walked out
into the bright summer sunlight and Isabel did not say
a word. Something made him suspect that although the
youngsters had not seen one another, she was somehow
tied to Berkeley by the *idea* of the presence of Jerry
Pracht.

"I think he made a lot of sense, Isabel," her father
commented. Thinking to himself, not only is MIT the
Olympus of science, but I've outmaneuvered the guy after all. Instead of having his son shipped to Cambridge,
we can go there ourselves and leave him here.

He then remarked out loud, "I'd say if Pracht comes

up with a big enough offer, we should take it and go to greener pastures."

June 28

A new book. And in a new medium: I've just opened a file in my very own laptop computer, for which I now have to provide eighty megabytes of my own memory. From now on, the saga of my personal life should be easier to keep private since I have encrypted the file and no one can access it without the password "sesame"—it's hardly original.

I was desperate to talk to Jerry about Karl's invitation, especially since Dad was putting unbelievable pressure on me. At first I was disappointed when Jerry gave me a pep talk about doing "what was the right thing for myself." I guess I was hoping he would get all passionate, and beg me to stay.

But it's typical of his generosity. I always know that he wishes only the best for me and would never make any selfish demands—although a part of me wishes he would.

"Look at it this way, Isa," he explained. "Starting this spring, Berkeley is going to be just a mailing address for me. So, the only difference in our currently unsatisfactory relationship will be in the size of the phone bill. Right?

"And frankly, I can see a lot of advantages in your going East. First of all—and I guess you never thought of this—MIT has practically a club or—perhaps I should call them a play group—of prodigies there. Granted, you'll be a graduate student, but at least there'll be a lot of undergraduates your age and I think that might make a major difference to your social life."

I felt like shouting no, Jerry, you make the only difference that matters.

After we hung up, I thought a lot about what he said and realized that if he was in fact going to be on the road so much, I might as well go and do my doctorate at the school Dad refers to as "the top of the mountain."

43

ISABEL

September 11
Jerry was right. Moving to MIT turned out to be a good idea in more ways than Dad and I had ever imagined. First of all, since I'm grown-up now (five foot five and a half in track shoes), nobody on the campus whispers, raises eyebrows, or points fingers as I walk past. A lot of freshmen look my age, and one or two of them are actually younger.

There's a math whiz from the Bronx High School of Science who's only fifteen and—lucky guy—he's got at least half a dozen kids his age to talk to. Probably the most amazing thing is that he lives in the dorm with other students.

Also I'm here incognito. This I owe to Karl, who arranged with the MIT press office not to make any noises about my arrival.

In a highly charged community like Cambridge, Mass., there are not as many undergraduates eager to pay thirty dollars an hour to be tutored by Isabel da Costa's father. But fortunately, one of the conditions of the offer Karl struck for me with Tech (which is how the locals refer to MIT) is that—despite my dad's objections—I'm obliged to work two afternoons a week as a teaching assistant instructing kids in the Intermediate Physics labs. My course work to prepare for the

Ph.D. won't pose a problem. The real challenge will be the dissertation. My M.A. thesis was a pretty hard act to follow. But I've got to come up with something even better—hopefully less controversial, if the two don't necessarily go hand in hand. I find it incredible, but even now letters attacking me continue to fill the journals.

Dad says—not entirely in jest—that now I know how Galileo felt.

In a sense, Isabel da Costa was living a double life. First, her assault on the Fifth Force theory had given her a worldwide reputation. There were scientists both pro and con, and she was variously regarded as illustrious or notorious.

Yet, on the campus of the Massachusetts Institute of Technology she was just another grad student sweating out the requirements for her doctorate.

Perhaps her most significant accolade was a follow-up article by Karl Pracht in *The Physical Review* reporting that he had repeated the various experiments and that her refutation of his argument had been correct.

Although some of the students occasionally invited Isabel to join them for a dinner or the movies, she was forced to limit her social activities to Kaffee and Klatsch in the common room, which housed what passed for a coffee machine. Isabel's day was divided between supervising and being supervised.

At MIT she encountered an array of new minds, if not more brilliant than those at Berkeley, at least with refreshing new hobbyhorses, for the university had no fewer than fifty full professors of physics.

Everyone on the faculty wanted to be her thesis adviser. For they knew wherever Isabel excavated, she would find gold and some of its glitter would inevitably shine on them.

As usual, she was breezing through her course work, and keeping the profs who taught her seminars on their toes. But they seemed to enjoy the challenge as much as she. In fact, Isabel could not recall ever being happier.

At least intellectually.

Even as a lowly T.A. she was granted a cubicle, grandiosely referred to as an office. But since it had a telephone and her very own computer terminal hooked into MITNet, the room had a legitimate claim to officiality.

In direct contrast to the unchanging routine of Isabel's life, Jerry's schedule was highly erratic: different cities, different time zones, different motels. But he never failed to phone her at a time when she would be able to talk privately.

Though they had not met face-to-face since midsummer, an astonishing intimacy was growing between them.

Jerry was young to be making the tour—especially on his own.

He was getting beaten fairly regularly, and began to count it a victory when he was not totally shut out by the big boys or speedily aced into oblivion.

Though not rising in the rankings, Jerry was nonetheless gaining a following—at least in Pracht's lab. For his career gave the scientists an aura of athleticism by association. Whether he knew it or not, he was fast becoming a hero to dozens of sedentary physics types, for whom he was their vicarious Sir Lancelot.

Also, even when he appeared briefly on the Cable Sports Network enacting the minor role of straw man for superstars like André Agassi to dispatch, Jerry was holding his own in another department.

A great many of the female sports fans were more interested in the good looks of the players than the quality of their play. And here Jerry Pracht gave even the flamboyant Agassi a run for his money.

Imagine the cannonade of emotions hitting Isabel all at once as she sat in the lounge watching him play, and hearing coeds sigh about his blond good looks.

She was at times joyful, proud, lonely—and embarrassed. For in one early qualifying round when Michael Chang took a mere forty-five minutes to relegate Jerry to the showers, a female graduate commented loudly, "Just imagine, that gorgeous hunk'll be hanging around Houston with nothing to do. I feel like calling him up and offering my company."

"You mean your services?" quipped a waggish undergraduate.

"Why not?" the girl replied. "He's fair game, and so am I."

"Well don't get too excited, honey. A guy like that has probably got his choice of half a dozen consolation prizes waiting outside the locker room."

This ostensibly harmless banter upset Isabel terribly, and she was barely able to reach the safety of her office before breaking into tears. To her delight, virtue was rewarded. Less than ten minutes later the phone rang.

"God, am I glad you're there, Isa," Jerry said with great relief as her heart soared. "I'm as depressed as hell. I just suffered a particularly ignominious defeat. Dink could have done better out there without a racket."

Her instinct told her it would be prudent not to mention that she had seen the match. "Want to talk about it?" she asked.

"I really want to forget it," he replied frankly. "But quite honestly, if I don't at least bitch a little, I'll never get it out of my system."

He launched into a self-deprecatory tirade about his bad performance, which lasted almost as long as the game he had actually played.

"Hey, Isa, I'm sorry," he said at last. "I know I'm boring you to stupefaction—"

"No, Jerry, that's fine," she reassured him.

"Part of the reason I was so upset," he continued, "was that I knew Paco was watching the game. The minute I hang up he'll chew me into little pieces. If I keep playing like this, I may not even get my job back at the club."

"Now you cut it out, Pracht," Isabel chided him. "I don't know anything about sports, but I know everybody has a bad day. Tonight was just your turn."

"Why is it, Isa," he asked affectionately, "that even though that kind of pep talk is as stale as a week-old bagel, coming from you it somehow makes me feel good?"

His compliment thrilled her.

"Do you think it has something to do with the way I feel about you?"

I hope so, she thought to herself.

"Anyway," he continued. "I know Paco's going to pull me off the road for a week of drills. I'll call you when I know where I am. By the way, if you ever feel as crappy as I did and want to lean on my shoulder—even over the goddamn phone—Dad can always get me."

He was reluctant to end the conversation, for he had another reason for calling. Finally, he confessed softly, "Isabel, I really miss you. Sometimes I get these fits of insanity that make me want to smash all my rackets on the floor and fly to see you."

She tried to conceal her excitement by joking, "And go back to school, of course."

"No." He laughed. "I haven't gotten that crazy yet. Good night, girl wonder."

As was their routine, Isabel would call Ray when she was ready to leave the lab, and he would come and walk her home—a prudent urban practice regardless of age.

"Get much done?" he asked as they strolled through the empty streets.

"A little," she murmured, omitting to mention how much her heart was full of Jerry's words.

"By the way," her father remarked ingenuously, "I saw your old friend on television tonight."

"Who's that?" she asked offhandedly.

"Why, none other than young Pracht, who got positively blown off the court. I must say he's not much of a tennis player."

That's okay, Dad, she thought. He's a hell of a human being.

By contrast with his daughter, Ray had a great deal of time on his hands—from the moment he accompanied Isabel to the door of the lab until he picked her up at whatever hour they would arrange.

True enough, he occupied himself with all the domestic chores—cleaning, shopping, preparing the food—and then sitting down to read through the mass of publications Isabel now subscribed to, abstracting for her those he thought of importance.

Yet it was hardly a fulfilling life, and he knew it. Still worse, it became increasingly clear to him that Isabel knew it as well.

One morning when she arrived at the lab at eight o'clock, Isabel found a Post-It notice from Karl Pracht fluttering on her door, asking her to come and see him at her earliest convenience.

Puzzled, she hurried to his office. Befitting his rank, the spacious room had a panoramic view of the Charles and the shining towers of the city beyond.

He offered her a cup of real coffee from his percolator. She took a sip and then asked, "What's this about?"

"Your dissertation, Isabel—or more specifically, lack of it. In all the time we've known each other, you've positively effervesced with theories, ideas, concepts—enough challenges to occupy the entire American Physical Society for a century. Isn't it strange that you can't settle on just one topic?"

Isabel shrugged.

"May I offer my own hypothesis?"

She nodded.

"It's Ray, isn't it?"

He looked at her, but she offered no comment.

"Isabel, sooner or later you're going to write your thesis and you'll be offered a cavalcade of professorships. At that point there'll be no evading the fact that your father will have played out the last syllable of his role. He'll have done his job brilliantly, and can rest comfortably on your laurels. But what the hell are you gonna do about him?"

For what seemed like an eternity, Isabel was mute. At last she protested weakly, "He needs me. He really needs me."

"We both know that," Pracht answered sympathetically. "The problem is, you no longer need him."

"Karl, let me be perfectly honest with you about Dad. . . ." She hesitated, then said almost under her breath, "I'm scared out of my wits."

The fax arrived late one autumn evening at the beginning of her second year at MIT. It had first been sent to the Department of Physics at Berkeley, the affiliation Isabel had listed in her controversial article.

The chairman then called the da Costa home in Cambridge. At first Isabel was surprised and delighted to hear her old adviser's voice. After they had exchanged warm greetings, he said something which made her squeal with delight.

"Yes, that'd be great. Fax it to the department. I'm sprinting there so fast it'll still be coming out of the machine. Thanks, thanks a million."

She hung up and turned to Ray.

"You'll never believe this, but the Italian Academy of Science has chosen *me* for this year's Enrico Fermi Award."

"The Fermi?" Raymond gasped. "That's just about as close to the Nobel as you can get in physics. When's the ceremony?"

"To be honest," she said, still shaking her head in disbelief, "I was so knocked out by the news I can barely remember anything else he said. Anyway, it'll be in the fax. Oh Daddy ..." She dissolved into tears of joy and threw her arms around him.

As they embraced, she thought, I can't wait till Jerry calls tonight.

"Isabel," Ray murmured. "I'm so proud of you."

"I couldn't have done it alone, Dad," she responded.

And as they hugged each other they realized something else that neither acknowledged: Isabel was now taller than her father.

The Enrico Fermi Prize was established by the Accademia Nazionale dei Lincei in honor of the man who had been Professor of Theoretical Physics at the University of Rome. He was one of those rare scientists at home in the practical as well as the theoretical field.

After receiving a Nobel Prize in 1938, Fermi immediately escaped Mussolini's fascism and emigrated to America, where he became a leading member of the team in Chicago that created the first sustained nuclear reaction—an experiment that culminated in the construction of the atomic bomb.

Like so many other scientific prizes, even the smaller ones, the award was not merely a plaque or statuette, but included a monetary gift as well. In Isabel's case, her bold work in the area of high-energy physics had now earned her seventy-five thousand dollars.

Their 747 landed in Rome's Leonardo da Vinci Airport at dawn. Three distinguished-looking gentlemen in charcoal-black suits met the da Costas as they disembarked: the president of the academy, Raffaele De Rosa, and two members of the executive committee.

As one of them presented the radiant, dark-eyed, sixteen-year-old with a large bouquet of flowers, what seemed like hundreds of cameras clicked and whirred from the roped-off areas beyond.

While the welcoming dignitaries were bowing and scraping and referring to her as *Signorina* da Costa, the paparazzi had no such reverence. Dozens of photographers shouted "Isabella, give us a smile!" "Run this way!" "Wave your hands to all of Italy."

While their baggage was being fetched for them, Isabel and Raymond were ushered past customs. Then the trio led them out to where a stretch Mercedes limousine waited.

Raymond, who was unaccustomed to imbibing anything but Miller Lite, had found himself unable to resist the charms of the Alitalia stewardesses who had foisted upon him several glasses of Asti Spumante. He swayed slightly as he trudged along in the company of two professors of physics, following a few steps behind his prize-winning daughter.

On the long journey into the still-sleeping city, one of the scientists read off, in heavily accented textbook English, the timetable of events that had been meticulously planned by the organizers. It included press conferences, luncheons, more press conferences, television interviews, two dinners in her honor—one of them the night before the big event, when her stomach would already be full of butterflies. All this would be built into the ultimate apotheosis, the official presentation of the awards in the Aula Magna of the university.

Isabel was expected to make an acceptance speech, after which all would retire to the Hotel Excelsior for the grand banquet that would conclude the program.

While her father had spent most of the flight relishing the amenities of first class, she had used the time to pore over her speech, which would be carried live on RAI, the Italian national television network.

The committee had spared no expense to demonstrate their appreciation of the young physicist's achievements. The da Costas' luxurious quarters in the Excelsior, which they had reserved for them, were graced by at least a dozen different arrangements of flowers.

Instinct drew Isabel to the most lavish of the bouquets. As she suspected, it was from Jerry: "Break a leg. Love, J."

She quickly hid the card in her purse.

Ray was so sozzled that he excused himself and went to his bedroom to sleep it off.

In contrast, Isabel ordered a continental breakfast and strong coffee so that she could best avail herself of the twelve hours' respite granted them before the ceremonial tornado began.

After working for about an hour, she rose from the graceful antique desk and tiptoed to her father's bedroom door. Hearing him snoring loudly, she hurried to the phone, extracted her little address book from her leather passport case, and dialed a number.

"Hello," she said in a cautious whisper, still frightened that Raymond might somehow overhear. "This is Isabel da Costa. You should be expecting my call. . . ."

She paused for a moment, listened, and then stated, "No. I won't have the money till the actual ceremony. But I've made sure your fee will be covered by a banker's check. It's as good as cash. Anyway, your merchandise had better be as terrific as you say, or the deal's off. Okay, see you then. *Grazie*."

44

SANDY

THE GREATEST day in Gregory Morgenstern's life was the blackest in Sandy's.

Scarcely three years after the publication of his discovery of the antibodies for liver cancer, Morgenstern was awarded the Nobel Prize for Medicine. As though the honoree had been an unsung hero for so long that the scientific community had rushed to redress their oversight as soon as possible.

The pain of the announcement was bad enough for Sandy. But the ceremony itself produced a veritable dagger in his heart. For Greg—the quintessential family man—had taken not only his wife to Stockholm, but his daughter and his granddaughter as well.

By some cruel trick of fate, photo editors all over America were drawn to the picture of the winner and his three ladies.

And ironically, Sandy's generosity had been the cause of this further distress. For, according to the terms of his divorce, Judy needed his permission to take Olivia out of the country.

He had wanted very badly to say no, for suddenly here was something he could deny Morgenstern, who had otherwise despoiled him of everything.

And yet Sandy could not be so hardhearted as to make his daughter a hostage to his own bitterness and rage.

He also calculated that if he insisted on his right of

veto, Judy would use it as ammunition against him for the rest of Olivia's minority.

"I really feel bad about this," Sandy admitted when Judy asked his permission.

"I think I can understand," she offered. "But I know you'll do the decent thing—whatever your feelings in the matter, you don't want to hurt Olivia."

Sandy sighed. "I'll give my consent on one condition."

"Sure, Sandy."

"That you never use the word decent to me again."

When his daughter returned from the ceremony, she innocently reported to Sandy on the phone, "It was really neat, Dad. You should've been there."

When Greg had first committed his intellectual robbery, Sandy had consulted Milton Klebanow, the greatest expert in patent law on the Harvard faculty, to find out if he could receive some modicum of justice.

At their initial meeting Klebanow was not wholly pessimistic. After all, Dr. Raven could produce the evidence of his own lab books, and they could find expert witnesses who would evaluate and testify to the importance of his contribution to the project.

As they spoke, Sandy was gripped with a sudden fear that—at the very moment they were chatting—Morgenstern or one of his minions might be confiscating his proof. The instant the consultation ended, he rushed in a panic to the lab to gather all the documents—including his contract. Obsessed with the notion of spies and espionage, he avoided using the university machines and photocopied them in a store on Massachusetts Avenue.

The next day, Klebanow phoned him at the faculty club, where he had found temporary refuge.

"I'm not a scientist," he began, "and the formulae are beyond my ken. But two things strike me. First, even I can tell you've done a significant amount of work, and second, it's too late to do anything about it."

Sandy's heart sank. "But yesterday you—"

"Yesterday I hadn't read your contract," the lawyer answered. "I don't suppose you ever have either. Otherwise you would have understood the clause that automatically assigns the rights to anything you create to the director of the lab—in this case, Professor Morgenstern."

Sandy's spirits nosedived. He knew that even if he had been aware of this clause, he would have trusted Greg enough to sign the contract anyway.

At the height of the emotional conflagration, he had resigned his post at MIT, confident that he could easily find another. He was correct, for universities like Columbia and Johns Hopkins, which were better informed on the nature of his role in the Morgenstern research, took the initiative and sought him out. After he wrote letters to several other major institutions, he was swamped with offers.

Yet the terrible injustice so embittered Sandy that he made a conscious effort to become a cynic. From now on, he determined, all his research would be motivated by advancement and rewarded with material gain.

It soon became clear to him that the big money was in combating the aging process. Everybody was afraid of dying. This, after all, was the universal enemy. A scientist who might slow the process—and especially one who could stop the clock—would have the world at his feet and millions in the bank.

Midnight oil was burning in laboratories all over the world as they studied the mechanisms that imposed limits on the life span. Legions of other scientists were also hunting for the genes that debilitated various organs of the body and contained the invisible clock of aging.

Hence, taking a page from his father's operating manual, Sandy "pitched" to all the establishments who interviewed him the idea of an institute to study cell degeneration.

In the end he accepted a professorship in microbiology, with a lab of his own, at Cal Tech.

He had a variety of reasons. There was, of course, the prestige, the high salary, the state-of-the-art facilities. Not least, though, was the promise of funding for an Institute of Gerontology. There was also the fact that his father was living in Beverly Hills.

And, by moving to the West Coast, he would be as far away as possible from Gregory Morgenstern.

Groundbreaking work had already been done in the field. At the University of Texas a team of doctors came upon a deadly pair of genetic activities: Mortality One, which, when switched on, sets a slow deterioration in motion.

After this there was Mortality Two, which finishes the job shortly and swiftly. Yet by deactivating these processes, they were able to stop senescence.

Sandy's own efforts concentrated on trying to halt the progress and reeducate these genes, and ultimately reverse their destructive activity.

Unlike diseases such as cystic fibrosis, which have been pinpointed to one particular chromosome, aging is controlled from perhaps as many as a hundred different sites in the genome.

Some aspects of aging are visible. Sandy himself was experiencing a trivial but painful example as he combed his hair each morning. He sometimes could not keep from counting the strands that came off in his hand.

This is but a benign indication that other systems are gradually failing. The telomeres—end bits of genes—lose a few base pairs whenever they copy themselves.

Little by little the losses add up, until they begin to cause damage. And yet Sandy and his colleagues discovered that an enzyme called telomerace can be used to prevent time's once inevitable erosion of DNA. In other words, as he joked, they could now "grow hair on a gene."

In spite of all his misanthropic protestations, Sandy had an unconscious human motive for his research.

For all subjects that attract scientists relate, however distantly, to something in their psyche. And perhaps Sandy's many projects were, at least in part, inspired by a preoccupation with his own father's growing old.

As a result of many years of exposure to the California sun, Sidney Raven had developed three black spots on his face. An expert dermatologist diagnosed them as malignant and surgically removed them. In his view, there was little immediate danger of the carcinoma spreading to more vital organs.

But the mere fact that his dad was coming ever closer to the limit of life spurred him into spending more and more time on his quest. Deep in his soul, he cherished the irrational thought that he could make his beloved father immortal.

There had been an additional element in Sandy's choice of university—one he had not mentioned to Sidney—for his move to Cal Tech would place him in the same time zone and the same city as the former Rochelle Taubman.

Yet, what little he now knew of her was almost exclusively from the media.

Although the split from Elliot Victor did not make banner headlines in a town where marriage is only a seasonal sport, the events that followed propelled Kim Tower once again, permanently it would seem, into the Hollywood firmament.

"Have you heard the news, sonny boy?" Sidney trumpeted down the phone.

"I've been in the lab all day, Dad."

"Well, it's stunned the town, but she's coming home in triumph."

"Who? What are you talking about?"

"Don't tell me you've forgotten Rochelle," Sidney
teased. "I can't tell you how proud it makes me feel.
They've just announced that Miss Kim Tower—aka Rochelle Taubman—is succeeding Sherry Lansing as head
of Fox. It's the highest executive position ever held by
a woman in Hollywood. As a matter of fact, my sources
tell me she's already on the lot."

"My God," Sandy exclaimed, "that's sensational.
Perhaps I should send her a telegram or flowers or . . .
something."

"Why not call her up, sonny boy? She'd probably be
glad to hear from you. Remember, you knew her when
she was a minnow. Anyway, suit yourself," Sidney philosophized. "I'm just going down to watch the dailies.
Why don't you drive in and meet me at Chasen's so I
can buy you the best bowl of chili this side of heaven?
We can raise a glass to Rochelle."

"Great idea. Want me to pick you up?"

"Don't bother, kiddo. I think I'll go home and
change. See you at eight."

Though not in the movie business, Sandy nonetheless
felt a pang of inferiority as he drew up in a mere
Chevrolet a few yards from Chasen's green-and-white-
striped awning and had to wait for the valets to park not
one, but two Silver Clouds.

When Sandy gave his name, the maître d' reacted
with a slight bow of the head and led him through the
lavish twilight of the restaurant to a rich red-leather
booth.

Declining the suggestion of a cocktail, he ordered a
glass of mineral water. When his eyes had grown accustomed to the semidarkness, he scanned the restaurant in
hopes of glimpsing a famous face.

Sandy was so engrossed in stargazing that he lost all
sense of time. Having spotted—so he thought—Paul
Newman and Joanne Woodward, he suddenly realized

that it was nearly nine and his dad still had not arrived. He flagged the waiter and asked for a phone.

"I'll bring one to the table right away, sir."

Moments later Sandy was dialing Twentieth Century-Fox.

One ring, two, three. Perhaps the studio was closed for the night. No, that was absurd. There was always somebody awake—even if it was only a lowly screenwriter.

Finally, a male voice answered. Clearly at this hour calls were rerouted to Security.

"Can you tell me if there's anyone still working in the projection rooms?" Sandy asked.

There was a pause. The man was no doubt buzzing the various numbers.

"I'm afraid there's no answer from any of them," he announced.

"Then, can you give me Sidney Raven's line, please?"

There was another pause.

"I'm sorry, sir," said the voice. "There's no one of that name on our list."

"Are you serious? I want Sidney Raven, R-A-V-E-N. He's been with Fox for years."

The man did not hesitate this time. He repeated like an automaton, "I'm sorry. There's no extension for anyone of that name. Now you have a good evening, sir."

The line went dead. And Sandy went into shock. After fretting for another fifteen minutes, he was about to dial again when his father suddenly appeared. Normally dapper and fastidious, Sidney was unkempt, disheveled, his shirt open and tie dangling sloppily down his chest.

"Christ, Dad, what's the matter?"

"I'm dead, sonny boy. You're looking at a walking corpse."

Sandy rose quickly, put his arms around the older man and helped him to sit down. "Let me get you a drink," he offered solicitously.

"I think I've had too much already."

Only then did Sandy realize there was whiskey on his father's breath.

"Please, Dad, what happened?"

"Are you kidding? What the hell d'you think takes place at a firing squad?"

"Here, Dad," Sandy responded, offering him some mineral water and trying to keep his own wits about him. "Calm down and tell me all about it."

Sidney emptied the glass and recounted the final moments of his professional life.

"When I went to see the rushes, she was there waiting. At first, I was flattered. Wow, I thought to myself, the head of the studio's barely moved in and she comes down to see my stuff."

"And?"

"And so we ran the film. It wasn't terrific, but it wasn't terrible either. Then the lights go up and she turns to me and says, 'This is crap, Sidney, total crap. And what's more, it's sixties crap.' She kept repeating that word again and again."

He shook his head in agony and then continued, "She told me I wasn't with it, I was out of touch. And then she said something even worse."

Sandy, sick at heart, did not want to hear it, but he knew his father needed the catharsis.

"What was it, Dad?" he asked.

"She called me a dinosaur. She said I was extinct and didn't even know it."

"Jesus—the bitch. Didn't she have any respect for your career?"

The older man shook his head.

Sandy's voice grew louder. "And what about the fact that you were the guy who started her off in the first place?"

"Come on, kiddo. This town has the highest amnesia rate in the world."

Sandy felt outraged and helpless. He could not imagine such behavior even among the most barbaric tribes in the jungle.

Though his worst fears had already suggested the answer, he felt compelled to ask, "So, what's going to happen? Will she put you on another one of those so-called 'youth' pictures?"

"Get serious. I'm over twenty-five, and what's left of my hair is gray. My kind of people don't get work in this business anymore."

"Don't be silly, Dad, you're exaggerating."

"I wish, I wish." Sidney sighed. "But believe me, sonny boy, *you're* too old for this game. If things end up like they're going, in a year or two every studio will be run by a squeaky-voiced high school kid—at a salary of twenty-five million a year."

"Listen, you've got every right to be upset," Sandy said soothingly. "But don't let her break your spirit. I'll buy you that chili dinner and we can go for a drive along the ocean."

The older man nodded.

Sandy beckoned to the waiter, who could not conceal his disapproval of Sidney's untidy appearance.

Watching his father eat mechanically, simply moving the spoon back and forth between the bowl and his mouth, Sandy realized he was a broken man.

And now he had an overwhelming reason for contacting Rochelle Taubman.

He had misgivings about leaving Sidney alone, and decided to sleep in the guest bedroom that he and Judy had once shared—so many traumas ago.

Paradoxically, Sandy was more agitated than his father. He tossed and turned all night, wondering what he would say to Rochelle when he confronted her—if she would even speak to him.

He was in the kitchen drinking a cup of black coffee when Sidney entered wearing a bathrobe.

"Hey, what are you doing here? You've got a lab to run."

"I know, Dad, but I was too bushed last night to drive home. So, if I can borrow a shirt and a razor, I'll head back. Will you be all right on your own?"

"Sonny boy, I've been all right on my own since the day I was born. Believe me. The past is past and today is the future. As Claude Rains said to Bette Davis in *Deception*, 'I've always had a great sense of tomorrow.' So I'll just sit here and make some phone calls."

Though his father's optimism was not convincing, Sandy was confident that he would at least be able to cope with the routine of life on his own.

Sandy shaved very quickly, arranged the thin strands of hair endlessly and finally, when he was satisfied, sprayed them. Before leaving, he gave his father a pep talk and promised to check in later on.

During the anguished hours of the previous night, Sandy had pondered whether it would be best to call Rochelle and straightforwardly ask for an appointment. He concluded that this tactic would then allow her simply to look at her agenda, protest its fullness, and sweetly suggest that he call another time.

No, Sandy had decided. It would be far better to appear at the studio entrance and have the guard announce his arrival. She might still refuse to see him, but somehow he felt his physical presence would add weight to his request.

And then he would face her and say what had to be said.

Although he had not yet found the words.

45

ISABEL

AT LAST the gala evening arrived.

Raymond da Costa donned the tuxedo he had bought for himself at Filene's. Isabel had been unable to choose between a light blue taffeta and a peachy silk and had, at Raymond's urging, bought both. Tonight, when she could vacillate no longer, Isabel resorted to a fundamental scientific method: she flipped a coin; the blue dress won.

The Aula Magna was packed with dignitaries, all bedecked, bemedaled, and bejeweled. Isabel sat onstage at the center of a crescent of chairs otherwise reserved for the high officials of the academy. Raymond sat in the front row, radiating pleasure.

Many of the distinguished guests could not help remarking how much tonight's honoree looked like a pretty Italian schoolgirl. They adored her before she even opened her mouth.

The actual presentation was made by Professor De Rosa. Both his voice and his gestures were fulsome. He praised Isabel's achievements to the sky and reminded the "grown-ups" present that, just as science knew no national boundaries, the same objectivity should apply to the scientists.

"In the quest for new discoveries, neither age nor gender should be considered. What counts is the achievement per se."

He then went into detail, describing the outstanding

work that Isabel had performed, which had forced even the most eminent of physicists to rethink their conclusions about the Fifth Force.

Then, with a verbal flourish, he introduced this year's winner, *"circondata d'onore."*

To enthusiastic applause, Isabel gracefully approached the podium. Cameras flashed like fireworks as Professor De Rosa shook her hand, kissed her on both cheeks, gave her the plaque and an envelope, and returned to his seat, leaving her alone in the limelight.

She laid her awards to one side as she prepared to make her acceptance speech. To everyone's surprise, she had no sheets of paper, not even cue cards.

With stunning poise she stood smiling at the guests, nodding her head to both sides of the hall in acknowledgment of their welcome.

A sudden hush fell as she began.

"Carissimi colleghi, gentili ospiti, desidero ringraziarvi per l'alto onore che mi fate assegnandomi questo premio, di cui mi sento indegna." Esteemed colleagues, distinguished guests. Thank you for the great prize that you have accorded me and of which I feel unworthy. . . .

At first the audience assumed that she had gone to the effort of phonetically memorizing a few words of Italian to flatter the country that was honoring her. But it quickly became apparent that Isabel would be speaking entirely in Italian.

Perhaps the most dumbfounded spectator was her father. She had read him the draft in English, without confiding that she would ultimately be delivering it in a foreign tongue.

Isabel began with some words of praise for Italian researchers, past and present, notably Rita Levi-Montalcini, who two years earlier had won the Nobel for her work on nerve cell growth. She then modulated skillfully into a history of the Fermi Prize itself.

She concluded by offering her views as to the moral

obligation of the modern scientist, "not merely to seek truth, but to *share* it."

Her select audience all understood her thinly veiled allusion to the selfishness in certain areas of the community. They knew that in the international rat race, many researchers were holding back their discoveries for the sake of personal glory rather than actually circulating them for the benefit of mankind.

The applause was tumultuous. If they could have given her yet another prize, they would have done so on the spot. The standing ovation lasted nearly five minutes.

The instant she could free herself, Isabel rushed off stage, where she nearly collided with Professor De Rosa. There were tears in the older man's eyes as he again kissed her on both cheeks and murmured, "You are the eighth wonder of the world. You—"

"Excuse me, sir," she interrupted urgently, "but I have to go somewhere for about a quarter of an hour. Will you please tell my father not to worry? I'll be back in time to join you before dinner."

She was in such a hurry to get away that she did not even notice Raymond's appearance in the distance.

De Rosa offered Ray his congratulations and faithfully conveyed his daughter's message. The information jolted Raymond into a sudden panic, and barely acknowledging the professor's remarks, he dashed out into the cobblestoned Via della Lungara.

Just in time for the greatest shock of his life, for he glimpsed Isabel climbing on to the back of a Lambretta, driven by what looked like a slim young man, whose features were obscured by his helmet.

Their chauffeur was waiting dutifully by the stage door and Ray hailed him.

"Gino!" he called out, pointing to the top of the narrow street where the Lambretta was just disappearing.

The driver nodded. "*Sì?*"

Ray responded with the only word he knew in any foreign language: *"Vamos."*

Gino understood the message, and both men ran to the Mercedes to give chase.

Some parts of Rome never sleep. Others rarely wake. And, as they followed Isabel and her companion, they passed brightly lit streets of crowded outdoor tables, with people laughing and singing as they drank and dined. Then suddenly they turned into a dark street behind the restaurants. Most of the stores and small workshops, obviously only used by day, were boarded up for the night. Only occasionally did a pale glimmer emanate from one of the upper floors.

Where the hell is she going? Raymond thought as his heart pounded. And is she going willingly? This was, after all, a country notorious for kidnapping.

"What is this area?"

"It's Trastevere. By day, there are many artisans at work."

"But what's she doing here at this time of night?" Ray growled. "She's the goddamn guest of honor."

"If you want my opinion," Gino offered in a heavy Neapolitan accent, "the young man may have caught her fancy."

Raymond nearly shouted that he had no interest in the driver's philosophy of life. But at that very moment the Lambretta swung into a narrow alley. Gino sped up and brought the limousine to a near-silent stop.

"I think is better we go on foot, signore," he whispered. "I know this is a dead-end street."

They turned the corner just in time to spot Isabel and her escort illuminated by a sliver of light from an open door.

The cyclist had taken off his helmet and flung back his head to remove the strands of long hair that had been covering his face.

Both men instinctively realized that they could move

more briskly, for Isabel and the mysterious man were now inside.

In a moment the two men were standing in front of an incongruously open shop whose interior light shone onto the fading gilt letters on the windowpane that identified the establishment:

GIULIANO
STRUMENTI A CORDA

They could hear the sound of several people talking, including Isabel saying, "I'm in a big rush, Mr. Carbone. I hope what you told Edmundo is true."

"It is, signorina, I promise you." The voice was of a man of well-advanced years.

Raymond and Gino now dared to take a closer look. The shop was small, with what appeared to be a workroom behind. Various colors and species of stringed instruments hung in every conceivable place, ranging from a delicate treble viola to several majestic double basses standing on the floor.

They saw the elderly man move toward a glass-fronted cabinet housing several antique violins, and withdraw one of them. It was dark amber, and the surface, despite superficial cracks visible through the varnish, was smooth and unblemished.

He handed it to Isabel, who held it as though it were a precious child as he continued his presentation.

"It is a Giovanni Grancino, about 1710. An amateur collector has owned it for the past thirty years, but following his death, the estate is selling the instrument. If I cannot arrange a private sale, it will go to auction at Sotheby's in London next week."

As Isabel placed it under her chin, he handed her a bow that seemed of the same era.

She took a deep breath and began to sound the open strings. The violin instantly came to life.

Isabel then launched into the Bach Third Partita. She

was so enraptured by the voice of the instrument that
she played the entire Preludio. At the end, the faces of
Carbone and the young man were transported, and both
clapped enthusiastically.

"That was magnificent, signorina," Carbone almost
sang. "You played that instrument like someone making
love."

"Well," Isabel smiled, "you've lived up to your
promise, and so will I. Here's a banker's check for
thirty-five thousand dollars."

"What?" he responded with disappointment.

"What's the matter?" Isabel asked.

"You haven't bargained with me," Carbone lamented.
"Thirty-five was my starting figure. I assumed we
would end up with somewhere in the high twenties."

"I'm sorry," said the confused sixteen-year-old. "But
I told you I had no experience in this sort of thing.
What can I do? The check's already made out."

"I tell you what, sweet, naive lady," he announced
paternally. "For that price, I will add the splendid bow
you have been using. Then you will have a real bargain.
If you like, I can bring it around to your hotel tomorrow
morning."

"I don't know." Isabel hesitated. "We're leaving so
early. Could you call me a cab so I can take it back with
me to the banquet?"

Then she suddenly remembered.

"My God, *the banquet.* I'm really late now—"

"That's okay, Isabel," her father interposed as he entered the shop.

"Dad! How did you find me?"

Ignoring her question, he went straight to the point.

"You really should've told me about this, darling," he
chastised her. "I'm genuinely hurt. But we can talk
about it tomorrow. For the moment, Gino's waiting at
the corner and we can just make it back in time for the
dinner."

As they careened through the streets of Rome—Gino

taking all the shortcuts he knew through the compli-
cated maze of thoroughfares between the Campo dei
Fiori and the Piazza Colonna, then on toward the Hotel
Excelsior—Raymond continued to berate her gently.

"After all, thirty-five grand is a big hunk of our win-
nings. You should have asked me so I could have had
the chance to say yes. I would've felt a lot better."

"No, you wouldn't," Isabel said quietly.

"What do you mean?" he asked.

"Because I bought it for Mom."

46

ADAM

THE COOPERSMITHS' grand tour began auspiciously
enough. They charmed the distinguished medical scientists (and doubtless Nobel nominators) from San
Francisco to San Diego. During the week they spent in
La Jolla, it seemed as if they had a meal with everyone
at the Salk Institute for Biological Studies—not least its
director, the legendary Jonas, conqueror of polio, and
his wife Françoise.

Salk, though into his ninth decade, had the lively
mind of a zealous schoolboy and was fascinated to hear
firsthand of Adam's discoveries.

He himself, it turned out, was far from resting on his
many laurels and was deeply involved in finding weap-
ons against the newest immunological scourge—AIDS.

Anya had been nervous about this dinner.

"I just couldn't get out of my mind that Françoise
had once been married to Picasso. And I'm ashamed to

say that I actually asked her what he was like to live with."

"What did she say?"

" 'Interesting.' "

"Well, I suppose that's an honest answer," he replied.

"Actually, one thing puzzles me," she continued. "Jonas Salk is one of the towering scientific minds of this century. He cured a disease that killed and crippled millions. Why didn't he get a Nobel Prize?"

Adam took a chilled bottle of Chardonnay and two glasses onto their balcony, which commanded a breathtaking view of the Pacific expanding into infinity.

"Well, Annoushka, I can only give you my own off-the-wall theory."

"Yes?" She smiled, lifting a glass to her lips.

"I think the boys in Stockholm sent their secret agents out to check on Jonas. They took one look at his institute and the paradise it's built in and thought that was enough for one human being."

Anya fixed him with her large brown eyes and asked, "If you had the choice, which prize would you prefer?"

"You," he answered without a moment's hesitation.

Hawaii was intended to be a vacation, but Adam's medical colleagues all pressured him for lectures—or at the very least, a state visit. He ended up working harder than ever.

Two days before their departure to the South Sea isles, the wire services ignited with the controversial and—to many—grotesque story that a sixty-two-year-old Italian woman had just given birth to a child.

Naturally, the sexagenarian mother in question was postmenopausal. But the doctors had fertilized a younger donor's egg with the older husband's sperm in vitro and transplanted it into Signora X's uterus. There, with the aid of copious hormonal support, she carried the pregnancy to term.

Adam was not impressed. As he told Anya, "I think

it's just a stunt. Since the ovum belonged to a young girl, the signora wasn't much more than an incubator. It would have been a *genuine* accomplishment if she could have provided her own eggs."

"Absolutely," Anya agreed. "And if you believe that passionately enough, we have a new project."

"I do and we have. In fact my mind's been racing all morning."

He opened a desk drawer, withdrew some hotel stationery and scribbled some basic principles.

"As a woman reaches the end of the fifth decade, her mid-cycle peak gradually diminishes and then disappears. Now we've already got the knowledge and drugs to stimulate moderately older women to produce at least occasionally promising ovulations. But you can't do this forever, and there are obvious hazards."

He then tossed the ball to her.

"How would you handle it, Doctor?"

"Well, since we have the luxury of speaking only theoretically, why don't we posit the 'simplest' scientific solution, namely defer the menopause altogether?"

"Good. A solution that women would welcome for other reasons as well, and it's no longer science fiction. Naturally, we'd have to hook up with a geneticist. Anybody come to mind?"

"Avilov," she quipped jokingly.

"I doubt if he's smart enough," Adam countered, his natural male rivalry aroused. "Actually, I was thinking along the lines of gerontologists like Raven, the *Time* magazine cover boy who's into reversing the genetic clock."

"I'm sure he would be flattered to work with you, darling," Anya offered.

"Actually, Raven's the least likely guy to want to embark on any collaboration. He's already been royally screwed out of one Nobel Prize. But maybe if we meet and he sees your honest face . . ."

He smiled at his wife and then suddenly remarked, "But isn't this supposed to be a vacation?"

"Come on, Adam, you thrive on challenge. Why not indulge yourself?"

He laughed. She read him like a book. Lately, despite the lectures, which he disparagingly referred to as "ideas from the freezer, defrosted for the occasion," he had begun to feel like a malingerer. Since the moment he met Max Rudolph long ago, he had never ceased to wrestle with apparently insoluble problems. Now he missed the excitement.

Adam borrowed his host's secretary the next morning and dictated a long letter to Dr. Sandy Raven, sounding out his willingness to participate in a project that was, as he put it, "down both our scientific alleys." Perhaps, Adam thought, despite Raven's justifiably misanthropic reputation, the biogeneticist would agree to put his anger on hold.

They broke their journey to Australia in Fiji, where only a third of the three hundred tropical islands were inhabited. At Suva he took advantage of their modern technology and called Heather to touch base. Though Anya had tried to write at least a postcard every day, this was their first live contact. Then they changed to a small two-propeller shuttle that took them to an islet which had more coconuts than people.

They arrived exhausted, and spent their first day sleeping late, strolling on the beach, and sleeping some more.

It was to battle fatigue that Anya ascribed the first incident.

The setting sun gave the sand a roseate glow as they walked back toward their palm-thatched *bure*, letting the waves lick gently at their feet.

Adam suddenly glanced at his watch and said, "Jesus—what time's my lecture?"

Anya laughed. "We'll order one of those delicious

cocktails, and you can address me on any topic that suits your fancy."

Counter to her expectation, Adam did not smile. "No, seriously, I've forgotten what time I'm speaking. I seem to recall your saying something about five-thirty—I'd better hurry and get my slides."

There was something in his tone of voice that gave Anya a frisson. She sensed that he was not joking, that he was genuinely confused.

"Darling, I knew you shouldn't have taken on so many commitments. I'm happy to say that you gave your last lecture two days ago in Maui."

His answer chilled her. For he gazed at Anya with the look of a little boy lost and asked, "Isn't this Maui?"

"No, my poor tired husband, this is Mana, one of the Fiji Islands, and the only obligation for this evening is rest and recreation."

Adam looked about him with an initial expression of mistrust. There was the endless beach, the undulating palms that had convinced him they were in Hawaii.

Then he retrieved the reins of his mental processes and joked, "I was just checking you for jet lag, Annoushka. I'm happy to say you passed."

Anya confidently dismissed her husband's harmless lapse and they proceeded to consume enough rum and coconut juice to make their geographical location irrelevant.

Five days later, tanned and relaxed, they boarded a Qantas jet to begin what would be a triumphal tour of Australia.

It was hard to tell who enjoyed his lectures more— Adam or the medical faculties he addressed in Perth, Adelaide, Melbourne, Sydney, and Brisbane. Beyond the sheer charisma of his physical presence, there was his ability to spellbind an audience by looking straight at them for several minutes at a time, rarely, if ever, glancing at one of his index cards.

They returned to Sydney for a few days of idleness and opera. Yet by this time they were beginning to realize the extra cost of fame.

For all its physical size—almost as large as the continental United States—Australia has a kind of small-town mentality. Not only were Adam's lectures written up in every city where he appeared, but since the nature of his achievement was so emotive—every person could sympathize with the trials of a childless woman—in the mere fortnight they spent down under, he became a celebrity.

He was invited on television shows he had never heard of, and to parties by people he had never met.

"You know, Anya," he confessed as they were returning in a taxi after a late-night fete, "I thought I was the most ambitious guy in the world. And now that Clarke-Albertson has taken care of our financial future, I would feast myself on adulation. But I've discovered I hate the publicity, like going into a store and being greeted with 'Hi, Doc!' and all that groveling I imagined would be so terrific."

"Well, you'd better get used to it, darling. Think of how much more famous you're going to be when you win the Nobel Prize."

As the cab pulled up to the Regent Hotel, the doorman rushed to welcome them. A few seconds later, when Adam took out his wallet to pay the driver, the man insisted, "Not a bit of it, Doc. It's been an honor to have you as my passenger. All I want's your autograph to give my kids."

As they walked arm in arm into the hushed luxury of the hotel lobby, Anya whispered lovingly, "Come on, Adam, tell the truth—you enjoyed that, didn't you?"

He smiled broadly. "You didn't even need to ask."

Thus ended the last happy day of their lives.

They spent the next morning shopping, and lunched on the Australian answer to New England lobster, Mortin

Bay Bugs, in a restaurant looking east over Darling Harbor.

A good night's sleep had restored Adam's effervescent spirit. He enjoyed Anya's breathless excitement at the prospect of seeing *Eugene Onegin* in Russian at the Opera House that evening.

"You know, I sometimes forget how hard it must be for you to have to live constantly in a foreign language."

"You mean Australian?" she joked.

Later that afternoon, he put on his "U.S. Drinking Team" track suit—a farewell present from the lab staff—to go out jogging, while she descended to have her hair done by the hotel coiffeur.

Yet when she returned to the room two hours later, she was puzzled to find it empty—with no note from Adam. Surely he couldn't still be running.

There was plenty of time, so Anya did not begin to worry—that is, until she was dressed and ready and there was still no sign of Adam.

At six o'clock she was concerned enough to want to call the police. At which moment they called her.

"Mrs. Coopersmith," the constable explained, "we picked up your husband wandering a bit dazed around the opera lobby, in his running gear."

Anya breathed a sigh of relief.

"He was sort of glassy-eyed, so security thought he might be on some kind of drug. He didn't resist or anything when we asked him to come along with us, and one of the chaps recognized him from the television. He was in a bit of a state. But when he calmed down, he asked us to contact you as soon as possible. It took us a bit of time because . . ." He faltered, and in an embarrassed tone confessed, "Uh, he couldn't remember where you were staying."

She found Adam addressing a small, respectful audience of policemen on the wonders of scientific research.

He was overjoyed to see her.

"Annoushka," he called out, "I'm so glad to see you. I've been telling these nice people how worried I was when you didn't turn up at the opera."

Anya tried to mask her feelings of embarrassment and worry by replying softly, "I'm sorry if I misunderstood. But I thought we were meeting at the hotel. I mean, the officer told me you'd forgotten where we were staying."

"Calumny," he retorted. "We've been in so many damn hotels these past few weeks, it slipped my mind for a second. I know we're staying at the Regent Hotel and it's room 1014. I bet you don't even remember the phone number: 663–2248."

She shook her head immediately, inwardly aware that he was desperately trying to prove his mnemonic power to the police.

"No, you're right," she said as calmly as she could. "But then, as long as I've known you"—she paused for a breath, to keep control of her emotions, and concluded with a heavy heart—"you've always had a photographic memory."

47

ISABEL

October 25
On the flight home, Dad was as sober as a judge. I
also wasn't very talkative. I had the distinct impression
that, had it not been such a monumental occasion, he
would've exploded at my buying Mom that gift.

I know I hurt him, but is it my fault that he can't recognize that a person has two parents and it's possible, even normal, to love both of them?

In any case, I had a sip or two of Chianti in a kind of farewell party to my old self.

For I know, whatever the future holds, my life will never ever be the same.

Buoyed by her Italian coronation, Isabel returned to Boston and immediately went to see Karl Pracht.

"Welcome home, Champ. How was Italy?"

"Very Italian, Karl. In fact, with what's left of the prize money, I'm gonna take you for the finest meal of your life."

"The *New York Times* picked up some nice quotations from your acceptance speech. I'd say you had a promising future in science."

"Speaking of the future . . ." She hesitated and then began to fidget. "Uh . . . I'm not so sure you're gonna believe this, Karl."

"Well, unless you're setting out to prove that my own Ph.D. should be revoked for malpractice, I think I'm ready for anything. So, what is it?"

"I was thinking about the Unified Field Theory," she murmured.

"Whose version? There're a lot of contenders."

"Uh . . . mine. I mean, I would like to try and see if I can formulate a complete hypothesis that interrelates the various energy forces."

"You're right," Pracht answered. "I don't believe it." He looked at her and continued, "Isabel, in another life you must have been a tightrope walker. No one respects your talents better than I, but as you're aware, Einstein was working on this when he died. Is there something perverse in you that wants to unravel the mystery that Albert left unsolved?"

"Karl," she countered, "I only said I'd give it a shot. There are a zillion other thesis topics, any of which would take me a year or eighteen months at the outside. Tackling the Grand Unified Theory is a real challenge. Besides, if I fail, won't it be at least character building?"

"Isabel," he responded. "I have to tell you that in my opinion, all G.U.T's are just hypothetical constructs—people talk about them, but nobody believes they're really possible."

"Let's say I waste a year or two," she said urgently. "I'll hardly be eligible for a senior citizen's pass on the bus."

Pracht reflected a minute and then pronounced, "I suggest you go out and buy a lot of aspirin."

"How come?" she asked.

"Because you're going to be hitting your head against a stone wall."

Unfortunately, Raymond did not share her enthusiasm.

"You can't be serious, Isabel. It's a pipe-dream concept. I can't even imagine any theory that could possibly unite gravity, electromagnetics, and the strong and weak nuclear interactions—they're so different."

"Come on, Dad, if I don't go for broke, somebody else will. After all, Weinberg and Salam got the Nobel in '79 for best effort so far.

"Their rest-mass energies are on the order of fifty to a hundred times the mass of a proton, but their theory can't be absolutely proved until the next generation of high-energy accelerators. Suppose I came up with a theory that everybody bought beyond any doubt? I mean, I've never been wrong yet, have I?"

"Well," Ray said sardonically, "I wouldn't call your Roman extravagance an intelligent decision."

"Oh, for heaven's sake! When are you going to stop hitting me over the head with Mom's violin? I mean, after all, it was my prize, I had the right to spend it in any way I chose. And, for the *nth* time," she protested. "I'd gladly have spent the money on *you*—all of it—but there's nothing you need. I mean—" She was trapped in her own rhetoric.

"And besides," he went on, taking the initiative, "I've just about outlived my usefulness as far as you're concerned, haven't I? It's a pity I'm too young for an old folks' home."

No one knew better than Raymond da Costa the potency of guilt in winning an argument with a child. Isabel ended the debate.

"Don't ever say that, Dad," she rejoined with emotion. "I could never forget how much you've sacrificed for me. If you're dead set against my doing it, I'll find another topic."

The guilt had crossed the net onto Raymond's side. His instinct for survival told him that his only alternative was magnanimity. He walked over, took her by the hands, and said in the most affectionate of tones, "Isabel, you're my little genius. Aim for the stars. If anyone can do it, you can."

At first Muriel was speechless. And then she exclaimed, "Darling, you shouldn't have. I'm overwhelmed. I'd be afraid to touch something so valuable, much less try to play it."

As Isabel watched ecstatically, her mother gingerly picked up the antique violin and the bow and then, lest she profane such an instrument, merely played some scales.

"Oh my Lord," she whispered. "This must have been made for the angels' symphony."

Muriel threw her arms around her daughter and hugged her tightly.

"You're such a naughty girl. You must've paid a small fortune for it."

"That's okay," Isabel replied lightheartedly. "The Fermi Prize *was* a small fortune."

"That was a wonderful thing you did for Mom, Isabel," Peter remarked that night when he and Terri, his live-in girlfriend, took his little sister out for a Chinese dinner. "Ever since you gave it to her, she's been dancing on air—not to mention playing the thing day and night."

"I'll bet Edmundo flips when he hears her play," Terri offered.

She was a pretty, blond coed, and clearly extremely fond of Peter. This added to Isabel's happiness. For despite his father's neglect, her brother had managed to keep his life on course. She had no doubt it would only be a matter of time before the two were married.

"Isn't it kind of hard," Terri inquired, "to win such a big prize and still be working for professors who probably can't even run a state lottery?"

Anxious to deflect the topic from her relentless achievements, Isabel asked, "How come Edmundo's in Argentina again? Has he got some kind of visiting conductor post?"

"I don't know," Peter answered. "But there's illness in his family. I don't even know who it is. Lately he's been going back there almost once a month."

"I know what you're thinking." Terri smiled. "But he's not playing *Captain's Paradise*. There's no other woman. He and Muriel are very devoted to one another. Actually, when he heard you were coming, he tried to postpone his trip, but you didn't give us enough warning."

"Well, I'm giving everyone fair warning now. I'm going into hibernation, and I won't be coming back out until I crack my thesis—or just crack. As I told you earlier, I've picked the toughest nut imaginable."

Peter reached over and squeezed her shoulder.

"Sis," he murmured lovingly, "from you I'd expect nothing less. Which reminds me—is your adviser still that guy Pracht?"

"Yes, sure."

"Wow," Peter enthused. "Do you hear that, Terri? That's Jerry Pracht's father."

At such astounding news, his girlfriend could only

echo, "Wow," and then, turning to his sister, ask, "He's incredibly cute. Have you ever met him?"

All Isabel could think of was, Am I blushing visibly?

"Well, yes," she temporized. "Once or twice."

"Is he as handsome in person?" Terri asked eagerly.

Indeed, though her boyfriend's sister was a worldwide celebrity, Terri had never before now evinced such interest in her academic life.

"He's absolutely gorgeous," Isabel answered with secret pride. "And you know something else—he's as smart as hell."

"I could tell that," Peter said. "I mean, the way he talked in his interview the other night."

"What interview? What other night?" Isabel demanded breathlessly. "I feel like I've been off the earth in orbit."

"Oh well, unless his dad told you, you probably wouldn't have heard about it, sis," Peter offered. "I mean, sports isn't exactly your bag. But in any case, two nights ago the guy played like there was a bullet up his—" Peter stopped abruptly.

"That's okay." His sister smiled, bursting with excitement. "You can say 'ass.' Anyway, what did he do?"

"Oh, nothing much," Peter said sarcastically. "He just knocked off Boris Becker in straight sets in the Australian Open."

Momentarily allowing her guard to drop, she murmured euphorically, "Gosh, I wonder where I can call him."

Peter and Terri laughed. "Becoming a groupie in your old age?" her brother teased.

"No—yes . . . I mean, he's a sort of a friend. By the way, do you know what this will do to his ranking?"

"Ranking?" Peter inquired with eyebrow raised. "Have you become a tennis nut too, sis?"

"For gosh sakes, I was just asking a simple question," she protested with embarrassment.

"To be perfectly honest, it was such an exciting

match that I didn't even pay attention to Pracht's new computer ranking. With the French Open and Wimbledon coming up, it doesn't matter."

"But it does," Isabel insisted.

Peter grinned. "Well then, let's put it this way, sis. All you have to do is spell T-O-P. Because, right now, that's exactly where your boyfriend is."

48

ADAM

ANYA WAS in the grip of panic, uncertain what to do. She thought of calling Charlie Rosenthal, but wasn't sure what time it was in Boston. Or if Adam would be angry.

He emerged from the shower in high spirits and insisted they go downstairs for dinner.

Though she fought to hide her concern, Anya was too upset by that evening's experience to be able to eat. By contrast, Adam ate heartily.

"What's wrong, darling?" he inquired cheerfully. He was almost manic now. "Are you disappointed about missing the opera?"

"No," she replied. Then quickly emended her answer. "Yes."

"I'm really sorry," he continued. "But you know this sort of thing can happen to anyone."

She nodded, thinking, No, not to anyone. And not *this*.

That night, he made passionate love to her and she tried to reciprocate his ardor. But she could not help wondering if his actions were an attempt to deny what had occurred.

Still later Anya could not sleep. Too restless to remain in bed, she got up and sat staring out the window with unfocused eyes. She had only been there a few minutes when her sleeping husband, sensing her absence, awakened.

"What's the matter, Annoushka?"

"Nothing, nothing. I had an upsetting dream."

Adam could not intuit the deeper truth in what she was saying, but he did sense she needed comforting, so he quickly got up, put on his bathrobe, sat beside her and took her in his arms.

"Anya, don't hold out on me," he implored. "Have I made you unhappy in some way?"

Though she squeezed her eyes and tried not to cry, Anya nonetheless began to sob. "Adam, I don't know how to say this or if you'll understand," she murmured, "but I think you're having some ... memory problems."

"No." He answered quickly. Perhaps too quickly. Perhaps because somewhere in his semiconsciousness he knew that his powers of recollection were slipping from him. "You're talking to the guy they call 'the walking medical database.' "

This gave Anya an acceptable way of breaking it to him. "I know, Adam," she began. "Then maybe you'll understand the history of this case."

"Ask me anything," he said, trying to make it sound like a playful challenge.

As delicately as she could, she described the signs and symptoms of a hypothetical patient who demonstrated behavior similar to his own.

"I know it isn't your field, but what sort of specialist do you think such a person should see?"

"Well, what you've described sounds to me like the sequelae of a minor infarct—a mild stroke that caused short-term ... forgetfulness. Your patient probably needs to see a neurologist. Now tell me what this is all about."

His eyes betrayed the anxiety that his voice attempted to conceal.

Hesitantly, like a soldier gingerly making his way across a mine field, Anya told him of his various lapses since that first unsettling incident on the beach in Fiji. There had been minor episodes in the intervening days, none important except as incremental evidence. Until today, when his actions had demonstrated that something was seriously wrong.

Adam listened mutely, then sat deep in thought. Finally, he said in a bland, toneless voice, "I remember ... I mean, I have a vague sense of not being able to remember." He paused and then finally confessed, "Anya, I'm scared. I'm terribly, terribly scared."

She put her arms around his neck and hugged him tightly. "Don't worry, darling, we'll take the first plane home, and whatever it is, there will be somebody at Harvard who will make it right."

Adam, at this point completely lucid, said to himself, Don't be so sure. You forget, Anya, *you* were a case beyond the fabled powers of Fair Harvard.

Strangely, Anya felt relieved. It was out in the open now and they were once again sharing everything, even his illness—whatever it might be.

"Of course, if we were doing a differential diagnosis," he continued in a vain attempt to be dispassionate about his own case, "we would have to allow for the possibility of a tumor—"

"Oh, no," she responded in a shocked whisper.

"But I wouldn't worry," he continued. "Those brain plumbers wield a mean laser. They can zap out the problem in a minute."

Anya was still too frightened to remark that her husband's analysis had not set forth the many alternatives and then eliminated them one by one.

He broke the silence. "Hey, you know something?

On second thought, I don't think we should go home because of this. For one thing, Hippocratic Oath or not, our learned colleagues do talk shop, and whatever minor thing I may have will still be grist for the cocktail mill. There are some terrific people here in Oz. Why don't we go to the university hospital and check the *International Medical Directory*?"

She nodded.

Miraculously, they were both able to get a few hours' sleep. They had breakfast in the room and then started out in search of a learned healer.

The librarian at the university hospital had herself attended Adam's lecture the previous week and was delighted to let the Coopersmiths use the computer database.

"Let me drive," Anya said, seating herself at the keyboard. This seemingly trivial action fulfilled a tremendous need in her to *do something*.

In a few key strokes they had retraced their tour of the Australian continent, and come up with a specialist not merely in Sydney, but one just a few floors away from where they were sitting.

"Why don't I go down and make an appointment?" Anya offered.

"No, no," Adam objected. "I feel—I don't know—naked. I mean, they *know* me here. You saw the song and dance the librarian gave us."

"Adam," Anya scolded him gently, "I don't think I'll be able to find a qualified penguin in Antarctica. Isn't Australia far enough from Boston?"

He thought for a moment and then responded, "Yes, but not as far off the beaten track as New Zealand. See what you can come up with."

She shrugged and returned to the machine.

Anya knew it would appeal to Adam the minute she called up the information: Otago University Medical School, Dunedin, on the South Island of New Zealand,

was barely accessible. Nonetheless, it boasted one of
the finest medical faculties in the world.

James Moody, the Chairman of Neurology, owned an
international reputation, and further inquiry confirmed
that his hospital possessed a state-of-the-art PET scanner which enabled real-time exploration of various brain
areas.

Anya was right. Adam was already making note of
Moody's phone and fax numbers.

When they first phoned, the New Zealander was
reluctant, since Anya was trying to be both de-
scriptive and discreet. He wondered out loud why Dr.
Coopersmith didn't enlist the help of one of his many
distinguished Australian colleagues.

But she persisted, and Moody relented. An appointment was set for two days hence.

In the intervening time, husband and wife practically
held their breaths. Their lifestyle had already changed.
By mutual agreement, he would no longer go off on his
outdoor jogs, but would do his daily mileage on a treadmill in the hotel fitness room.

Though outwardly the two doctors reassured one
another, inwardly they trembled at the prospect of
Moody's diagnosis.

From Sydney they flew to Auckland, then changed for
a connecting flight to Dunedin, where they spent a
sleepless night watching practically every film on the
hotel network. Early the next morning, making a detour
to give blood at the first floor lab, they appeared punc-
tually at nine A.M. at the offices of the professor. He
was in his mid-fifties, leathery skinned, with a full head
of white hair and—rare quality in a neurologist—an
outgoing personality.

After taking the shortest of histories, he suggested affably, "I know how worried both of you must be, so
why don't we skip all speculation and go right to the
machines?"

Moody had been especially accommodating to the Coopersmiths' request for discretion. Only a radiology technician was present, with the professor offering to provide another pair of hands where needed. Moreover, he generously invited Anya to look over his shoulder at the screen in the control room.

First Adam had an injection of specially treated glucose—the primary energy source for the brain's activity. Several minutes later he was strapped to a table, as the futuristic eyes of the scanner transmitted to the screen images of sections of his brain.

Moody paid special attention to the frontal occipital lobes. Almost immediately Anya had turned her gaze from the monitor to the physician's face, hoping to discern a telltale expression.

At one point Moody seemed to squint. Or was it a frown? Or perhaps simply her imagination.

"Well, what did you see, Doctor?" Adam asked anxiously as the professor and Anya came into the imaging area to help him off the table.

"I wish you'd call me Jamie," he replied. "In any case, we'll be more comfortable downstairs in my office. I'll go ahead and order us some coffee and we can chat."

Adam took Anya's hand. There was a strange expression on his face.

"Now I know what it's like to be a patient," he murmured, adding, "to be straight-armed when I ask a direct question."

"Well . . ." Moody began, letting the rest of his sentence dangle ominously in the air.

Adam jumped in, hoping that by offering one he could will a diagnosis.

"Tumor—right, Jamie?"

"No tumor, Adam," the professor replied. "At least none that I can see."

Analyzing every syllable, Adam had diagnosed

Moody's last remark as the old mock-modest naive ploy. *As far as he could see,* suggesting that perhaps a greater diagnostician might have discerned one.

"Did you find anything out of the ordinary?" Adam asked with an urgency that tried to pin the man down.

"I did detect slight traces of neurofibrillary tangles and a few ominous plaques . . . surrounding a core of amyloid protein."

"Leading to what conclusion?" Adam demanded.

Even Moody could not say the words. He half evaded pronouncing the verdict by simply citing the initial letters.

"I'm afraid it looks like A.D."

"No," Adam erupted, "not Alzheimer's. That's way off base, Moody. I'm only forty-four years old. Couldn't a tumor produce the same . . . erratic behavior?"

The professor did not reply immediately.

Although petrified, Anya somehow found the strength to ask, "Is it possible you could be mistaken, Doctor?"

"Of course he is," Adam shouted in a burst of denial. "Whatever lapses I may have had are the result of fatigue. My memory's perfect. In fact I can quote verbatim the symptomology of A.D. to show how wrong he is."

Anya exchanged glances with the professor, whose tiny nod suggested they allow her husband this pedantic catharsis.

Adam became a torrential encyclopedia: "Biochemical abnormalities associated with neuron failures include accumulation of aluminum, disrupted nerve-cell membrane, phospholipid metabolism and decreases in neurotransmitter substances such as—"

"Please darling," she gently implored him, "your memory is phenomenal, but the scanner doesn't lie."

"Yeah, but how can we be sure this guy's reading it right?"

Moody did not take offense. He swiveled around, took a textbook from the shelf, put it on the desk, and almost by itself it fell open at the appropriate page.

Then he handed the tome to Adam and said, "With respect, Dr. Coopersmith, I ask you to look at those pictures—and draw your own conclusions."

The book had two color images taken by a PET scan.

Moody then explained, "The one on the left side is an image of a healthy adult brain. Looks like a cheese and tomato pizza, doesn't it?"

Adam did not reply, for he was staring at the contrasting photo, that of a patient with Alzheimer's. To use simplistic terminology, it looked merely like tiny leftovers on a blue plate.

Moody then handed over four Polaroid color photographs. "These are the ones we took this morning."

Adam snatched and stared at them.

Anya peeked over his shoulder, trying not to give voice to her horror. For the dominant color was turquoise, with what looked like stains of blue ink.

Then Moody said gently, "You will of course want to have a second opinion. But I would remind you of two things. In rare instances Alzheimer's has attacked people in their twenties. Mid-thirties is no longer that rare, and as for mid-forties . . ."

He turned to Adam and continued, "Believe me, Dr. Coopersmith, I wouldn't stick my neck out with someone of your stature unless I were pretty sure."

"What—What do you suggest I do?" Adam asked helplessly.

"What can I tell you that you don't already know?" the neurologist answered as softly as possible. "You're aware this thing isn't static. It goes in only one direction, and the younger you are, the faster."

Adam was mute, his fists clenching the arms of his chair till the knuckles were white. Finally he worked up the courage to ask hesitantly, "Dr. Moody, what sort of time frame do you envisage?"

The New Zealander shook his head. "I can't specu-
late at this point. I can only suggest that you consider
going home and putting yourself in the care of a Boston
physician."

Anya agreed. "I think that's very wise."

"Do you have any children?" he inquired.

"Adam has a daughter from his previous marriage,"
she answered for him. "Heather's fourteen."

Moody shook his head sympathetically. "I can see
this is going to be very difficult for you, Dr. Coopersmith—for both of you. I'm terribly sorry."

During the long journey home, Anya lost count of the
number of times Adam tried to console her. "You don't
deserve this, darling. Why should something like this
have to happen to you?"

It was at moments like this that she remembered the
accepted wisdom that there is nothing more helpless
than a terminally ill doctor.

49

SANDY

SANDY RAVEN turned off Pico and drove up to the inner
gate of Twentieth Century-Fox. The officer in aviator
sunglasses was a familiar figure who had been there as
long as Sandy could remember.

And he, in turn, had a photographic inventory of everyone who had ever passed through his portal. He even
recalled the first visits Sandy had made as a wide-eyed
teenager. Yet his nomenclature was always up-to-date.

"Good morning, Professor Raven. Nice to see you."

"Good morning, Mitch."

But this time he did not automatically lift the barrier. Instead, he came out, clipboard in hand, and inquired, "Who're you gonna see today?"

Sandy's heart began to pound. Struggling to keep his composure, he asked as offhandedly as he could, "Would you mind calling Miss Tower's office and asking if she could give me a few seconds?"

The guard did his best to camouflage his surprise, then asked with extreme politeness, "Do you have an appointment, sir?"

"Not exactly. It's sort of a last minute thing. But I'll be glad to wait for as long as necessary."

"Right, Professor. I'll call her office."

He returned to his booth and closed the glass window so that Sandy could not possibly hear the conversation. Yet he tried to decipher its contents by analyzing Mitch's body language. All he managed to recognize was discomfort at the beginning and a sigh of enormous relief at the end.

Then the sentry emerged. "A-okay, Prof. She's gotta watch the morning rushes from Europe, but she'll do her best to fit you in before then. Do you need directions to her office?"

Heartsick, Sandy was on the verge of exploding. Come off it Mitch, cut the obsequious crap. This is where my father spent half his life.

He simply nodded to the officer, who continued, "Very fine. And guest parking is—"

"I know," Sandy snapped.

He quickly rolled up his car window and proceeded around to the main building. There were V.I.P. spaces with the names of the executives stenciled on the asphalt. Though his father had parked there for many years, the caretakers had never allowed the paint to fade. Yet this morning—as Sandy had half expected—

the name was completely effaced. Indeed, it had already been reallocated to one "F. F. Coppola."

He angrily drove to the visitors' lot, and leaving his car, slammed the door behind him.

Marching back toward the main building, he passed through familiar sets which were now ghost towns. Relics of the time when half a world separated him from Rochelle Taubman. And he could worship her in secret.

He stormed up the stairs to the first floor, stopped to recomb his hair and straighten his jacket, then proceeded to the double doors that bore a gold plaque:

KIM TOWER
HEAD OF PRODUCTION

As he turned the knob, he realized to his embarrassment that his palms were sweaty. Hopefully, she would not offer to shake hands.

Two secretaries—one male and one female—guarded the inner sanctum: the first was a blond beach-boy type, the second an elegantly groomed woman in her mid-thirties.

"Well, hello, Professor Raven," she greeted him with an expert smile. "I'm Eleanor, Miss Tower's secretary. My my, you're just like your father. The family resemblance is quite striking. Miss Tower is tied up in a phone call, but you're next on her schedule. Can I offer you a cup of coffee?"

"No thank you," Sandy replied tersely.

"Tea? A soft drink perhaps?"

In his anger, Sandy wanted to refuse even the tiniest gesture of hospitality from anyone associated with Rochelle. Yet, feeling inexplicably tired, he nodded at the suggestion of a Diet Coke.

"With or without caffeine?" Eleanor asked.

Sandy opted for the stimulant, thinking it would help him in what he expected would be at most a ninety-second encounter.

Moments later the intercom buzzed and he heard Rochelle's voice asking whether he had arrived.

"Yes, Miss Tower. Shall I show him in?"

"No, no," said the voice. "He's an old friend. I'll come out and greet him personally."

One deep breath later, the inner door opened and there, in all her power and glory, stood Rochelle Taubman.

Sandy had never paid much attention to women's fashions. His sartorial observations had been limited to telling Judy that she looked nice or, under extreme duress, responding with candor as to why he really did not like what she was wearing.

But he knew from all the interviews that Rochelle bought her clothes at a place called Milestones, which specialized in making good bodies look better, and great bodies radioactive.

She smiled. "Sandy, what a marvelous surprise. I'm so happy to see you. Do come in."

Thankfully, she did not offer her hand, nor—as he had worried during the night—did she offer her cheek to kiss.

"Sit down," she said, motioning to one of the Barcelona chairs that formed a semicircle in front of her enormous marble desk. She returned to her own leather throne. "Gosh, it's nice to see you," she remarked, a smile playing on her face. "Would you like something to drink?"

"No thanks," Sandy answered quietly. "Eleanor was a charming hostess."

There was a sudden silence, during which Sandy stared at her, wondering if she would give the minutest sign of anxiety. Or *any* emotion.

Finally, she asked, "What brings you to Tinseltown?"

Christ, he thought to himself, the *L.A. Times* announced my university appointment, but she probably doesn't read anything but *Variety*.

"Actually, I'm based out here," he replied. "I mean, I'm at Cal Tech. In fact, I'm part of their new genetic engineering program."

"Genetic engineering? That must be thrilling work. I wish I had the time to read more, but I'm fascinated by the whole subject of DNA."

"You know about DNA?" he asked with surprise and a tinge of condescension.

"Just a bit. We had Jim Watson's *Double Helix* in development. But the screenwriters couldn't lick it."

The second silence was longer.

Even Rochelle could sense that the magic of her beauty, the opulence of her office, its shelves lined with Oscars, was ceasing to mesmerize Sandy.

Wisely, she took the initiative. "I'm sorry about your father. . . ."

Unbelievable, he shouted inwardly. She's acting as if he was in a car accident, when she was the one who ran him down.

"I'm sorry too." Sandy frowned. "But neither of us feels as bad as the man who gave twenty years of his life to this studio."

"And lost almost that many millions," she added in subdued but emphatic tones.

"I don't believe that, Rochelle," he countered. "I mean, those pictures he made during the first years were real gushers—and on a tight budget."

"I'll give you that," she said. "Sidney *was* an asset to the studio—in a different era. Sandy, you work in science. God knows that's changed since we were kids."

Her civility was killing him. He was determined not to be the one to raise his voice.

"Excuse me, Miss Taubman, but to the best of my knowledge, motion pictures are not an exact science."

"That's just the point." She leaned over her desk for emphasis. "In this business the most important quality is intuition. Our statistics tell us that the vast majority of our audience are teenagers. Now how can you expect a man in his sixties to understand today's youth culture?"

Sandy was outraged by her sophistry—and yet amazed by her resilience and the dexterity with which she continued to hit the ball over the net.

"By that reasoning, Rochelle," he rejoined, "all pediatricians should be little kids."

She was stymied for a moment, then chose humor as the medium of response. "That's very clever, Sandy. I mean that."

She glanced at her Rolex and stood up.

"Oh my God, I'm late for a screening, and I know Sergio hates to be kept waiting. Give me a ring sometime and we'll do lunch."

Then Sandy exploded. "Rochelle!"

There was a barely susceptible flash of triumph in her eyes: she had finally cracked him. And dealing with hostility was not only her forte, but one of the prime secrets of her success in Hollywood.

"Yes?" she answered primly.

"Forget his loyalty and all the years he broke his back for this studio. Think about just one thing—your own career."

She did not react, leaving him off balance to continue his tirade.

"I mean if it hadn't been for my father, you wouldn't be in this office right now."

Perhaps she was unaccustomed to being told the truth. But suddenly her temper flared. "That's your opinion," she said with a hostile smile. "Personally, I think it's a considerable overstatement. Anyway, it was nice seeing you, Sandy."

With that she disappeared. Leaving him still consumed with rage.

How could he have ever loved this monster?

50

ISABEL

SOME OF the greatest scientific discoveries are not made, but stumbled upon.

Columbus, seeking a new route to the Indies, and happening upon America. Sir Alexander Fleming, finding that a mold he had left in his lab over the weekend accidentally contaminated a staphylococcus culture and stopped the bacteria growth, thus giving the world penicillin—and earning him the Nobel Prize.

Many investigators report sudden apocalyptic answers to questions that have plagued them for years—when they are least expecting them: on the golf course, in the shower . . . and still more mundane places.

Isabel would forever ascribe her great brainstorm to some scientific fairy godmother.

Rising early one morning in her third summer at MIT, she splashed water on her face, brushed her teeth, made a cup of coffee, sat down at her desk, pencil in hand, and began to think.

With her mental faculties still half slumbering, Isabel started to doodle, just to bring thoughts into focus. Then, suddenly, she began to write figures, which gradually became equations.

Continuing to work furiously, she felt a sudden craving for carbohydrates. Padding barefoot into the kitchen, she took out two frozen waffles, toasted them, saturated them with maple syrup, and carried them back to the desk for a high-calorie breakfast.

Gobbling the rich food, she glanced at the paper again. It suddenly looked like someone else's work. She could scarcely believe that the entire formulation had come to her complete, in a single burst of inspiration, like a great melody coming whole to a composer's imagination. As flawless as a snowflake.

She thought to herself: This could be it.

But how could it be so simple? I made a few basic calculations and it all poured out. Did everyone just overlook such an obvious idea?

Forty-five minutes later she poked her head into Pracht's office.

"Karl, can you spare me a few minutes?"

"Sure, of course." He smiled. "What brings you here so bright and early?"

"An idea has just popped into my head. Can I walk you through it?"

"Be my guest."

Without another word she hastened to the whiteboard, picked up a colored marker and began by setting out the first principles from which she developed the theory, explaining all her assumptions and showing where she had deviated down a new path.

Finally she concluded. "Well, what do you think, Karl?"

"Frankly, I'm having trouble making it sink in. I mean, a theory in physics always tries to be the simplest explanation, and your hypothesis is an exquisite example. It's also extremely elegant and self-consistent and agrees with earlier work. In other words, it's magnificent."

"Thanks." Isabel smiled with elation.

And yet, Pracht's brow was furrowed.

"What's bothering you, Karl?" she asked.

"Well actually, Isabel, my mind's already rushed to phase two. I mean there's no question this will cause a stir because of its sheer beauty. But there'll always be doubters. After all, there were objections to Einstein's

Theory of Relativity, only it was verified by a solar eclipse in 1919. And you don't make any predictions that are observable. If only we could come up with a way of demonstrating that you're right."

"Well," she replied, not daunted, "we're neither of us on the experimental side. But if you've got time, we could kick around some ideas."

"Isabel, for you, I've always got time."

Just then Pracht's intercom buzzed. "What is it, Alma?"

An unexpected voice preempted his secretary. "Dad, Isa's not in her office."

She fairly bounded from her seat. "My God, Karl, it's Jerry—isn't he supposed to be flying to England?"

"Are you out there?" the professor shouted into his machine.

"No, I'm right here." His smiling son practically walked through the door without opening it.

Isabel was so excited she unabashedly threw her arms around him and they kissed.

Without letting go, Jerry smiled mischievously. "Hi, Dad. Am I interrupting?"

"On the contrary. I think *I* am," his father joked. Then: "Aren't you supposed to be in Wimbledon?"

"I routed myself through Boston so I could see my special friends here. I've got till the day after tomorrow."

"Great. By the way, nice going with Becker."

"Thanks, but don't expect an encore. I was just lucky. Anyway, were you guys working?"

"We certainly were," Karl pronounced. "You arrived at a historic moment—Isabel has just come up with a new Unified Field Theory."

Jerry was staggered. "You're putting me on."

"Have I ever exaggerated as far as Isabel is concerned?"

"No," Jerry conceded. He turned to her. "This is fantastic, Isa. Congratulations. Can I take you to dinner?"

"I'll have to check with my social secretary," she replied playfully. "Now, why don't you take a walk around the block while your dad and I talk business?"

"No," he smiled. "I want to hear this for myself. I probably won't understand it, but can I at least listen?"

"Fine," the elder Pracht agreed, warning, "Some of this may be a little abstruse, but I'll explain it to you later."

Jerry smiled broadly. "I'm sure Isa will take care of that."

She returned to the whiteboard and repeated her earlier performance—with a few more refinements that came to her on the fly. At the end of her exposition, Jerry clapped.

"Brava, brava," he exclaimed. "That's a guaranteed Nobel winner."

"Your dad's pressing me for even more," Isabel complained with mock frustration.

"What else do you want, for heaven's sake?" Jerry demanded.

"Well," the elder Pracht replied amiably, "a demonstration would be kind of nice."

"Come on," Jerry rejoined. "Didn't Weinberg win the Nobel in '76 for his version of the UFT? I don't recall your mentioning any experimental proofs either then or since."

"That's precisely why it would be great to have Isabel go him one better," Karl said, gesturing with a professional index finger.

"Well," Jerry turned to Isabel, "what sort of conditions do you need?"

"A monster source of energy—and not even the five-hundred-GeV accelerator at CERN in Geneva could rev up enough."

Jerry thought for a moment and then his face suddenly lit up. "How about a supernova?" he asked excitedly. "When a star collapses there's a tremendous gravity field and a massive amount of energy."

He stepped to the board and quickly listed some of the conditions at the core of a star just after it implodes.

"It's lucky I'm usually knocked out in the early rounds," he joked. "I've had plenty of time to read."

Isabel brightened. "I think you're on to something, my stargazing friend." And now, pad in hand, she eagerly buried herself in fresh calculations.

"Wait a minute," Pracht interposed, waving his hands like a basketball referee. "I don't think this is going to work. Admittedly, the ion temperature in a supernova is high, but it's only a hundred KeV or so. You need a *million times that*. And if that weren't bad enough, there's so much hot matter around, no light or other signal from the core could get through—except the neutrinos, of course."

"Hold it, Dad, hold it," Jerry shouted. "What about the shock wave?"

Isabel pondered briefly and then exploded with joy. "Jerry, you're unbelievable. Now, both you guys follow me."

In an instant she was at the whiteboard once more, a veritable geyser of ideas.

"The star shrinks down incredibly fast, until it reaches a point where it hits bottom and rebounds, sending this really fast shock wave," she began. "Now, theoretically, we've got all the needed elements present—we've provided the energy, as well as huge magnetic and gravitational fields. I calculate that there should be some telltale signature of unification by the release of microwaves, something in the nature of a wavelength of about four centimeters."

Pracht, who was reveling in these youngsters' animated dialogue, played the troublemaker. "This is all very well, but I don't think I'll live long enough till the next supernova."

"You don't have to," Jerry replied. "There *was* one in February 1987—"

"—when the blue star Sanduleak detonated," Isabel finished his thought.

"Bingo!" The elder Pracht cheered as his son regained center stage.

"Astronomers in Chile caught onto it really early," Jerry explained, "and studied it with every possible instrument. But the most sophisticated data would have been at CISRO in Australia. I mean, their hemisphere got the best view of it. It just so happens that one of my old buddies from the Astronomy Club is working there. I can call and persuade him to send us the tapes."

"Can we have 'em do it Federal Express?" Isabel asked excitedly. "I'll pay the freight."

"No, no, no," Jerry overruled her. "This is my treat." He picked up the phone and grinned at his father. "Dad can pay for this call."

Since there is always someone awake at the Observatory, in a matter of minutes Jerry had determined that the team at CISRO did indeed have numerous twelve-inch reels of tape covering the history of Sanduleak on their old VAX780 computer, and were happy to oblige him by making copies.

"That's absolutely brilliant," Isabel beamed. "Do you want to write this up with me, Jerry?"

"No way," the young man answered. "*This* part is fun, but that would be like work. And you know my allergy to anything academic."

"Jerry," Karl admonished his son good-naturedly. "If you don't stop playing the eccentric, I'm going to tell Isabel your deep, dark secret."

"No, Dad. *Please*."

"What's this?" Isabel demanded, her curiosity aroused to fever pitch.

There was now no holding back. Pracht disclosed the classified information.

"Jerry's actually not a high school dropout."

"I am too," Jerry insisted perversely.

Ignoring him, his father spoke directly to Isabel.

"What really happened is that he was *kicked out* for conduct unbecoming—"

"See?" Jerry interposed.

"But with his courses at the Planetarium, he'd already earned enough credits to graduate, so they gave him a diploma as a going-away present."

"Is this true?" Isabel demanded.

Jerry shrugged uneasily. "Well, kind of . . ."

"Listen," Karl suggested. "Why don't you sit down and tell Isabel all about it, while I get on the phone and see about having her theory published."

She slumped into a chair and breathed a weary sigh. "Must we, Karl? Maybe this is so outrageous some people might be hesitant to print it."

"You're right, and even if they aren't, there are so many guys out there waiting to shoot down whatever you do next. That's why we need a strategy. Now, everything submitted to *Physical Review* is subject to peer evaluation—and even then the editors could still make hamburger meat of any article they wanted to savage."

But he knew his politics.

"Make it short and concise so we can send it in as a *letter*. That way no reviewer can get his claws into it. And you can go public without being mugged or muzzled. It's almost axiomatic—the biggest discoveries in modern science have had the smallest write-ups."

Isabel broke her silence. "Do you think this can wait a day, Karl?" she asked with a touch of melancholy.

"What's another twenty-four hours?" Pracht replied. "It's waited since Sir Isaac Newton. But this is so uncharacteristic of you, Isabel. Are you getting cold feet?"

"No," she said. "It's just that whenever we announce this, the whole carnival will start again. Frankly, that's the only part of my scientific career that I've really hated. All I care about is the work."

"But Isa," Jerry said, "You have to realize how important your discovery is."

"Right," his father echoed. "There's a lot of talk

nowadays about what occurred after the Big Bang. The current thinking is that everything was extremely hot and therefore energetic. And at this primal moment, all the forces of nature were united and mixed intimately together. And what you've done can actually prove it. This is so amazing—a real godsend. You'd better be prepared for the brightest spotlights you've ever faced."

51

ADAM

CHARLIE ROSENTHAL cried.

He had been a doctor for more than twenty years, and the only other time he had lost control was when his son had fallen off his bike and lay unconscious in the hospital.

"I'm sorry, Adam. I'm so sorry," he sobbed. "You're my best friend. And what kills me is that there's not a goddamn thing I can do to help you."

Adam put his hand on his colleague's shoulder. "Hey, take it easy," he said gently. "The worst is yet to come. Save your tears for then. Meanwhile, tell me what specialist is going to get the pleasure of my case."

"I've asked around and there's no question about it—the guy you should see is Walter Hewlett at Mass. General."

"What makes him so special?" Adam asked phlegmatically.

"He won't be treating you from a textbook, Coopersmith. His own father died of Alzheimer's."

Adam began to shout hysterically. "What the hell sort

of doctor are you, Rosenthal? You know the worst part
of Alzheimer's is not dying."

"Right, Adam. Right," Charlie responded nervously.
"It's just—well . . . the deterioration part—"

"—is worse than death," Adam finished his thought.

But Charlie replied urgently, "Listen, except for
AIDS, there's no other area in medicine that's being as
thoroughly researched. This isn't just a palliative pep
talk."

"I know, Charlie. They're already aware that one
defective protein is made from a gene on Chromosome 21. But none of it'll be in time to do me the
slightest good."

"Well, old buddy, why don't you talk that over with
Walter? He's doing some work with neurotrophic cells.
I mean, *somebody* had to be the first to get a shot of
penicillin and not die of an infection. Besides, Hewlett's
going to make history and pay a house call."

Charlie put his arm around his suffering colleague as
they walked from his book-lined study into the half-
furnished living room where Joyce was talking to Anya
by the light of the gas-burning fireplace, which magnified their shadows against the bare wall.

As the two women rose and started toward Adam, he
suddenly exploded into ferocious rage.

"What do you people think you're doing?" he bellowed. "Coming into my house like this, invading my
privacy—bothering Anya?"

Charlie tried to calm him. "Take it easy, Adam.
You've known Joyce for years. You were best man at
our wedding."

Adam's reply electrified Charlie like a lightning bolt.
"Who do you think you are?" he ranted. "The two of
you are probably here to poison me."

Anya tried to reorient him. "Darling, the Rosenthals
are old friends."

But Adam snapped at her as well. "Don't tell me

lies," he retorted. "Just get them out of here before I call the police."

Charlie addressed Anya, his eyes broadcasting shock and sorrow. "I think we'll go now. Make sure he takes those pills. Hewlett'll be here before nine. Call me if you need anything."

"Stop talking to my wife," Adam shouted.

Charlie and Joyce exchanged a quick glance with Anya, who left the room to show them out.

Less than a minute later she was back in the living room with Adam. He was bent over, holding his head.

"What's the matter?" she asked.

"My head, it feels like it's splitting open," he replied.

"Don't worry, Adam, the doctor will be here in a little while."

"What doctor?" Adam asked in continuing confusion. "All I need's an aspirin."

"Just sit here and rest while I get you one," she said aloud, inwardly realizing that she herself was now afraid to be alone with him.

Anya returned with a glass of water, two aspirin, and the little yellow pill that—with luck—would becalm him till the doctor arrived.

What most surprised Anya was that, for a senior scientist, Walter Hewlett was so young.

"Thank you for coming over, Doctor."

"It was the least I could do, Mrs. Coopersmith. Your husband won't remember, but I was his student when he had to take over Max Rudolph's course in mid-year. He was a great lecturer."

Was, Anya thought to herself. I guess I must get used to having him referred to in the past tense.

They entered the living room and found Adam staring at the fire. He looked at them quizzically.

"Adam, this is Walter Hewlett," Anya explained matter-of-factly. "He's a neurologist at Mass. General. By sheer coincidence, he was a student of yours."

"Really?" he remarked in what seemed a normal tone. "Since I only gave an actual course when I filled in for Max, that must have been in 1979. Am I right?"

Hewlett smiled. "That's exactly when it was. You've got quite a memory, Dr. Coopersmith."

"Would either of you like coffee?" Anya inquired, hoping to placate Adam by giving the impression that this was a social call.

"That would be fine," the young specialist answered. And then, turning to the man who was both his host and his patient, asked, "And you, Adam?"

"Watch out for caffeine," Adam replied, shaking an admonitory finger. "It actually causes cholesterol."

He paused for an instant and smiled at Anya. "But I guess I don't have to worry about that, do I, darling? Bring me a cup as well."

Hewlett opened his attaché case and pulled out a large manila envelope. "With your wife's permission, I've looked over the reports and the photographs you brought along from New Zealand."

"New Zealand?" Adam asked quizzically. "Why would I go to New Zealand?"

"Well," Hewlett answered, "I know you're tired and it may have slipped your mind. But as I hope you know, I'm a neurologist and I believe you have a problem."

"Really?" Adam reacted glassy-eyed.

Walter nodded. "I mean, naturally we'll want to take our own scan. But to my mind, the pictures you brought along substantiate Moody's diagnosis." The young doctor paused and then said tentatively, "I think you've got Alzheimer's."

Adam's reply was quite unexpected.

Still staring into the fire, he answered in a monotone, "So do I."

In the days that followed, he was driven to communicate. All his waking hours became an incessant dialogue with Anya. He had a lifetime of things to tell her—and a cruelly short space in which to do it.

Their lovemaking took on a kind of urgency, a sort of unspoken communion in which the intensity of his touch reassured her that he knew exactly what he was doing. And what he was trying to say.

His hands were articulate in silence. They spoke with an eloquence that transcended words.

When he kissed her, it was for all eternity.

Certain people had to be informed. First and foremost, there was Heather. Since Adam was declining swiftly, she was doomed to lose him well before his actual death.

That meant telling Toni.

Anya called Lisl, who came over immediately, to "help put the house in order."

She proved a welcome source of strength for Anya, who up to now had had no one to support her.

Lisl insisted on being the one to tell Heather and Toni. She reported her surprise on their reactions. Unexpectedly, Toni wept openly.

And Heather was too stunned to cry.

"May I see him?" Toni begged.

"I don't know," Lisl answered candidly. "That's something I think Anya has to decide. But he wants to see Heather very badly."

She looked at her goddaughter and said gently, "Shall I pick you up tomorrow after school?"

Heather nodded mutely.

Anya—on whose shoulders the burden would weigh the heaviest—knew that the rest of Adam's life would be a series of cruel ironies, for which she had to prepare herself as well as possible. One example was the letter received by Adam's secretary at the lab:

* * *

Dear Professor Coopersmith,

I was flattered to receive your letter and read your proposal with enormous interest. You're right in thinking that we are psychologically in tune.

I'm especially interested in arresting cell degeneration—not with the aim of postponing death, but extending *life*.

The ethics of your project pose no problem, Adam, because if the research is successful, we'll be not merely prolonging life but delaying the aging process so that an eighty-year-old mother will be neither senescent nor a freak, but enjoying the same good health that a woman of fifty now enjoys.

This sort of thing sounds outrageous to journalists, but then, they don't take into consideration that in 1850 the average American died at forty-five; by the end of this century, life expectancy will already be double that.

In this context, the notion of enhancing the time of a woman's fertility would be altogether appropriate in the new biological lifestyle.

In short, I would be most eager to discuss this with you further.

> Yours sincerely,
> Sandy Raven, Ph.D.
> Professor of Genetic Engineering

Because she wanted to keep Adam's mind alive as long as possible, Anya read him the letter and even went through the charade of discussing it with him.

"He's really interested," Anya said with forced optimism. "I mean he wrote such a long and thoughtful letter."

"And what are you going to do about it?" Adam asked bitterly. "Tell him I'm taking early retirement?"

She tried to smile. "I'll think of something," she said softly.

He sat for a moment and then said, "Contact him,

Annoushka, start the project with him yourself. Then
you can work. . . ."

His voice trailed off.

52

ISABEL

RAYMOND DA COSTA was outraged.

"How could you do such a thing? Don't you think I
deserved to know before anybody?"

He had never gotten angry with her like this. Never
had he fired off verbal bullets of recrimination.

"I'm sorry, Dad," Isabel said softly, "but there was
no point in showing it to you until I knew I was on the
right track."

"What you're saying is that you thought it would be
too far above my head."

Isabel was trapped. In truth, she could have explained
it to Ray in terms he would have understood, but had
balked at the prospect. And she herself could not comprehend why she had wanted to deny him the pleasure
of priority.

Suddenly her father was seated at the kitchen table,
his head in his hands, crying.

Isabel felt cold and frightened. Perhaps, in a reflex of
self-protection, she had been too brutal, she thought.
Was he going to crack?

"Dad, I apologize. I realize now I should have told
you first."

She stood motionless, painfully aware that their rela-

tionship had been torn in a way that could never be
healed.

Just then the telephone rang. She picked up the receiver.
"Yes?" She listened for a moment and then said, "I
told him." She paused and added, "Of course he was
happy. Anyway, eight o'clock's fine."

As she hung up, Ray snarled, "Jerry Pracht?"

Isabel nodded. "En route to Wimbledon. He's invited
me for dinner."

"He's a kid. He hasn't got a chance."

"He beat Becker—"

"Who had the flu. He was playing with a 102-degree
fever. The kid'll get knocked out in the first round."

Isabel lost her temper and shouted, "Even if he
doesn't get the ball over the net once, it won't make me
care for him any less!"

She looked at her father.

"Please," she said, taking the initiative. "I don't want
to hurt you."

"Well, you've certainly done a good job of it without
trying."

"Come on," she implored. "Let's go out for a nice relaxing jog and I'll tell you about my thesis idea."

Raymond's feelings were almost instantly assuaged.
"I'd like that, Isabel," he said warmly, "but lately, I prefer to discuss my science sitting down. Can we do it
over a glass of iced tea when you get back?"

"Sure, Dad, sure, that'd be lovely," she answered
quickly.

Moments later she emerged in her running clothes
and went to kiss him on the forehead.

"Now, don't do anything foolish while I'm gone,"
she cautioned.

"What would you regard as 'foolish'?" he asked, trying to be good-natured.

"Like clean the house again," she joked.

* * *

She spent most of her run castigating herself for being so harsh with Ray. He had given her so many years. Couldn't she have taken a few more days to let him down more gently?

She entered the apartment and was genuinely relieved to see that his mood—at least superficially—had radically changed. He had prepared a huge glass pitcher of tea with sprigs of mint.

She quickly showered and put on jeans and a shirt, unpacked her notes, placing various papers around the table, and prepared to deliver her second presentation of the day.

Ray sat there enthralled by his daughter's genius. It not only sounded right, but—like many great discoveries—seemed as if it had always been waiting there in full view.

At the end of her exposition, he rose enthusiastically and said, "This calls for a celebration."

"Thanks, Dad. Tomorrow we can—"

"I knew this was going to be brilliant," he interrupted her. "So while you were out, I went and shopped for all your favorite things. I'm preparing the most fantastic dinner you've ever seen."

"But, Dad," she protested gently, "Jerry's coming over to pick me up."

"This is a great occasion for you," Ray muttered frantically, still on his own wavelength.

It did not escape her notice that, totally out of character, her father had not spoken in the first person plural.

Clearly, he was determined to hang on at any cost.

She spoke to him with emphatic calm, like a parent to a hysterical child. "I'm going to go and change now, Dad. And then when Jerry comes, we'll be going out."

He appeared not to assimilate her remark and continued to set the table.

Twenty minutes later she reappeared dressed in her best silk blouse and blue skirt. To her dismay, Raymond was still fussing with the dinner arrangements. Significantly, a third place had been set.

"Dad, I told you—"

"You can both eat here," he said, the words tripping out in a tone bordering on hysteria. "I mean, Jerry's a nice boy, a fine boy. There's more than enough for him to . . ."

Isabel stared at her father. The man she had once revered as omniscient and infallible was now reduced to a helpless frenzy. She was gripped with a pity that consumed her body. And, surprisingly, a feeling of anger. For she suddenly allowed herself to resent the cloistered isolation in which he had kept her nearly all the days of her life.

The front door intercom buzzed then, and Isabel picked up the entry phone receiver, listened for a moment, and then said quietly, "I'll be out in a moment."

She turned back to Ray, just in time to hear him gasp, "P-Please . . ." He clutched his chest and sank to his knees.

"What's the matter, Dad?" she asked with mounting terror.

"Don't leave me now." Raymond's face reddened and he began to sweat.

Managing to keep a cool head, Isabel pressed the entry phone button and implored Jerry to hurry inside.

He took charge immediately.

"I'll handle this, Isa. You just call 911 for an ambulance."

"Don't," Ray murmured with difficulty, "I'll—be—all right. Just stay—"

He lost consciousness and fell back onto the floor.

For Isabel it had been a horrible feeling of déjà vu.

She remembered the trauma of Ray's Berkeley attack and her fear while waiting for the doctors to pronounce their verdict. Only now there was one important difference. Jerry Pracht was by her side. And the news—at least the medical diagnosis—was far less ominous.

"There was no cardiac implication," the senior resident at Cambridge City Hospital explained. "I don't know if he's been taking his beta blockers regularly, but he must have had some sort of shock that drove his blood pressure sky high. We've sedated him and, considering his history, we'll monitor him for two or three days."

Since her father would sleep till morning, Isabel acceded to Jerry's suggestion that they have a bite. But, unable to exorcise her feelings of guilt, the highest gastronomic level she would allow herself was Dunkin' Donuts.

Jerry had been wonderful that evening. Strong and protective, revealing enormous compassion. She had never imagined she could . . . love him more. But she did.

While they were on their third helping of French crullers, he affectionately broached another subject.

"Hey, remember a million years ago, when we were originally going out to have something fancier than this?"

"Yes?"

"Well, I was going to make a big deal about it because I had something important—at least what I thought was important—to tell you."

"Tell me now."

"Events have somewhat diminished its significance," he said. "I've come to the conclusion that our relationship has no future if we're only united by a telephone wire."

For a moment Isabel misunderstood and thought he might be about to leave her.

"Anything else?" she asked uneasily.

"Yeah. We should live in the same city."

Her heart melted. "I'd like that," she whispered. "I'd like that very much."

"You damn well better. I'm giving up eccentricity for you. Can you imagine the embarrassment? And I'll cease to be known as 'Pracht the dropout.' "

"They're not going to call you that anyway," Isabel responded. "In a week they'll be calling you 'Pracht the Wimbledon champion.' "

He looked at her with surprise. "Are you serious?" he asked softly.

"What do you mean?"

"Do you for one minute believe I'm going to get on that plane tonight and leave you with a father in intensive care?"

"Jerry, don't be stupid. I've got lots of friends—your father, for a starter."

He shook his head and said quietly, "No, Isa. We're going to play this by the book. I'm going to be your man and I'm going to stick by you when you need me."

"But what about—"

"Bouncing a ball on a grass court? Eating strawberries? I don't think that outweighs leaving you on your own. Besides, my beating Boris was sheer luck. Cinderella only happens once."

When he took her to her apartment, he saw the look of helplessness on her face as she opened the door.

"Isa, please don't mistake what I'm about to say. But I think we'd both feel better if I didn't leave you alone tonight."

For a moment she did not know how to react. Then she whispered, "Thank you."

And felt immensely relieved that she had found the courage to say it.

53

SANDY

"TELL ME the truth, Dr. Raven, do you have a sex problem?"

Sandy was caught off balance. "I don't understand."

"Well then, maybe it's me. I always thought I turned men on."

"Denise, you're an extremely beautiful girl, but . . . you're a colleague."

The woman gave a throaty laugh. "You make it sound so formal. Anyway, it never seemed to stop anyone before. Actually, I thought you'd be flattered that I find you so attractive."

"Please . . ." Sandy held up his hand, almost like a boxer blocking a punch. "This is starting to embarrass me. I *am* flattered, but—"

"Cool, cool." She backpedaled. "That's okay, Sandy. I'm sorry I came on to you. I didn't mean anything. I guess you haven't got a sex problem—as such."

"Oh?"

"No, I think you just have a problem—about sex."

In truth, though the young researcher's attempt at seduction had been exceptionally crude, it was not the first instance of its kind. Ever since he appeared as an eligible bachelor on the university scene, women had set their sights on him. Yet the fact that he sidestepped every opportunity and retreated into a cocoon of monastic abstinence had begun to worry his father.

Sidney could understand that his son had been burned

badly and was still too injured to brave emotional involvement with the opposite sex, but earthy sensualist that he was, he believed religiously in the value of "a regular, healthy roll in the hay."

He had for years frequented a veteran concubine—as he referred to her—in Santa Monica. Out of affection for her client and concern for his son, the woman prescribed a friend of hers for what she felt was ailing Sandy.

But the younger man was firmly evasive. "I know you won't believe this, Dad. But I get complete satisfaction out of my career."

"You're right. I don't believe you. You know what they say about all work and no foreplay?"

Sandy tried to smile at his father's homey witticism.

As he approached his fortieth birthday, Sandy found himself leading two separate lives.

His public persona was the distinguished scientist at Cal Tech, running his institute, organizing seminars, and directing dissertations.

This was the personage frequently invited to address meetings of his professional colleagues, who were all anxious to hear about the latest findings in his exciting research.

Yet he did not enjoy these appearances, mainly because he felt—and often rightfully so—that many in the audience were whispering about the unhappy "MIT scandal" he was trying so vainly to forget.

At these functions there were always women aplenty. But Sandy managed to reject all temptations, which, ironically, seemed to multiply exponentially with his every refusal. After all, he was a star. And for a variety of reasons, many of the young female scientists just beginning their upper climb in his field were anxious to know him better. But he was so numbed, he was unable to perceive his own loneliness.

Once, in desperation, he forced himself into an adventure in hopes of recharging his interest in romance.

He spent a weekend with a vivacious blond from Solvang, a transplanted Danish village located on the outskirts of Santa Barbara.

Their sex was joyful and uninhibited. Sadly, their conversation was less so.

It was reassuring that Sigrid Jensen was a tenured chemist at USC and did not need Sandy for anything but himself. She even knew his history. Naively, she hoped to help exorcise his demons.

"For heaven's sake, Sandy," she urged, "why can't you believe that I don't want to steal anything from you—I just want to share your thoughts."

Sandy shook his head. "I know, Sigrid," he said. "You're very nice. And believe me, I appreciate what you're saying."

She grasped him by the shoulders. "Listen, Sandy, you're a wonderful man. I can't apply for the job of your psychiatrist—but I hope you'll call me if you need a little human contact. For what it's worth, I really like you."

He smiled warmly, "It's worth a lot, Sigrid." He touched her hand and whispered, "Thanks."

Yet he never could bring himself to call her again. Perhaps because he feared that if he did, she might get too close to his bruises.

On the weekends, however, the hermit became a hunter. Sandy spent all his waking hours stalking the explorations of others.

Just as some people made a hobby of browsing for antiques at various country locales, Sandy would tour the unique backyard emporiums dotting the Bay Area. The all-pervasive technosphere of northern California— especially Silicon Valley—had engendered a spate of cottage industries. Dozens of young geniuses were working in their parents' garages, all trying to develop newer biotech wonders.

Sandy would hear about their work on the student grapevine, and actually seek them out. These adolescent dynamos were fired by a confidence bordering on recklessness. They shrank from no challenge, however outwardly daunting. Moreover, such was their enthusiasm that they focused their efforts more on the sheer joy of finding the end of the rainbow, all but ignoring the attendant pot of gold.

Their predecessors were men like the legendary Dr. Herb Boyer, who made history with a little company called Genentech.

At least, it was little at the beginning.

Once upon a time—in 1978, to be exact—Boyer and his staff were working out of a modest lab on the San Francisco docks. Their breakthrough was the synthesizing of insulin—a protein essential for the metabolism of blood sugar and especially vital to sufferers of diabetes, whose bodies cannot manufacture it on their own. This had been a pipe dream for so long that its success, though spectacular, was not surprising. It sold like hotcakes.

Two years later his company, Genentech, was floating on the stock market. On the very first day of trading, Boyer's share of the enterprise had risen to a value of eighty-two million dollars. Quite an act to follow, yet they were not short of emulators. There are at least a hundred thousand genes in the body, all with different base pair sequences. There were numberless new worlds for these young Columbuses to find.

Sandy was excited. He felt in his element as he drove from one garden shed to another, marveling at the undiscovered scientific potential of the younger generation. He would sometimes spend hours with the ecstatically honored teenagers, running through their demonstrations, looking over their data and making suggestions.

They were flattered that someone of his eminence

took an interest in their projects. Sometimes, Sandy also bought an interest.

On the surface, he was looking for a new Herb Boyers. In another, deeper sense, he was also trying to find himself before the fall. For his own intellectual curiosity had remained almost as limitless as the youngsters'.

By the late 1980s the university was paying him a basic six-figure salary plus a share of royalties in anything they might jointly patent. So the outlay of a few thousand dollars to buy half the shares of some fledgling's scientific dream seemed like a fantastic deal for both parties.

Yet Sandy was scrupulous in all his dealings with them. He was not about to visit the sins of the previous generation on the next.

Despite everything, at the still-unsullied core of his soul Sandy believed in professional integrity. Though he could easily have demanded a share of the credit as well, he had no desire to usurp their glory and enhance his reputation at the expense of theirs. He could never hurt another human being as he had been hurt. Which, in a way, explained the deepest emotion he felt toward these young scientists—that of a protective father.

Although he was deeply involved in many of his own projects, he nonetheless remained in close contact with the progress of the group he affectionately referred to as "his kids." And they were among the privileged few who possessed his unlisted home phone number.

This was in fact the only area of his life that resembled something like emotional involvement.

Sandy had always been enthusiastic about NeoBiotics. In this tandem operation, Francis, nineteen years old, and his "senior" partner James, twenty-one, were devising an AIDS test so simple and swift that it could be administered in the privacy of any doctor's office, and yield accurate results in less than five minutes.

When it appeared that they would be the first to get

FDA approval, Sandy put them in the hands of a good lawyer, who proceeded to negotiate for the initial public offering for the company. Their stock came out at five dollars. By the time the green light came from Washington, it had increased tenfold.

The younger partners sent Sandy a jubilant fax, "Thanks a million!" An hour or so later, a normally diffident Francis, emboldened by his very first taste of champagne, called to correct his mistake. "I guess we should have said thanks a lot of millions, huh?"

Sandy, for whom seven-digit checks were now almost a mundane occurrence, merely smiled. "It's only money," he philosophized.

"Yeah," the boy replied euphorically. "But it feels nice, doesn't it?"

"I guess so," Sandy said obligingly. He had long wondered why wealth was not everything it was cracked up to be.

But he was genuinely happy. For them.

There were other pleasures.

Vectorex was a husband and wife enterprise. It was so small at first that its founders not only worked in a garage—they lived over it. But Jennie and Doug Wilson thought big—and ultimately succeeded in perfecting a technique for delivering the retroviral repair man to the exact location of the genetic damage.

When they reached the market eighteen months later, their vectors—coming from the Latin "to carry"—instantly became the geneticists' favorite medium of delivery. This was a real gusher. The Wilsons bought a car for the garage—and the house attached to it.

The couple's subsequent achievement brought Sandy even more joy: they named their firstborn son after him.

"Hey kid. You really know how to pick winners," Sidney enthused. "I oughta take you to Vegas for a weekend."

"Don't bother, Dad. Those six-foot showgirls aren't my type."

"What makes you so sure—I mean, that's not what I mean," Sidney protested, finally organizing his thoughts and urging, "Come on Sandy, isn't this a dream come true? Don't you want to buy anything?"

"Yeah," his son responded sardonically. "As Groucho said, 'I'd like to buy back my introduction to Greg Morgenstern.' "

Sandy did his best to please his father and derive some enjoyment from his newfound wealth. He voluntarily increased the child support he paid to Judy, and established a very substantial trust fund for their daughter—which he never mentioned to Sidney.

And when Olivia came out to visit in the summers, he insisted that she fly first-class.

But what about himself?

Mostly out of inertia, he was still living in the same apartment he had taken when he first moved to the West Coast. Now he needed more space—if only to display the many awards and trophies he was receiving.

When he walked into his local up-market real estate agency, the branch manager—an elegant brunette in her mid-thirties—was breathless with excitement.

For Elaine—as she immediately insisted upon being called—could not believe the good luck that had brought Sandy—as she immediately insisted upon calling him—into her life. It was not simple avarice, for she met well-heeled clients every day.

But Sandy was so unspeakably eligible—cleanly divorced, self-sufficient, warm and friendly. And a professor.

So determined was she not to let this one slip through her fingers that she invited him to dinner that very evening at her home, "for an in-depth discussion of your needs."

Normally Elaine took potentially lucrative clients to one of the fancier eateries, but she did not want to risk meeting a friend and possible rival who might demand an introduction.

Among her many talents was cordon bleu cookery, and she whipped up a meal that was close to perfection.

Sandy was genuinely pleased.

"I'd never believe you could get this type of food outside Paris."

"That's where we went on my first honeymoon," she remarked. "Do you go often?"

"I had a congress there once."

Elaine blushed. "Oh Sandy, you naughty boy. You shouldn't be telling me that."

He politely laughed at what he assumed was her attempt at humor.

And pleased that she'd seemed to find favor, she smiled back.

Elaine was sure she'd reached first base. Moreover, her profession licensed her to ask innumerable personal questions. She had succeeded in putting Sandy so at ease that he not only discoursed at length about his family situation, but was almost lulled into narrating the story of his downfall at the hands of Gregory Morgenstern.

"What about you, Elaine?" he inquired.

"Usual Hollywood scenario," she answered, forcing an insouciant smile. "Husband a producer, married twelve years, turned me and his Jaguar in for newer models. Then *she* divorced him and he went bankrupt, so I became the breadwinner. I was lucky. Now, every so often, I write him a check."

"Oh, that sounds very generous," Sandy said gallantly. "Do you have any children?"

"Two teenage girls. Lovely, lively, and exhausting." Before he could ask, she offered, "I, uh, they're sleeping at a friend's."

No sooner had she spoken these words, than she realized her miscalculation. How could she have foreseen that Sandy was one of those rare men who would have actually welcomed dinner with a family? For his part, he suddenly felt claustrophobic, and after a short but decent interval for coffee, excused himself to return to the lab.

Elaine consoled herself with the fact that she would have many other opportunities. She politely commented on Sandy's dedication to his work, and promised to call him the next day with a list of possibilities.

It seemed to be the story of Elaine's life: she won the commission but lost the man.

In the end, she found Sandy an unlisted gem—a seventeen-acre estate just south of Santa Barbara, with an almost overbearing twenty-room, Spanish-style house. Not an easy commute, but worth it for its privacy and European atmosphere.

She could not help but sense that part of the attraction of this property was the fact that in its distant past, when California was Spanish, it had been a monastery. In any case, it needed a lot of renovation—which explained its "bargain" price of two and a half million—but Sandy fell in love with it. And Sidney—whom he had of course consulted—pressed him to buy, hoping that his son's emotional life would expand to fill the rooms.

Sidney put up only token resistance when Sandy urged him to move into what his father grandiosely referred to as the "Raven Compound." "Without you, we can't be a family," Sandy insisted.

How could Sidney Raven refuse the lure of an entire wing of his own, with a separate pool and patio for entertaining his own guests? Not to mention a twenty-seat screening room.

"Holy moly," he exclaimed. "Now all I need is something to screen."

At which point he turned to his son again and demanded, "Now, how about you, sonny boy?"

"I've got a pool too," Sandy countered.

"Nah, you know what I mean. When are you gonna *splurge* on yourself?"

"What do you call this whole deal?"

"Basic, sonny boy, basic. Like a gal's black dress—you gotta buy some diamonds to go with it."

"A tennis court?" Sandy suggested.

"Sure, why not."

"Neither of us plays."

"There are teachers. And Olivia would really like it."

"Yeah," Sandy agreed. "I'll get in a builder this week to give us some quotes."

"Okay," Sidney pursued. "That takes care of your daughter's treat. Now, back to you. What have you always dreamed of but never thought you could ever have?"

Sandy thought for a moment and then answered half jokingly, "A Nobel Prize."

"No. That you can't buy—at least I don't think so. But dream up something crazy—something really wild."

Sandy obliged his father and attempted to let his imagination run amok. Finally, almost as a capitulation perhaps, he answered, "What would you say if I built my own lab?"

"You mean right in the compound?"

"Yeah. A kind of mini-institute. I could transfer some of my work here and even have lab assistants on duty day and night. Well?"

The old man smiled. "It isn't the harem I would have constructed, but it's something, sonny boy."

It took longer to get the planning permission than for the industrious crew of Mexican–Americans to erect the imposing low-roofed laboratory building in a vaguely Spanish style, set in a secluded corner of the estate. Before he moved in, Sandy, ever in the vise of paranoia, took steps to protect his future inventions, hiring a security company to patrol his grounds at all times.

He even installed a direct phone line to his office at

Cal Tech to reduce his on-campus time to the barest minimum.

His daughter's visits were the high point of Sandy's year. And yet, in a way, they also saddened him. For Olivia had grown up so swiftly that he wished he could make time stand still and have her be his darling little girl forever.

Yet he had also used their time together for propaganda purposes. The two of them played a special game in which they made up songs composed of the silliest-sounding scientific words. For example, to help her learn physics, Sandy boned up on the latest advances and wrote ditties like "If You Knew SUSY," the name standing not for a girl, but for supersymmetry theory.

There was also "Every Quark Needs a Squark," not only a love song, but an accurate physical statement. Their subatomic bestiary included everything from particles and sparticles to winos and zinos. It was a high-tech *Alice in Wonderland*.

Young Olivia had laughed with delight at his true tales of left- and right-handed genes, the fingers on a flu virus, and even the adventures of the scientists working on gloves for them.

"Did you know, honey, that the smell of oranges and lemons is due to the right- and left-handed forms of an otherwise identical molecule?"

"Actually, I did."

"What?"

"Yeah, you taught me that last summer."

His indoctrination had worked.

"Guess what, Dad," Olivia exclaimed the very instant she deplaned on her next visit. "My science teacher says I have real aptitude for chemistry. Doesn't that make you proud?"

"I was already proud, honey," he replied, inwardly congratulating himself. Then, unable to keep from testing the waters, he remarked, "Besides—your grandpa Greg's a Nobel Prize winner."

"I know," she retorted. "But you should hear the way he talks about *you*."

I'm not sure I should, Sandy thought to himself.

"He says you're the brightest scientist he's ever met in his life."

Jesus, the sonovabitch never ceases to surprise me, he thought.

In the corner of his own lab-within-a-lab, Sandy installed a special bench for his daughter, who, by force of circumstances or by nature, had become a deep thinker at a remarkably early age. She also showed an interest in her father's private life, although this was an area where she had to tread lightly.

One day she came up to Sandy in the lab with a tattered movie script under her arm.

"Hey, Dad. You should really read this. I mean actually *read* it."

"What is it honey?"

"One of Grandpa's old screenplays. He asked me for an opinion because he's thinking of shopping it around again. Remember 'Frankie'?"

"Oh, yeah," Sandy remarked. "Musical chromosomes. That project was before its time."

"Right," his daughter agreed. "But I was thinking of the love interest."

"Did it have one?"

Olivia's eyes twinkled. "If you believe Grandpa, every good story has to." She hesitated and then braved, "Even yours."

Aha, so that was where it was leading. Sandy laughed to himself.

"Frankie's way of finding a wife should appeal to you," she continued.

"Oh?"

"Yeah. He concocts her in a test tube. Sound interesting?"

"Sort of," Sandy equivocated. "But what makes you think *I* would do it that way?"

She smiled wistfully. "Because honestly, Dad, you don't seem to want to try any other."

He was touched and amused. Clearly his daughter understood that he was still so affected by the betrayal and acrimonious divorce, that even after so many years, the only partner he might trust was one he himself could create in the laboratory.

By now the new science had even permeated the awareness of schoolchildren. Olivia's generation had grown up knowing what DNA was, and she also knew about the Genome Project, and took pride in the fact that her father was contributing to the great undertaking in Washington.

"Tell me, Dad, when you guys finish mapping every single gene in the human body—all hundred thousand of them—does that mean every disease will be cured?"

"Oh, we'd still be a long way from that, honey. Having a map doesn't mean we'll have a vehicle to get there. But sometime in the next century, when you're a full professor, you might be able to perform the last act of curing ever necessary."

Olivia secretly resolved to do just that.

Even prostrate on the Hollywood scrap heap, Sidney remained ever hopeful, and still held captive by the Hollywood myth that just one picture—just one—could reverse the tide of his fortunes.

Naturally, Sandy offered to bankroll one of his father's cinematic projects, but the older man was a proud patriarch.

"No, sonny boy," he insisted. "Like Sinatra, I gotta do things my way."

Father and son now shared a curious trait. They were

each preoccupied with showing Rochelle that she had
been wrong to underestimate him.

At the outset, Sidney had found it difficult to find a
company that would employ him even without a salary,
and with just an illusory promise of points of the profit.

And yet he was a veteran with a track record. Admittedly, it was for what the trade regarded as "schlock,"
but that was precisely what the television industry demanded. And with the passing of time, the stigma of
Kim Tower's banishment began gradually to fade.

One of the network chiefs, whose first job in the
business had been as Sidney's office boy, sensed what a
potential treasure the old man still was.

When pictures for the tube have schedules of fifteen
days, they must be shot in precisely that time and not an
hour more. Sidney had a reputation as a dependable
producer who got pages filmed. His former assistant
signed him on.

Sidney was so stirred emotionally when the young
man reached across the desk and shook his hand, that
he was unsteady on his feet. Though he tried to drive
home carefully, he could barely keep his mind on the
road.

When the electronic gates opened, he drove straight
to Sandy's lab and hurried in without even knocking.
He burst into his son's inner sanctum and blurted out,
"Hey, kiddo—great news—I'm in business again!"

Sandy was elated. "Oh Dad, that's wonderful."

As he embraced his father, they both broke down and
began to sob.

Sidney was a man reborn. He tackled his new duties
with gusto. Though he had his own kitchen, he and
Sandy dined together most nights. With persistent frequency, Sidney would turn the discussion to the latest
medical therapies.

"The audience loves diseases, kiddo. They can't get
enough of them—as long as the people get cured in the

final minute. That's why we stockpile AIDS stories—as soon as the doctors lick it, we can be on the air within a week."

His father went wild when Sandy told him of the true case of a woman in South Africa who had given birth to her own grandchildren. He had read about it in one of the journals.

"Can you believe it, Dad—a woman gave birth to her own grandchild?"

Sid's eyes widened. "What's that, sonny boy? Can you run that by me again?"

"It was in South Africa. It seems her daughter couldn't have kids, so the doctors took out the girl's ova, fertilized them in vitro, and then implanted them in her mother. Nine months later—"

Sidney's expanding imagination finished the thought. "I dig, I dig. The baby's not just a double daughter, she's also a grandchild—and her own aunt!"

The thought suddenly sent them both into hysterics.

"Isn't that wild?" Sandy gasped.

"Yeah. It's absolutely dynamite." He then leaned over and whispered conspiratorially, "Who else have you told about this, sonny boy?"

"No one, Dad. But I told you, it was published in—"

"I'll take down that stuff later. Right now, you have another 7UP, while I go and make some calls."

Fifteen minutes later a radiant Sidney reappeared.

"Did it, kiddo—did it. I caught Gordon Alpert at home and cut a deal with CBS to develop 'My Mother Had My Baby.' Like the title?"

"Yeah, Dad. It's neat."

"Well, I got you to thank for it, sonny boy. I owe you one."

"Forget it, Dad. You already gave me."

"What do you mean?"

"Well, look at it this way," Sandy reasoned. "That

film and I have something in common. We're both Sidney Raven Productions."

The old man beamed with love.

54

ISABEL

IT SCARCELY made a column of newspaper space, but it wrote headlines in their lives.

When Jerry Pracht, citing cartilage problems, withdrew from the 1991 Wimbledon tournament, there were modest expressions of disappointment, of curiosity deceived and hopes frustrated. But hardly an uproar or a dirge.

After all, 127 other players did appear, and there was no guarantee that he could even have gotten through the quarterfinals. On the other hand, Michael Stich, the underdog, not only reached the finals, but defeated Boris Becker to win the title that year.

"You see, Pracht," Isabel chided him playfully. "That could've been you out there after all."

"Would you believe I'm happier right here—next to you?"

She smiled at him, and answered, "Yes."

So much had changed in just a single night.

As Isabel slept in a flat infused with genuine and profound affection, Raymond was alone in the cold, impersonal atmosphere of Cambridge City Hospital.

Unlike his previous experience, he was not eager to go home. He realized how irrational—and foolish—his behavior had been. Part of him was terrified that he had already lost Isabel for good. But it was unmistakably clear to him that if henceforth he was to play any part in her life, it would be a minor—and supporting—one.

At one juncture in his sleepless wanderings in the long corridor of the night, he was tempted to call her up and plead forgiveness. But he could not muster the nerve. Now he prayed for only one thing—the dawn, and an end to the ordeal of uncertainty.

In the natural order of things, this was the moment when girls of Isabel's age would ordinarily be leaving their own families. They, in turn, would then have to suffer one of the normal traumas of parenthood, the empty nest.

The only problem was that Raymond da Costa *had* no nest of his own.

She officially became Dr. da Costa in late June. In two separate communications she was notified that although she would not receive her Ph.D. till the next graduation ceremony, she was already entitled to the privileges of that rank.

She also received an offer to be instructor of physics at MIT, effective immediately—with automatic elevation to assistant professor when her degree was awarded. The starting salary would be $45,000 per annum.

Isabel knew that the charade of parent and child to which she had been a willing accomplice for so many years had inevitably to end.

But how?

Ray returned from the hospital chastened and docile. But he had nonetheless returned.

He still spent his time taking care of the household chores—even reading and going through the journals to mark articles for her to read. But Isabel was too young and energetic to need a maid, and too junior an academic to need a research assistant, a post for which, in any case, her father did not have the credentials. Still, his behavior made it very clear that he was grateful to be welcomed on whatever level she would take him.

Two days after Jerry had called, a couriered package arrived for Isabel containing no fewer than five reels of computer tape. Her boyfriend had enlisted the help of a Physics Department computer consultant as they transferred the data into Isabel's computer.

As he'd sat in Isabel's office finishing the setup, Jerry murmured, "See how easy this is, honey? Electronics will do all the work for us. Say, I hope you don't mind my bivouacking in your cell?"

"No." She smiled. "It's nice to have you in such close quarters."

"Just to keep us both sane," he suggested, "why don't I work the night shift and you can have your own office during the day?"

"That's very generous of you."

"Isa, I'm a generous kind of a guy."

She laughed. "You're also crazy."

"But crazy nice," he responded, his eyes twinkling.

She and Jerry had a business meeting every morning at seven-thirty. He reported his progress as he went through the painstaking process of studying the Sanduleak tapes. Yet their conversation always seemed to come around to Raymond.

"My dad's told me that from time to time he's come across all sorts of jobs that would have suited Ray perfectly—stuff like technician or science teacher, but your father just didn't want to hear about them."

"That was in a different life," Isabel observed. "I honestly think he'd jump at the chance to make a graceful exit. Anyway, I've got this sudden urge to have a place of my own with a view of the river. But I can't simply ask him to move out. I mean, frankly, I'd be worried about him living alone."

Their dialogue even spilled over into their lunch break.

"You know, strictly speaking, Raymond shouldn't be your concern," Jerry counseled gently.

"I know," she conceded. "I'm just telling you straight out I'd be uneasy."

Jerry nodded. "I understand, Isa. What you're saying in so many words is that you're a human being."

"Then there's the question of money," she continued. "I have no idea what he has in the bank, but my salary will be plenty. And there's also the cash from the Fermi Prize. I've got almost thirty-eight thousand left. What if I transferred it to his account?"

"I'd say it's more than enough to ransom your freedom."

"Do you honestly think so?" she asked anxiously.

"Isa, the real question is whether *you* do."

By early July, Karl Pracht deemed the 985-word abstract of Isabel's thesis suitable enough to qualify as a letter. He immediately faxed it off to the editor of *The Physical Review*, who—such is the speed of modern science—accepted it within the hour.

Its appearance a month later caused a stir that re-echoed in every physics lab in the world. The daring young girl on the flying trapeze had done it again. This time, at an ever greater height, and with no net below.

Isabel da Costa, former child prodigy, now grown-up and an assistant professor of physics, might have changed in many ways, but she had not lost her intellectual audacity.

And, in fact, her formation of the Unified Field Theory was the closest the human mind had yet come to solving this ultimate conundrum.

She was aware that her own sleeplessness would be matched by radioastronomy groups around the world, who were even now searching for the minutest telltale sign that would give support to her theory.

In the first weeks after publication, she lived her life on automatic pilot. She jogged at daybreak and stopped at the department on her way home, to await the morning mail and see if any of the journals had printed a response.

She would then meet Jerry in the lab to continue their frustrating investigation of every centimeter of tape. And yet the tension mounted to such a degree that Isabel could not even concentrate on the search for evidence that could silence her critics with irrefutable proof.

Sometimes she was so nervous by the afternoon that she would drag him to endless classic films at the Brattle, just to pass the time.

Since he knew she was worried about her father's recuperation, Jerry always insisted that they rejoin him for dinner, and then pray that there was a ball game on TV so that he and Ray had something superficial to talk about.

Afterward, when he left the apartment, he was unable to go home. Instead he returned to study the microwave radiometer data.

When the bouquets finally came, they were all theoretical. In the ensuing months, scientists throughout the world, whether grudgingly or admiringly, came out in print to acknowledge Isabel's brainstorm. But none was able to suggest an empirical manner in which to *test* its validity.

Jerry was nothing if not diligent. As his tennis rackets gathered dust in the closet, he continued his obsessive scrutiny—but without success. In fact he grew so monomaniacal in his quest, there were times when Isabel urged him to capitulate. As she joked, "Just let me be a genius in the abstract."

"No dammit, remember Einstein."

"Ohmigod, him again?" she cried with mock exasperation. "When in doubt—trot Albert out!"

"Listen, Isa, it took nearly forty years before his general relativity theory made it out of pure math into real physics. Then at last when they came up with the quasars, pulsars, and possible black holes, it suddenly became very relevant."

"Okay, Jerry, maybe you're right. If you want to keep on banging your head against a stone wall—keep at it, as long as it's *our* stone wall. But I just don't want to put the rest of our lives on hold even for the sake of proving the best idea I've ever come up with."

"Even if it means a Nobel?"

"There are one or two more important things in the world," she countered.

"Really?" he asked with a teasing smile. "Like what?"

"Like maybe having one or two nontheoretical children with you."

"Oh." Jerry beamed. "That's a nice idea. But since I seem to be involved in both projects, I'd like to see you have your cake and eat it."

It was nearly four in the morning when the phone rang. Isabel picked it up drowsily.

"Isa!" Jerry was in a state of unbridled euphoria. "I've got good news and bad news."

"What're you talking about?" she asked groggily. "Where are you?"

"Where I've been every night for the past half century, at 'our' office—and that's the bad news. Last night while you were snoozing, I came to the absolute end of the Aussie tapes. I can now tell you with certainty that they give us mega zilch."

"God, that's a downer. What's the good news?"

"The good news was my sudden notion that they didn't catch the explosion early enough. Our last possible chance was to get the data right from the source. So I did what I should have done long ago. Somewhat misleadingly referring to myself as 'Pracht from MIT,' I contacted Las Campanas in Chile, where the blowup was first spotted. And down there they've got tapes starting only an hour after the event began.

"I got them to send the data on Internet, from the moment they saw the blast. I've looked it over, and guess what?"

"Please hurry, I'm going to faint."

"There was a small peak at—would you believe—4.0175 centimeters, which faded into the noise after a few hours. But it was there. The guy calculated that, based on the decay rate, it must have had a pretty high amplitude at the beginning.

"What's more, none of the theorists he consulted could explain why the peak should have been where it was in the first place. But your theory takes care of all that, doesn't it?"

"Oh, Jerry. I'm so excited I don't know what to say—I owe you so much. Thank you, thank you for everything."

"You may not believe this, Isa," he joked, "but I'm actually happier than you . . . since I don't have to see any more of those crazy expressionistic films."

Isabel laughed. And then—if such were possible—he endeared himself to her even further by saying softly, "Hey, listen, let me speak to Ray, he deserves a bit of congratulations too."

She glanced at her father's bedroom door, and was sorely tempted to tell him the news. But she realized that since he was on such strong medication, it might be dangerous to wake him.

"He's zonked at the moment. If I let him rest, he'll enjoy it more later. But I will call my mom."

"Yeah, I guess you're right. But if you want to know the truth, I'm beat too. I'll drop over tomorrow morning at eight sharp with an assortment of pastries. Well, Isa, as they say in California, have a nice day."

The moment he hung up, she dialed the West Coast.

Muriel's number seemed to ring endlessly. Isabel assumed that her mother was in deep slumber and would wake slowly, but to her surprise, the sleepy voice that finally answered was Peter's.

"Hi," Isabel said jauntily. "What're you doing home?"

"Terri and I are just house-sitting for Mom," he answered. His tone seemed strangely subdued. And even when she told him the news and he congratulated her, he did not perform his characteristic verbal cartwheels.

Isabel began to sense that something was wrong. "Where's Mom?" she asked anxiously.

"I wasn't supposed to tell you, but she's taken the red-eye to Boston."

"Why?" Isabel asked. "Did someone from Berkeley—"

"No," he cut her off. "It's nothing to do with you. There's a . . . a kind of problem. I'm sure she'd want to talk to you herself."

"You're scaring me. What's going on?" Isabel persisted.

"Listen, I've said too much already. I think you'd better hear the rest from her." He reluctantly conveyed the details of Muriel's flight. She would, in fact, be arriving within the hour.

"Peter, is this something very serious?"

Her brother hesitated and then said gravely, "Yeah, sort of."

"As in life-and-death serious?"

There was silence, followed by a whispered, "I guess so. Just try to stay loose till you see her."

Isabel put down the phone. She, who had been so exuberant scarcely an hour earlier, was now shaken to the core of her being.

Her mother was flying to Boston with ominous news. Whose life, she wondered, was in danger?

55

SANDY

SANDY FORGED professional links with as much zeal as he avoided sentimental ones. Since he was based on the West Coast, it was only natural that he established ties in the Pacific science community.

A great deal of work on aging and longevity was being done in Japan—at Keio University, in Tokyo, and at Osaka Bioscience Institute, to cite but two of the laboratories where he had ongoing collaborations on "immortality genes."

And yet the most important discovery in Sandy's life was Kimiko Watanabe. To be precise, it was she who found him.

They had in common not merely a passion for science, but a history of personal loss. Kimiko's husband, a geneticist, had died of cancer at an obscenely early age, leaving her with twin sons, a pension ample to raise them—but no means of *spiritual* support. Yet he had shared so many of his scientific ideas with her that she almost felt capable of carrying on his work—with the slight obstacle that she only had a high school degree.

Given token encouragement by his former colleagues, Kimiko applied to study genetics at half a dozen Japanese universities. And was turned down flat.

One day, while she was rummaging through her late husband's files, she came across an offprint from *Experimental Gerontology* on "Synthesizing Telomerase." It was inscribed to Akira Watanabe with warmest personal greetings from the author, Sandy Raven, Ph.D., California Institute of Technology, USA.

She now recalled her husband mentioning the stimulating conversations he had had with his colleague on the other side of the Pacific. For reasons she could not comprehend, this spurred her into making a reckless gesture.

Perhaps it was because her countrymen tended to view Americans—especially Californians—as being freer spirits, less bound by convention. In any case, Kimiko thought it might be a worthwhile gamble writing to Sandy and asking his help.

Her instincts were perfect. He read her letter and immediately sensed a fellow victim. He spared no effort in arranging for Kimiko to spend a trial year at Cal Tech as a special student. Although there were no further guarantees, she jumped at the chance, and, packing the boys, made the long journey—across more than just an ocean—to Pasadena.

Aware that this was a once-in-a-lifetime opportunity, she worked like a demon, and at the end of the year was offered a place in a formal degree program on a full scholarship.

In the months preceding her arrival, she and Sandy had exchanged dozens of faxes. On several occasions he had telephoned her to confirm the details of her travel and housing arrangements. He even helped her to make initial contacts with the local expatriate Japanese community.

And yet, curiously, from the moment she arrived, all personal contact ceased. Communication between Sandy's office and Mrs. Watanabe was now through his redoubtable secretary, Maureen.

At first Kimiko was working too hard to notice. But gradually the silence became so pronounced that she began to worry that she had in some way offended her benefactor.

But even if that were so, the good news that she would be staying on provided the perfect pretext for righting things with Sandy.

Merely through their telephone conversations, Maureen had grown to like Kimiko a lot. Her voice was gentle, her manner charming. On such small things the course of history can turn.

"Will it be possible for me to see the professor in person for a moment?" she appealed to Maureen. "I know how busy he is and I would not take up much of his time."

Maureen knew her orders. Sandy's schedule was strictly classified and only she knew on which hours of which day in a given week he would be coming to the campus.

Moreover, to maximize his privacy, Sandy would frequently alter his plans. His swift visits were confined to the lab team meetings, conferences with his grad students, and whatever dreaded administrative tasks he had to perform.

His secretary's brief was clear: "Don't clutter up my life." And yet on this occasion Maureen felt insubordination would in the long run be the wiser course.

"Listen, Kimiko. My boss is a bit of an oddball, and even I can't guarantee that you'll get to see him. But why not take a chance on coming by on Tuesday, at say four o'clock . . ."

"In the morning?" she asked affably.

"No, he's not *that* weird. Anyway, come around and I'll do the best I can."

Maureen herself was surprised.

The grateful visitor was so pert and petite that she looked like a young graduate student. She was dressed modestly but elegantly in a green skirt and matching sweater which set off a single strand of pearls. Her dark eyes seemed to sparkle with life.

When Maureen buzzed Sandy to announce Mrs. Watanabe's presence, he bristled.

"No way, I've got a meeting with the dean," he complained.

Overhearing the dialogue, Kimiko self-effacingly announced that she had to leave. The secretary motioned her to remain as she responded through the phone to her boss, "Come on, Sandy—that isn't till four-thirty. Why don't you just pop out for a quick hello?"

Sandy acceded grudgingly, while simultaneously shoring up his defenses. Reluctantly, he went out to shake hands with the grateful young Japanese woman— and send her on her way.

He had pictured Mrs. Watanabe as a woman with rings of worry around her eyes, drained of humor, tired, and very likely embittered by the harsh blows fate had dealt her. He did not expect her to be pretty. Certainly not young and vibrant, with a flawless porcelain complexion.

She smiled as she held out her hand, and with the hint of a respectful bow politely uttered, "I had to come by and thank you so much for everything, Dr. Raven."

The cloistered Sandy was momentarily tongue-tied. Her radiance had pierced his defensive armor. He recovered sufficiently to ask, "Do you have time for a cup of coffee?"

"But you have to see the dean," Maureen scolded mischievously.

Sandy ignored her and motioned the lissome visitor to follow him into his office, while Maureen grinned with satisfaction.

Kimiko monopolized the time with varied expressions of gratitude. The best way to thank Sandy, she had correctly planned, was to show how much she had learned at Cal Tech—and to demonstrate a knowledge of his work.

As she talked, Sandy searched his mind for a pretext to see her again.

He tried to look at her without staring. Her presence was unsettling: her face, her figure—why, after years of looking at women as if they were broccoli, did he suddenly notice how shapely this one was? Part of him longed for her to leave so he could return to his sheltered life, while another part longed to keep her there.

Yet she diffidently rose, thanked him for his time and, again with a trace of a bow, prepared to take her leave.

"No—wait," he spluttered, pressing a button. "You haven't even had coffee. . . . Maureen, uh, would you bring us two espressos? And, uh, call the dean and say I'll be late."

As she prepared the refreshments, Maureen found herself humming "Some Enchanted Evening."

Meanwhile, Kimiko was herself hearing sounds of her own. An emotional wake-up call.

After the initial formal awkwardness, she began to see Sandy as something more than a figure in a white lab coat. For there was no mistake about the way this intense, intelligent man was gazing at her. She was on the verge of blushing.

What really captivated Sandy was the strength of her personality. The conversation had quickly passed from a routine discussion of her courses to the real center of her life: the twins.

One minute she was talking about Hiroshi and Koji, and the next he was discussing Olivia and how much he missed her. She found his unabashed pride in his daughter enormously endearing.

He in turn noticed the obvious pleasure she took in talking about her boys.

"I am happy to say that they are very industrious. I mean, they have a difficult schedule since I also send them to Japanese school in the afternoons."

"Yes." He nodded. "I've heard about your high-pressure academic system. To be frank, it sounds a bit severe."

"It's a way of life," she answered. "They'll have to sink or swim in our society. You must come and meet them sometime. I suppose you are probably too busy."

"No," he swiftly replied. "As it happens, I'm very free at the moment. When would be convenient for you?"

Had Kimiko suggested that very evening, he would have readily accepted. But being diplomatic, she proposed dinner the following week.

Sandy spent the intervening days absorbing all the latest books on Japanese culture and society. He was determined to make a good impression, and was too insecure to believe he already had.

What he liked most of all was the fact that she made no attempt to camouflage her motherhood. The boys sat at the table with them in their modest apartment near the campus, making polite informed conversation when spoken to.

At the stroke of eight they excused themselves and retired to their room to study.

"What time do they go to sleep?" Sandy asked.

"Never before midnight. They have two sets of homework."

"Well, at least they can catch up on the weekends."

She laughed. What a lovely shape her mouth was, he thought.

"They go to school all day Saturday."

"God—do they ever rebel?"

"No, they understand. It's normal in Japan."

"Just a guess, but I'd say *you* don't go to sleep before three."

"You're right, Sandy. But you got me this chance, and I don't want to disappoint you."

"You haven't. And yet we Americans have a saying,

all work and no play ... You're a very attractive woman. In fact, I only wish I were ten years younger."

"Why?" she looked at him with undisguised affection. "You are not exactly an ancient person. And you are a very attractive man."

She can't mean that, he thought. I'm too much of a nerd for someone like her.

Still, they talked until midnight. When she excused herself to say good night to Hiroshi and Koji, Sandy realized that it was time to go. Yet when she returned, they continued talking for another hour. Only then did he force himself to take his leave, but not without making another date.

"What about Sunday?" he asked. "The boys deserve a little break. Why don't I take you all to Universal Studios?"

"Oh, they would love that," she responded.

"It's a little silly, but I thought you might enjoy it too," he remarked.

"I know I will."

With its fires and floods and man-eating sharks and other catastrophes, the studio provided dozens of opportunities for reassuring hugs.

Long after he dropped them back at their apartment, Sandy could still feel the touch of the boys on his neck, and especially of Kimiko's hand slipped spontaneously into his as they walked back to the car.

"What do you normally do on weekends?" Kimiko asked.

"Well, as you probably gathered, I live a peculiar life. On weekends I go shopping."

"There's nothing strange about that," she offered.

"In San Francisco?" he asked jovially. "It's a few hundred miles away."

"Yes," she acknowledged. "That is a bit unusual. Is there something special there?"

Revealing his enormous enthusiasm, he told her about the garages and their brainy proprietors.

She nodded. "That seems like an important part of your work. You should not let us disturb you."

"Then why don't you come with me?" he quickly added, "I mean, the boys too."

She thought for a split second. "I would have to propose one condition or I would not feel right."

"Name it."

"I would have them miss Japanese school so we could go on a Saturday. Otherwise it would not be fair to you."

Two days instead of one? It was a bounty that he dared not dream of.

They left at dawn and drove slowly on the Pacific Coast Highway, stopping for an early coffee on the pier at Monterey, where Sandy bought little bowls of food for the boys to feed the seals.

A short while later he booked them all into a luxurious three-bedroom suite near the top of the Four Seasons Clift Hotel in San Francisco. They immediately left again to explore Silicon Valley.

Here Kimiko saw another side of Sandy. Whereas he was timid with adults, even with her at times, he was a kind of benevolent godfather with the young scientists. The fledgling inventors adored him and treated her and the boys like colleagues, especially after they realized that she understood perfectly what they were talking about.

That evening they went to the crystal-chandeliered French Room for dinner on their own, leaving the boys to eat in the room. Kimiko had not forgotten their obligations—the makeup work their Japanese teacher had set for them as a condition for missing school.

Yet she only pecked at her food, and Sandy realized at once what was wrong.

"Kimiko," he said earnestly, "how can we be friends

if we don't tell each other the truth. You're having real qualms, aren't you?"

She nodded nervously.

"But you're right," he insisted. "I feel exactly the same. We shouldn't have left them up there on their own."

She nodded again.

A moment later he had settled the bill and they were back in the elevator to rejoin Hiroshi and Koji. When they had completed their second dinner, as a special treat he ordered them all waffles and ice cream for dessert.

At last the boys were asleep, and Kimiko and Sandy were alone. Really alone.

He knew what he wanted to happen, but was afraid that one false move would shatter the perfection that they had shared so far. And yet in accepting his invitation to come away, she must have known this moment was inevitable.

He just could not tell how she had prepared to face it. Then she told him without words, excusing herself to take a shower and reappearing primly, but fetchingly, in the towel bathrobe provided by the hotel.

She sat down on the same couch.

"You have the figure of a young girl," he whispered.

She smiled and took his hand. "If you say so, Sandy." And then she added, "I must tell you I feel very shy."

"That's two of us," he confessed. "Only I feel more than that."

She put her finger on his lips. "No," she cautioned. "This is right, Sandy. We both know what we are doing." She hesitated and added, "And we both want to."

Thus began the most important project of rejuvenation Sandy had ever undertaken.

His own.

* * *

Two months later Sandy struck gold—literally and figuratively. He identified a group of genes that promoted aging in skin cells, and during various trials succeeded in reversing the degeneration. It may not have been permanent, but it looked as if the process could be repeated indefinitely.

Though he had tried to avoid all sensationalism by publishing the details of his discovery in an article in a recondite journal, the beavers of the wire services translated his findings into laymen's language. Overnight, Sandy Raven became a household name.

It was then that the editors of *Time* magazine made the first contacts that would ultimately lead to a cover story.

The media touted him as the creator of the ultimate—and especially Hollywood—dream: a chemical that held out the promise of eternal youth.

His placid and comfortable life was suddenly invaded from every quarter. Calls, faxes, letters—a few desperate people even turned up unannounced at his lab; it would not be long before they found the estate.

Sandy was so harassed by the three-ring circus that he fled with his father to Lake Tahoe, where they rented a bungalow under the name of Smith.

The first few days were idyllic, as they took long walks in the pure, serene mountain air.

In the comfort and isolation of their Tahoe chalet, the two men watched a carnival of avarice as the auction for Sandy's discovery reached dizzying heights.

When Corvax beat out Clarins and Yves St. Laurent with an advance against royalties of fifty million dollars, Sandy was not gratified—he was outraged.

"Think of it, Dad. You can't get these guys to give a million bucks for a cancer lab. But the prospect of being able to make old women look a little younger can get them to cough up fifty million without even batting an eyelash."

"Listen, don't knock the dough," Sidney answered

philosophically. "It's the only drug in the world you
can't overdose on. And, as Liz Taylor said in *Cat on a
Hot Tin Roof*, 'You can be young without money, but
you can't be old without it.' "

In their tranquil retreat, the two had many heart-to-
heart conversations lasting well into the night.

"You may be a big-time scientist now, sonny boy, but
you're not too old to take advice from your dad."

"Of course not. What did you have in mind?"

"Well," the elder Raven began his homily, "let's start
with your life."

"What about it?"

"Look at you," Sidney scolded. "You live in your
private lab with your private assistants, surrounded by
your private electronic surveillance gizmos. I've never
known anyone more devoted to the betterment of mankind and more careless with the betterment of himself.
Take it from your old man, all the money in the world
ain't worth more than a hug and a kiss from a good
woman. Am I making sense?"

"Yes." His son smiled.

"Kiddo, there's nobody been more disappointed than
me by the female gender. Love is more dangerous than
Russian roulette—'cause *five* of the chambers got
bullets. Still, there's always that chance you'll come
up with a winner. As the song goes, 'It's a many-
splendored thing.' "

Sandy looked at him sheepishly and murmured, "You
know, don't you?"

Sidney smiled back. "Was my Hong Kong guess on
target?"

"Well, you've got the right hemisphere—she's Japanese." Sandy grinned. "Only how did you—"

"I'm not Sherlock Holmes, sonny boy. I just kinda
guessed that the rental of this joint didn't include the
picture in your bedroom of the Oriental gal and her two
kids. Is she as nice as she looks?"

"Nicer," Sandy replied, his affection showing. "I

mean, I feel very comfortable with her, with all of them."

"I'm a little old to start learning Japanese. Do the kids speak English?"

"Better than you and me."

"Good," Sidney commented. "I like the sound of this more and more. I especially like the look on your face when you speak about ..."

"Kimiko."

"Kimiko Raven." He tried it out. "It sounds different."

"Well, she *is* different," Sandy asserted.

Sidney looked at his son's face and saw new life. "I love her already," he said with feeling. "I love her for what she's done for you."

On Thursday afternoon of the week in which Cal Tech had straightforwardly broken the news of Sandy's discovery, a gaggle of journalists and photographers burst into the lab where Olivia Raven, now a freshman at MIT, was trying to concentrate on that week's experimental assignment in first-year physics.

She had been dodging them for days, but now they had her cornered. They surrounded her, snapping photos from every conceivable angle to show the great man's daughter at work.

Exasperated, she burst out, "Will you leeches get the hell off my case?"

The commotion caught the attention of her instructor—herself no stranger to the predators of the press. By sheer force of personality, she ordered them out and locked the door.

The teacher then took the dazed and disoriented young girl to her office, made her a cup of tea and tried to calm her.

"Olivia, what you just saw was the ugly side of science. The newspapers are absolutely carnivorous when it comes to stories of so-called laboratory miracles.

Imagine what they would have done if they could have interviewed God after He split the Red Sea?"

Olivia laughed lightly and the muscles of her face relaxed.

"Well, I guess if anyone should know, it's you, Dr. da Costa," she commented.

Isabel nodded. "If I could get some of my students to apply themselves as doggedly to their lab exercises as these clowns do to their photographs, we could probably have found a cure for AIDS. And please, Olivia, just call me Isabel. We're practically the same age. Anyway, I think it's safe enough for you to go back and finish your acoustics experiment."

Only when they were back in the street did one perceptive reporter realize in frustration, "Holy shit, I just remembered—the broad in the white coat was the girl physics genius. Did any of you guys get shots of them together?"

For once the press did not win. Despite their global resources, the paparazzi were unable to find Sandy Raven. They looked in Paris, Rome, even Tokyo. But they did not think to scour the numerous tourists visiting the Buddhist temples, Shinto shrines, gardens, and traditional houses of Kyoto, the cultural center of Japan.

For Sandy was here, visiting one of its twenty universities—privately.

In a journalistic sense, it was a pity. For it would have made an ideal photograph for *People* magazine: the famous American scientist, a ravishing Oriental girl, and twin Japanese boys.

All very happy.

56

ISABEL

ISABEL DA COSTA cursed the many times she had almost taken driving lessons, but foolishly changed her mind, thinking them a waste of time away from her research. She phoned for a cab, and minutes later when it arrived, the driver buzzed so aggressively that the noise woke her father.

Ray shuffled, confused, into the living room just as she was heading for the door.

"Are you leaving?" he mumbled drowsily.

Flustered, Isabel tried to explain quickly so she could make her escape.

"I—I'm going to the airport—"

"Eloping with Jerry, are you?" he asked half seriously.

"No, Dad, don't be silly. In fact, he'll be here at eight. Tell him I'll be back as soon as I can."

She hurried out, leaving Ray standing lost in the midst of an invisible fog.

Muriel, exhausted from lack of sleep, was scarcely able to believe her eyes when she saw her daughter at the airline gate.

"How did you find out?" she asked, her worried tone in contrast to the strength of her embrace.

"Never mind that. Why didn't you tell me you were coming?" Isabel countered. For a split second the little girl in her came close to blurting out her own good news. But she suppressed the selfish urge.

Muriel was caught off guard and struggled to fabricate a plausible excuse.

"Well, I know you're in your office all day, so I was just going to shoot up there and surprise you right after my appointment."

"What appointment? What the hell is going on?"

Muriel held her daughter's hand in both of hers and, forcing back the tears, tried to find the words.

"Edmundo's ill—very ill." She paused, gathered the courage and then uttered the words, "Huntington's disease."

"Oh, Mom, I'm so sorry. But I still don't understand why you didn't call me."

Muriel interrupted her daughter. "There's a professor at Mass. General who's developed a radical cure. But it's still in the final stage of FDA trials—and I've come to see if there's any way I can get him to try it on Edmundo anyway."

"I'll go with you," Isabel insisted.

"No. Believe me, this is something you want no part of," Muriel objected with startling severity.

"If you put it like that, Mom, there's no way on earth I'm going to leave you alone for a minute."

Muriel shook her head in defeat and then realized that, for form's sake, she had at least to murmur, "Thank you, Isabel."

With time to kill, mother and daughter had breakfast in a crowded coffee shop near the hospital. The bleary-eyed, white-clad customers were obviously going off duty. The livelier ones, about to enter into the fray, were exchanging the essential news that encompasses a Boston doctor's life: red cells and Red Sox.

Despite her mother's obvious reluctance, Isabel could not withhold a torrent of questions.

"Mom, I don't know anything about this disease."

"Let's put it this way. It's a kind of neurological time bomb. Ultimately everything falls apart."

"Aren't there any chances for recovery?"

"One hundred percent fatal," Muriel stated emphatically. "There's no cure."

"But you say this guy at MGH has something?"

"A genetic link. They've got a drug that works on rats," Muriel said bitterly, "and several other laboratory animals. The only thing they don't have is approval to try it on people."

"Is there any hope they might make an exception?"

"Well, the government sometimes allows things on 'compassionate' grounds. I'm just praying to God that this doctor is strong on compassion."

He was tall and broad-shouldered, his black eyebrows flecked with gray.

"Good morning, Mrs. Zimmer," he said in a heavy Russian accent, holding out his hand. "I am Professor Avilov. Would you come in please."

Isabel rose at almost the same time. "I'm her daughter. May I come too?"

"Her daughter?" Avilov reacted with startled interest. "Well, I should think—"

"No," Muriel said emphatically. "I don't want her involved."

"But, my dear Mrs. Zimmer," he answered with exaggerated courtesy, "by the very nature of the disease, is she not very much involved?"

"No, Edmundo's not, I mean . . . her father's Raymond da Costa," Muriel protested.

The Russian scrutinized Isabel's features and a sudden glow of recognition crossed his face. "Ah, are you not the famous physicist?"

Isabel nodded wordlessly.

"Let me tell you what an honor it is to meet you," Avilov pronounced with deference. "I greatly admire your achievements."

Then turning again to her mother, he said, "I had no idea, Mrs. Zimmer. But the fact that you have such a world-respected person in your corner, so to say, might help with the wretched bureaucrats in Washington."

He stared at Muriel, waiting for a reply.

"Will you not reconsider allowing Dr. da Costa to accompany us?"

Though emotionally battered and physically exhausted, Muriel could still sense that this pompous professor, whose assistance she so desperately needed, would not be satisfied unless Isabel joined them.

"Very well," she sighed in capitulation.

They followed him into his large office, which was decorated with diplomas in many languages. He seemed to be a member of every academy of science in the universe.

"Please, ladies, sit down." He gestured gallantly as he positioned himself behind his massive wooden desk. Occupying center stage was a large color photograph of his blond wife and three children, all smiling like a toothpaste ad.

Avilov eyed his visitors and then pronounced, "Well . . ."

Neither woman could fathom the significance of this portentous monosyllable.

The great man then launched into a kind of lecture, punctuated with patronizing repetitions of, "as I am sure you already know."

"Huntington's is, as I am sure you already know, one of the real 'nasties.' No cure. No remission. No hope. Nothing. Up till a few years ago they did not even know where in the human genome it was to be found."

He addressed Muriel with groveling condescension.

"All of this must be very familiar to your daughter. But if there is anything you wish me to explain, do not hesitate to ask."

"No, no," she replied softly. "Please go ahead."

"Work done in this very lab by my distinguished colleague Professor Gusella determined that the Huntington's disease gene resides on a strip of Chromosome Four. It was the first time in history anyone had used DNA markers to figure out roughly where a gene was located when they had no other clue.

"From this auspicious beginning, a cooperative effort was organized, including some participants from Dr. da Costa's own MIT. Our strategy hinged on a new type of DNA marker called Restriction Fragment Length Polymorphisms—or RFLPs, as we refer to them in the lab.

"After our painstaking explorations, we now had the Huntington's gene, so to say, in our clutches.

"It was here that I myself, a minor player in this great drama, stepped briefly into the limelight. I was fortunate enough to clone the offending gene, and by using recombinant DNA, produce a protein which seems—at least in the laboratory—to restore the structure of Chromosome Four to its normal healthy state."

He ceased emoting to the world and once again addressed Muriel. "This, I take it, dear lady, is the reason for your visit."

"Yes, Professor," she answered as deferentially as she could, aware that the way to this man's heart was through his ego.

Avilov propped his chin up on his right hand. He emitted one of his random "Well's" and began to ponder. A moment later he became voluble again.

"As you must realize, Mrs. Zimmer, you are not the first ... petitioner I have received. Huntington's is a dreadful malady, and my heart goes out to the many sufferers whom I hope someday to help. Yet imagine the irony when I, as a former Soviet citizen, say I am strangled by what is here called 'red tape.' Unfortunately it is true.

"I am certain my restructured gene would work as well with humans as it has with mice. But in the past, our appeals have fallen on deaf ears."

Muriel lowered her head.

"And yet," Avilov boomed suddenly, "I see here a potential advantage."

"What, Professor?" Isabel asked, breaking her long silence.

The Russian suddenly pointed his finger at her and uttered yet another single syllable: "You."

"I don't understand," she responded.

"Perhaps, Dr. da Costa, you are not aware of your own eminence. But the outside world regards you as a scientific giant and—speaking proudly as a newly naturalized American—a national hero. If the authorities in Washington were led to believe that you were in fact Edmundo Zimmer's child, they would surely consider this appeal with new—and dare I say—favorable eyes."

Muriel dissolved into tears. Isabel embraced her mother while continuing to address the eminent scientist.

"But that's absurd, Professor Avilov. Anyway, how could they see *his* life or death as being relevant to me?"

Muriel's sobs now became more audible.

"But surely, Dr. da Costa," Avilov replied with raised finger, "you are aware of the genetic dimension?"

"Frankly, no."

"Well, let me put it to you in the proverbial nutshell. Huntington's is one of the primary autosomal *dominant* disorders. Affected individuals have a *one in two* chance of passing it on to their offspring. Were it known that a scientist of your magnitude were in such jeopardy, I am sure we would get, so to say, the green flag to treat the patient."

"My God," Isabel whispered, and then asked Muriel, "Do Francisco and Dorotea know about this?"

Muriel nodded. "They both insisted on being tested. I tried to persuade them not to. Francisco was lucky, but now Dorotea knows she's living out an inescapable death sentence."

"Oh, that's horrible," Isabel gasped.

Avilov could not keep from smiling inwardly at what fortune had so unexpectedly brought to his office—not only a surefire method of accelerating government approval, but a world-famous patient to publicize its success.

"Dr. da Costa, if this therapy were sanctioned, you would be helping not only your stepfather and stepsister, but countless others who could be saved if it proved efficacious."

Isabel clutched Muriel by the shoulders and said passionately, "Mom, I'll go along with it. It's our one chance to save them."

At this moment Muriel, overcome with emotion, grasped Isabel's hands. "There's something you have to know," she said. "This affects you in a way you never realized."

"I don't understand."

"You're in danger, darling. I mean, it's my fault." She began to weep. "I don't know how to say this."

Isabel grew alarmed. "Mom, for God's sake, what are you trying to tell me?"

"It's actually the truth, Isabel. Edmundo is your natural father."

At first, praying she had misunderstood, she gaped at her mother.

"Darling, try to understand. My marriage was falling apart and Edmundo was so warm and caring. He genuinely loved me. . . ." She hesitated. "We had an affair and"—her voice lowered to a barely audible whisper—"you were conceived. After Ray became so obsessed with you, there was no way I could ever tell him."

"Stop it! I don't want to hear any more of this."

She had let go of her mother who, by now, was weeping uncontrollably.

"In fact, if you must know, one of the reasons I let him manipulate you was because I felt so guilty."

"I can't believe this, I simply can't believe this," she repeated in a paroxysm of denial.

She was staggered, stricken with self-doubt, racked with a terrible uncertainty as to who she really was. For emotionally, she had always defined herself as Raymond da Costa's daughter. She had lived with him. And for him.

At this point she again grew aware of the Russian doctor's presence.

"My dear Dr. da Costa, I am a physician. I will hold all of this in confidence."

"Professor Avilov," Isabel declared. "I've changed my mind. I won't be a party to this unethical travesty."

He straightened himself, manifestly taking offense. "But it is now urgent that you yourself be tested."

"I don't give a damn," she snapped.

"But Isabel," her mother pleaded, "don't you realize you're in danger?"

Abruptly, Isabel buried her head in her hands.

"You owe it to the world," the Russian argued unctuously. "You are perhaps the greatest scientific mind in modern physics, and have a fifty-fifty chance of carrying the gene for Huntington's disease."

"Thank you," Isabel retaliated furiously. "You've just cast a giant shadow over my entire life."

"Not necessarily," Avilov remarked with an incongruous grin. "I can draw your blood and within a week you will know your fate. After all, it could be good news."

Though Isabel stood motionless and silent, he could sense that his words had struck home.

She still did not reply.

"Perhaps I should leave you two alone to talk about this," he suggested, feeling a sudden urge to retire.

She glared at her mother, who was living in her own private hell.

"You expect me to talk to the woman who screwed

up my life—and my father's? What she did was unfor-
givable."

"But if there hadn't been Edmundo," Muriel said
pleadingly, "you wouldn't be you!"

Isabel seared her mother with eyes of fire. "Do you
expect me to thank you for that?"

She stormed out of the doctor's office.

57

ISABEL

THOUGH THE heat was sweltering, Isabel walked the entire distance home from Avilov's office.

What she had experienced was like the turning point
in a Greek tragedy. In a matter of seconds she had gone
from a person whose whole life had been blessed to one
not only cursed, but possibly doomed to death.

She didn't hurry. There was so much to think about.

Curiously, it was not her own uncertain destiny that
was preoccupying her most, even though it was possible
that on some day in the future she would turn a corner
and come face-to-face with the Angel of Death. At this
moment her principal concern was the fate of the man
who, from her earliest memories, had loved, cherished,
and protected her.

And she was not even his biological daughter.

Isabel knew in some sense it would no longer matter
to him. After all, love is not genetically transmittable,
and he had lavished it upon her for years. And recipro-
cally, she had given him all the affection a natural father
could have dreamed of.

During the lengthy exploration of her thoughts, she resolved to make things right again. To give Ray what he had earned by sacrificing his own life.

She swore a fervent oath that he would never, never learn of Muriel's betrayal.

And now when she thought of Jerry, she was pierced with aching loneliness.

The happiness he had brought her was real. Yet how could their relationship continue? She felt tainted, no longer worthy of him.

She arrived back at the flat—overheated and drenched with sweat.

There was an eerie feeling that the apartment was somehow emptier. Her father's bedroom door was closed. Perhaps he was escaping from the brutal Cambridge heat by taking a siesta.

Suddenly, feeling parched from her long hot walk, she went into the kitchen, opened up the fridge, poured some lemonade, and went back to the main room, which was the coolest because they had kept the shutters closed.

She sat down, took a swig and looked around. The place looked unusually tidy. Magazines and journals that were normally scattered everywhere were piled up neatly.

Glancing at the table they used for work and meals, she noticed a long sheet of lined yellow foolscap propped up between the salt and pepper.

Knowing instinctively what it would say, she picked it up with dread.

Dearest Isabel,
You have been a wondrous, loving daughter, more than someone mediocre like myself could ever have deserved. You are a blessing and a gift that I was honored to enjoy for all those years. Too many years.
I realize that I've overstayed my welcome in your

life and that your rightful place is with people of your own age—like Jerry, who's a wonderful boy.

I don't deny that what I am doing hurts me deeply, but I do it out of the profoundest love I have for you.

Among the many offers Pracht passed on (perhaps to get rid of me?) there was a last minute opening for a physics teacher in one of those fancy prep schools for future Ivy Leaguers who are already full of themselves.

I guess my claim to fame as your father is my best recommendation. When I called him this afternoon, the headmaster said he would take me sight unseen.

As soon as I get settled, I'll make contact and give you my new address and phone. (Remember, I may be letting you go, but I'm not completely letting go of *you*.)

From now on, I'll be acting like a grown-up parent with grown-up children. I'll look forward to Thanksgiving, Christmas, birthdays, and whatever festivals we can concoct.

I leave behind the only gift I withheld from you— your freedom.

> Be happy, my beloved daughter,
> Your loving father

Isabel was at a loss for words. She knew—the way a patient on a local anesthetic knows—that a part of her flesh was being torn away. But all she could sense was the anguish she would feel when the shock wore off.

She put her head in her hands. Suddenly her world was spinning in a centrifuge, whirling all her thoughts asunder. She, who had always played the indomitable Miss da Costa, ever cheery and composed even in the most pressured of circumstances, fell apart and began to sob.

She was not aware of the passage of time, and was jolted by the piercing ring of the phone.

"Isa, I waited so long the breakfast rolls got stale. Did you meet some cuter guy or something?"

She was overwhelmed with relief to hear his voice. "Oh, Jerry, am I glad to speak to you."

"Well, you didn't give me that impression all day," he chided playfully.

"Please, Jerry, listen. It's been the worst day of my life. Traumatic would be an understatement. Can you come over for dinner?"

"Why don't you let me take you out for a change? I mean, we could be alone."

She paused for a moment and then said softly, "We'll be alone. Dad's gone."

"What the hell happened, Isa?"

"I'm still in such shock. I'm not sure I understand yet, but I think he had a sudden attack of guilt. Anyway, he's taken a job in a prep school."

"Well," Jerry argued, trying to see the bright side, "this could be the best thing that ever happened to both of you. Is that why you're so upset?"

"Would you believe me if I told you that's the least of the earthquakes?" she replied. "But why don't you let me tell you in person. My invitation was a very special one—I mean, in my whole life, I've never really cooked for anyone but me and Dad. Is it okay if I make something basic? I mean, I'm not exactly Julia Child. Will you settle for spaghetti and meatballs?"

"Fantastic. I'll come by at seven."

Still in a hypnotic daze, she went out to the supermarket and bought the ingredients for dinner, not forgetting Sara Lee brownies, should all else fail.

The phone was ringing insistently as she opened the door. Quickly setting down her packages, she hurried to answer it.

"Isabel—please don't hang up. We've got to talk." It was Muriel. "I've checked into the Hyatt Regency. Would you have dinner with me?"

"Sorry, I've got other plans," Isabel said tonelessly.

"Yes, of course—Ray—"

"No, Mother, not Ray," she replied pointedly. She resented the inference that everyone in her life regarded her as a social misfit.

"Well, when?" Muriel asked helplessly. "I mean, now that this terrible thing is out, it has to be dealt with."

"Look, I can't think about it now. I'll call you back in the morning."

"Can't we even set a date for breakfast? Say eight o'clock?"

"All right, fine," Isabel replied exasperatedly. "I'm sorry, I have to go now."

Just when Isabel had reassured herself that the worst was over and she could now unburden herself to Jerry, she realized that yet another dark cloud had fallen on her life.

She was in love with him and secure in the fact that her feelings were reciprocated. She had always assumed that their relationship would develop in time and that he would eventually ask her to marry him.

But not *now*. Not with her appalling heritage.

The doorbell rang. And suddenly, despite what was weighing heavy on her heart, she laughed with joy. He was that dear to her.

Jerry had a bottle of that sparkling red concoction known as Cold Duck, as well as a bouquet of roses, but his most precious gift was irrepressible good humor.

Impulsively she threw her arms around him.

He smiled. "Hey, I think I'll go out and come in again for more of the same."

"Don't be silly," she coaxed him. "Sit down so that I can depress the hell out of you."

"Where's Ray?"

She handed Jerry the note, and watched his expression as he read it. He was clearly moved.

"God, it took a lot of guts to write this. He's a hell of a guy. You should be very proud of him."

Somehow the approval of the man she loved, his

words of unabashed affection, had a paradoxical affect on Isabel. She began to cry.

"Isa, what's wrong?"

"I've just found out he's not my father."

"I don't understand."

She gathered the courage to tell him everything. About who Edmundo really was. And who Ray really wasn't.

"You know something," Jerry remarked. "The fact that he doesn't even know, makes what he did all the more—generous."

For the moment Isabel did not have the courage to mention Edmundo's illness; selfishly perhaps, since she did not want to run the risk of scaring Jerry away on this of all nights.

"Does it sound crazy that I'm angry with my mother for giving birth to me?" she asked.

"That's a real tough one," Jerry replied. "Frankly, I can't help feeling at least a little grateful . . ." He held both her hands and squeezed them affectionately.

Oh, if you only knew the worst part, she thought.

By the middle of dinner, with some credit perhaps to the wine, they managed to talk of things other than parents, heredity, and fidelity.

It was growing late, nearing the time when Jerry usually made his chivalrous departure.

He stood up, moved closer and put his arms around her.

After they had kissed for a few moments, Jerry asked gently, "Isa, last time when your dad was ill, I spent the night here on the sofa."

"Yes, I remember."

"If you don't mind, I'd like to stay again, but this time with you."

Their eyes met and, without any touch of hesitation or scintilla of fear, Isabel answered softly, "Please, Jerry, I'd like that very much."

58

ADAM

IN A way, Alzheimer's disease is like going through the torture of drowning—again and again. Just when the victim has lapsed into unconsciousness, he suddenly succeeds in finding his way above water to snatch a breath of reality. This is simply another reminder that he is *not* dying ... yet.

Paradoxically for the sufferer, it is more painful at the beginning when his periods of lucidity are longer. In the end those around him become the victims. For they know that though he is not lost to the world, he is lost to *them*.

But even before the light completely fades, there is an unending series of humiliations.

Adam fought like a demon when they tried to take away his driver's license. He was determined to preserve this tenuous symbol of independence.

Since she had so much to do to protect him, Anya enlisted the help of Terry Walters, a beefy black male nurse with considerable experience in dealing with this ruthless disease.

He was so skillful and good-natured that it was not clear whether Adam knew precisely why he had been hired.

As the disease advanced, the patient became more depressed and lethargic, but Terry convinced him to jog, matching him stride for stride, alert and ready to catch him if he stumbled.

The addition of a nurse also enabled Anya to go about the difficult business of living two lives: hers and Adam's. She visited the lab daily, collecting the data gathered from various experiments and bringing it home, explaining to the staff that the prof had picked up a nasty virus on the journey that he simply could not shake.

In lucid moments he wrote comments in the margins of the reports, and Anya made sure his modifications were adopted. If his mind was blurred—as was the case with growing frequency—she would pretend to talk to him. And when he stared glassy-eyed, unable to understand the problem, she tried to imagine what the old Adam would have done and conveyed the response to the staff.

In the brief time they had spent together, they had learned to think as one—which gave Anya the courage to enter areas where she would never have trespassed.

She had no alternative but to tell Prescott Mason. He was genuinely shaken. Perhaps behind that PR man's facade there was a human being after all.

Moreover, he added, for what it was worth on the scale of things, he would continue to work on their behalf because he believed in what they had done.

Ever the pragmatist, Mason chose to regard his client's tragic circumstances as just another kind of deadline. Up till now, he had been subtle and low-key, operating on the assumption that he would make his big move in three or four years. But after what he had just learned, he had to go into high gear.

In some areas Anya proved to be an undreamed-of asset. As MR-Alpha became more and more widely used and its effectiveness recognized, there were increasing requests to interview Adam. But it was clearly too dangerous to allow him to talk to the press.

Mason easily convinced the papers that mattered to interview this wife of the nineties, not walking a humble ten paces behind, but standing together with her husband in the vanguard as they charted new territory and made medical history.

In private, Anya longed for those fleeting—ever rarer—moments when Adam would be himself. It was like a reunion with someone resurrected for a quarter of an hour. But the price was going through the agony of watching him "die" again.

Prescott Mason labored tirelessly. On more than a dozen occasions in the most important research centers in the country, Mason took previous Nobel laureates and respected nominators into his confidence and explained that Adam Coopersmith was dying.

Naturally, he argued, Adam would have been chosen in due time. But perhaps the cruelest and most arbitrary Nobel rule was that the award could only be given to a man alive at the time of the voting—though ironically, if the recipient died of joy one second after receiving the official news, his widow could collect the prize.

By the spring, Mason had made considerable headway. He had obtained almost forty "congressional suggestions" that he knew of, and nearly twenty recommendations, sent by letter and fax to Stockholm.

Except when she had to be at work, Anya never left Adam's side. Sometimes she would drive him to the lab, and, though he was occasionally confused and disoriented, she would walk him swiftly down the corridor, encouraging him to respond to the friendly waves and greetings, "Hi, Prof."

Previously an annoyance, the glass wall in Adam's office now served a useful purpose. It proved to the staff that, in some sense at least, he was still *there*, "on the job." Anya seated him behind his huge desk, always made sure he had a book in his hand.

But members of the staff, accustomed to bringing their problems directly to Adam, began to resent what they thought was Anya's usurpation of his role. She would take their reports, assure them that the prof

would look them over that evening and return them
with comments in the morning.

Why, they wondered, was he letting her take over?

Anya was aware that she was unpopular. But she
counted it as a small price to pay. Because on the larger
scale of things, they seemed to be getting away with it.

Whenever possible, she would go to her own work
station in the lab while simultaneously keeping an eye
on Adam through the glass, should someone try to
reach him directly.

Yet with each passing week, they had to deprive
Adam of more and more of the trappings and privileges
of adulthood. In moments of distraction—for Terry,
though dedicated, did not work around the clock—
Adam had occasionally wandered to the garage and
tried to drive off.

It was not enough that they had appropriated his license, they had no choice but to confiscate his keys. At
first he was angry and resentful. Then, as his perception
continued to blur, he barely noticed the infringements
on his autonomy.

Finally, Anya had to resort to the ultimate pacifier.
She now came into the lab at midnight and tried to do
some serious work for three or four hours, while Adam
sat in his office in front of an electronic baby-sitter,
staring at the screen of a portable television that he had
long ago bought her.

At that hour the place was all but deserted. At an appropriate moment, when the two or three remaining
workers popped out for a late snack, Anya would help
put on his coat and walk him quickly to the car. But she
knew this charade would not last for long.

His condition worsened. In fact, one night Adam was
so agitated that Anya begged Terry to work overtime
and stay with him while she went to check on their various projects.

Just as she was waiting for the down elevator, she

was accosted by Carlo Pisani, Venice's gift to the women of Boston.

"Hello," she answered his greeting. "How's your work coming?"

"You should know," he said pointedly. "You've already critiqued it."

"Well," she reacted, flustered, "it sounds very exciting. I mean, naturally, Adam's told me something about it."

"Please, Anya," he protested, "don't treat me like a fool. It's *you* who told *him*." He paused for a moment and then asserted, "I think the two of us should talk." His tone was knowing, but she was unable to tell how much he had discovered.

"Why, of course, Carlo," she said uneasily. "Any time it's convenient."

"Now," the Italian said insistently.

"At this hour?"

"What we have to say is long overdue. I want to know why you have kept me in the dark."

"I don't understand," she responded with growing panic.

"You could have trusted me," he persevered. "In fact, if you had, it would never have come to this. I respect you as a scientist. We could have worked together."

She shrugged, at a loss for words.

"Anyway," he said, "since you locked the front gate, I had to resort to the only approach that would be off limits to you."

He then continued, with a trace of satisfaction, "Last night I waited nearly two hours in the men's room hoping he'd come in to use it before going home. And, of course, he did."

Still trying to maintain an outward calm, Anya casually asked, "And what did he say to you?"

"He didn't have to talk, his actions said everything." Pisani spoke with something approximating compassion. "I almost cried when I saw it. This brilliant, splendid man, was so pathetically disoriented . . . that he pissed in the middle of the floor."

"Oh Jesus," Anya said, letting down her guard and covering her face with her hands.

"He's a very sick man," Carlo murmured in a tone that sounded strangely conspiratorial. "We have to talk now."

Anya could merely nod. She was crying. Not for herself, but for Adam's degradation. "Why the sudden urgency?"

He hesitated and then said softly, "Because there are other people waiting."

"I don't know what you mean."

Carlo could not suppress a touch of pride as he pronounced a single word, "Stockholm."

A million volts of electricity struck her dumb. She was terrified that all was lost. Finally, she managed to say, "*You*—you're their spy."

"I could think of nicer ways of putting it, Anya." He then added mildly, "Now, don't you think we should continue this in Professor Coopersmith's office?"

She nodded in defeat.

As they entered Adam's sanctum, even Pisani was impressed by the number of citations lining the walls. On previous visits he had been too focused on seeking his mentor's opinion to notice the decor.

She placed herself behind the ramparts of Adam's desk and asked, "What are you going to do?"

"That depends on what you tell me."

Anya was torn. It would be difficult, if not impossible, to lie to him, for he had medical as well as research credentials. She had to take the risk of appealing to his sympathy—if he had any.

"You're correct," she whispered. "My husband is ill."

"We already know that," Pisani replied quietly.

"Well," she asked anxiously, "what does 'Stockholm' think it is?"

"I'm not sure. But I do know they've heard he's . . . degenerating."

For a moment Anya's fear gave way to anger. "Why is the committee so worried? Even if he were short-listed and died before the voting, their stupid rules would make him ineligible. As if death could diminish a man's achievements."

"True. But in this case it might depend on the cause of death. If, for example, he were suffering from something like AIDS, that might pose problems."

"I don't believe it," she protested. "How could that possibly affect his suitability for the Nobel Prize?"

"Let me put it this way," he explained. "If Adam had *cured* the disease, they would give him the prize and a twenty-one gun salute. On the other hand, if he died of it, in some quarters that might reflect on his moral suitability."

"You mean, even if he were a hemophiliac and caught the virus from a blood transfusion?"

"That might still be a negative image. The cynics would always say the transfusion was a cover-up for something worse."

Rather than engage in protracted debate, Anya concentrated on helping her husband. "Well, Carlo, I can assure you that Adam's illness has absolutely nothing to do with the HIV virus."

"Of course not," Carlo pronounced. "In fact, all the external signs and symptoms seem to point to a brain tumor. I assume he's been scanned."

Anya nodded. Let him draw his own conclusions, she thought.

"Is it operable?"

She shook her head.

"Oh *Dio*," the Italian moaned. "He's so young. He had so many years of achievement in front of him."

"Forget the eulogies," Anya retorted. "He's done more than enough to qualify for the prize."

"I agree. I quite agree."

"Then what will you say in your report—or however you communicate?"

"I will tell them ... it is now or never."

"How did you get here, sweetie?"

Adam was propped up in bed, freshly shaven by Terry and dressed in elegant pajamas.

"Lisl picked me up," his daughter replied. "Say, Dad, you look terrific."

"I feel terrific," Adam replied. "I mean, I hope you don't believe those rumors about my being sick. I'm just taking a long time to get over the jet lag from Australia. By the way, did you get our postcards?"

"Yeah. The best photos were from Fiji. Did you guys have a good time?"

"So-so," Adam answered, and then whispered emotionally, "I missed you like hell, honey. I wish you could have come along. How's school?"

A look of fear crossed Heather's face and she was barely able to speak loud enough for him to hear.

"Hey, Dad, stop trying to make it easy on me. I realize I'm not supposed to know what's going on, but I'm getting the distinct impression that you might not be around for my college graduation."

Adam lowered his gaze. "I'm sorry, Heather," he said with anguish. "I really am. I can't bear the idea of ... not being there for you."

His daughter covered her face. "Oh, shit. That's such a brutal way of putting it."

He shrugged helplessly. "I don't know what else to say."

She looked at him and was engulfed by a tidal wave of love. "Oh, Daddy," she cried, "please don't die. Please don't ..."

She moved closer to the bed, putting her head next to his on the pillow, and sobbed uncontrollably.

After a moment she felt that something had changed.

She looked at her father and realized his face had suddenly frozen.

"Dad—are you okay?"

Adam stared at her for a moment longer and then burst out irascibly, "Who let you in here? This isn't Harvard Square, you know. What do you want?"

In an instant Anya was there and put her arm around Heather's shoulder. The young girl did not refuse the gesture of comfort.

"What's wrong with him?" Heather gasped, terrified.

"It's part of his condition. Try not to be upset," Anya said as reassuringly as she could, inwardly castigating herself for not cutting off the conversation just a few moments earlier.

"Does this mean he won't know me anymore?"

"No," she replied, trying as hard as possible to sound convincing. "In fact, if you come to the kitchen for a cup of tea, he might . . . calm down again in a little while."

Heather and Anya sat at the table as the last rays of the sun retreated from the garden. Heather looked at Anya's soft, sad face and murmured, "You live with this all the time. How the hell can you bear it?"

The older woman let her glance drop and confessed in a whisper, "Sometimes I don't know."

59

ISABEL

JERRY PRACHT awoke to the sound of quiet sobbing. He got out of bed, covered himself incongruously in Isabel's paisley bathrobe, and went into the living room, where he found her seated by the window staring out at the rising sun and apparently grieving at the prospect of a new day. He went over and tenderly touched her shoulder.

"Isa, what's wrong?" he asked softly. "Is it something about last night?"

She put her hand on his. "No, Jerry, that was beautiful. I just wish it could have lasted forever."

"But it can—"

"No," she interrupted. "It's what I have to live with starting today."

She turned and looked at him. His expression told her unambiguously that she could trust him completely.

"Listen, I told you a lot of terrible things last night. Things I wanted you to know. But I left out the worst."

"Go on," he said lovingly. "Nothing could ever scare me away."

"Want to bet?" she challenged him. "Try this."

She then told him the truth about the specter of her heredity.

"So you see," she said with a gallows humor, "instead of being supergirl, I turned out to be a leper."

He put his finger gently on her lips. "I don't want you talking that way, Isa. As far as I'm concerned, you're the same person I've always known and loved. And nothing you've said will make me walk out on you."

She threw her arms around him passionately. "I won't hold you to that," she whispered. "But it'll be nice to have you around as long as you can bear it."

"I'm going to do more than that, I'm going to help," he insisted. "Now, let's deal with things in chronological order. First there's your mother."

"Whom I hate."

"At this moment, anyway," Jerry acknowledged. "But the fact remains she's waiting for you in the hotel dining room, and I think the best thing is to get her on a plane home as soon as possible."

"That's for sure," Isabel replied. "I just don't know how I'm going to face her without—I don't know—doing something violent."

"*We're* going to face her together, Isa. I'll stick with her till she has to go to Logan, and I'll make sure she gets on the plane."

"But what do I say to her?" Isabel pleaded, at her wit's end.

"As little as possible. I mean, be sensible, there's no way you can undo what she's done. But there might be steps you want to take."

"You mean to save Edmundo?"

"The hell with him. I'm only thinking about you."

At first Muriel was annoyed that Isabel had not come alone. But it did not take long for her to realize that this young man was an important part of her daughter's life. In fact, she now recalled many veiled allusions in their phone conversations to "this terrific tennis player." And despite her feelings of apprehension and dismay, it gave her some comfort. She accepted his presence without question and motioned for him to sit down and join them.

Correctly assuming that Isabel had told Jerry everything, she spoke freely.

"Professor Avilov must have called me a dozen times since we last talked. Needless to say, he's anxious to try his therapy on Edmundo. But I think the price is your letting him test you."

Isabel shook her head in confusion while Jerry answered firmly, "I'm not sure I'll allow her to do it, Mrs. Zimmer. I mean, first of all, if she tests positive, there's nothing she can do about it except live in constant fear of an early death."

"You're not a doctor," Muriel objected firmly.

"Mom, he's my best friend," Isabel rejoined emphatically.

"I appreciate what he means to you," Muriel said diplomatically, longing to regain her daughter's good graces. "But even if Avilov weren't making it the precondition for treating Edmundo, wouldn't you want to know for yourself?"

Again Jerry seized the initiative. "Excuse me, but there's a whole ethical question involved here. This is not something like AIDS, where Isa's being positive or not might endanger other people," he insisted. "And I don't see where she owes Mr. Zimmer—or you, for that matter—any sacrifice."

"But what if you had a family history of Huntington's disease," Muriel argued. "Wouldn't you want to find out?"

"No," he retorted. "I wouldn't want anyone to find out—least of all my insurance company. At the risk of sounding sanctimonious, I think these long-term predictive genetic tests will open a Pandora's box of medical abuses."

"That's very high-minded of you, young man," Muriel fought back angrily. "But you don't have anything to lose."

Jerry rose furiously. "On the contrary, Mrs. Zimmer, the most precious thing in my life's at stake," he said softly, putting his arm around Isabel. "The girl I'm going to marry."

Even in the depth of depression, Isabel was thrilled by Jerry's declaration. She took his arm as he continued to address Muriel.

"Now, if you don't mind, I've taken the liberty of booking you on the noon flight to San Diego. I'll go downstairs and wait in the car so you two can have some time to talk."

He kissed Isabel and left mother and daughter to face each other.

Muriel tried to break the ice. "He's quite a fellow, that young man of yours. How long have you two known—"

"It's none of your business," Isabel snapped.

"You must be very angry with me."

"I don't think that word is adequate, Mom," she said sharply. "You betrayed Dad's trust."

"But can't you look at it another way?" Muriel countered. "Edmundo is not just your natural father, his genes are very likely the reason for your gifts."

"Come on," Isabel said bitterly, "you surely don't expect me to thank you for what you did."

"All I would ever ask for is a modicum of understanding. God knows I did something wrong, but I'm certainly being punished."

Just then an alien voice interrupted them.

"Good morning, ladies, may I join you?" It was Avilov himself, jovial and expansive.

Muriel looked up and answered helplessly, "Of course." Ever observant, the Russian professor noted the place setting that had been Jerry's and could not keep from probing.

"Or have I interrupted something important?"

"Oh, don't worry, Professor," Isabel remarked sarcastically. "My mother's not seeking a second opinion. No one's going to try to steal your thunder."

"I was not interested in my 'thunder,' Dr. da Costa. I

am after all a physician, and my prime concern is saving lives."

"And getting a lot of publicity for yourself," Isabel added.

"I think you're being unfair," Avilov protested.

"Frankly, I don't care what you think," Isabel rejoined.

Muriel could not bear it any longer. "Can't you two stop bickering—a man's life's at stake."

Isabel was about to protest that there was more than one potential victim in this medical tragedy, but Avilov anticipated her intervention.

"Quite correct, Mrs. Zimmer. That's why I've come to announce my decision."

He paused dramatically to increase their concentration on his words.

"I've made special arrangements to treat Maestro Zimmer with my new therapy."

"Oh, that's wonderful," Muriel replied.

"Of course, I can give no ironclad guarantees. But nowadays, many advanced medical techniques are being practiced in highly modern clinics in the Caribbean. There you do not need FDA approval to administer experimental drugs. I suggest that we all make arrangements as soon as possible to fly to St. Lucia."

"Thank you, Doctor. Thank you." Muriel was close to tears.

"Fine," the Russian stated, standing as abruptly as he had seated himself. "I will liaise with all parties concerned." He added, "And that of course includes you, Dr. da Costa."

"Please don't, Professor Avilov. If I never hear from you again, it'll be too soon."

Jerry Pracht knew there was only one absolute way of reassuring Isabel.

"Isa, let's get married right away."

"What?"

"You heard me. And if you want me to, I'll even ask your father's—and by that I mean Raymond's—permission."

"There's no way I'd let you. I'm a genetic time bomb."

"But Isa, I love you."

"Me too," she responded. "Which is why you can't go through with this. I have no choice, but you do."

"In that case," he stated, "I've changed my mind."

"About what?"

"About your taking the genetic test. At least that would give me half a chance of getting you to say yes."

"To be honest, that's the only reason I'd go through with it. Otherwise, I agree with everything you said to my mother. I haven't been able to sleep since I heard the news. And even if the results are terrible, at least I'd know. On the other hand, if we let Avilov do it, there's not much chance of keeping the results under wraps."

"I agree. For all the bull about ethics, scientists can blab as much as anybody if a celebrity's concerned."

Isabel sighed with disappointment.

"But the field is not lost," Jerry announced. "This may sound perverse, but I've asked around and located the one person in the world who's least likely to divulge our secret to that fat Russian shit."

"But what makes this individual so scrupulous?"

"It's his first wife." His eyes twinkled. "She's now married to Adam Coopersmith at Harvard, and even though she's working in immunology now, when they first came over, she worked as 'Ivan the Terrible's' flunky, and actually helped him develop the Huntington's test. Between you and me, I think she probably did most of the work. And from everything I hear, she's a wonderful person. Apparently Avilov really treated her shabbily."

"Actually, I can't imagine him acting any other way."

Fifteen minutes later Jerry had booked an appointment with Dr. Anya Coopersmith.

* * *

Preoccupied though she was, Isabel could not help but feel an inexplicable kinship between herself and the still youthfully attractive Russian doctor.

As Anya sat across the desk in her office at Harvard Medical School, her face—especially her eyes—seemed to emanate a sympathy that could only have been nurtured by a personal acquaintance with tragedy.

She fully understood the need for discretion, and even insisted on drawing the blood herself.

"Gosh." Isabel flinched. "I'm really scared of injections."

"Everybody is." Anya smiled. "But before I passed my U.S. boards, I worked as a lab technician. I still pride myself on my needlework."

Her concern for minimizing pain extended to the psychological as well. After taking the blood, she promised Isabel, "The very minute I learn anything, I'll call you."

"Day or night," she pleaded.

Anya nodded understandingly. "Don't worry. My husband taught me never to keep a patient waiting a second more than necessary for news."

"He must be a very special person," Jerry remarked.

"Yes." There was a tinge of sadness in her voice. To keep up appearances, she said in parting, "I'm sure Adam would like to meet you. Perhaps we can have dinner or something."

"That would be terrific," Isabel responded. "But first things first."

"You're right," Anya Coopersmith smiled wanly. "First things first."

Earlier that week, they had gotten their first letter from Ray on the gold-embossed Coventry Prep School paper. The timing was perfect.

Rather than sit around all weekend waiting for the phone to ring, they drove down to see him. Despite the fact that they were obliged to hide so much, it was an enjoyable outing.

Perhaps the most surprising aspect of their visit was the fact that Ray had already begun to establish the rudiments of a social life. He probably was unaware of how often the name Sharon came up in the conversation. She was the head of the girls' athletic program and a divorcée.

"She's a lovely girl. You've got to meet her the next time you're down," Ray emphasized, perhaps an oblique way of requesting that the two of them come again soon.

Raymond's change of heart seemed to be unshakable. For now, far from resenting his daughter's relationship, he seemed to sense in Jerry someone who, like himself, was totally devoted to Isabel. He even embraced the young man warmly as they exchanged good-byes.

When they reached Cambridge, there was a message on the answering machine to call Dr. Coopersmith at her home.

"I thought you would be nervous, so I rushed the test through," she explained. "Anyway, I'm overjoyed to tell you that Isabel's chromosomal makeup doesn't—repeat, does not—have a dominant Huntington's gene. That means you can look forward to a long, productive—and reproductive—life."

Nonetheless, Anya invited the couple to come back in for another personal chat.

This time she offered an extensive explanation of what the data meant. Not only was Isabel herself in no danger of developing Huntington's, there was no risk whatever to any children she and Jerry might have.

"You'll just have to worry about dying from something else," Anya said. Again, like a shadow, that strangely sad smile crossed her face.

"I propose old age," Jerry offered.

"That's a very good one," Anya agreed. "What's more, there's all sorts of exciting work being done on longevity. We're not far from an average life span of more than one hundred years."

"God," Jerry blurted, "can you imagine an entire century of that asshole, Avilov?"

He caught himself too late, and quickly turned to Anya. "I'm sorry, Dr. Coopersmith."

"No, not at all," she concurred. "I agree. A few months of Dmitri is enough for a lifetime."

They all laughed.

Twenty minutes later, as they were walking down the corridor hand in hand, Isabel whispered, "Do you know how many kids the Coopersmiths have?"

"Well, he's got a girl from a first marriage, but I don't think he has any with Anya."

"I could tell," Isabel commented sympathetically. "There was such a terrible look of loss in her face when she mentioned babies."

She stopped and said with deep emotion, "Thank you."

"For what in particular?" he smiled.

"For being you. And for being willing to stay with me either way."

60

SANDY

IT WAS only in 1994 that the money radically changed Sandy Raven's life. That year, *Forbes* magazine added his name to their golden honor roll of the four hundred richest people in America.

Yet even this formidable publication could not specify his net worth to the last penny. But since the humblest person on their list was worth $300 million, it could be said without fear of contradiction that Sandy was extremely well off.

The night before the issue appeared, his lawyer, Nat Simmons, who had been privileged to see an advance copy, called him with the sensational news.

Sandy's reaction startled the attorney.

"Dammit, Nat. Can't we stop them?"

"First of all, the thing's been printed in a zillion copies. But why would you want to? People kill—or at least lie—to make this stupid list. Are you afraid women will start to lust after your money?"

"Yeah," Sandy replied sardonically. "Something like that."

"Well, there's nothing to worry about on that score," Nat reassured him.

"What do you mean?"

"Because they already do. Anyway, my professional advice is that when the audience applauds, you should take a bow. Good night, Sandy. I hope you sleep off the lousy mood you're in."

Sandy hung up and walked out on to the patio, where Sidney, against doctor's orders, was sneaking in a few rays of California sun, and offhandedly told him the news.

"That's great, sonny boy," the old man enthused. "Who would have dreamed that the son of a small potato guy like me would—"

"Come on, Dad," Sandy cut him off. "You're the real businessman in this family. I just got lucky."

"Yeah," Sidney remarked. "Like King Midas."

"Dad, if you recall," Sandy said, "King Midas was a very unhappy man."

"Maybe," Sidney replied, "that's because there was no Mrs. Midas."

* * *

As usual, the *Los Angeles Times* gave a big play to the local citizens who had made that year's "Four Hundred."

Now elevated to the pantheon of plutocracy, Sandy was besieged by telephone calls from adoring well-wishers—many of whom he had forgotten he even knew.

He told Maureen not to put any of the callers through, so he could at least have a few hours of hands-on time in the lab.

She disobeyed him only once. "I know what you said, but this one I know you'll want to take."

He was certain it wasn't Kimiko, since she used his home phone. In fact they had spoken earlier that morning. So he barked: "Unless it's from Stockholm, I can't imagine anyone I'd like to speak to."

"I can," she replied knowingly.

"Try me," he challenged.

She answered simply, "Kim Tower."

It opened a torrent of feelings. The object of his childhood longings, the princess who, in reverse fairy-tale fashion, had turned out to be a dragon. And nearly destroyed his father. The lodestone of his strongest passions of love and hate, whom for sanity's sake he had tried to banish from his consciousness. Now she who had ignored or—on some rare occasions—deigned to recognize him only to disparage him, was suddenly telephoning of her own accord.

"Okay," Sandy capitulated. "Put her through."

He could feel his blood pressure mounting as he waited for the connection.

"Hi, sweetheart," she purred. "How does it feel to be the talk of the town?"

"I don't know. How should I feel?"

"Like a nuclear firecracker," she suggested, and segued quickly into further greetings, asking sweetly, "How's Sidney? I hear he's doing a great job at CBS. Give him my best regards."

Sandy was too astounded to be outraged. Her presumption was breathtaking.

"I'll pass it on," he said dryly.

"You'll never guess why I'm calling you," she said coquettishly.

"Don't tell me." Sandy could barely hide his sarcasm. "The studio wants to do the story of my life."

She laughed. And the sound was still like crystal.

"Actually, that's not such a bad idea," she responded with glossy Hollywood hypocrisy. "Rags-to-riches is always boffo stuff. But anyway, why don't we get together, break bread, and talk about old times?"

Old times? Sandy thought to himself. What do we have to reminisce about? But then she had lit the fires again. And for reasons conscious and unconscious, he thought, what the hell. . . .

"That would be great, Rochelle."

"What about tonight at the Bel Air? It's Friday, and we can stay up extra late."

"Fine with me. I only hope you recognize me after all these years."

"Dollface," she replied, "lately your picture's been in the paper more than mine. After all, I've never been on the cover of *Time*. See you at eight. By the way, it's my treat. *Ciao*."

"What the hell do you think she wants?" Sandy asked his father.

"Whatever it is," said the older man, "it's dollars to doughnuts her body's included."

"What?" His father's blunt cynicism unsettled him.

In truth, in the many years they had known each other, he had dreamed of making love to her. But time had so metamorphosed the protagonist of his fantasies that he could no more conceive of a sexual encounter with "Kim Tower" than he would with a female divinity depicted on a Grecian urn.

He arrived early to find that she had arrived even

earlier and was already ensconced in a corner where she could survey the room.

Her hair was light blond at the moment, and even at a distance she looked like the magnificent superstar she might have become had it not been for her consummate lack of talent.

Still, she had the aura of success about her, glittering like the precious rocks she wore everywhere—especially the necklace with the diamond ankh, the popular Egyptian love symbol, which pointed like a jeweled road sign directing the attention of all who beheld her to the cleft between her magnificent breasts.

This time she offered him her glowing cheeks to kiss. Simultaneously, the sommelier poured the champagne. By the time they were seated, Rochelle could already raise a glass and toast his success.

"To the greatest star I know." She smiled.

"A slight exaggeration," Sandy retorted with graceful humility.

"You know, I always knew you'd make it, Sandy," she continued. "I mean, even when we were classmates, you were so brilliant that I figured you for either winning the Nobel Prize or getting elected President."

At this hyperbole, Sandy could only comment, "Well, I don't think we have to worry about either of those happening."

"Come on," she contradicted him. "If the Swedish Academy can honor a maverick like Kary Mullis, they can overlook your extreme wealth and still honor your fantastic brain."

Once again he marveled at the breadth of her knowledge. She may have merely digested news bites, but she had the mind of a computer database and was fully aware of the idiosyncratically colorful character who had won the Nobel Prize for chemistry in 1993.

She gazed at her grade school admirer as if seeing him with new eyes. And while she was doing so, he admired the expertise of her plastic surgeon. There was not the slightest scar in sight, though she had been re-molded to look twenty years younger than their mutual age.

She, on the other hand, was lying through her brilliantly capped teeth when she cooed, "You know, you haven't changed a bit. Do you use your own magic formula?"

Sandy self-consciously touched the crown of his head as if trying to cover the growing bald spot, and thought to himself, Ah, that's it. She wants the Fountain of Youth. Does she actually think I'm going to give her free samples?

"Rochelle," he said with a diversionary smoke screen of flattery, "it's my professional opinion that good genes are better than any medicine. And you are terrifically endowed. I mean, I don't think you'll ever age."

"Really?" She smiled. "Do you really think so?"

His feelings were stirred. Gradually he could feel his defenses weakening. He was so bedazzled that he temporarily suppressed his anger at her long-ago cruelty to his father. And, despite everything, he still wanted her.

"I have an idea," she said, leaning closer to him. "Let's go to my place for coffee. You haven't seen it, have you?"

Goddamn stupid question, he thought to himself, but played along.

"As a matter of fact, I have." He surprised her. "I mean, when *Life* did a spread on your spread. It looks fabulous."

"Wait till you see the view," she murmured. "In any case, shall we talk some business first?"

"Why not?" By now he was bursting with curiosity at the reason for her sudden rediscovery that he existed.

"As I'm sure you know, I've got a sensational record as head of production. I've given the boys on the board some really terrific Christmas and Fourth of July presents."

"Yeah, your instinct's phenomenal," Sandy commented, still wondering where all this was leading.

"Well, it's not that they don't pay me a living wage. But dammit, I'm just a salaried employee," she continued, making it sound as if she were the janitor. "The big money goes to the studio bosses.

"For a long time now I've been looking for an opening to make my move, and I think the time is really right. I happen to know that our chief stockholder, the intrepid George Constantine, is financially overstretched and is trying to lay off big chunks of the company."

"Well, then now's your chance," Sandy said encouragingly. "Why don't you go for it?"

"With what?" she inquired in an unconvincingly helpless tone. "Even with my track record, the banks are still fundamentally sexist. To them I'm some kind of female airhead who's had a few lucky breaks. If I had a penis, I'd be golden. But as it is, I can't get anybody to subsidize me for an LBO."

Ah, Sandy realized, it's my money.

"I don't even know what an LBO is," he lied. "Isn't it a cable TV network?"

"No, silly," she answered with an indulgent smile. "Don't you have bankers and portfolio managers and stuff? 'Leveraged buyouts' are how the rich get richer. And with your kind of collateral, you could easily raise enough cash to relieve Constantine of his holding." She paused, looking at him meaningfully.

"Naturally, you and I can make some arrangement. Stock options and so forth. But that goes without saying. I mean, what are friends for? If nothing else, I've given you the inside tip-off, right?"

"Right," Sandy answered in a strangely flat tone.

"Well?"

Sandy evaded her question, stroking his cheek in a deliberate gesture of deep thought. "It's something to sleep on."

"I agree. Do you have a driver waiting?" she asked, subtly changing the subject.

"No. Actually, I drove myself."

"Rolls?" she inquired.

"Chevy."

"You're quite a character, Sandy. I have so much admiration for people who live beneath their means." She flashed a brilliant smile. "I've got a Lamborghini that can make it from here to my place in under five minutes. Are you interested?"

"Rochelle," he replied in the understatement of his life, "I've always been interested."

But in ways not even you could imagine.

In a town that imposed draconian punishments for speeding, she drove jauntily down Sunset Boulevard, then cornered expertly up Benedict Canyon to a pair of iron gates that opened automatically at the touch of a dashboard button.

Sandy could not help but appreciate the symbolism.

Not that he would have expected it to be any other way, but her home was just like a lavish movie set, with a second swimming pool right in the middle of the living room.

And yet not a servant in sight.

"Come on, dollface," she murmured sweetly. "Let me show you what a great cup of coffee I can make with just a few spoons of Nescafé."

He followed her into a room whose sophisticated machinery could well have surpassed the kitchen of the hotel at which they had just dined. Everything sparkled: glass, metal, hidden lights, the works.

"You were married once," she remarked offhandedly.

"Yeah," Sandy nodded. "It didn't agree with me. Or to be more specific, it didn't agree with her. But I'm certainly not bitter. I've got the most wonderful daughter."

"Oh, really?" she gushed. "You must tell me all

about her." Quickly adding, "Sometime. But for the moment, let's be selfish."

"In what way?" Sandy inquired.

"What about a little skinny dip?" she asked with non-chalant eroticism. Before he could respond, she gracefully undid the zippers and stepped out of her dress.

Despite her long-ago appearance in *Playboy*, he was still self-conscious about seeing his childhood friend unclothed. Somehow he felt he was spying on the young and innocent—was she ever really innocent?—Rochelle Taubman whose homework he had cheerfully done and whom he had once dreamed of seducing. But whether it was the aerobics, genetics, or merely plastic surgery—her body was magnificent.

"Come on, honey," she coaxed. "What are you waiting for?"

"I don't know, Rochelle," he answered softly. "But I think I'd prefer to pass."

She stared at him in disbelief. "What's the matter, Sandy? Scared you're not man enough?"

Her taunt helped him at his moment of indecision. He stood up. "No, Rochelle," he answered. "I think it's the other way around. You're not woman enough."

"What?" she shrieked with outrage. "I always knew you didn't have any balls. You're nothing but a chickenshit little eunuch. Go to hell."

At this point his soul had broken free.

"Thanks a lot for the dinner," he said.

"Did you hear me?" she shouted furiously. "I said go to hell."

He stared at her with genuine indifference and answered, "You know the funniest thing, Rochelle—I've been there all this time, and only just realized it."

Sandy knew he had his work cut out for him that weekend, and drove straight to the airport without even going home. He made the necessary arrangements on his car phone.

He called Kimiko to explain he had to fly urgently to New York and would try to return by the following evening.

"Is everything all right?"

"It will be by the time I get back," he said warmly.

"Do you want me to pick you up at the airport?"

"Yes," he replied. "I would like that very much."

The following Monday, since Kim's first meeting of the day was off the lot, she did not pull up to the studio gate until nearly eleven. Usually the minute he caught sight of her red Lamborghini, the guard would lift the barrier so she could zoom through without having to change gears.

Today, for some reason, the barrier remained in place.

"What's happening?" she called out in mock anger. "Have you lost your touch? Open the drawbridge."

"Uh, hello there, Miss Tower," the officer said uneasily. "How're you doing?"

Kim had exhausted her patience and good humor with this minion. Instead of responding to his question, she merely barked, "Up, Mitch. Move your ass."

The sentry remained by the side of her car, a part of him savoring the moment. It was a role he had played on countless occasions, but never on so grand a level.

"Miss Tower, I don't know exactly how to say this, but . . ." He paused and then concluded, "you're not on my docket."

"I . . . what?"

The man nodded. "As you know, the lists are changed each morning. I guess you don't work here anymore."

Kim had a short fuse, and she exploded. "Listen, mister, I'm giving you exactly ten seconds to cut this misplaced April Fool's gag and let me in—or you'll never work in this town again."

The security guard stood steadfast. In fact, his tone became more solemn. "With respect, ma'am, you're blocking the entrance. I'm afraid I'm going to have to ask you to move."

"Balls!" she snapped, reaching for her car telephone. "I'm going to get George Constantine on the phone right now and we'll see who leaves this spot first."

Naturally, the studio boss's line was preprogrammed number 1, and Kim immediately reached him on the other coast. After the tycoon said a brief hello, he remained impeccably calm as the wrath of hell poured into his ear.

After a moment he took a breath. "Listen, sugar," he explained cordially, "you of all people should know the way the system works. It's a revolving door—one day you're in, the next you're out. I'm afraid this is your day to be out.

"But as a token of my gratitude I'd like to give you some valuable advice. If I were you, I'd use the twenty-four hour hiatus before we make our announcement to fly to Paris and buy dresses or whatever makes you happy. You don't want to be here when the spit hits the fan."

The phone went as dead as Kim Tower's status in the town.

Mitch was staring at her, his face fully showing the satisfaction that his superior rank had now been established. Before retreating, Kim had to ask him the sixty-four-million-dollar question.

"By the way," she said with artificial sweetness, "can you tell me who's head of production as of this morning?"

"Oh," said Mitch with a poker face. "I guess you mean Mr. Raven."

"Who?"

"Mr. Sidney Raven, Miss Tower," he replied. "Now you have a nice day."

61

ISABEL

SOME CLINICS are born out of need, some out of philanthropy—and others out of sheer desperation.

While the more medically sophisticated nations of the world continue to impose strict clinical protocols before ratifying experimental drugs for use on humans, the terminally ill refuse to wait. After failing to sway their own medical bureaucracy, they circumvent it by going to one of several special hospitals that have recently opened on tiny Caribbean islands previously known for their beaches and rum punch.

Many establishment physicians denigrate these operations as heartless and exploitative. While in certain cases this is a valid accusation, in others genuine cures are being realized. Numerous hopeless cases are alive today having acted as human guinea pigs beneath the swaying palms.

True, a large proportion of the "cures" offered by these institutions have been like Laetrile, an antitumor drug originally derived from apricot pits by two California doctors, which has produced little more than dashed hopes and large bills.

The dubious benefits of this remedy did not dissuade a stream of patients whom more traditional methods had not helped.

In other cases, for example under the Reagan and Bush administrations, while strict American legislation forbade the medical use of tissue from aborted fetuses, it became available in the islands. Brain surgeons were therefore able to try radical procedures that advanced the fight against such maladies as Parkinson's disease and even Alzheimer's.

Although they did not broadcast their presence, representatives of all the multinational drug companies made regular, if low profile, visits to these farflung enterprises, and even major universities turned a blind eye when distinguished senior members of their faculties dashed off to the Caribbean for what they euphemistically referred to as "working vacations."

Now, Dmitri Avilov waited on the runway of the airport at St. Lucia, a lush and verdant paradise of volcanoes and valleys.

Though only the second largest of the Windward Archipelago, it held two special attractions for the former Soviet scientist: the ultramodern facilities of its private Clinique Ste Hélène, and the compelling coincidence that this tiny country—one-fifth the size of Rhode Island—had already produced two Nobel Prize winners, though none as yet in medicine.

Uncharacteristically sporty in his open short-sleeved shirt, Avilov scanned the cloudless skies for signs of the Piper Comanche ferrying the Zimmer family from Caracas, where they had flown in from Buenos Aires.

He was tense. For all his confidence before patients, he was deeply apprehensive about the new genetic therapy he was about to undertake.

While one of the ancillary advantages of risking experimental techniques in faraway places was the fact that doctors could quite literally bury their mistakes, he was still frightened that if he failed, albeit in so remote a place, somehow the word would get out. And while his formal academic job would not be imperiled, his international reputation might be irreparably damaged.

On the other hand, if he succeeded, his long-cultivated romance with the press would bring attention to the little island that had witnessed his major breakthrough.

A moment later the drone of the small plane became audible. In another instant it was visible, circled the field, and gracefully touched down. The pilot jumped energetically from the cockpit and hurried to open the passenger door. A dark-skinned nurse in a blue cotton pantsuit came quickly down the steps carrying a small satchel.

After scanning the various people waiting outside the terminal, she motioned to a white minibus. The orderlies who had been waiting in its air-conditioned comfort drove out onto the field and entered the plane. Then together they bore out Edmundo Zimmer, his face gray with impending death, placed him onto a stretcher, and carried him back to their vehicle.

The other passengers—Muriel, Francisco, and Dorotea—followed, shielding their eyes from the harsh Caribbean sun.

The local authorities insisted that the new arrivals go through an elaborate customs procedure that even the great professor could not circumvent.

Finally, Muriel and the Russian went in the minibus with Edmundo, while Francisco and Dorotea followed in a rickety taxi that bounced them dizzy.

When they regrouped at the Clinique Ste Hélène, Avilov proposed, "There's no point in waiting. The actual 'operation' has already been performed on the samples I took from his bone marrow. We have merely to infuse the recombinant cells and set them to work transforming the murderous gene. I think we can get right on with that."

"I agree," Muriel responded, then cast a glance at Francisco and Dorotea, who both nodded concurrence.

"In that case," the Russian continued, "I'll see to it that he's installed in a room and start the transfusion. Since there'll be no immediate results, may I propose that the rest of you go to the hotel and unwind from the journey."

"I want to stay with him," Muriel insisted.

"So do I," the two others echoed almost in unison.

"As you wish," Avilov acceded. "But I would insist that you be present only one at a time."

As the professor had predicted, nothing dramatic happened for several days. Avilov had returned temporarily to Boston to attend to other matters and other patients. When the rest of them weren't visiting the hospital, they relaxed on the beach.

One night at dinner Dorotea confided, "I've spoken to several doctors, and all of them seem to concur that Avilov is on the right track. I asked if—since we're in a 'rule-free' zone—he would try the therapy on me as well. And he agreed."

"Isn't that taking a big risk?" Muriel asked.

"No," the younger woman replied, her voice revealing both anger and fear. "I can't live waiting to be sick. If he can't cure me, I'd rather die immediately."

Francisco tried to dissuade his sister, but she was adamant.

On his return, the Russian was delighted. "A very wise decision," he trumpeted. "There's still time for you to be a happy mother of children—healthy children."

He was so effusive that it almost seemed as if he was willing to help get her pregnant also.

There was little to do on this distant paradise. The newspapers were all three days old. In her room, Muriel found a pamphlet with a brief history of the island, which mentioned as one of its tourist attractions a seventeenth-century cemetery whose residents provided a historical panoply of the various waves of emigrants to this island—thence to the North American colonies. According to the brochure, there was even a fellow with the exotic name of "Uriel Da Costa."

"Do you think he might be a relative?" Francisco asked.

"I doubt it. But it would give us something to fill the afternoon."

"Okay, *vamos*."

It turned out to be a mixed blessing.

Francisco was able to translate the epitaphs, which were all in Spanish or Portuguese. And yet, amid the worn and beaten gray stone slabs, they discovered three perceptibly newer ones.

Upon investigation, they were staggered to see that this trio of graves dated not only from the twentieth century, but from the past five years. And the deceased were neither Portuguese nor Spanish. One headstone read, "Mary Donovan, 1935–1989."

Francisco, who read Muriel's thoughts, immediately approached the caretaker and asked who these people were. The old man shrugged, and mumbled a few words.

Francisco was furious when he returned, and Muriel asked anxiously, "What did he say?"

Her stepson imitated the man's French accent, " 'Zey ill—zey die—I bury.' "

"Were you able to ask him what they died of?"

"He said just two words—'La Clinique.' "

They were both alarmed and incensed, but during the interim had agreed not to impart this information to Dorotea. They were waiting on the runway to confront Avilov when his chartered plane from Boston touched down.

He seemed offended by their attitude.

"I do not wish to discuss such matters in public. Let me first get this vital genetic material to the hospital and then we will talk."

When they were finally back in the acceptable privacy of the doctor's office, Francisco exploded. "Why didn't you come clean with us about your failure rate?"

"Because I have none," he insisted coolly. "Don't

forget, there are doctors performing other procedures on this island."

Muriel fixed him with an intense gaze and demanded, "Was Mary Donovan a patient of yours?"

The Russian fidgeted uneasily. "I regard that question as unethical," he mumbled.

"It doesn't matter," Muriel responded. "You've just answered it."

Avilov suddenly panicked. "But you don't understand, Mrs. Zimmer," he babbled. "The woman was practically dead when she got here. It was too late. But the treatment did her no harm—"

"I would have believed that more readily had you told me in Boston."

"If I had, would you still have come?"

"I don't know." Muriel shook her head. "I certainly would have thought twice."

"Have you told Dorotea?" he inquired.

"No," her brother answered. "Not yet."

"Then at least give me a week's grace. I'll keep her retrovirus in cold storage, and you can see for yourself if Edmundo makes any progress."

Muriel could not help wondering how many other human guinea pigs he had treated. And whether, in clinics on other islands, there had been more Mary Donovans. No doubt she would have to wait till his data was published. And yet her instinct told her that the Russian would be emphasizing the positive results and might even succumb to some selective amnesia when it came to patients who had been too sick to be helped.

It took merely five days to discover that Dorotea's fate would be reversed. Indeed, Avilov's success was proof that even the devil himself could work miracles.

Whatever his motivation, he was a superb scientist. With each passing day it became apparent that Edmundo had become a unique medical phenomenon: a victim of Huntington's in remission.

It was a momentous achievement.

Perhaps even worthy of a Nobel Prize.

62

ISABEL

"Isabel, you've gotta grow up."

The twenty-three-year-old star of the MIT physics faculty laughed. "I'm doing the best I can, Jerry," she responded. "If you've noticed, you pay full price for me at the movies."

"You know what I'm talking about," he protested. "You've held out long enough. It's time to pick up that phone and call your mother.

"I can understand you feel this urge to 'punish' her. But whatever the messy circumstances, there's no question about her loving you. Think about how much she suffered when you and Ray walked out on her."

Isabel sighed. "Dammit, Pracht, you're so maddeningly mature—at least when it comes to other people." She paused for a moment and said softly, "I'm scared."

Jerry took her by the shoulders. "I can see that. You're worried she might already be a widow, and wonder how you'll react if . . . Edmundo is dead."

"Are you thinking of taking up psychiatry?" she asked, half serious.

"I just want to help straighten out your head so you can transfer that emotional energy you're wasting on worry—to loving me."

"Jerry, I couldn't love you more."

He smiled. "How do you know if you haven't tried? Call her, Isa—call her now."

Jerry kept his hand affectionately on the nape of her neck as her trembling fingers dialed area code 619 and the other numbers. There were several rings, and then—

"Hello?"

"Mom, it's me."

"Oh, Isabel, how wonderful to hear your voice. How are you, darling?"

"Never mind me," she protested, inwardly relieved by the affectionate welcome her mother had given her. "How's everybody at your end? I mean, especially ... Edmundo."

"Would you believe that we're all fine? So far the gene therapy's worked wonders, and there don't appear to be any side effects."

"That's wonderful."

"How's that young man of yours? You won't believe how angry Peter is that I didn't get his autograph. I didn't know I was in the presence of such a sports star."

"You had other things on your mind," Isabel allowed.

"Yes, I certainly did," her mother answered, and then inquired tentatively, "You will invite me to the wedding, won't you?"

"Listen, you'll be pleased to know that Jerry and I agree we're both too young to get married—which is such a grown-up decision we're thinking of changing our minds. Anyway, if and when, I promise I'll invite you."

In the silence that ensued, Muriel's relief was palpable. Then she asked, "And Edmundo?"

"Mom, Jerry and I have talked ourselves hoarse about this. He's made me see that I'm foolish to be angry at—your husband. On the other hand, I've made *him* see that I only want one father. Am I making any sense to you?"

"I'm afraid so, darling." Muriel paused and then said softly, "Anyway, I'm really glad you called."

"So am I."

The moment she hung up, a broad smile of joy and relief crossed Isabel's face.

"I did it, Jerry. Thank you."

"I'm glad, Isa. You look very happy."

Her next volley of words caught him off balance.

"Now it's your turn."

"What do you mean?"

"I mean now *you've* got to grow up."

"What are you talking about?" he demanded.

"Well, you allege you want to marry me . . ."

"What do you mean allege? Don't you think I'm serious?"

"I'm perfectly willing to love you as a tennis pro—or even as a high school coach if you want. But I refuse to marry a scatterbrain who doesn't know what he'll be doing in two weeks. Honestly, Jerry, it's unsettling."

As he listened to her scolding, a broad grin crossed his face.

"I knew this would happen," he said histrionically. "You've gone totally bourgeois on me."

"You're right. Deep down I'm a very conventional person."

"Want to hear a terrible confession?" he offered. "I've discovered that I am too. So I'm going to hang up my racket—that is, until we have kids to teach—and join the family business. Now, you can't get more bourgeois than that."

"You mean you're going into physics?" she asked excitedly.

"Not the theoretical kind," he replied with emphasis. "I'll leave it to the likes of you and my father to hang around dreaming up theories. I like to go hands-on."

"You mean like microwave radiometer tapes?"

"Yeah, that kind of stuff—and of course telescopes. I mean, look at it this way: If I grow up and get a degree,

I might actually get to work in a grown-up observatory." He smiled sheepishly. "Have I succeeded in glossing over the fact that I'm selling out?"

"It doesn't matter if you have a good reason," she answered affectionately.

"Well, I can't think of a better one than you, Isa— except I have one non-negotiable demand."

"I tremble—what is it?"

"To get my goddamn bachelor's, I actually have to go through intermediate physics. And I want you as my instructor."

She began to laugh. "All right, but I'm warning you right now, fool around in my class, I'll flunk you without mercy."

He took her in his arms. "That's the way I want it, Isa, without mercy."

"Yes, Jerry," she answered. "But with all my love."

Several weeks later, with profoundly mixed feelings, Isabel received an inscribed advance copy of Avilov's article scheduled to appear in the *Journal of Genetic Therapy*. Though of course none of the patients was mentioned, she could still deduce from the data curve that since the procedure had been successful on several subjects of Edmundo's age, it had clearly worked on Edmundo himself. But then, her mother had already supplied even more substantiating evidence.

From a strictly professional standpoint she could not fault the science of the paper. The man would not win any personality awards, but he certainly knew his stuff. Even without the use of emotive adjectives, he could make his achievement sound so dramatic that it reached the front page of the *New York Times*.

The article also speculated on the ramifications of his accomplishment. Without question, the ability to create a retrovirus that would not only arrest the progress of such a grave disease but also restore health, brought the possibility of cures for such catastrophic illnesses as Alzheimer's that much closer.

The profile also made it clear that the former Soviet academician had proven to be a quick study in the ways of capitalism.

Though no figures were specified, it was obvious that the Swiss pharmaceutical giant underwriting Avilov's work had been more than generous. And although the interviewing reporter had admired his subject's work, he could not totally conceal that he regarded Avilov as devoutly materialistic. He quoted the scientist's description of himself as a man "with a beautiful wife, three gorgeous kids, and four vintage sports cars."

By happy coincidence, the most important event in the scientific calendar was about to take place. The various committees in Stockholm were meeting to choose laureates in Medicine, Chemistry, Literature, and Physics. Their official announcements would be made in October, and the awards themselves presented on December tenth, the anniversary of Alfred Nobel's death.

Nomination forms had gone out to the usual constituencies—previous recipients, heads of departments in the outstanding universities of the world, and assorted other dignitaries.

There were also self-propelled candidates who did not wish to leave anything to chance and who openly solicited letters of recommendation from influential colleagues. This was the inevitable topic of conversation whenever scientists gathered.

One evening when Jerry and Isabel, MIT freshman and assistant professor respectively, were having dinner with the elder Pracht, Karl remarked, "It's unbelievable, but that Russian at Harvard has been shameless enough to write unctuous letters to all the Nobelists on the MIT faculty. God knows why, because he doesn't know any of them personally."

"He's just ruthlessly ambitious," Isabel commented, without revealing her personal relationship with him.

"No, he's more than that, he's incredibly astute," Pracht replied. "You'd be amazed, but one or two of the boys actually felt their egos being stroked and dropped a little note to Stockholm. I don't have to tell you that when it gets down to the nitty-gritty, every letter helps.

"But of course, this year it's a foregone conclusion in physics," he stated, smiling at his future daughter-in-law. "I hope your Swedish is good enough to give an acceptance speech."

"But I was just beginning to enjoy the bliss of semi-anonymity, dammit," Isabel protested.

"You can always turn it down." Jerry grinned. "I mean, Jean-Paul Sartre refused the Literature Prize in 1964."

"Yes," his father agreed, "only that got him even more publicity."

"But I genuinely don't want it," Isabel said plaintively. "I mean, it's the traditional grand finale to a career, and I've barely started."

Jerry smiled. "Don't sweat it, honey. Remember, Marie Curie won it twice—and that was at a time when women were barely allowed to win it once."

63

ADAM

BEHIND EVERY Nobel Prize there is not merely a lab book, but a saga. Of personal sacrifice, of pain, of disappointment, and rarely—very rarely—of unadulterated joy.

Isabel da Costa defied all the odds, growing more human as she became a legend.

It could be argued that, considering the nature of her discovery—and the early recognition by the Italian Academy—there was really no doubt that the Nobel would be hers. And there was no reason why the Swedish Academy should defer it.

Her achievement completed the final dimension of Einstein's theory of the universe, and there was no hesitation among the Royal Swedish Academy of Sciences about giving her the prize. The vote was almost unanimous, with only a single dissenter raising the issue of her tender age. He was immediately overruled.

As one elder statesman put it, "We shouldn't argue by actuarial tables. For once let's honor Alfred Nobel's words and give it to the achievement without worrying about the nature of the achiever."

The meeting lasted less than forty minutes. Isabel's victory was secure.

Everyone in the Stockholm establishment knew that the big battles to be fought that year would be for the award in Physiology or Medicine. In this category, the procedure differed radically from all the others.

Despite the initial canvassing of names, the soliciting of further information from knowledgeable individuals—and yes, the discreet inquiry into private lives—the names on the Nobel Committee's list are treated as suggestions and are far from final. For its job is merely to propose five candidates as guidelines to the Nobel Assembly, which would do the actual voting.

The assembly consisted of fifty Swedish doctors of all specialties, who had the right to reject all the nominees of the Nobel Committee and pick a candidate purely of their own choosing.

Of course, some aspirants to the award saw this as an advantage.

Naturally, those working for Prescott Mason on Adam's behalf also exploited this idiosyncrasy. A number of medical practitioners totally unknown on the international scene found themselves wined and dined to an unprecedented degree.

The lobbyists for Clarke-Albertson concentrated on lighting the fires of doctors with known rhetorical gifts, for after the nominating committee went through the motions of presenting its short list, the floor would be open and the battle would commence.

As one jovial Swede put it, "If the meeting ran long enough into the night, you probably could wear them down into giving the prize to Dr. Dolittle." But in any case, the results would very much be in the hands of the local physicians.

Dmitri Avilov had laid the groundwork with foresight and patience. As early as the days when he had been a Soviet academician, he had paved the way to personal honor by visiting Sweden every year and giving generously of his time, both socially and scientifically.

He had also continued a long and steamy relationship with Dr. Helga Jansen, a microbiologist at Uppsala University, which so simmered in her memory that she would have gone to the barricades for him even had he not already been one of the leading nominees.

Not only did Avilov have grass roots support, but the timing of his paper's appearance could not have been better.

Adam Coopersmith was not personally known to any of the electors, but the drug company had succeeded in disseminating the "secret" of his grave illness.

Moreover, beyond the obvious sympathy for the brilliant scientist dying young, there was another important consideration that could not be ignored. By giving the award to Adam, they would also be honoring the work of Max Rudolph, who had been cruelly denied the kudos he deserved.

There were, of course, three other names on the nominating committee's list, and the meeting traditionally took on an air of a Gilbert and Sullivan operetta when a local boy named Gunnar Hilbert would annually nominate himself.

By any standards, there was an extraordinary amount of lobbying. In the early stages Sandy Raven's name was mentioned in fleeting conversation. Yet it was the unspoken consensus that he had already enjoyed his fair share of recognition and reward.

Then suddenly Lars Fredricksen, a respected senior member of the panel, demanded the floor and turned what seemed to have been an inevitability into bedlam.

"Honored colleagues, with all the sympathy in the world, I think we should not allow the Nobel Prize to become like another Oscar—which has been known to have been awarded to actors simply because they were suffering from grave diseases," he said. "I don't believe that scientists should be swayed by either pity—or, for that matter, jealousy."

He looked at his audience. His presence and his argument had checked them.

"If Coopersmith's illness qualifies him, why should Raven's good fortune *dis*qualify him? After all, on the scale of absolute scientific achievements, his—"

Suddenly his assistant was at his side, signaling for his attention. He eyed the young man, who handed him a slip of paper which he quickly examined. "Mr. Chairman, I have more to say on this matter but—for good and proper reasons—I request a fifteen-minute recess."

"As a gesture of respect to the distinguished character of the speaker, the request is granted. We will reconvene in a quarter of an hour."

The physician rushed to a telephone.

"This is Fredricksen—" he began.

"Yes, Lars, good to hear your voice. I hope I'm not too late?"

"Actually, if you had called in an hour or so, I would have been able to give you good news."

"And what might that have been?"

"That your candidate had won the prize. I was making headway. I think I am very close."

"Thank God—I mean, thank God you haven't succeeded yet."

"What do you mean, sir?"

"It's a long and complicated story, Lars. But briefly, I've changed horses. What would you say about Adam Coopersmith's chances if you were to back down?"

The Swedish scientist was confused. "But if I understood my instructions, Coopersmith is precisely the candidate you wanted me to block. Believe me, it was not easy, there was enormous compassion for the man."

"Good, good—that means you can go back in there and harness that sympathy."

Fredricksen sighed wearily. "I know I'm in your employ—"

"Don't make it sound so crass, Lars. Let's just say I like to give tangible demonstrations of gratitude."

"However you wish to phrase it, the end result is that I've done your bidding. If this is what you now wish, then I'll do the best I can to urge the selection of Coopersmith."

Though he sensed the conversation was about to conclude, the doctor felt impelled to make a statement of principles.

"Would you allow me to speak my heart, sir?"

"Why, of course. I would expect no less."

"To be perfectly honest, if I had all the time been free to express my own sentiments, I would have voted for Coopersmith from the beginning."

"I'm very glad, Fredricksen. So long."

Tom Hartnell hung up and sat for a moment, staring pensively out at the pond on his Virginia estate.

That phone call had been one of the hardest he had ever made in his life. For he had abandoned a quest that had driven him intensively for years—revenge against Adam Coopersmith.

He turned to his daughter and said with a sigh, "And that's really what you wanted, honey?"

Toni lowered her head and answered softly, "Yes, Dad."

"After everything he did to you?"

"There are limits," Antonia Nielson answered. "Adam's suffered enough. Let him die with something. Besides, he deserves it."

At this, her father would not suppress a grin. "Skipper, if people always got what they deserved, I'd have been out of business long ago."

A moment later she rose, father and daughter embraced affectionately, and she left to catch her plane.

Seated once again at his desk, the Boss realized that he still had to dispose of the other thoroughbred in this horse race. He pressed a button on his automatic phone and a raspy voice answered, "Hi, Boss."

"Good evening, Fitz. Sorry to disturb whomever you're doing."

"That's okay, my captain. What can I do you for?"

"Sell my calls."

"You mean Corvax? All of them?"

"You read me well, Fitz."

"Damn," the stockbroker muttered half under his breath.

"Listen, if you put your other clients on to my little speculation in longevity, that's your tough luck. Oh, and use the proceeds to buy Clarke-Albertson at the market price. Good night, Fitz."

The scope of Adam's life had been reduced to the one room on the ground floor that contained his bed. The two upper stories stood empty of furniture, as if emphasizing the hollowness of his earthly triumph.

It was a little after four A.M. in the Coopersmith house on Brattle Street. Anya sat talking quietly to Charlie Rosenthal. She had long since given up hope of getting a night's sleep, refusing medication because she worried that Adam might regain consciousness while she was in a drugged slumber.

"He seemed pretty stable to me," Charlie remarked with more hope than conviction. "I mean, I'm almost positive he knew me just then."

"He did, he did," Anya insisted, anxious to assuage Charlie's fears that he was no longer able to convey his compassion to his best friend.

To buttress her reassurance, she took him into her confidence and confessed, "Do you know the most amazing thing? Up until a week ago we still had the remnants of a . . . sexual relationship."

"Yeah. That's one of the paradoxical aspects of the disease. While it's insidiously closing down all the systems, it keeps the sex drive intact for a long time."

"You know," Anya said hoarsely, "it doesn't matter if he recognizes me or not. The important thing is, *I* know him. If we never have another conversation, as long as I can watch him sleep or look in his eyes—even when they're looking past me—that's enough. Can you understand that?"

Charlie nodded. "Absolutely. It's like so many of the mothers with sick newborns I've treated through the years. It doesn't matter if their baby's not aware . . ."

His voice trailed off, for he had suddenly remembered he was talking to a woman who had been afflicted not only with a terminally ill husband, but with the tragedy of childlessness.

Anya understood. But she now had an outlet for her maternal instincts.

"No," she said kindly. "You're right. In a way, Adam has become my child. And as long as I can give him my love, nothing else matters."

The phone rang. "My God, who could it be at this hour?" Anya wondered aloud.

"It might be my service," Charlie explained apologetically. "I'm sorry. I'll take it."

He walked over to the phone, answered, and then

said immediately, "I was wrong. At crazy four in the morning somebody wants you, Anya."

She moved slowly. After all, there was nothing that important in the outside world. And she did not care who wished to communicate with her from that alien territory.

"Mrs. Coopersmith—I should say Dr. Coopersmith—this is Professor Nils Bergstrom of the Karolinska Medical Institute in Sweden. Forgive me if I've awakened you."

"That's all right," Anya mumbled absently. "I wasn't sleeping."

"I assume you have some idea of why I'm calling," he said gently.

"I can guess," Anya whispered, wondering if she would have the emotional strength even to thank this man for what was clearly intended as a gesture of kindness.

"It gives me deep satisfaction to inform you—in strictest confidence—that at noon today in Stockholm, two hours from now, we will announce this year's Nobel Prize in Medicine. And the academy will honor the invention of MR-Alpha as first put forth in the *New England Journal* by you and your husband and his team."

Professor Bergstrom continued to speak, but his words were merely a meaningless flow of syllables pouring over Anya's consciousness.

She once again thanked him and hung up.

Now, with tears streaming down her face, she stared at her husband's friend. "He's won—Adam's won the Nobel Prize."

The impulse to rejoice was so strong in Charlie that he succeeded momentarily in forgetting his friend's terrible affliction. He bounded from the chair. "Fan-tas-tic! Have you got any champagne?"

"Yes," she replied diffidently. "But I don't feel it's proper before—you know—Adam is told. I mean, made aware."

Immediately chastened, he agreed. "You're right. So what I'll do is stay with you till he has a clear moment. If you don't mind, Anya, I'd really like to share his happiness. It would mean a great deal to me."

"Of course." She nodded. A moment later they were in Adam's bedroom looking down at him. His face—still unlined and still handsome—wore an expression of tranquility.

"Should we try to wake him?" Charlie asked.

"We both want to, so let's take a chance," she replied.

Anya touched him and said softly, "Adam."

Her husband's eyes slowly opened. He gazed at her and for a moment said nothing. His glance then fell on Charlie. Then back to his wife.

"An-Anya," he murmured. "How are you, darling?"

She exchanged glances with Charlie. "He's lucid. We can tell him. He may forget it in half an hour, but at least he'll understand now." She took his hand.

"Adam, we've got something wonderful to tell you," she began. "You've won the Nobel Prize. It won't be officially announced for another two hours, but you've won."

He looked at her incredulously and shook his head. "No, no, you're wrong," he objected.

"But Adam—"

"No, *we* won," he corrected her. "Without you . . ."

And then, abruptly, there seemed to be a short-circuit in his brain. His eyes glazed and he became silent as a stone, no longer present.

"He knew," Charlie insisted. "He was all there when you told him. Don't you agree?"

She nodded. Then the two of them helped settle the disoriented patient back in bed.

Later, Anya was scrambling some eggs for Charlie before he left for the hospital, when the phone rang again. It was Prescott Mason.

"Have you heard?" Triumph colored his voice.

"Yes," she responded quietly.

"Splendid news, isn't it?" Mason shouted like a cheerleader, clearly angling for a pat on the head.

"Yes, yes," she agreed. "You did a good job."

"Listen, Anya," Mason said emotionally, "I don't deny that we lobbied. But they don't give out Nobel Prizes without merit." He hesitated, and then added softly, "Now comes the hard part. At least for you."

"I don't understand," she protested.

"There's no way Adam can face the press. We'll have to convince them that he's temporarily sidelined. I mean, you'll have no problem fielding any questions, will you?"

Her heart sank. "Must I?"

"Listen, dear," Mason urged, "this is for him. If you can keep saying that to yourself, it'll help you get through it."

She shrugged. "But what about the ceremony? I hate to think how he'll be by December."

"Be brave, Anya," Prescott responded affectionately. "Let's take this one day at a time."

She hung up and looked at Charlie.

"I heard," he said softly. "That guy's voice is like a megaphone. Listen, Anya, I don't know how the hell I can help, but I'll get back here as soon as I make my rounds. You shouldn't be alone at a time like this."

"Thanks, Charlie," she murmured sadly.

"Yeah," he answered. He then turned on his heels and left.

Once outside, Charlie breathed a sigh of relief and thought, Where the hell does she find the strength?

And felt glad that he was able to get away from all that ceaseless suffering.

The moment she was alone, Anya immediately called Lisl Rudolph, for in a real sense, this was her prize too. The older woman cried.

For Max.

For Adam.

For herself.

"Lisl, I want you here with me when the reporters come. And I don't mean to help me out. I want you to be a living reminder of how much this prize belongs to Max."

A few minutes later, Terry Walters arrived to begin his day of nursing. Anya had been so preoccupied that she hadn't checked on Adam for nearly an hour.

Moments later she was startled to hear Terry roar, "Holy shit!" This was followed by the heavy tread of his footsteps as he raced into the kitchen. "He's gone— your husband's gone!"

"What do you mean?"

"I mean, he's not in his bed. He's not in the john. He's not anywhere. What the hell could have happened?"

Anya was frozen with fear. Earlier in his illness there had been occasions when Adam had left his bed like a sleepwalker and wandered around the backyard. Lately he had not seemed well enough to go AWOL. And she could see through the kitchen window that he was not in the garden.

She and Terry thought as one. They opened the door to the garage and had their worst fears confirmed.

One of the cars was missing.

Alzheimer's had slowly but relentlessly deprived Adam Coopersmith of all his faculties. Now and then he had revisited his old life with enough awareness to make him despondent. The only thing he had not dared tell Anya was that he had resolved not to surrender to the disease its ultimate prey—his dignity.

There was no doubt a neurological explanation for the sudden—and inevitably transitory—return of his rational faculties. And yet, though no scientist has discovered the location of the human will, they all recognize its existence and respect its inscrutable power.

Adam's whole life had been one of increasing mastery of his environment. As a youngster this was epitomized in his skills as a diver. He had trained his body to obey his thoughts and perform actions of extreme beauty.

His enormous inner strength prefigured the character of his scientific career, in which he strove to correct nature's mistakes. The prize he had just received was ample testimony to his success.

Moreover, the news from Stockholm had provided a neural stimulus, giving him a physical renewal he was unlikely to experience again.

He knew this was the moment to act. He sat up in bed and, like an automaton, dressed himself and put on track shoes—an act he had not performed without assistance for several months. Car keys were strewn carelessly on the hall table. He picked up a set.

The garage door had been left open, so the only sound he created was the soft purr of Anya's Ford Tempo as he backed out into the street.

As he drove toward the lab, Adam meticulously observed the rules of the road. He carefully stopped at red lights. He did not exceed the speed limit.

He even parked in the correct space in the garage.

He took the elevator to the eighth floor in hopes of making a final visit to his lab. But the moment he spied several night owls still at their benches, he turned and walked to the fire door.

Then, with dignity and grace, he mounted the steps and walked out onto the roof.

Adam knew where he was and why he had gone there.

He was not frightened.

He walked slowly to the edge and stood erect and proud as he surveyed the city bathed in the glow of the morning's early light.

Then, calling upon distant but distinct memories of his body's flights through space, he sprang forward. And dove into the void.

EPILOGUE

Our souls, whose faculties can comprehend
The wondrous Architecture of the world:
And measure every wandering planet's course,
Still climbing after knowledge infinite,
And always moving as the restless Spheres,
Will us to wear ourselves and never rest,
Until we reach the ripest fruit of all,
That perfect bliss and sole felicity,
The sweet fruition of an earthly crown.

CHRISTOPHER MARLOWE
Tamburlaine the Great

LATE ON the afternoon of December tenth the nobilities of blood and mind packed the Grand Auditorium of the Concert Hall in Stockholm for the culmination of a week of celebrations: the climactic ceremony at which the Nobel Prizes were presented to the winners of the year.

Unlike most theatrical productions, this event had spectators on both sides of the footlights. For seated in several semicircular rows on stage were some 150 members of the Swedish academies, in their white ties and evening dress, for all to see.

The rows of black and white figures were only occasionally punctuated by colored gowns—a graphic illustration of how small a role women have played in Nobel history.

At precisely four-thirty, on a raised platform behind

488

them, Niklas Willen's baton signaled the Stockholm Philharmonic Orchestra to begin the Royal Anthem. The audience rose as Their Majesties, King Carl XVI Gustav—young and regal, dressed in conservative black—and Queen Silvia, dazzling in a red dress, with a shining coronet on her auburn hair, entered from the right-hand side of the stage.

Exactly one minute later—the Foundation's schedule is Swisslike in its precision—to the strains of the Rákóczy March from, of all things, *The Damnation of Faust,* the new laureates entered in procession through a curtain of flowers, passing as they did a dramatically lit bust of Alfred Nobel, the inventor of dynamite and presiding genius of this event.

They took their seats in red velvet armchairs, across from the royal party.

From a modest black podium bearing a large gilt copy of the Nobel medal, the chairman of the Foundation delivered a brief introduction.

The awards were then bestowed in the order listed in the benefactor's last will and testament.

Physics was first.

In presenting Isabel da Costa, Professor Gunnar Nilsson wasted few of the precious words accorded him. He placed her in a progression that began with Galileo, then reached—and surpassed—Einstein. He also gratified the audience by noting the phenomenon of her age:

"She now displaces Sir William Bragg—who received his award at the tender age of twenty-five—as the youngest ever recipient of the prize."

The royal party led the entire auditorium in a standing ovation for her.

Radiant in a dark blue satin gown, complemented by a single strand of pearls, Isabel had no airs of childhood precocity about her. For the little girl with the dark curls was now a handsome woman, whose dignity was ample demonstration that the circus aspect of her life was over.

They expected her to speak in Swedish, and she did. But only a single prefatory sentence: *Ers Majestät, Ärade ledamöter av akademien, Jag tackar Er för denna stora ära.* "Your Majesty, members of the academy, I thank you for this great honor."

The rest of her strictly rationed words thanked "my father, Raymond da Costa, without whose devotion and sacrifice I would not be here today, and my fiancé Jerry Pracht, for his loving, moral, and emotional support." He had made Isabel promise not to mention any scientific assistance she "thought" he might have given her.

The two men singled out for her special recognition sat side by side in the audience—each in his own way profoundly moved. Although he had promised Isabel not to shed tears, Ray was on the verge of involuntarily breaking his vow when Jerry clasped him affectionately and whispered, "Congratulations, Dad."

The single obligation of all laureates is to deliver a lecture at a time of their own choosing. Isabel had deliberately scheduled her own for the day after the festivities, lest the nature of her remarks cause too much of a stir.

For, counter to the cynics who argued that the moment she left the podium "she would turn her brain off like a lightbulb and just have babies," she intended to use the occasion to call the "definitive" nature of her work into question.

She was bent on proving that her own achievement was not the be-all and end-all of physics. If there was no one on a par to criticize her work, she would have to take on that responsibility herself. And so she proclaimed, "The theory for which you are honoring me could not be proven in the world as we know it.

"For the true unification of all forces can only be seen at temperatures so high they cannot be reached in any lab—nor found even in the fiery fury of a supernova.

"They were united long ago at the birth of the world and may yet be unified again when the great gravitational forces cause the universe to collapse. Thus, the answer will lie forever beyond our experience and our understanding."

She was determined to leave the way open for more scientific exploration. And concluded with graceful eloquence, "Nature and Divinity still have enough secrets to make humility the most important watchword of any physicist."

Traditionally, the ceremonies themselves are rarely characterized by high drama. Any strong feelings aroused by the selections would have been vented back in October, when the announcements were first made.

This year was an exception, at least as far as the award in Physiology or Medicine was concerned. At this moment an extraordinary tension gripped everyone in the Grand Auditorium.

The spectators waited breathlessly and the reporters with pens poised.

Two months earlier, when he had called her on the morning of the fateful decision, Professor Bergstrom had not felt it necessary to mention to Anya that the institute had voted that the year's award be shared. To him, the important thing was that Adam was one of the recipients and there was a human urgency to convey that information.

Sandy Raven, inexplicably abandoned by his most passionate supporter, Lars Fredricksen, had quickly fallen by the wayside. And although Adam was now a certain winner, thanks in great measure to the efforts of Helga Jansen, the doctors had been persuaded that whatever else they decided, they had to honor general advances in cellular transformation to combat disease—a rubric that would cover not only Adam's achievement, but also that of Dmitri Avilov.

When the announcement was made, the electors had not been aware that Dr. Coopersmith's wife had once been married to the corecipient of the award.

But it was not long before the press unearthed this piquant bit of information. Furthermore, their thorough investigations also revealed that the parting had been far from amicable. Indeed, during the intervening years, Dmitri and Anya had never exchanged a word or appeared in each other's presence.

When the hypersensitive organizing committee learned of this, they nervously cooperated in "desynchronizing" the two scientists' schedules to minimize the strain on Anya. At the parties and receptions during the early part of the week, Anya, accompanied by the Rosenthals, Lisl, and Heather, managed to avoid any communication with Dmitri. She and Avilov were not even seated together on the stage.

But there would be no evading him when they would be summoned by His Majesty, King Carl XVI Gustav.

Their imminent appearance on the podium therefore took on a heightened dramatic dimension.

At last Anya Coopersmith and Dmitri Avilov were both invited to come forward to receive their honors. All present were struck by the physical contrast between them. She seemed like a delicate sparrow, he like an unruly bear.

The king bestowed the prizes, first to her as her late husband's representative, and then to him. Each of them now had an instant to express their thanks.

Even at so sublime a moment, Avilov was still petty enough to want to punish Anya for being there. And he had the secret means of doing so. For only she could comprehend the hidden significance of his seemingly innocuous expression of affection for his wife and family.

"I owe many gratitudes, but I wish especially to

thank my wonderful wife and beloved children. For it is
for them, and their future, that we scientists do our
work. And without them our life would have no meaning."

Anya had expected unpleasantness, yet she did not
anticipate how much it would hurt. Not the remark itself, but the mere fact that he would be so hostile to her
on this sublime occasion.

Her own speech balanced gratitude with regret.

"This is for me a time of great joy and profound
grief. Your recognition of the achievement of my husband, and before him Max Rudolph, rewards not merely
work of enormous scientific imagination, but of great
human compassion.

"That the progress of science is truly like the ancient
Greek torch races is nowhere better demonstrated than
in the lamp Max Rudolph passed to Adam Coopersmith
and which I have the humble honor of holding before
you today. It illuminates this podium as I accept this
award in their names."

She caught a sudden glimpse of Lisl, gazing up at her
with tear-filled eyes, moved beyond words. Instinctively, Heather put her arms around her godmother.

In the normal course of events, joint recipients always
make some polite reference to one another's accomplish-
ments. But the feelings between Avilov and his former
wife were anything but civil. Indeed, during their entire
appearance center stage, both had managed to smile at the
king and the audience, but not each other.

The press was disappointed but not despairing. They
could not keep their feelings bottled up forever. Sooner
or later, their true emotions would show.

During the early part of the week, Anya had been
numbed by ceremony. Though she had steeled herself
for this awesome moment, she nonetheless felt a
wrench in her soul. And a feeling of pain beyond
words. At that moment she missed Adam more than

ever. If she could, in some way, she would have given her life for his.

The presentation was followed by a magnificent banquet for thirteen hundred guests in the Blue Hall of the Stockholm Statshus.

For Isabel, the best moments were those that appealed to the child in her. She was transported by the almost make-believe moment when she stood before the eyes of the world, facing a real king to receive a certificate and a twenty-three-carat gold medallion whose obverse showed a profile of Alfred Nobel, and whose reverse depicted the Genius of Science uncovering the veil of Nature. As on all the medals, there was a Latin quotation drawn from Virgil: "Those who have enhanced life by newfound skills." A check for one million dollars was at that moment being wired to her bank in Boston.

But for her the money was less exciting than the fabled Ice Cream Parade.

At the conclusion of the banquet, a seemingly endless phalanx of white-gloved and epauletted waiters marched across the marble floor, bearing scoops of pink on silver platters.

Isabel even insisted that Ray break his rigorous diet so they could all enjoy this delicacy.

Avilov had hounded Isabel for days, desperate to establish his personal credentials with her. Ever on the lookout for an opportunity to inform the world that he had saved this girl's stepfather from certain death.

As his behavior was unsettling Isabel and impinging on her unsullied enjoyment of this high point in her life, Jerry buttonholed the Russian at one of the elegant receptions.

Wearing an expression that belied his words, he said, "Professor, I'd be very grateful if you would keep the hell away from my future wife."

"I beg your pardon?" Avilov responded, eyebrows raised.

"Perhaps I can put it more scientifically so that someone of your intellectual level can understand," Jerry countered. "How about 'keep your slimeball hands off my girl or I'll break every bone in your goddamn body'? Am I getting through to you, Doctor?"

Avilov nodded and moved away with extraordinary speed. To Jerry's enormous satisfaction, he made no further attempts to engage Isabel in conversation.

In a real sense, Jerry had also acted in Ray's defense as well—if not as a bodyguard, as a soul guard. For in establishing a barrier between the da Costas and the Avilovs, he would be certain that Ray would never learn the truth about his daughter's paternity.

At the dinner, Anya and Dmitri were once again diplomatically separated. After the extravagant dessert and toasts, the guests repaired to the Gold Hall, where an orchestra was tuning up to play for dancing.

It was at this point that Dmitri made a final attempt to force Anya to acknowledge his scientific apotheosis.

As the musicians struck up a waltz, he strode over to her and with a deferential bow murmured, "May I have the honor of this dance, Anya Alexandrovna?"

She smiled beatifically. And a part of her, she had to admit, felt an irrepressible surge of triumph.

"I'm afraid I'm not allowed to," she answered politely. "Doctor's orders."

Her glance indicated the physician in question, who was seated at her left.

"Hi there, Dmitri," Charlie Rosenthal called affably. "I hope you're enjoying the party—I mean, it's your night too."

"Thank you, Dr. Rosenthal," Avilov answered grudgingly. "May I ask what brings you to Stockholm?"

"I'm here in a professional capacity," Charlie declared. "Dr. Coopersmith's my patient. May I tell him, Anya?" he asked.

She nodded her permission.

"It's this way," Charlie explained to the professor. "Anya's pregnant."

Avilov's jaw dropped. "What? That is impossible."

"No," Charlie explained. "It's completely possible. Idiopathic reversals of ovarian failure are well-documented in the literature. I'd give you the references—but the proof is right here."

The Russian was flustered. "Oh, yes, of course," he babbled. "But I mean, I . . ." He composed himself and forced a smile in Anya's direction.

"You must be very happy, Dr. Coopersmith," he said.

"I am, academician Avilov," she replied, deliberately recalling his former status.

Anya's announcement had the anticipated effect on Dmitri's pride. Even after so many years, he felt obliged to explain what now paradoxically could be regarded as his failure.

"Well, Dr. Rosenthal," he proclaimed, "another triumph for medical science."

"No," Anya corrected him. "It is quite simply a miracle."

The Nobel Prize ceremony is a concerto for numerous soloists. And its final chord is not sounded in the auditorium or Golden Hall.

For early the next morning the victors, all lodged in the famous Grand Hotel, are awakened by the sound of singers heralding the advent of St. Lucia, the Swedish Festival of Light.

To each of them standing at their windows, this moment had its own special significance.

Dmitri Avilov delighted in the very name of this holiday as a reference to the site of his own triumph. But then, even the day after the banquet, he was already hungry again. And he could not comprehend that the larder of honors was bare.

To Anya the gentle flutterings of new life within reminded her that Adam had not only been there in Stockholm, but would remain with her forever.

Isabel and Jerry gazed out at the choristers, arms around each other.

"Beautiful, isn't it?" she murmured.

"Isa, this whole thing has been beautiful. But the best part is that it's over. Now we can concentrate on something really important."

"Oh? And what is that, pray tell?"

"Each other."

They had won the ultimate prize.

hungry again. And he could not comprehend that the days of hunger was over.

To Anya the gentle strangeness of new surroundings delighted her, that Alexi had not only freed them all Stockholm, but would remain bad had forever.

Liana and Harry gazed out at the exhilarating land around each other.

"Regardless," said the announcer, "the play itself, the whole thing has been beautiful. No matter how it ended it's over. But we can concentrate on something really important."

"Oh? And what is that play self?"

A cheered once more.

They had won the ultimate prize.

ACKNOWLEDGMENTS

As a twentieth-century stranger in a twenty-first-century world, I owe many debts for the patient advice I received from experts at the cutting edge of science.

It was a privilege to visit their labs and talk to the next generation of pioneers they are training. Excitement was in the air.

Dr. Joseph Hill and his wife Dr. Deborah Anderson, both Professors of Immunology at Harvard Medical School, were a constant source of advice and information. It is, in fact, Joe's own research on multiple-miscarrying women that he "lent" me for use by Adam. It was the opposite of plagiarism—an act of unprecedented generosity.

Dr. Jack Strominger, Higgins Professor of Biochemistry at Harvard, was patient, hospitable, and generous with his time and expertise. He knew both the dynamics of science *and* the psychodynamics of the world of scientists. Merely to be in his presence and hear him discourse was an education—and a pleasure. Indeed, as I was concluding this novel, yet another of his students—Dr. Richard Roberts—received a Nobel Prize for Physiology or Medicine.

One of the new breed of geneticists—Dr. Tali Haran of the Technion, Haifa—was exceptionally articulate in conveying the thrill of scientific revelation.

A great discovery *I* made in the course of writing this book was that my Harvard classmate W. French

Anderson '58 had made medical history: on September 1, 1990, he performed the first official gene-therapy trial on a human patient.

The Anderson team at NIH successfully infused a four-year-old girl suffering from a severely compromised immune system with cells which had been altered, thus giving the promise of life to this otherwise doomed child. French has since gone on to other triumphs. He welcomed me into his lab, let me join his (unbelievably hectic) life and talk with his inspired and dedicated staff.

How could I have known that the quarter-miler with the locker next to mine would someday prove to be *the* Doctor of *the* Class?

The "humanoid mouse" that saved the Boss's life is actually the invention of another student of Jack Strominger's, Dr. Mike McCune of Systemix, Inc. Mike and I had many a conversation when it was five A.M. California time. True researchers, I suppose, never do sleep.

For the astronomy, physics—and his constant friendship—I have Earl Dolnick of the University of California at San Diego to thank. He has the rare gift of being able to make the most complex ideas accessible to the simplest of laymen.

And as for Stockholm, I am pleased to record my debt to Birgitta Lemmel of the Nobel Foundation—for whom no question was too difficult—or too trivial.